THE VELLHOR SAGA VOLUME 3

DWARVEN PRINCE

MARK STANLEY

First published by Dragontale Publishing Limited 2024

Copyright © 2024 by Mark Stanley

All rights reserved. No part of this publication may be reproduced, stored or transmitted in any form or by any means, electronic, mechanical, photocopying, recording, scanning, or otherwise without written permission from the publisher. It is illegal to copy this book, post it to a website, or distribute it by any other means without permission.

This novel is entirely a work of fiction. The names, characters and incidents portrayed in it are the work of the author's imagination. Any resemblance to actual persons, living or dead, events or localities is entirely coincidental.

Mark Stanley asserts the moral right to be identified as the author of this work.

First edition

ISBN: 9798340538796

To my readers who relish in the chaos and bloodshed of battle, but who can also appreciate the emotional turmoil our heroes go through—thank you for stepping into the shadows with me.

Together, we've waded through blood, betrayal, and the kind of moral dilemmas that make you question if being a hero is really worth the trouble.

If you're looking for a tale with a light at the end of the tunnel, you've taken a wrong turn into the dark depths of Draegoor. But if you're here for the grit, the grim, and the occasional laugh in the face of certain death—well, welcome home.

Enjoy the carnage

Contents

ᚠᛟᚲᚢᛋᛋ (Glossary)		I
Prologue		1
1	Shadows of Leadership: The Blade of Justice	5
2	Forging Strength from Shadows	14
3	Echoes of Resolve	28
4	Trials of Trust and Destiny	42
5	The Cost of Leadership	56
6	A Fragile Alliance: The Cost of Unity	68
7	Bonds of Blood and Fire: A Path Forged in Shadows	80
8	Bonds Forged in Battle	98
9	Trials, Trust, and Triumph	109
10	The Path Forward: Allies, Ancient Power, and New Trials	119
11	A Stranger Among Us	125
12	Whispers of Betrayal	141
13	The Captive and the Fallen	152
14	The Price of Treachery	163
15	Lost and Found	177
16	A Call to Arms	193

17	The Edge of Despair	203
18	Forged in Duty	214
19	The Wolves of War: March to Hammer	223
20	Through Blood and Flame	236
21	A Race Against Time	248
22	Broken Bones, Unbroken Will	260
23	Of Shadows and Sacrifice	266
24	Bound by Shadow, Freed by Love	279
25	A Sword Raised, A Crown Bound in Darkness	289
26	A Fortress Fallen, A Power Awakened	301
27	Through Stone and Steel	315
28	Lost to the Darkness	326
29	A City Turned to Ash	332
30	A Heart Torn Between Love and War	336
31	The Man in the Mirror	342
32	Vengeance First, Mercy Last	348
33	The Path of Dragons	357
	Afterword	366
	About the Author	369

ᚱᚢᚾᛖᛋ (Glossary)

ᚱᚨᚲᛖᛋ (Races)

Dwarves - Renowned for their discipline, training, and superior craftsmanship, Dwarves are a formidable race in Vellhor. Their society is steeped in traditions of hard work and bravery, governed by a complex political structure involving clan chiefs and their elective council. Characterized by their short stature and robust builds, Dwarves are respected for their resilience and dedication to their craft.

Elves - Elves are distinguished by their mastery of magic and their deep-rooted traditions. Standing no taller than five feet, they possess slender, elegant features and maintain a profound connection to nature, particularly the Great Elven Forest. Elves are revered for their wisdom and their ability to wield powerful magic.

Humans - Humans in Vellhor possess the ability to practice magic, though they are not as adept as the Elves. Integral to the world's dynamics, humans contribute through various trades and play significant roles in conflicts and alliances. Their versatility and adaptability make them key players in the realm.

Drogo - The Drogo Mulik are a fierce and chaotic race of lizard-like people, feared across Vellhor for their brutal nature.

Standing over seven feet tall, Drogo warriors have scales and an intimidating, dragon-like appearance, with muscular builds and savage demeanors. Known for their aggression and lack of discipline, the Drogo are unpredictable and dangerous enemies, making them a constant threat to the peace of Vellhor.

ᛏᚠᚱᛏᚺᛪᛁᚵ (Main Characters)

Gunnar - Dwarf - Heir to Clan Draegoor, Gunnar is a stalwart figure among the Dwarves. His leadership and combat prowess are legendary, marking him as a key defender of his kin. As a seasoned warrior, Gunnar skillfully navigates the treacherous political landscapes and protects his people against relentless threats, including the fearsome Drogo Mulik.

Anwyn - Elf - Anwyn, an outcast from Elven society, resides with her parent in the Great Elven Forest, outside of Stromyr. Graceful yet formidable, Anwyn's role becomes crucial in the united front against her adversaries. Her isolation has forged a strong, resilient character, preparing her for the challenges ahead.

Kemp - Human - Kemp, a mage of rare elemental affinity, stands as a beacon of magical prowess within the human kingdom. His journey involves honing his natural talents while navigating the societal expectations placed upon a young mage. Kemp's abilities and dedication make him a pivotal figure in the realm's magical community.

Ruiha - Human - Once a feared assassin and a former member of the Sand Dragons gang, Ruiha's life is a testament to resilience and transformation. Trained by Faisal, a dangerous and manipulative figure, she executed his commands for eight long years. However, a moment of moral awakening led Ruiha to defy Faisal, putting her own life at risk and embarking on a path of redemption.

ᚱᚢᚾᛖᛋ (Glossary)

ᛊᚢᛈᛈᛟᚱᛏᛋ (Supporting Characters)

Dakarai - Drogo - Dakarai is a character who grapples with familial and societal pressures. His devotion to his people is unwavering, but the internal conflict regarding his son's chosen path places him in a challenging position. Dakarai's struggle reflects the broader tension within Drogo society.

Elara – Drogo – Elara is an exiled Hedgewitch who joins Kemp, Ruiha, Dakarai and Magnus on their journey to the Scorched Mountains. She becomes a vital character to the story and aids Gunnar in his quest to save Anwyn.

Lorelei - Lorelei, a Fae of the forest, is Anwyn's steadfast companion and guide. Her ethereal presence and magical abilities significantly bolster Anwyn's own powers, providing crucial support and wisdom throughout their journey.

Havoc - Havoc, a newly bonded Stonesprite to Gunnar, possesses remarkable control over earth and stone despite his infancy. Gunnar's steady influence balanced his chaotic and unpredictable nature, creating a powerful and dynamic partnership.

Karl - Karl is a jovial dwarf known for his loyalty and bravery. As a close companion of Gunnar, Karl's unwavering support and spirited personality bring both strength and humor to their adventures.

Magnus - Magnus, Gunnar's younger brother, is also a seasoned Dwarven warrior. Known for his light-hearted banter and camaraderie, Magnus provides both a formidable presence in battle and a source of morale among his comrades.

Thalirion - Thalirion, an Elf who stands by Anwyn, plays a critical role in the efforts to unify Elves and Dwarves. His wisdom and guidance are instrumental in forging alliances and overcoming the deep-seated divisions between their peoples.

Thraxos - Thraxos is a Sage at the Tower of Absence, a formidable half-human, half-bull Minotaur from the realm of Stepphoros. Towering over most, his fierce appearance belies a deep intellect and a refined, gentle demeanor. Thraxos is both a guardian and a mentor, respected for his knowledge and strength.

Uleg - Uleg is a stoic and formidable dwarven warrior known for his unwavering loyalty and physical prowess. His battle-scarred visage and imposing stature make him a fearsome presence on the battlefield. Despite his intimidating appearance, Uleg harbors a deep sense of honor and a commitment to protecting his comrades at all costs. A quiet wisdom matches his strength and resilience, earned through countless battles fought in defense of his people.

Brenn - Brenn is a dwarven warrior and the youngest member of the Snow Wolves. His mischievous demeanor and sharp intellect often mask a deeper, more complex character driven by a personal quest for redemption. Brenn's skills make him an invaluable asset in the fight against the dark forces threatening their world.

Fellron (deceased) - Fellron is a Daemonseeker of the Shadowforged, trained extensively in the Dark Arts. His piercing eyes and enigmatic presence exude an aura of foreboding, making him a figure shunned and feared by the rest of dwarven society. Despite his ostracization, Fellron remains resolute in his duty, embracing the darkness to protect his kin from threats they scarcely comprehend.

Junak – Junak is the leader of the Drogo Mulik, having attained his position through his strength. He believes himself to be the Herald of Nergai, the draconic deity revered by the Drogo.

ᛚᛟᛏᛖᚱᛁᛟᚱᛁᛋ (Locations)

Vellhor - Vellhor is a vast and diverse realm, rich with ancient forests, towering mountains, and bustling cities. It is a land where magic flows freely, and its inhabitants, ranging from Elves and Dwarves to Humans and the Drogo Mulik, coexist in a delicate balance.

Nexus - Nexus, also known as the Echo Realm, is a shadowy, mist-laden dimension where time and space shift unpredictably. It is a place where the living and the spectral converge, and the very air is thick with an otherworldly aura. Nexus serves as a testing ground for those who enter, challenging them to confront their deepest fears and uncertainties.

ᚠᛚᛗᚴᛏᚺᚱᚠᛦ (Map)

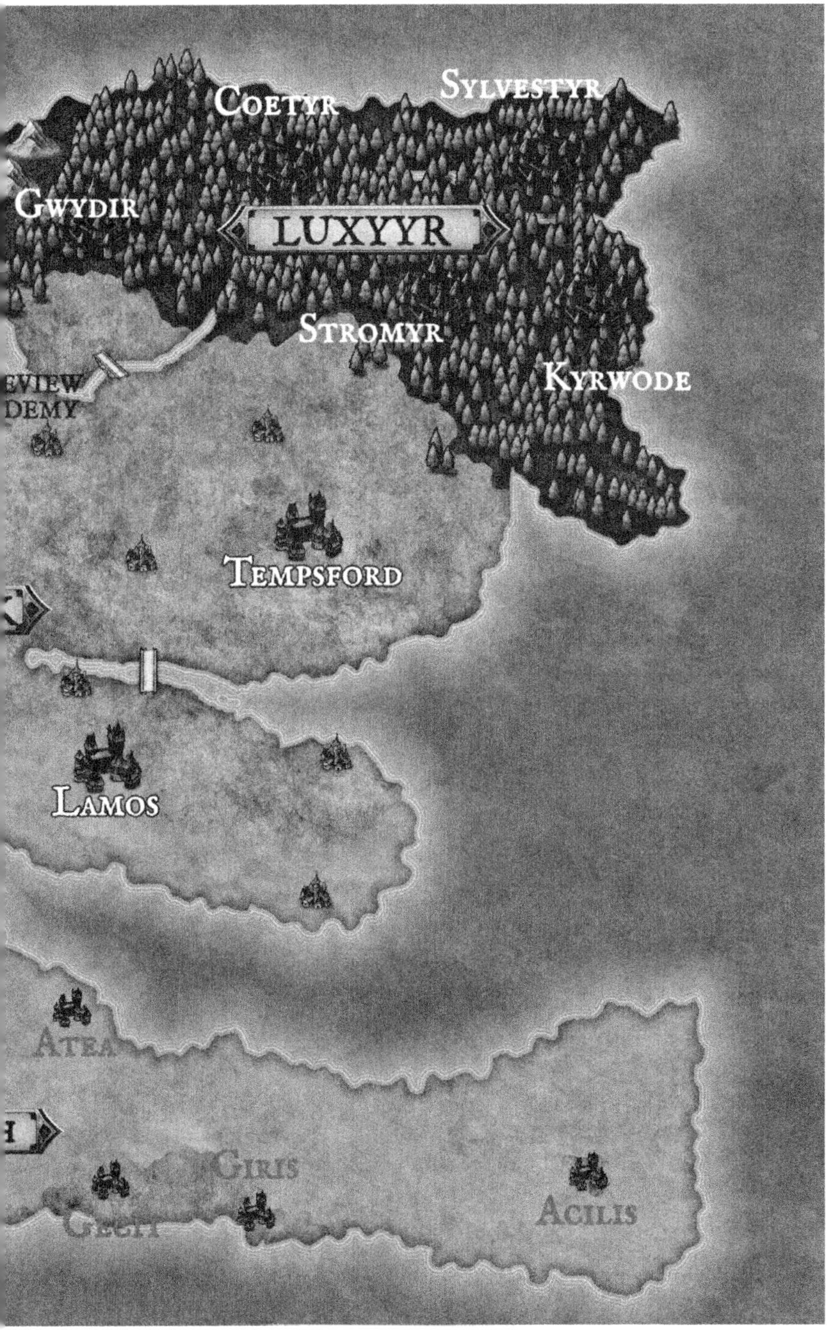

Coetyr
Sylvestyr
Gwydir
LUXYYR
Stromyr
Kyrwode
Tempsford
Lamos
Atea
Giris
Acilis

Prologue

"A leader's heart is forged in the fires of doubt, tempered by love, and tested by the weight of duty. Only when he embraces both his strength and his fear, will he unite the shattered and heal the broken."

Gunnar

Gunnar stepped into the chamber, and the sheer grandeur of it all struck him like a hammer blow. The air was thick with the heady fragrance of burning incense, mingling with the faint, musty aroma of ancient parchment and burning torches. The walls, a testament to centuries of unparalleled dwarven craftsmanship, gleamed with intricate carvings that seemed to come alive in the flickering torchlight. Each stone whispered of ancient battles and hard-won victories, echoing the legacy that now rested on his shoulders. Gold and gemstones sparkled from the very rock, a silent, glittering reminder of his new status as Dwarven Prince.Yet, amid all this wealth and history, a seed of doubt gnawed at him. Could he ever measure up to the legacy of those who had come before? As his gaze drifted to Anwyn's bedside, the weight of his responsibilities pressed harder, his chest tightening with the enormity of it all. Ready or not, his time had come. The question was, would he rise to the occasion, or crumble beneath the weight of his destiny?

He moved to Anwyn's bedside, his steps slow and deliberate. She lay motionless on the plush silk bed, her honey-colored hair spilling like liquid sunlight across the pillow. The sight of her, so still and fragile, pierced his heart like a dagger. The warm glow of the lanterns cast an ethereal light on her delicate, serene features. Despite the pallor of her magically induced coma, her beauty remained undiminished. Gunnar's heart ached with worry for her, a pain that gnawed at him constantly. He longed to brush his fingers against her porcelain skin, to feel the warmth of her breath against his hand. But the fear of disturbing her fragile state held him back. For now, all he could do was sit vigil and pray for her recovery.

Lorelei's delicate, shimmering form darted closer, her tiny face etched with worry. She whispered tinkling words in the tongue of the Fae, hoping to reach Anwyn's spirit. The sound was like a gentle breeze, soothing yet filled with urgency. Gunnar, lost in his own turmoil, barely registered her presence. His world had narrowed to the rhythmic rise and fall of Anwyn's chest, each breath a fragile promise that she was still with him.

Gunnar's rough hand gently held hers, the contrast between his calloused skin and her delicate fingers stark. He had spent endless hours here since her coma began, his mind consumed with finding a way to heal her. The room bore silent witness to his despair, the walls absorbing his whispered vows and muffled sobs. The fiery spirit that had drawn him to her lay dormant, and he desperately missed the spark that had once danced in her eyes. Their bond, forged in battle and bloodshed, had never had the chance to blossom in peace. Now, in his home, with the illusion of peace finally present, he longed for them to have the chance to explore their relationship further.

His shoulders slumped, a deep sigh escaping his lips. His gaze remained fixed on Anwyn's face, the one constant in his chaotic world. "Anwyn," he whispered, his voice a mix of pleading and desperation. "I will find a way to save you, no matter what it takes."

The echo of his words lingered in the air, a promise to the sleeping figure who had come to mean so much to him. Just as he was about to lose himself in his thoughts, the sound of approaching footsteps pulled him back to the present. He blinked, focusing on the here and now, pushing away the swirling storm of emotions. He squared his shoulders, drawing strength from the resolve that had seen him through countless battles. Gunnar looked up to see his brother Magnus entering the chamber, his presence a steadying force amidst the turmoil.

Magnus filled the doorway, his strong posture tinged with concern. The soft light caught the worry lines etched into his face, highlighting the shared burden they both carried. His eyes, mirrors of Gunnar's own, reflected the silent pact between them—duty above all.

"Gunnar," Magnus called gently, his voice echoing off the stone walls. "Father needs us in council."

Gunnar tightened his grip on Anwyn's hand momentarily before he reluctantly let go. He stood, his stature imposing despite the weariness in his eyes. "What does he want?"

Magnus's gaze softened as he glanced at Anwyn. "It's about the council. There are murmurings of dissent. Some do not believe uniting under one leader is the right path."

Gunnar nodded, though doubt gnawed at him. "They fear change, even when it is necessary for our survival."

Magnus moved further into the chamber, placing a reassuring hand on Gunnar's shoulder. "We need a strategy to get them on board. You have the strength to convince them, but we must plan carefully. You are our prince now, and soon, you will be more."

With one last look at Anwyn, Gunnar followed Magnus out of the chamber. Each step felt like a march toward an uncertain destiny. His heart felt heavy, a fire of determination burning within him, but doubt shadowed his resolve. He wondered if he could truly unite the clans, especially once they learned about his ability to practice magic—a fact he had yet to disclose to his father. Would they see him as a leader or as a threat?

As the doors closed behind them, the torchlight flickered, casting long shadows that danced across the room. And in the quiet of the chamber, Anwyn's chest rose and fell in a steady rhythm, as if even in her deep slumber, she waited for him to fulfill his destiny. The silent room held its breath, bearing witness to the unfolding saga of love, duty, and the quest for unity.

1

Shadows of Leadership: The Blade of Justice

"Justice sought in anger can blind the heart, while true power is found in mastering one's own darkness."

Gunnar

The council chamber was a stark contrast to the hushed and somber atmosphere of Anwyn's bedside. Here, the air was thick with the pungent smell of burning incense and the acrid scent of torches, mingling with the undercurrent of tension that hung in the air like a storm about to break. As Gunnar entered alongside Magnus, his gaze swept over the faces of those assembled—his father Erik, with his fiery temper as unmistakable as his red beard; Uleg of the Snow Wolves, stern and unyielding; Arvi, the calm diplomat; and Ruiha, Kemp, and Dakarai, whose expressions were a mix of concern and uncertainty. Each represented a vital piece in the intricate puzzle of uniting the scattered Dwarven clans.

The stone walls seemed to vibrate with the echoes of passionate arguments, each voice carrying the weight of the clans' fates. Erik's voice was already booming, cutting through the din. "We can't waste time pandering to their whims! Braemeer, Hornbaek, and Uglich need to understand the urgency of unity. Our survival depends on it."

Uleg grunted in agreement, his voice as cold as the northern winds. "Erik's right. We must show strength, not beg for cooperation."

Arvi, ever the voice of reason, raised a hand. "But force will only breed resistance. The clans must feel they have a choice, that their voices are heard in the council. Otherwise, we risk rebellion."

Ruiha, Kemp, and Dakarai exchanged uneasy glances. The stakes were high, and the path forward was anything but clear. Gunnar doubted if they truly grasped the intricacies of Dwarven politics. They were capable, but the delicate dance of clan alliances and ancient rivalries, not to mention the deeply rooted traditions of the Dwarven Council, were complexities that eluded even the most seasoned leaders. This realization only added to Gunnar's sense of isolation and the weight of responsibility pressing on his shoulders.

Magnus stepped forward, his voice cutting through the heated debate with a commanding authority. "Enough. We need solutions, not more arguments. Gunnar, what do you propose?"

Gunnar felt the eyes of the council turn to him, the weight of his title pressing down like a mantle of stone. The grand chamber, once a place of pride, now felt stifling. Taking a deep breath, he pushed aside his doubts and met his father's gaze. "Father, everyone," he began, his voice steady despite the turmoil churning within him. "We must find a balance. Strength is vital, but so is diplomacy. The clans need to see that unity benefits us all. We need a plan that addresses their concerns while demonstrating our resolve."

Erik's face reddened, his impatience evident. "We don't have time for coddling! Action is needed, not words."

Gunnar stood taller, his presence commanding, his voice firm. "Father, if we act rashly, we risk alienating the very clans we need to unite. Remember, I am the Dwarven Prince now. Our actions must be measured and strategic."

A silence fell over the room, Erik's eyes narrowing in challenge, but Gunnar's words held. The council members looked to him, a mixture of skepticism and hope reflected in their expressions.

Arvi nodded, his approval clear. "Gunnar is right. We need to draft a proposal that addresses the concerns of Braemeer, Hornbaek, and Uglich. Show them the benefits of unity, and ensure their voices are heard in the council."

Ruiha leaned forward, her gaze sharp with thought. "Perhaps we offer them a greater say in the council, rotating leadership roles, or shared decision-making on key issues?"

Magnus added, "And we can promise mutual defense pacts. Each clan will benefit from the strength of the others."

Gunnar felt a spark of hope igniting within him. "Excellent suggestions. We will draft a proposal incorporating these elements. We'll meet with the leaders of Braemeer, Hornbaek, and Uglich individually, show them respect, and listen to their concerns. It won't be easy, but together, we can forge a united front."

Erik grumbled but nodded, the fire in his eyes dimming as he acknowledged the wisdom in Gunnar's words. Uleg crossed his arms but remained silent, respecting the decision.

As the council adjourned, Gunnar felt a slight easing of the burden on his shoulders. The path ahead was fraught with challenges, but for the first time, a glimmer of hope pierced the darkness. He turned to Magnus as they left the chamber. "We need to prepare immediately. The longer we wait, the more uncertainty will fester."

Magnus nodded. "I'll gather our best scribes and strategists. We need to present a united front, and quickly."

Yet, as Gunnar left the chamber, his thoughts inevitably returned to Anwyn. He had vowed to save her, and that promise weighed heavily on his heart. But he also bore the responsibility of uniting his people. The two missions seemed inseparable, their fates intertwined in ways he couldn't yet fully grasp.

Gunnar paused at the chamber's entrance, steeling himself. The challenges ahead were immense, but he was determined to meet them head-on. His people needed him, and so did Anwyn. With renewed resolve, he strode forward, ready to face whatever trials awaited him.

Ruiha

Ruiha stormed out of the council chamber with Kemp and Dakarai, her thoughts a raging tempest of frustration and unwavering determination. The convolutions of Dwarven politics slipped through her fingers like sand, and she didn't care. Her focus was a burning arrow aimed squarely at revenge against Junak, her former slaver.

Kemp walked beside her, his eyes—dark smoky tendrils—betraying a flicker of uncertainty that contradicted his usually timid nature. Ruiha stole a glance at him, her mind wrestling to reconcile the sinister appearance with the kind-hearted young man she once knew. His prosthetic hand, a masterpiece of dark, shadowy material, perpetually flickered with black and purple flames, casting an eerie glow that unsettled her. It was a constant, haunting reminder of the darkness that had seeped into their lives.

She remembered Kemp before all of this—before the battles, before the magic that had changed him so profoundly. He had been the epitome of kindness, his smile a beacon of hope, his hands always ready to help. Now, his eyes, once warm and inviting, were shrouded in an enigmatic, smoky turmoil that mirrored his inner conflict. And that hand—a symbol of the price they had all paid, a reminder of the dark forces that had become a part of their reality.

Ruiha felt a pang of sorrow for the boy he had been, even as she respected the strength he had gained. But alongside that sorrow was a seething anger at the injustices that had brought them here. She steeled her resolve, knowing that their current mission was not just about revenge, but about reclaiming the lives they had lost.

"Ruiha," Kemp began hesitantly, his voice barely above a whisper, "do you think revenge will give you closure?"

Ruiha's jaw tightened, her eyes narrowing into slits of steel. "Closure?" she echoed, bitterness dripping from her words. "I don't care about closure, Kemp. I want Junak dead. He has to pay for what he's done."

Kemp's eyes flickered, the smoky tendrils swirling faster. "But—"

"No," Ruiha interrupted, her voice cutting through his like a blade. "This isn't about feeling better. It's about justice. It's about making sure he can't hurt anyone else."

Dakarai, on her other side, nodded slowly. His large, reptilian eyes—typical of the Drogo—gleamed with a mix of gratitude and fierce determination. "I understand," he rumbled, his voice like distant thunder. "The Dwarves have given us sanctuary, but I want to return to my lands free from Junak's tyranny. His death is necessary for that."

Ruiha glanced at Dakarai, appreciating his unwavering support. Unlike the dwarves with their labyrinthine political games, Dakarai understood the raw, unfiltered need for freedom and justice.

"We all have our reasons," she said, her voice softening slightly. "The Dwarves can play their games. We have a more direct path."

Kemp looked down at his flickering hand, the black and purple flames casting eerie shadows on the stone floor. "I just hope... I hope we're doing the right thing."

Ruiha placed a hand on his shoulder, feeling the tension radiating from him. "We are," she said firmly. "We'll navigate the politics, but we won't let them distract us from our mission. Junak's reign of terror ends."

Dakarai's boots echoed against the stone walls, his expression resolute. "We owe it to those who suffered and died under him. We owe it to ourselves."

Ruiha nodded, a surge of determination coursing through her veins. The path ahead was shrouded in uncertainty, the Dwarven politics a confusing web she had no patience to untangle. But her mission was crystal clear. Junak would fall, and she would make sure of it.

As they walked away from the chamber, the flickering torchlight cast long, shifting shadows on the walls—a dark reminder of the challenges and battles yet to come. But Ruiha's resolve was unshakeable. Junak would fall, and she would see to it personally.

The alliance with the dwarves was a means to an end, nothing more. Her true battle lay with the tyrant who had shattered her life. And she would not rest until she had taken everything from him, just as he had taken everything from her.

Kemp

Kemp walked beside Ruiha and Dakarai, his thoughts churning with a tumultuous blend of fear and determination. His gaze, dark and brooding, flickered with an uncertainty that mirrored the storm within him. His prosthetic hand, forged from shadowy material and perpetually wreathed in black and purple flames, felt like a constant reminder of the darkness that had infiltrated his life. He caught Ruiha glancing at it and quickly looked away, memories of the past and the price they had all paid flooding his mind.

The winding corridors of the Dwarven stronghold stretched before them, their walls adorned with intricate carvings depicting the history of a proud and ancient race. The air was thick with the scent of earth and stone, the oppressive weight of the mountain pressing down on them. Kemp battled the voice whispering insidiously in his mind. "She's right," it hissed, "Violence and death are the answer." He clenched his jaw, desperately trying to silence the whispers that clawed at his resolve.

The Dwarven city was a marvel of engineering, its halls lit by glowing crystals embedded in the walls, casting a soft, ethereal light. Statues of Dwarven heroes stood sentinel, their stone gazes unwavering, as if judging the resolve of those who passed. Kemp had urged Ruiha to seek another path, one that didn't involve more bloodshed, but even as he spoke those words, doubt gnawed at him. Was violence truly the only way?

He shook his head, trying to dispel the thoughts. He had found a way to silence the voice, at least temporarily. It was a painful process, one he dreaded but accepted as necessary. He called it the Shadowfire Purge, an internal cleansing that involved summoning the dark flames that coursed through him. The flames seared his spirit, burning away the whispers and leaving him with a few days of blessed silence.

Kemp steeled himself, knowing what he had to do. He would perform the purge tonight, away from prying eyes. The pain would be intense, but it was a small price to pay for peace of mind. He promised himself he would speak to Thraxos about it when he returned from their mission.

Thraxos and Thalirion had journeyed across the Endless Bridge to the remnants of the Sacred Tree, seeking any scrap of magic or spirit that might save Anwyn. Kemp hoped they would find something, anything that could help.

As they walked, Kemp forced himself to focus on the task at hand. "Ruiha," he said softly, his voice trembling slightly, "I know you want revenge, but we need to be careful. There are consequences to every action."

Ruiha's eyes hardened, her expression resolute. "Consequences be damned, Kemp. Junak must pay for what he's done. I won't rest until he's dead."

Kemp nodded, swallowing his fears. He understood her pain, her need for justice, but he couldn't shake the feeling that they were treading a dangerous path. The voices in his mind began to stir again, but he shut them out, focusing on the promise he had made to himself. Tonight, he would purge his spirit, and for a few days, he would find some semblance of peace.

The flickering torchlight cast long shadows on the stone walls, their dark shapes shifting and twisting like the uncertainties that plagued Kemp's mind. The carvings on the walls seemed to come alive in the dim light, the stories of ancient battles and lost heroes echoing their own struggles.

Kemp's thoughts wandered to Thraxos and Thalirion, hoping

they would return soon with the hope they all desperately needed. Thraxos, with his calm wisdom and unwavering resolve, was a pillar of strength for them all. Thalirion, ever the optimist, had a way of finding light even in the darkest of times. Until then, Kemp would endure, drawing strength from his friends and the fragile hope that one day, they might all find peace.

They reached a massive iron door, the entrance to the chamber where they would meet with the Dwarven council once more. Kemp took a deep breath, steeling himself for the political maneuvering ahead. The Dwarves were meticulous and cautious, their politics a web of alliances and rivalries that Kemp found exhausting.

But as the door creaked open and they stepped inside, Kemp felt a flicker of hope. They were not alone in their fight. With allies like Thraxos and Thalirion, and the strength they drew from each other, perhaps they could overcome the darkness that threatened to consume them. Kemp glanced at Ruiha and Dakarai, drawing comfort from their presence. Together, they would face whatever challenges lay ahead. And, together, they would shatter Junak's grip and forge a new destiny, reclaiming the lives that had been ripped away from them.

2

Forging Strength from Shadows

"True strength is not measured by the battles one fights and wins, but by the fears one faces alone."

Kemp

Kemp awoke to an unusual stillness, a cherished respite from the incessant whispers that plagued his every waking moment. The absence of voices was a welcome balm, soothing his mind in a way he hadn't experienced in ages. He lay motionless, savoring the silence that enveloped him like a protective cloak, contrasting sharply with the usual cacophony that twisted his perception and threatened his sanity.

Drawing a slow, deliberate breath, Kemp hesitated to disrupt the fragile peace that had settled over him. Memories of the previous night lingered—memories of the excruciating Shadowfire Purge. The mystical ordeal had tested not only his physical endurance but also exacted a toll he hadn't anticipated. Amidst the agony and the flames that consumed him, he had glimpsed a fleeting peace. The purge had silenced the insidious whispers, granting him precious moments of clarity. This reprieve, however brief, was a treasure he cherished above all.

With a cautious movement, Kemp rose from his bed, the cool touch of the stone floor grounding him in the present. He dressed methodically, each action a deliberate choice to reclaim control over his body and mind. Glancing into the mirror, he noted the dark circles etched beneath his eyes, testament to countless sleepless nights, and the new lines that marked his face, evidence of the internal battles waged. Yet, amidst the weariness, a spark of resolve flickered. The purge had been brutal, a confrontation with both inner darkness and the fear of losing himself. But it had gifted him this moment of tranquility. Kemp knew it was ephemeral; the whispers would return, as inevitable as the dawn. But for now, in this fleeting moment, he allowed himself a rare, fleeting smile.

Once dressed, Kemp made his way through the quiet corridors towards the training grounds, where he knew Ruiha would be.

Her presence was as constant as the steady echo of dripping stalactites in their subterranean world—a beacon in his tumultuous world. As he walked, he reflected on the stark contrast between their coping mechanisms. Where Kemp sought solace in the Shadowfire Purge to quell his inner turmoil, Ruiha channeled hers through disciplined physical training. He admired her strength and fortitude, qualities that seemed to shine brighter amidst adversity.

His footsteps echoed softly in the dimly lit halls, the flickering torchlight casting shifting shadows that danced like specters from his nightmares. Thoughts turned to his conversations with Ruiha during these early mornings. Though she seldom spoke of her past, the intensity in her eyes and the ferocity of her training spoke volumes. Kemp sensed that she, too, wrestled with her own shadows, perhaps not so dissimilar from his own.

Approaching the training grounds, the distant clang of metal on metal reached Kemp's ears. Ruiha was already deeply engrossed in her regimen, each strike against the training dummy resonating like a drumbeat, inviting Kemp to join her in battle. Pausing at the entrance, Kemp drew a steadying breath. The tang of sweat and steel hung thick in the air—a stark reminder of the world they inhabited. Did Ruiha find in her training the same respite Kemp found in the aftermath of his purges? Did she, too, experience that fleeting release, however brief, with each precise strike?

Entering the training grounds, Kemp's gaze fell upon Ruiha. She moved with the fluid grace of a storm, every motion a testament to her warrior's heart. Watching her, Kemp felt a pang of envy. Her method of confronting inner turmoil seemed almost elegant compared to his brutal purges. He approached her silently, his presence unnoticed for the moment, affording him a brief moment to observe.

Ruiha's brow was furrowed in concentration, her features etched with determination. Beads of sweat glistened on her olive skin, evidence of the intensity of her efforts. Kemp couldn't help but feel a kinship with her struggle, despite their differing approaches. They were both warriors engaged in battles unseen by others, battles that left scars upon their souls.

Clearing his throat softly to announce his presence, Kemp watched as Ruiha paused mid-strike and turned to face him. Recognition flickered in her eyes, a silent understanding that surpassed mere acknowledgment—as if she had anticipated his arrival, ready to share in the burdens of their silent wars.

"Morning," he greeted quietly, breaking the silence that hung between them. Ruiha nodded in response, a faint smile tugging at the corners of her mouth. In that simple exchange, Kemp felt a connection that eased the weight of his own burdens. They were kindred spirits in their own right, confronting their demons one day at a time.

"Kemp, come join us!" Ruiha unexpectedly called.

He hesitated, feeling somewhat out of place, but her invitation was genuine, her smile encouraging. Drawing in a deep breath, he stepped onto the field. Ruiha handed him a practice sword, while Dakarai gestured for him to adopt a stance.

Kemp gripped the sword, feeling its unfamiliar weight in his hand. As he attempted to mimic Dakarai's stance, he felt awkward and exposed, the cool metal of the blade an alien presence in his grip. His shadowed hand twitched as if frustrated, complicating his movements. Stepping forward, he attempted a basic strike, but his motions were clumsy, his swings wild and uncoordinated. Each misstep brought a surge of frustration, embarrassment coloring his cheeks.

Patiently, Ruiha and Dakarai offered guidance. Ruiha demonstrated a sequence of moves, her movements flowing like liquid against the morning light, while Dakarai's adjustments to Kemp's grip were precise and thoughtful. Despite their efforts, it was apparent that Kemp's talents lay elsewhere. His strikes lacked power and precision, his footing unsure.

As the session progressed, Kemp's frustration mounted. Sweat beaded on his brow, testament not just to physical exertion but to the inner turmoil that gripped him. Glancing at Ruiha, he couldn't help but contrast her unwavering focus and effortless grace with his own faltering attempts.

A profound sense of inadequacy washed over him. He felt like a scholar thrust into a warrior's dance, a familiar and disheartening sensation. Yet amidst the frustration, a flicker of determination ignited within him. Meeting Ruiha's gaze, he sensed not judgment but understanding and support. Drawing a deep breath, he resolved to persevere, recognizing that even incremental progress held value.

After hours of grueling effort, Kemp finally lowered the practice sword, shoulders slumping with exhaustion. Every muscle ached, protesting the unfamiliar strain. Sweat trickled down his temples, stinging his eyes. He turned to leave, burdened by the weight of his perceived inadequacies.

"Kemp, wait. Try your magic," Ruiha called after him, her voice carrying a note of encouragement that halted him in his tracks.

He froze, back still turned to her. The mere thought of wielding his dark magic sent a chill down his spine. Memories of past failures, of chaos and unintended harm inflicted, flashed through his mind. He could almost hear the cries of the Drogo warriors caught in the wake of his uncontrolled fury. Shaking his head as if to dispel the haunting images, Kemp struggled against the overwhelming fear. The idea of unleashing that volatile force terrified him more than any foe he could face with a blade.

Turning slowly, he met Ruiha's unwavering gaze. There was understanding in her eyes, and a determination that both comforted and unsettled him. She believed in him, even when he couldn't summon belief in himself. The stark contrast between her confidence and his own self-doubt left him feeling exposed, vulnerable.

"Ruiha, you don't understand," Kemp began, his voice wavering with emotion. "Every time I've tried before, I've only caused harm. I don't want to risk it, not here, not with you."

Stepping closer, Ruiha's expression softened. "Kemp, we're here to learn and grow together. Your magic is a part of you, and together we can help you harness it."

Her words hung in the air, offering a glimmer of hope that he hesitated to grasp. Drawing a deep breath, Kemp felt the knot of anxiety tighten in his chest. He wanted to believe her, to trust that he could master the chaos within. But the fear of failure, of causing harm once more, remained a potent deterrent.

Still, the unwavering support in Ruiha's eyes gave him pause. Perhaps, just perhaps, she was right. Maybe this time could be different. Slowly, he nodded in tentative agreement, though doubt lingered like a shadow at the edge of his thoughts.

"Please," urged Dakarai, stepping forward with genuine curiosity and encouragement in his reptilian eyes. "Show us what you can do."

Kemp hesitated, heart pounding in his chest. Casting a glance at Ruiha, who nodded reassuringly, he drew in a deep breath and turned towards the row of training dummies standing at the field's edge.

Closing his eyes, Kemp focused inward, feeling the unsettling stir of dark energy within him. The Shadowflame, a swirling vortex of black and purple, flickered to life around his shadowed hand, casting eerie reflections upon his face. The power surged like a tempest, barely contained, threatening to consume him if he let his guard slip.

With a flick of his wrist, he unleashed the dark fire on the dummies. The flames arced through the air, a torrent of raw, chaotic energy. Impacting their targets, the dummies exploded into bursts of dark fire, crumbling into ash. But these were no ordinary dummies—encased in frosteel armor, they were designed to withstand even the fiercest blows. Yet despite their robust defenses, Kemp's Shadowflame incinerated the armor, leaving only puddles of molten metal pooling beneath where the dummies had stood mere moments earlier.

The display was both awe-inspiring and terrifying, a stark reminder of the volatile power Kemp wielded. Opening his eyes, Kemp saw the residual wisps of dark flames lingering in his hand. Silence settled over the field, heavy with the scent of charred wood. His heart raced, a mixture of relief and lingering fear coursing through him. Turning to the onlookers, he searched their faces for reactions.

Ruiha, Dakarai, and the Snow Wolves stared in a mix of astonishment and awe at the display of power. Yet Kemp felt no pride, only a deep sense of embarrassment and frustration. He couldn't control this magic, and the thought of its destructive potential weighed heavily on him. What use was such power if it could only bring destruction?

Ruiha approached him, her eyes wide with a mix of awe and concern. "Kemp, what you just did… that was incredible. You truly have a remarkable gift."

"It's not a gift," Kemp muttered bitterly. "It's a curse. I can't control it, and all it does is destroy."

Dakarai stepped forward, his reptilian eyes filled with understanding. "Kemp, every weapon can be used for good or ill. It's in how you wield it that matters. With guidance and practice, you can learn to master it."

Kemp looked between them, seeing the sincerity in their eyes. For the first time in a long while, he felt a flicker of hope. Perhaps, with friends like Ruiha and Dakarai at his side, he could find the strength to transform his curse into a blessing. Yet the path ahead seemed daunting and uncertain, the weight of his abilities pressing heavily upon him.

As the training session concluded, Kemp resolved to persevere, to push himself further in mastering his magic. He knew he had a long journey ahead, but with allies like Ruiha and Dakarai supporting him, perhaps he could discover the means to harness his power responsibly, turning potential destruction into protection and healing.

Gunnar

Gunnar sat by Anwyn's bedside, his rugged face etched with layers of worry. The dim light from the candles cast long shadows on the stone walls, flickering gently as if trying to comfort him. Anwyn lay still, her breath shallow and her once vibrant spirit seemingly dimmed. Gunnar reached out, taking her hand in his, the weight of his helplessness pressing down on him.

Havoc, his bonded Stonesprite, still the size of his forearm, rumbled softly at his feet. Normally mischievous and full of energy, Havoc had been subdued since Anwyn fell into her coma, his usual antics replaced by a quiet, watchful presence. He stayed close to Gunnar, sensing his distress and offering silent support, for which Gunnar was grateful.

A soft knock on the door broke the silence, pulling Gunnar from his anxious thoughts. His heart quickened as one of his attendants entered, bowing respectfully. "My lord, Thalirion and Thraxos have returned from their journey to the Sacred Tree."

For a moment, Gunnar's mind whirled with a mix of hope and fear. The sacred tree was ancient and powerful, a place of mysteries and forgotten wisdom. If Thalirion and Thraxos found anything, it could be the key to saving Anwyn. He felt a glimmer of hope light up within him, like a beacon in the dark.

"Bring them in immediately," he said, his voice a mix of urgency and anticipation. He held his breath, his thoughts racing. Would they have the answers? Could they bring Anwyn back from the brink?

Moments later, Thalirion and Thraxos entered the room. Gunnar searched their faces, looking for any sign of success or failure. His heart pounded, each beat echoing his desperate need for good news.

"Thalirion, Thraxos," Gunnar greeted them, his voice a mix of relief and desperation. "Did you find anything at the Sacred Tree that could help her?"

Thalirion shook his head slowly, his expression somber. "We scoured the remnants of the Sacred Tree, seeking any clue, any ancient wisdom that might aid Anwyn. But, alas, we found nothing that could directly help her."

Gunnar's shoulders slumped, feeling as if the weight of their words had physically pressed down on him. A cold draft whispered through the room, and Gunnar glanced at the flickering candles, their shadows dancing with a more ominous air. Despair clawed at his insides, gnawing away the hope he had clung to. His mind raced, desperately seeking a solution, but finding only a void of uncertainty. "There must be something we can do," he said, his voice tinged with a plea that belied his usual stoic demeanor. The thought of losing Anwyn, of not being able to save her, was a torment he could barely endure.

Thalirion moved closer to Anwyn, his eyes filled with sorrow as he examined her. He muttered ancient words under his breath, the syllables resonating with a haunting melody that sent shivers down Gunnar's spine. "I will try some more spells, though I fear they may be in vain."

Thalirion began to chant softly, his voice a soothing murmur that filled the room. A gentle light emanated from his hands, casting a warm, golden glow over Anwyn's still form. The light flickered and danced, weaving intricate patterns across her pale skin. Gunnar watched intently, his eyes tracking every movement, every shimmer of light.

As the minutes passed, the brilliance of the light began to wane, its once vibrant glow fading to a faint glimmer. Thalirion's brow furrowed, lines of worry deepening on his face. His chanting faltered, and the light sputtered, flickering one last time before it extinguished completely. Thalirion's hands dropped to his sides, his shoulders heavy with unspoken concern.

Gunnar watched intently, his heart aching with each passing moment. "Please, Thalirion, there must be something we haven't tried."

Thalirion lowered his hands, the glow dissipating entirely. He looked at Gunnar, his eyes filled with regret. "I am sorry, my friend. Her spirit is deeply wounded, and my spells cannot mend it."

Gunnar clenched his fists, fighting back the frustration and despair threatening to overwhelm him. The room seemed colder now, the shadows from the candles growing longer and darker. "We cannot give up. There must be another way, another source of knowledge or power that can heal her."

Thalirion placed a reassuring hand on Gunnar's shoulder. "We will not give up. We will seek out every possible avenue, consult with every Sage and healer we can find. Anwyn's spirit is strong; she has endured so much already. We must have faith that we will find a way to restore her."

Gunnar nodded, his determination renewed. "The candles flickered, their light steady once more, as if responding to Gunnar's newfound resolve. "Thank you, Thalirion. We will find a way. We must."

As Thalirion and Thraxos prepared to leave, Gunnar turned back to Anwyn, gently squeezing her hand. "Hold on, Anwyn. We will not rest until you are well again. I promise you."

The room fell silent once more, but this time, the flickering candlelight held a promise of hope, a testament to the unwavering resolve of those who loved her.

Gunnar remained steadfast by Anwyn's bedside, his heart sinking at the creak of the door. He couldn't tear his gaze from her pale, serene face, her soft breaths a fragile lifeline.

"Gunnar," came Erik's steady voice, interrupting his vigil.

Reluctantly, Gunnar looked up. Erik stood in the doorway, his imposing frame casting a shadow that darkened the room further. Yet, Gunnar's focus remained on Anwyn, her presence consuming his thoughts.

"Father," Gunnar responded numbly, his voice devoid of its usual deference, more a reflex than true acknowledgment. He returned his gaze to Anwyn, his concern overshadowing all else.

Erik approached with resolute steps. "The council is gathering. The clan leaders await in the grand hall. It's time."

Gunnar's shoulders slumped. "I can't leave her, not now. What if she wakes? What if she needs me?"

Erik sighed, impatience flickering in his eyes. He didn't grasp the depth of Gunnar's love for Anwyn. "I understand your concern, son, but our oaths to the clan are as binding as your vows to her."

Gunnar's heart twisted. The weight of his responsibilities pressed like a mountain. He felt torn between duty and his need to stay with Anwyn. Looking back at her, helpless in her stillness, he whispered, "Why now? Why leave her like this?" The injustice threatened to overwhelm him.

Erik's grip on Gunnar's shoulder tightened. "Leadership demands sacrifice. Anwyn's condition is tragic, but the realm's future hinges on this moment. Discord could shatter our kingdom."

Gunnar closed his eyes, Erik's words settling heavy. They were true, but they offered no solace. The thought of abandoning

Anwyn, even briefly, felt like betrayal. Leaning down, he pressed a gentle kiss to her forehead, promising, "Hold fast, Anwyn. I'll return to mend what's broken," the pledge more to himself than to her.

Rising, Gunnar squared his shoulders, the mantle of leadership weighing heavy. He turned to Erik, resolve hardening. "Lead on. The clans must see their king, and I will not falter." The words felt hollow, but he clung to them for strength.

Erik nodded approvingly. "Show them the resilience I've forged in you, my son."

As they exited, Gunnar glanced back at Anwyn, silently vowing to return and fight for her with all he had. The grand hall beckoned, bringing with it the daunting task of uniting fractious Dwarven clans. But Gunnar knew he must succeed—for Anwyn, for his people, for their kingdom's future.

Standing at the grand hall's entrance, Gunnar's heart pounded beneath his armor. The council chamber, with its high ceilings adorned in Dwarven history, did little to ease his anxiety. The task ahead was monumental: to unify fiercely independent clans into a cohesive kingdom.

The air thickened with torch smoke and murmurs of dissent. Magnus and Uleg stood beside him, their faces resolute. Gunnar took a deep breath, trying to steady his nerves. The leaders of the clans were gathered, their expressions ranging from skeptical to openly hostile.

"Esteemed leaders of our noble clans," Gunnar began, his voice carrying more force than he felt. "As we stand on the precipice of change, I ask not only for unity but for a covenant to shield against encroaching darkness. Our enemies thrive on division."

Bojan, leader of the Hornbaek Clan, spoke first, his face stern with skepticism. "Gunnar, you speak of unity, but what guarantee do we have that our traditions and independence will be honored? Hornbaek has stood firm for generations; we will not yield lightly."

Gunnar felt frustration rising, but Magnus's reassuring nod steadied him. "Chief Bojan, your traditions are the cornerstone of our realm. This union does not seek to dilute our heritage but to fortify it with combined strength and shared wisdom."

Durik, towering leader of the Braemeer Clan, leaned forward, his red beard ablaze. "Aye, Bojan speaks true. We of Braemeer value autonomy. We are smiths, farmers, and miners, not warriors. Why should we trust a council that may not understand our needs?"

Gunnar's pulse quickened. Durik's challenge required careful handling. "The council we propose will reflect our realm's diversity. Each clan's perspective will bolster our decisions, ensuring no voice is lost to the majority's echo. Your skills as smiths and miners are as vital as any warrior's blade."

Gadrin, shrewd leader of the Uglich Clan, reclined, his coppery fingers steepled. "And power—who holds the reins of this kingdom? We will not be pawns in another's game."

Gunnar drew a breath, feeling the tension in the room. Turning to Magnus, he nodded. "**This charter," Magnus announced, unrolling the document, "outlines a balanced governance. Each clan leader serves on the council, with equal say. We propose mutual defense pacts— an attack on one, is an attack on all. This is not subjugation, but a shared destiny under one banner."

The leaders exchanged glances. Tension lingered. Words alone would not sway them. Gunnar needed to show his intentions were true, and the benefits of unity real.

In the weeks that followed, Gunnar, Magnus, and Uleg met with each clan leader. The discussions were intense, filled with fiery arguments and pointed demands. Gunnar listened patiently, offering reassurances, even as the weight of his responsibilities pressed down on him like a boulder. In those moments of reflection, he found his strength, a steady resolve that refused to waver. But when night fell, doubt crept in, whispering insidious fears into his mind. Faces haunted his thoughts: Bojan's accusing glare, Duric's fierce intensity, Gadrin's measured calm. They all watched him, silently questioning if he was truly up to the task.

Some nights, those doubts threatened to consume him: What if he failed? What if the clans remained divided, forever fractured? But then he would think of Anwyn, lying in her coma, her face serene as if dreaming of a better future. He imagined the moment she would awaken to find the dwarven kingdom united, stronger than ever. That vision ignited a fire within him, a blaze of unquenchable determination. Each morning, he rose with the resolve of an unbreakable mountain, his purpose clear. The future of his people depended on him. He could not, would not, falter. He would unite the clans. He would bring Anwyn back. He would shape their destiny.

3

Echoes of Resolve

"Inaction allows darkness to grow, but even the smallest spark of determination can ignite a flame that lights the path to unity."

Gunnar

In Bojan's underground hall, the stone walls loomed like ancient sentinels, each crack a whisper, each fissure a silent scream. Gunnar's fingers traced the cold, unyielding surface, feeling the rough-hewn texture beneath his touch, each groove a testament to the relentless hands that had shaped them. The air was thick, laden with the scent of earth, sweat, and iron—a heady perfume of toil that seemed to seep into his very bones. It was the smell of Dwarven labor, of centuries of sacrifice and unbroken endurance, wrapping around him like a shroud. Gunnar breathed it in, feeling the weight of history pressing down, a tangible force that grounded him in the here and now while tying him to the past.

The rhythmic clanging of chisels and hammers filled the hall, a relentless drumbeat that echoed off the stone, each strike a note in a symphony that spoke of both creation and destruction. The sound was as much a part of the Hornbaek as the blood in their veins, a living, breathing pulse that bound them together. Gunnar let the noise wash over him, each strike a reminder of the burden he bore, the legacy etched in every line of his face, every scar on his soul. The walls seemed to whisper back, their silent voices woven into the shadows, urging him to honor, to fight.

He closed his eyes, and the hall seemed to come alive around him. He could almost see the faces of the old chiefs, their eyes hard and unyielding, staring back at him from the darkness. Each one had felt the weight of duty, each one a link in a chain that stretched back through the ages, forged in the fires of struggle and tempered in the blood of their enemies. They watched him now, these silent specters, their gaze a challenge and a promise. Gunnar felt their presence like a chill at his back, a constant reminder that he was not alone. That he could not fail.

Bojan's footsteps cut through the air, and Gunnar turned to see him step into the hall, his stout figure outlined against the flickering torchlight. The dwarf was a mountain in his own right, all muscle and resolve, carrying the scent of smoke and earth. His shadow loomed large, dancing on the stone walls as if the mountain itself acknowledged him. Gunnar straightened, meeting Bojan's gaze with a nod of respect.

"Your stonework is unparalleled," Gunnar said, his voice a low rumble that echoed through the hall. "The precision, the care—you honor your ancestors with every strike. As part of a united kingdom, your craft will not only be celebrated but protected. We will establish a guild, one that ensures your techniques are passed down, your contributions recognized for the masterpieces they are."

Bojan grunted, his eyes flickering with a mix of pride and caution. "Words," he said, his voice like gravel grinding in his throat. "We've heard plenty of those before." His gaze was steady, a challenge in its own right. Gunnar could see the doubts, the fears etched into the lines of his face, the wariness of a man who had seen too many promises broken.

"Aye, words," Gunnar replied, his tone steady, unwavering. "But words are where we begin. Trust is earned, and I mean to earn it. We share the same Dwarven blood, the same stone. We've been shaped by the same hands. You give me time, Bojan, and I'll show you more than words."

From the shadows, a voice cut in, sharp as a blade. "And what makes you different from the rest, *prince*?" It was Keldar, his eyes glinting like steel, arms crossed over his chest. He was known for his fiery temper and sharper tongue, a dwarf who had never been afraid to speak his mind.

Gunnar turned to face him, a faint smile touching his lips. "What makes me different, Keldar?" he said, his voice calm, laced with steel. "Maybe nothing. Maybe everything. But I know this: I'm here, and I'm not going anywhere. We'll either stand together, or we'll fall apart. The choice is yours."

The silence that followed was heavy, thick with the unspoken weight of history and the future. Gunnar felt the eyes of the past on him, their gaze a constant reminder of what was at stake. He stood tall, feeling the stone beneath his feet, the hammer's song in his ears, and the ancient spirits in his blood. This was his place, his duty. To honor the past, protect the present, and fight for the future, no matter the cost.

Keldar broke the silence with a huff and a shake of his head, just as he was about to talk, Gunnar interrupted. "I understand your mistrust. But this is not just about promises; it's about survival. Alone, we are vulnerable to our enemies. Together, we stand a chance to thrive."

Keldar's eyes flashed with anger. "Thrive? At what cost? Our independence? Our traditions diluted by your politics and schemes?"

Bojan raised a hand to calm Keldar. "Peace, Keldar. Let Gunnar speak." Turning to Gunnar, he continued, "You ask much of us. Trust is earned, not given lightly, especially in these times."

Gunnar nodded solemnly, his resolve steeling against his own uncertainties. "I do not expect your trust overnight. But consider the threats we face—the growing darkness in the Scorched Mountains, the barbaric Drogo that seek to plunder our lands. A united front is our best defense. No, our only defense!"

Keldar remained unconvinced. "Words." He brought his hand up to his mouth and blew, sending an imaginary pile of dust scattering from his palm. "Words are like the wind, *prince*. They drift, they scatter, they mean nothing once the storm comes." His voice was rough, each word a challenge hurled into the silence of the hall. "Show us actions." He scoffed, his eyes narrowing as they locked onto Gunnar's. "Prove your commitment to our cause."

Gunnar stepped closer to Keldar, his voice low but resolute. "I intend to. After the war is over, I will return with the resources to fortify your defenses and the scholars to document your techniques. In the meantime, I will live among you, learn from you, and stand by your side in battle if need be."

The hall fell silent, the weight of Gunnar's words hanging in the air. Bojan's expression softened slightly, a glimmer of hope in his eyes. "Very well, Gunnar. We will hold you to your promise. Show us you mean what you say, and Hornbaek will consider your proposal."

Gunnar bowed respectfully. "Thank you, Bojan. You have my word."

As Gunnar left the hall, the rhythmic sounds of chisels and hammers resumed, but the air was charged with a new tension. The future of Hornbaek, and perhaps the entire kingdom, now hung on the actions of a conflicted prince determined to prove his worth to a wary clan.

Gunnar settled on his bed in the lavish room Bojan's household had prepared for him and sighed deeply. Throughout the negotiations with Bojan, he had fought to keep his thoughts from constantly drifting to Anwyn's well-being. He could still see her vacant eyes, hear her breathing in his mind. The weight of the day's discussions pressed heavily on him, but the ache in his chest for Anwyn's safety overwhelmed all other concerns. Now, alone in his room, the silence was deafening, amplifying his worry. He wished he could focus on anything else, but his mind stubbornly clung to thoughts of her.

Ruiha

Ruiha's sword danced through the air, a blur of silver against the dim light. Sweat stung her eyes, but she welcomed the burn. Her muscles ached with each swing, each thrust, but she ignored the pain. Pain was something she could control, unlike the frustration boiling inside her. She paused just long enough to gulp down water, then resumed her drills, her blade carving invisible enemies from the air.

Each strike was a release, a physical outlet for the storm in her mind. Gunnar's endless talks, the council's ceaseless debates—it all grated on her nerves like a whetstone on steel. The Dwarves had the strength to crush Junak and his Drogo, but instead of wielding it, they wasted time talking. Deliberation over action. Hesitation over decisive blows.

Her sword crashed against the training dummy, splintering wood, as if she could split her frustration in two with a well-aimed swing. She could see Junak's face in the wood, taunting her, as if he knew they were all tangled in webs of their own making. "Why do they hesitate?" she muttered under her breath, her words a growl, each one punctuated by the whistle of her blade. She swung harder, faster, as if sheer force could cut through the fog of indecision that held them all captive.

Her arms screamed with effort, lungs burning, breath coming in ragged gasps. This was the kind of pain she understood, a simpler agony than the gnawing frustration inside her. Every muscle burned, every nerve screamed, but she welcomed it. Pain she could handle. Uncertainty, inaction—those were the true enemies.

She pictured Gunnar in the council chamber, surrounded by cautious dwarves, all too afraid to make a move. Her blade sliced through the air, a mirror to her thoughts. Every swing was a question unanswered, every thrust a frustration voiced. Why did they delay? Every moment they waited, Junak grew stronger, and their chances of victory grew thinner, like the edge of a worn blade.

Ruiha's sword crashed into the dummy again, and this time it shattered, sending shards of wood flying. She stood, chest heaving, her mind still caught in the rhythm of her training. If only she could break through their indecision as easily. She couldn't bear the thought of standing still, of letting herself drown in the council's endless words. She needed to move, to act. Anything to avoid feeling powerless.

Lost in the relentless rhythm of her training, she didn't notice the soft scuff of boots on the stone floor behind her. The sound was swallowed by the echo of her own breath and the crackling tension in the air.

"Ruiha," a voice broke through her focus, steady but tinged with concern.

Ruiha halted mid-swing, her blade poised in the air. The

familiar voice cut through her intense focus, startling her. She turned to see Kemp standing at the edge of the training grounds, his eyes filled with a mix of worry and affection. The sight of him was like a splash of cold water, a stark contrast to the raw energy she had been pouring into her training. For a moment, the fury and frustration coursing through her stilled, replaced by a flood of conflicting emotions at the sight of him.

"Kemp," she said, lowering her sword, "what is it?"

Kemp hesitated at the edge of the training circle, his gaze flickering from Ruiha's flushed face to the shattered remains of the training dummy. His mouth tightened, a hint of concern creasing the corners of his eyes. "I thought you might want to take a break," he said gently, stepping closer with cautious steps. "You've been at this all day."

Ruiha wiped the sweat from her brow with the back of her hand. "I need to keep moving. I can't just sit and wait while they debate and negotiate. It's driving me mad."

Kemp nodded his head in understanding. "I know. But you also need to eat. Come for a walk with me, and let's get something."

Ruiha hesitated, her frustration still bubbling beneath the surface like a boiling pot ready to overflow. She felt the tension in her muscles, the unresolved anger that training had only barely begun to dissipate. "I don't want to stop," she muttered, her eyes flicking back to the shattered dummy. It stood as a testament to her pent-up fury. "I need to take this out on something."

Kemp gave her a gentle smile. "I understand. But you haven't eaten since yesterday, and you're not going to be any good to anyone if you collapse from exhaustion."

Her stomach growled loudly, betraying her resolve. She sighed, sheathing her sword. "Alright, fine. Let's go."

As they walked through the winding underground tunnels of

Draegoor, the cool, damp air wrapped around them, a refreshing change from the stifling heat of the training grounds. The dim light cast long shadows on the rough-hewn walls, their flickering dance creating a soothing rhythm. The steady echo of their footsteps mingled with the distant clinks and clatters of Dwarven activity, a comforting reminder of life bustling around them.

With each step, Ruiha felt the tightness in her shoulders gradually easing. The tension that had coiled within her like a spring began to unwind, replaced by a reluctant sense of calm. The rhythmic cadence of their walk, combined with the familiar presence of Kemp beside her, acted as a balm to her frayed nerves. She inhaled deeply, letting the cool, mineral-scented air fill her lungs, and slowly exhaled, feeling a small measure of her agitation dissipate into the ancient stone around them.

Kemp walked beside her, his shoulder occasionally brushing against hers in the narrow confines of the tunnel. The further they ventured into the subterranean labyrinth, the more the distant clamor of dwarven activity faded, giving way to an almost serene silence. Kemp's voice, soft and steady, began talking of their time at the Olive Tree.

He recounted their shared adventures and the secrets they had whispered in the tavern. With each story, the tension in Ruiha's chest began to loosen, like ice slowly melting. She could almost feel the warmth of the sun filtering through the trees, hear the rustling of branches in the breeze, and smell the dusty scent of Lamos.

As Kemp continued, she felt the wall she had built around herself begin to crumble. The familiar cadence of his voice, the warmth of his words, started to chip away at her defenses. She realized how much she had missed this, missed him, and the connection they shared. A small, hesitant smile tugged at her lips, and then, unexpectedly, a laugh bubbled up, surprising her with its suddenness. The sound felt foreign, as if it belonged to someone else, yet it was also incredibly comforting.

The laughter bridged a gap to a part of herself she had thought lost, buried under layers of anger and frustration. It rippled through her, light and unexpected, like the first warm breeze after a long, bitter winter. In that fleeting moment, she remembered what it felt like to be happy, to share light-hearted moments without the weight of the world pressing down on her. The sound seemed almost foreign to her ears, a relic from a time when her days weren't consumed by the constant grind of war and politics.

She looked at Kemp, a flicker of surprise in her eyes, as if he had pulled some magic trick by making her laugh. The tension in her chest loosened, the iron band of worry that had been squeezing her heart for weeks finally easing. It was strange, she thought, how a simple moment of levity could remind her that there was more to life than the battlefield, more than the endless debates and strategies that filled her waking hours.

"I missed this," she admitted softly, glancing at him. "I missed you."

Kemp looked at her, his eyes filled with a warmth that made her chest tighten. "I missed you too, Ruiha. There were times I thought I'd never see you again. When I awoke in Nexus without you, I feared the worst."

She swallowed hard, the memory of that battle a raw wound. "When I saw you disappear, I thought I'd lost you forever."

They walked in silence for a moment, the weight of their shared experiences hanging in the air. Eventually, they arrived at a cozy tavern nestled within the cavern walls. The smell of hearty food and the sound of laughter greeted them as they entered.

They found a table in a secluded corner of the tavern, the warm glow of lantern light casting a comfortable ambiance around them. When their drinks arrived, Kemp took a tentative sip of the dark ale and immediately grimaced, his expression twisting in a way that was both comical and endearing. Ruiha couldn't help but laugh, the sound genuine and light.

"Still can't handle foreign delicacies, can you?" she teased, her eyes sparkling with amusement.

Kemp shook his head, a reluctant smile spreading across his face. "Some things never change. Remember the first time I ate in Lamos? I thought I was going to die." He chuckled, the memory evidently as vivid for him as it was for her.

As he spoke, Ruiha was transported back. She remembered her initial skepticism, the way he offered her that bloody flower. She almost laughed out loud again at the memory.

For a moment, the weight of their current troubles lifted. Ruiha realized just how much she had missed these simple, shared moments. The familiar banter, the laughter, the sense of camaraderie that had always come so easily between them. It was a reminder of the bond they shared, a bond that had endured despite the hardships.

As they reminisced, Ruiha felt a renewed sense of closeness to Kemp. The walls she had built around herself continued to crumble, replaced by the warmth of their shared history. The sense of normalcy, however brief, was a balm to her weary spirit.

They laughed, reminiscing about their escape from the Olive Tree, and for a while, the world outside seemed less daunting.

After they finished their meal, Kemp leaned back in his chair, his demeanor shifting slightly. "I have to see Thraxos after this," he said, his tone guarded.

Ruiha raised an eyebrow. "What for?"

Kemp hesitated, looking down at his shadow hand, then shook his head. "It's nothing you need to worry about. Just—need some advice."

She sensed he wasn't telling her everything but decided not to press him. "Alright," she said simply.

They left the inn, and Ruiha returned to the training grounds. Picking up her sword again, she felt a renewed sense of purpose. The time with Kemp had been a balm to her weary soul, and now, she was ready to face whatever came next, knowing she wasn't alone.

Kemp

Kemp watched Ruiha's determined stride back to the training grounds, each step resonating with unwavering resolve that sparked a flicker of admiration within him. As she vanished from sight, Kemp turned and ventured deeper into the labyrinthine tunnels. The rough-hewn stone walls closed in around him, intermittently lit by flickering torches. His every footfall echoed in the oppressive silence, reflecting the tumultuous thoughts racing through his mind.

His shadow hand tingled, a constant reminder of the burden he bore. Dark, ethereal energy pulsed through his veins, unsettling yet familiar. He flexed his fingers, watching as shadowy flames wreathed around them like living tendrils. The sensation was both intrinsic and alien, an embodiment of his inner conflict.

Kemp's mind swirled in a tempest of anxiety and uncertainty. Since merging with the Dragon Crown, his shadow hand had become increasingly unmanageable, especially in moments of violence. It seemed to possess a will of its own, a tethered but rogue entity. It wasn't just a loss of control he feared; whispers haunted him, suggesting the darkness was consuming him. He could feel it in his bones, an insidious force gnawing at his resolve.

Navigating the labyrinthine corridors, memories flooded Kemp's mind of the first time he gained control over the shadow hand. Magically attached after a perilous surgery following an attack by a Shadowwing in Nexus, it had initially felt like a gift—a powerful tool born of necessity. Yet, despite its undeniable power, Kemp had always seen it as a curse, starkly contradictory to his essence. Now, it felt like a chain tightening around his soul, a constant reminder of the survival price he paid.

It was Thraxos who had saved him, who had affixed the shadow hand. Now standing before the towering Minotaur, a mix of apprehension and hope churned within Kemp. Thraxos represented stability in their chaotic world, his wisdom and strength unwavering. Kemp trusted him implicitly yet feared exposing his deep struggle. What if Thraxos couldn't help? What if the darkness had taken too deep a hold?

Kemp shook his head to clear the dark thoughts. He had to trust in Thraxos. The cavern housing Thraxos's quarters loomed ahead, its entrance framed by jagged rock. Kemp hesitated, feeling the cool draft of underground air brush against his skin. Shadows clung to the vast space's corners, deepening its natural gloom. In the center, Thraxos's massive silhouette loomed, his hulking form stark against the flickering torchlight as he studied a map on a stone table.

Kemp's heart raced; he swallowed hard, the bitter taste of fear on his tongue. He shook off the darkness, forcing a lighter tone into his voice. "Kemp," Thraxos rumbled, his voice echoing through the cavern, "What brings you here?"

Kemp hesitated, the weight of his secret pressing down on him. He glanced at his shadow hand, dark energy coiling and uncoiling. Before he could respond, he summoned a lighter tone, "How did your trip to the Sacred Tree go?" Thraxos's shoulders sagged slightly, a rare sign of dejection. "We found little more than charred remains. Whatever power it held is long gone."

Kemp nodded solemnly, sharing in the disappointment. "Is there hope for Anwyn?" he asked.

"There will be a way," Thraxos replied with determination. "We just need to find it."

Kemp knew he could delay no longer. Thraxos's perceptive eyes studied him closely. "You didn't come all this way for that," Thraxos said, his voice softer. "What truly brings you here?"

Kemp felt the weight of his shadow hand, its dark energy a constant reminder of his struggle. The words were heavy on his tongue, but he pushed through. "I... I need to talk to you about something."

Thraxos set aside the parchment and turned his full attention to Kemp. "Speak," he said, his expression inscrutable. Kemp took a deep breath, feeling the shadow hand pulse in response. "My shadow hand... it's been behaving strangely since I merged with the Dragon Crown. It's as if it has a mind of its own."

Thraxos's brow furrowed slightly, but he remained silent, his dark eyes fixed on Kemp. "Initially, I thought it was a side effect, something I could manage. But then, I started hearing voices—dark whispers, especially in moments of danger or violence. They... they tempt me to embrace the darkness."

Kemp's voice wavered, the fear and uncertainty now evident. The shadows around his hand seemed to writhe in agitation, reflecting his inner turmoil. Thraxos's eyes narrowed, urging Kemp to continue.

"I fear the crown is corrupting me," Kemp admitted, barely above a whisper. "It's like poison seeping into my thoughts. But I've found a temporary solution—a Shadowfire Purge. It's excruciating, but it grants me a few days of peace."

Thraxos's expression shifted, a flicker of shock crossing his face. "Does it hurt?" he asked softly. Kemp nodded. "Yes, tremendously. But the silence it brings is worth it."

Thraxos regarded him silently for a long moment, his gaze intense. "This is troubling news, Kemp. The Dragon Crown's influence is stronger than we anticipated. I will speak with Thalirion. Together, we will find a permanent solution."

Relief surged through Kemp at Thraxos's words. "Thank you. I... I didn't know who else to turn to."

Thraxos placed a massive hand on Kemp's shoulder, his reassurance grounding him. "You are not alone in this fight. We will find a way to rid you of this darkness."

Kemp nodded, feeling a weight lifted from his shoulders. "I appreciate it, Thraxos." As Kemp departed, the flickering torchlight casting long shadows behind him, he felt a glimmer of hope. The road ahead would be challenging, but with Thraxos and Thalirion at his side, he was prepared to confront whatever lay ahead. The darkness within him might be formidable, but Kemp was determined to overcome it, whatever the cost.

4

Trials of Trust and Destiny

"Trust is a fragile bridge, built slowly through action, but shattered in a moment of doubt."

Gunnar

In the fiery forges of Braemeer, Gunnar faced clan chief Duric and his retinue, the air thick with heat and tension. Each dwarf's face was set in hard lines, grim and skeptical, their eyes reflecting the dancing flames. The heat was oppressive, seeping into Gunnar's skin and clothes, making every breath feel like a gulp of molten metal. Around them, the forges blazed, casting long shadows that flickered on the stone walls, while the ceaseless roar of flames and the relentless clang of metal on metal filled the cavernous space.

Duric stood at the forefront, his broad chest rising and falling like bellows with each breath. His red beard was damp with sweat, glistening in the forge light, beads of perspiration trickling down his cheeks like molten iron. His eyes, sharp and appraising, flicked over Gunnar, weighing him as if he were a piece of ore fresh from the mine, judging his worth before the hammer even struck. Duric's gaze held a challenge, a silent question that burned as fiercely as the fires around them.

"We are smiths, farmers, and miners," Duric stated, his voice a low growl. "We do not seek war."

Gunnar met Duric's intense gaze, feeling the weight of skepticism pressing down on his shoulders like the heat of the forges. "And that is exactly why we need you," Gunnar replied, his voice steady despite the tension in the air. "Your knowledge of the earth and its riches will be the foundation of our united kingdom."

As he spoke, he envisioned the vast landscapes and hidden resources that lay beneath, the potential they could unlock together. "We will create a council, ensuring that every clan's needs, including Braemeer's, are understood and respected." Gunnar's mind raced with possibilities, imagining a future where cooperation and mutual respect paved the way for prosperity.

Duric's eyes narrowed. "A council, you say? We already have a council, Gunnar, and this one isn't led by one dwarf!"

Gunnar met Duric's eyes with calm determination. "Yes, Duric, we have a council, but it is flawed," he said, his voice steady but impassioned. "The current council fails to truly represent the needs and wisdom of each clan. Look at what happened to my own father when Wilfrid betrayed him. That could have been you!"

Duric's expression remained skeptical, but Gunnar noticed a flicker of curiosity. "Go on," Duric said, crossing his arms.

Gunnar took a deep breath, his mind racing to find the right words. "Imagine a council that not only ensures every clan's voice is heard and valued but also offers us protection from the looming threats of the Drogo and Nergai. The current council gives us each a voice, yes, but we need more than that now. We need unity and strength to face the dangers that are closing in on us. This new council will be our shield and our sword, a coalition where each clan's unique strengths are harnessed to defend our kingdom."

Duric's expression remained skeptical, but Gunnar noticed a flicker of curiosity. "Go on," Duric said, crossing his arms.

Gunnar leaned forward, his voice growing more urgent. "The Drogo and Nergai are not threats we can face alone. They are your closest neighbors. They are powerful, relentless, and they seek to destroy everything we've built. By creating a council that not only represents every clan but also coordinates our defenses and strategies, we can stand a chance against them. Braemeer's knowledge of the earth and its treasures, Uglich's expertise in metallurgy, Hornbaek's skill in mining, and Draegoor's warriors—all these will be crucial in our efforts to fortify and defend our lands."

Duric raised an eyebrow. "And who gave you this grand vision? Surely, it wasn't just your own ambition."

Gunnar hesitated for a moment, then spoke with reverence. "Draeg, the god of chaos, came to me in a vision. He set me on this mission to unite our clans, to forge a kingdom where we can all thrive and protect each other."

Duric chuckled, a skeptical grin spreading across his face. "Draeg, you say? The god of chaos is guiding you to bring order to our kingdom? Sounds like he's pulling your leg, Gunnar."

Gunnar met Duric's laughter with unwavering conviction. "Draeg may be the god of chaos, but he also understands the necessity of balance. He showed me that our current disunity only leads to weakness and strife. By embracing change and working together, we can create a kingdom that endures and is strong enough to withstand any threat."

Duric's expression softened slightly, though his skepticism remained. "It's a fine tale, Gunnar. But why should we trust that Draeg's vision is in our best interest? Chaos isn't exactly known for bringing prosperity."

Gunnar nodded, understanding Duric's doubts. "Chaos can lead to destruction, yes, but it can also lead to renewal and growth. Draeg's message was clear: our unity is the key to our survival and prosperity. This new council will be a testament to that vision, ensuring that every clan's needs and voices are heard and respected, and that we are prepared to face our enemies."

Duric's eyes narrowed, his brow furrowing as if he could see the future laid out before him, full of promise and pitfalls. He sighed, the sound a mixture of frustration and contemplation. "Very well, Gunnar. We'll consider your proposal. But know this: if this council fails to protect all clans equally, it will be the end of your grand vision." His voice carried the weight of countless years of tradition and the unspoken threat of what failure could bring.

Gunnar felt a surge of relief as he stepped forward, clasping Duric's hand with a firm grip. "Thank you, Duric. I promise you, we will create a council that honors and empowers every clan." His words were as solid as the stone around them, a vow made in the heart of the mountain, where nothing could hide from the heat of the forge.

Gunnar

The forges spat orange light into the shadows, painting the cavernous halls of the Braemeer Clan in the colors of fire and ash. Gunnar and Duric moved through the flickering gloom, the heat curling against their skin, the air heavy with the tang of molten metal. Shadows danced along the stone walls, silent specters bearing witness to the brittle pact being forged between them. The tension still simmered in the air, thick and cloying, like the smoke that drifted from the forges, a constant reminder that words alone couldn't snuff out the flames of doubt.

Duric's eyes, usually hard as granite, held a glimmer of something that might have been curiosity, sparked by Gunnar's talk of unity and protection. As they ventured deeper into the halls, the clamor of hammer on anvil faded, replaced by the low murmur of dwarves passing by, their eyes a mix of suspicion and hope, watching the two of them. Gunnar could feel the weight of those stares pressing on his back, like the forge's heat, pushing him onward. The burden of their expectations sat heavy on his shoulders, as if he were already carrying the mountain.

Just as they neared Gunnar's chamber, the ground beneath them gave a sudden shudder. A low growl rumbled up from the earth, growing into a roar as the ceiling above cracked and groaned. In a heartbeat, the cavern erupted, the floor heaving, stones breaking free from the roof and crashing down. The air thickened with dust, choking the cries of the dwarves as they scrambled to safety, some trapped under the fallen rubble, their desperate voices swallowed by the chaos.

Gunnar's heart hammered, not with fear, but with a cold, iron resolve. He reached deep, drawing on the magic that thrummed through his veins. Time slowed, the chaos unraveling into a sluggish, nightmarish dance. Stones hung in the air, suspended in a cruel mockery of gravity, each movement a ripple in the fabric of reality. Gunnar moved through the chaos like a blade through flesh, precise and unerring. Where others saw chaos, he saw a pattern, a path. His hands gripped boulders as if they were nothing more than pebbles, each action calculated, every motion a piece of a puzzle he alone could see. He guided the trapped dwarves out of the debris, his voice calm, steady, a lighthouse in the storm.

To the dwarves watching, Gunnar became something more than a dwarf—he was a phantom, a force of nature bending time and space to his will. In moments that stretched into an eternity, he had the last of the trapped dwarves free. The dust settled, and the cries of panic turned to murmurs of awe, disbelief hanging in the air like the residue of magic.

But not all eyes were filled with gratitude. Duric stood apart, his face a mask of conflicting emotions. Awe, yes, but suspicion too, hard and sharp. Braemeer had suffered under the hand of Drogo shamans before; they knew the sting of sorcery's betrayal. As Gunnar turned to face him, Duric's eyes narrowed, his voice cutting through the air like a knife. "What did you just do, Gunnar? How did you move like that?"

Gunnar met Duric's gaze, the silence between them heavy, charged. "I've been blessed with something known as Elven Blood," he said, voice steady, resolute. "A gift to aid us in our darkest hours, to protect, to lead."

Duric's face twisted, anger creeping in where suspicion lay. "Magic," he spat, the word heavy with disgust. "Dark magic. And you expect us to trust you? To follow you? How do we know it hasn't already poisoned you?"

Gunnar's frustration flared, a spark catching in the dry tinder of his soul. "This power isn't dark, Duric. It's a tool, nothing more. I saved lives today. Draeg himself told me of a prophecy. I'm meant to unite us, to lead us against the Drogo and Nergai. This magic is our salvation."

Duric's sneer deepened, his voice rising. "Prophecy? Or just a convenient excuse to grab power? I've seen what dark magic does, Gunnar. It corrupts. It destroys. I won't let you endanger our people with your sorcery."

The tension in the chamber was suffocating, the air thick with Duric's anger and Gunnar's desperation. The forges, usually a roaring backdrop, were muted, as if even the flames held their breath. Gunnar felt the chasm between them widen into a gulf, the realization striking him like a blow. His act of heroism had driven a wedge deeper than he'd intended.

"I swear to you, Duric," Gunnar said, his voice raw, edged with desperation, "I'm not corrupted. I want to fulfill Draeg's vision, to protect our people. We have to stand together."

Duric's eyes were as cold as the mountain stone. "You've lost my trust, Gunnar," he said, voice low, simmering with anger. "Without that, you're just another fool with a taste for power. You want to lead? Do it with courage, with strength, not by hiding behind cursed magic."

The words cut Gunnar deep, each one a twist of the knife. His heart pounded, every beat a painful reminder of the widening gulf between them. "Duric, you don't understand," he pleaded, stepping forward, hand outstretched. "This power is a tool. Nothing more. Draeg himself—"

"Enough!" Duric's shout cracked through the chamber, a warhammer shattering stone. The echoes filled the silence that followed, hammering the finality of his words home. "I've heard enough, Gunnar. You think I don't see what you've become? A dwarf who thinks he can twist the world to his will with magic is no leader. He's a tyrant waiting to happen."

Duric stepped closer, face inches from Gunnar's, his breath hot and metallic. "We know what happens when leaders bend the rules. You're not risking just your own neck—you're risking all of ours. You think the others won't see it too? Won't whisper about the changes they see in you? They will fear you, and they will be right to do so."

Gunnar's mouth opened, but the words were trapped, caught in the web of Duric's accusation. The certainty that had driven him faltered, crumbling under the weight of Duric's glare.

"Duric," he rasped, voice barely a whisper, "I'm trying to do what's right. For all of us."

Duric's eyes were dark coals, smoldering. "What's right?" he echoed, voice laced with contempt. "Right isn't turning your back on your kin, on your blood. Right isn't wielding powers no dwarf should touch. You want my trust? Throw that magic into the deepest pit and bury it. Lead with your hands, your heart. Not with sorcery."

Gunnar's hand fell, heavy and useless at his side. Duric's gaze was as unyielding as steel, the silence stretching between them, thick with unspoken words and broken trust. The forges hissed in the background, the sound like the last breath of dying hope.

"Duric," Gunnar tried once more, voice cracking with the weight of it, "I need you to trust me. Just this once."

Duric's voice was ice. "You had your chance. You've squandered it. I won't follow a leader who dabbles in dark arts. You saved a few lives, maybe, but you've lost the trust of many more. And that's a price too high to pay."

With that, Duric turned and walked away, his footsteps echoing in the cavern, each one hammering Gunnar's heart deeper into despair. Gunnar watched him go, the weight of his mission pressing down on him like the stones he'd moved. The air thickened around him, the shadows deepening, threatening to engulf him.

He stood alone, the dwarves he'd saved watching him with a mixture of gratitude and fear. The stench of sweat and smoke lingered, and the certainty of the path ahead seemed to slip through his fingers like sand. Gunnar clenched his fists, the metal of his gauntlets cool against his skin, grounding him. He couldn't abandon his quest. Not now. Draeg's prophecy still burned in his mind, a beacon in the darkness.

As Duric's footsteps faded, Gunnar vowed to find a way. He

would bridge the divide, prove the purity of his intentions. He would unite the clans, lead them against the Drogo and Nergai, no matter the cost. The road ahead was treacherous, but Gunnar felt the steel in his spine, the resolve that would not be bent or broken. He would show them all that Draeg's vision was true, and lead his people into a future where they stood united, strong, unbreakable.

Ruina

"How was your date with Kemp?" Dakarai teased, swinging his practice sword in a wide arc towards Ruiha's head.

Ruiha deftly tilted her head, the blunted blade slicing through the air mere inches from her ear. With a fluid motion, she planted her foot firmly, her balance impeccable. Her leg extended like a piston, driving her heel forward with precise force. The ball of her foot connected with Dakarai's midsection, a perfect alignment of muscle and intent. The power of her strike was not merely in brute strength but in the flawless execution, channeling her energy into one explosive movement. The impact was swift and brutal, sending Dakarai reeling, his breath escaping in a ragged gasp.

"Sorry, Dak... did you say something?" Ruiha quipped, a playful glint in her eye.

Dakarai tried to catch his breath, coughing. "I... no," he managed, wiping his mouth.

Ruiha chuckled softly, a sound both light and triumphant. "That's what I thought," she said, her voice carrying a blend of amusement and confidence, echoing through the training grounds as she lowered her stance, ready for the next move.

The clang of practice swords and the sharp breaths of exertion filled the training grounds. Ruiha's eyes never left Dakarai's as they exchanged blows, her movements swift and precise, his strength formidable yet met with equal skill. With one final, decisive swing, Ruiha disarmed Dakarai, sending his practice sword clattering to the ground.

"Alright, you win this round," Dakarai conceded with a good-natured grin, rubbing his ribs where Ruiha's kick had landed earlier. His eyes sparkled with mischievous respect, acknowledging her superiority in their never-ending dance of blades. "How about we get some lunch? I'm starving."

Ruiha nodded, a thoughtful expression crossing her face. They sheathed their swords and made their way to the mess hall, the scent of roasted meats and freshly baked bread wafting through the air. The rich aroma wrapped around them, a comforting embrace as familiar as their sparring sessions.

They found a quiet corner, plates filled with hearty fare, and sat down. For a moment, they ate in companionable silence, the camaraderie of warriors who had fought side by side evident in their easy manner. But Ruiha's mind was elsewhere, her thoughts heavy with concern. Dakarai noticed the furrow in her brow, the way her gaze seemed distant.

"What's on your mind, Ruiha?" Dakarai asked, his tone gentle, a stark contrast to the teasing banter they had shared earlier.

She sighed, setting down her fork. "It's Kemp. I've been worrying about him a lot lately."

Dakarai leaned in, his expression serious. "What happened?"

Ruiha took a deep breath, her eyes darkening with the weight of her thoughts. "The other day, he told me he needed to speak to Thraxos. There was something in his eyes, Dak—something I've never seen before. It was as if he was haunted by those shadows."

"The Shadow Hand?" Dakarai asked, his voice barely above a whisper.

Ruiha nodded. "He's struggling to control it, but lately it seems to be getting worse. When he looked at me, it was like he was pleading for help, but he didn't want to burden me with it. He's changed so much since we lost each other. He's not the sweet, innocent boy I met all those years ago. He's seen too much—done too much to be that boy anymore."

Dakarai reached across the table, placing a reassuring hand on her arm. "Ruiha, Kemp is strong, but he doesn't have to face this alone. I'll have a word with him, see if I can get him to open up."

She looked at him, gratitude and worry mingling in her eyes. Her voice trembled slightly, "Thank you, Dak. It means more than you know."

He gave her a reassuring smile. "We're all in this together, Ruiha. Whatever it takes, we'll help Kemp get through this."

As they continued their meal, the weight on Ruiha's shoulders felt a little lighter. She knew Dakarai's words were sincere, and that together, they would face whatever darkness lay ahead. The bond between them was forged in battle and strengthened by loyalty, a bond that would see them through the trials to come.

Ruiha glanced at Dakarai as he ate, wondering if he saw Kemp as more than just a friend. Dakarai had lost his own son in Junak's brutal raid on his home, a loss that had carved deep lines of grief into his face. She often wondered if Kemp's presence had filled some of that void, giving Dakarai someone to care for and protect. The way he had spoken about Kemp, the concern in his eyes, it was almost paternal. Ruiha hoped that this connection might help bridge the gap and bring Kemp the support he desperately needed.

As these thoughts swirled in her mind, she felt a renewed sense of determination. They would help Kemp, not just because it was their duty, but because they were family, bound by ties stronger than blood. She and Dakarai would face the encroaching darkness together, their united strength a beacon of hope against the shadows threatening to consume them.

Kemp

Kemp had been waiting outside Thraxos's chamber for almost an hour, the cold stone walls sapping warmth from his body as time dragged on. The corridor was dimly lit, shadows flickering from the torches mounted at intervals along the walls. The echo of distant footsteps mingled with the low murmur of the torch flames, creating a symphony of solitude. Just as he was about to give up and retreat to his own room, the distinctive low rumbling voice of Thraxos echoed down the corridor, a deep bass that seemed to vibrate through the very stones.

Kemp straightened, his heart quickening with a mix of anticipation and anxiety. As Thraxos turned the corner, his massive frame filling the hallway, Kemp noticed that he was not alone. Walking beside him was Thalirion. The sight of the Sage, as calm as the sea in storm, brought a slight ease to Kemp's tensing muscles.

Relief washed over Kemp as he saw them together. He desperately hoped they had found time to discuss his Shadowfire and the Dragon Crown, the two elements intertwined with the dark whispers that plagued his mind. These whispers, though faint now, promised to swell into a cacophony by morning, as they had many mornings before. The whispers had begun to return as he had waited, faint now, but he knew from bitter experience that by morning they would be too loud to ignore.

Thraxos's eyes, sharp and intelligent beneath his formidable brow, met Kemp's as they approached. "Kemp," the Minotaur rumbled, his voice both a greeting and an acknowledgment of the wait.

"Thraxos, Thalirion," Kemp replied, inclining his head respectfully. "I hope I'm not intruding, but I need to speak with you both. The whispers—they've started again."

Thalirion's gaze was piercing, his silver hair catching the torchlight. "We sensed as much," he said, his voice as calm as it was firm. "We know, Kemp. Come inside. We have much to discuss."

Kemp followed them into Thraxos's chamber, the door closing behind them with a weighty thud. The room was warm, a fire crackling in the hearth, casting long shadows that danced upon the walls lined with ancient tomes and artifacts.

"Sit," Thalirion said, motioning to a chair. "We have indeed discussed your Shadowfire and the Dragon Crown. It seems these forces are more entwined than we feared. We believe there is a way to help you, but it will not be easy."

Kemp sat, feeling the weight of their words settle over him. "I'll do whatever it takes," he said, his voice steady despite the fear gnawing at his insides.

Thraxos leaned forward, his expression grave. "The Shadowfire is a force of great power, but it is also a curse. It feeds on your doubts and fears. To control it, you must confront these whispers, face the darkness within you."

"And the Crown," Thalirion interjected, his sharp eyes reflecting the flicker of the firelight, "it seems to resonate with your Shadowfire in ways we did not anticipate. This interaction could be both a curse and a key."

Thraxos nodded solemnly. "This means your path might be harder than we thought, but also more crucial. The Crown and the Shadowfire together—it's a rare conjunction that could either doom or save."

Kemp felt the room's warmth drain away, replaced by the cold touch of destiny. "What must I do?" he asked, more to himself than to his mentors.

"Your journey will be perilous," Thalirion continued, his voice low. "You must seek Chronos of the Forgotten Realm. Only he can untangle the threads of your fate intertwined with the Crown and the Shadowfire."

"And I will be alone," Kemp stated, more a declaration than a question.

"No," Thraxos replied, placing a reassuring hand on Kemp's shoulder. "Ruiha and Dakarai will stand by you. Their strength and loyalty, combined with your courage, form a tapestry of fate no dark force can easily unravel."

Kemp nodded, words failing him. He thought of Ruiha's unwavering support, of Dakarai's steadfast presence. They had faced many challenges together; this would be no different.

"Where must I go?" Kemp asked, the weight of the task settling in his bones.

"There is a place beyond the Scorched Mountains, in the land of Sandarah," Thalirion answered, his voice echoing slightly in the chamber. "A land shadowed by ancient curses but also rich with forgotten magic."

Kemp nodded, feeling a mixture of fear and determination. As he left the chamber, the whispers still lingered at the edge of his mind, but they seemed quieter, subdued by the resolve now burning within him. The path ahead was fraught with unknown dangers, yet with the guidance of his mentors and the support of his friends, a flicker of hope remained. He would master the Shadowfire, tame the Crown, and reclaim his destiny.

The darkness would not claim him. Not now, not ever.

5

The Cost of Leadership

"Strength lies not in the magic you wield, but in knowing when to lay it down for the sake of others."

Gunnar

Torchlight pierced through the narrow windows of Gunnar's chamber, casting long shadows on the rough stone walls. He stirred beneath his heavy blankets, the events of the previous day weighing heavily on his mind. Duric's rejection and the deep-seated distrust of his magic had left him conflicted, and as he lay there, the path ahead seemed shrouded in uncertainty.

Gunnar sat up slowly, rubbing the sleep from his eyes, and reached out with his mind to Havoc. The Sprite, his loyal companion with a body like living granite and eyes that shimmered with deep violet hues, responded with a gentle pulse of warmth and reassurance.

"*Havoc,*" Gunnar thought, seeking the solace of their telepathic bond. "*I'm not sure what to do. Duric's distrust runs deep, and I fear that staying here may be a waste of precious time.*"

The Stonesprite's voice resonated in his mind, calm and

steady. "*Gunnar, moving on without Duric's support will make your task far more challenging. The Braemeer Clan's influence is substantial, and their endorsement could sway others. Leaving now might weaken your position with Uglich and Braemeer.*"

Gunnar sighed, feeling the weight of Havoc's words. "*But how can I convince Duric? His hatred for magic is strong, and my attempts have only driven a wedge between us.*"

Havoc's response was thoughtful. "*Leadership isn't merely about persuasion but about proving one's value through actions. Show Duric and his followers that your magic is a tool for good—begin by addressing a need they cannot deny.*"

Gunnar marveled at the change in Havoc. When had the chaotic hatchling he had first met matured into such a wise and steadfast ally? He remembered when Havoc's energy was wild and unpredictable, a storm of youthful exuberance that often left chaos in its wake. Now, the Sprite radiated a calm confidence, a stark contrast to the frenetic creature of the past. It struck Gunnar how time had shaped both of them, transforming youthful chaos into something enduring and profound.

Taking a deep breath, Gunnar nodded to himself, feeling a renewed sense of determination. "*You're right, Havoc. I will stay and find a way to weave my magic subtly into our daily efforts, proving its worth.*"

With a newfound resolve, Gunnar rose from his bed and prepared for the day. He donned his armor and strapped his battle axe—a gift from Karl that held immense power and personal value—to his side, feeling the familiar weight of responsibility settle upon him. As he moved towards the door, Havoc's voice echoed in his mind. "*Let's approach today with strategy. Observe first, then act.*"

Gunnar paused, a pang of guilt tugging at him. He knew how much Havoc wanted to help, how the Stonesprite's presence had always been a source of strength. But the Braemeer Clan was not ready to meet Havoc. If they feared his magic, what would they think of meeting a mystical Stonesprite?

"*I appreciate your offer, Havoc,*" Gunnar replied, his tone gentle but firm. "*But introducing you now might confirm their worst fears. Let's build trust first.*"

Havoc's response was tinged with disappointment but also understanding. "*I understand, Gunnar. Just know that I'm here if you need me, even from a distance.*"

Gunnar nodded, grateful for Havoc's wisdom and patience. "*Thank you, Havoc. Your support means more than you know.*"

With that, Gunnar left his chamber, the sounds of the bustling forge filling his ears, a constant reminder of the industrious nature of the Braemeer Clan. The forge's heat hit Gunnar like a physical wall as he entered the central hall. The sight of the clan leader's stern face and the skeptical glances of his retinue only served to strengthen Gunnar's resolve.

"Duric," Gunnar called, his voice steady and clear. The hall fell silent as all eyes turned to him. "I seek another audience with you."

Duric's eyes narrowed, but he nodded curtly. "Very well, Gunnar. Speak."

Gunnar stepped forward, his gaze unwavering. "Yesterday, I acted instinctively to avert disaster. It's clear now that my swift actions, though well-intentioned, have stoked fears rather than assuaged them. I propose a demonstration—a day without magic—to show you that my skills and my dedication to Braemeer's well-being extend beyond my abilities as a Mage."

Duric crossed his arms, his expression guarded. "A day? And if you succeed?"

Gunnar took a deep breath. "Then grant me a week, a month—enough time to prove that magic, under control and used wisely, can be beneficial. It's not just an external power, but a part of who I am, as much as my resolve, my intelligence, and my loyalty to this clan."

The room was silent as Duric considered Gunnar's proposal. The skepticism in his eyes was still present, but there was also a hint of curiosity. "Very well, Gunnar. You will work with us. But know this: if you falter or show any sign of deceit, you will be cast out."

Gunnar nodded, his heart pounding with determination. "Thank you, Duric. I will not let you down."

The following days were charged with purpose as Gunnar immersed himself in the clan's daily routines, leveraging his broad knowledge from beyond their borders to introduce new methods in smithing and mining, enriching the traditional ways of the Braemeer. His efforts were not just physical but intellectual, proving that his contributions could enrich their culture and economy.

Evenings were spent around the great hearth, the flicker of firelight casting dancing shadows on the stone walls. Gunnar listened intently to the stories of the clan, shared his own tales of distant lands, and spoke of his vision not as a prophecy dictated by a god but as a shared dream of a united and prosperous kingdom. He highlighted the strengths and values of the Braemeer Clan, showing them how crucial their contributions would be.

Duric watched him closely, his skepticism gradually giving way to a grudging respect. The turning point came during a particularly grueling day in the mines. Once again, a sudden cave-in trapped several miners. Cave-ins and rockslides were common, and between the clans, hundreds if not thousands of

Dwarves perished each year owing to them.

Without a second thought, Gunnar leaped into action, shouting commands to the nearby miners. "Secure that shaft! Quick, bring the supports!" His voice was steady, cutting through the chaos as Dwarves scrambled to follow his lead. Dust filled the air, and the ground trembled beneath their feet as they moved debris and propped up unstable sections of the tunnel.

Sweat poured down Gunnar's face as he heaved a massive boulder aside, revealing a trapped miner beneath. "Stay calm, we've got you," he said, his voice gentle but firm. He directed a group to carefully lift the dwarf to safety, then turned to the next pile of rubble.

As Gunnar worked, a sinking feeling settled in his chest. He could hear the faint cries of another Dwarf further down, trapped beneath an immense slab of rock. He knew the seconds were ticking away. His mind raced, thinking of the battle magic he possessed, knowing that with a mere thought he could halt time, move the impossible, and save the trapped miner.

But he also knew what that would mean. The suspicion and fear of his magic would resurface, undoing all the progress he had made with Duric and the Braemeer Clan. His heart ached with the weight of the decision. Gritting his teeth, he pressed on, using only his physical strength and strategic mind to guide the rescue.

Finally, with the last of his strength, Gunnar pried open a narrow passage, pulling the remaining miners to safety. All but one. The final cries had faded, replaced by a haunting silence. Gunnar's hands trembled as he stood there, staring at the immovable slab that sealed the fate of the lost Dwarf.

His heart pounded, heavy with exhaustion and guilt. He could have saved them all with a single spell. The sight of the fallen Dwarf haunted him, a stark reminder of his choice. But deep down, he knew the truth: using his magic would have only proved Duric's fears right. Their trust was fragile, like glass. One spell, and it would shatter. And in the end, he would be the monster they believed him to be.

Later that evening, as the rescued miners were tended to and the clan gathered to mourn their lost comrade, Gunnar slipped away to a quiet alcove, seeking solace in his connection with Havoc. He closed his eyes, reaching out with his mind. "*Havoc, I failed him,*" he thought, the weight of his guilt pressing down on him. "*I could have saved him if I had used my magic. Now, his blood is on my hands.*"

Havoc's response was immediate and comforting, yet laced with a profound truth. "*Gunnar, the sacrifice of that Dwarf, though tragic, may save thousands if you can convince the clans to unite. Sometimes, we must bear the weight of individual losses to achieve a greater good.*"

Gunnar's breath hitched as he absorbed Havoc's words. The pain of the loss was a sharp, unrelenting ache, but the wisdom in Havoc's voice provided a sliver of solace. "*I know you're right, Havoc. But it doesn't make it any easier.*"

"*It never will,*" Havoc replied gently. "*But remember why you are here. Honor his memory by continuing your mission.*"

Drawing a deep breath, Gunnar nodded. The resolve within him hardened. "*I will. For his sake and for the sake of all our people.*"

As the night deepened and the Braemeer Clan began to disperse, Duric approached Gunnar. His face was etched with lines of grief and contemplation. There was still a guarded look in his eyes, but also something new—an understanding, a flicker of respect. Gunnar met his gaze, knowing that while he carried the guilt of one lost life, he also carried the hope of a united future.

"You've proven yourself a hard worker and a capable leader, Gunnar," Duric said, his voice measured. "But the question remains: can you lead us without your magic?"

Gunnar met Duric's gaze with unwavering conviction. "I believe so, Duric. The strength of our people lies not in one individual, but in our unity and collective effort. My magic is a tool, but it is not the essence of who I am or what I stand for."

Duric shook his head slowly, his dirty beard swaying hypnotically. "Magic is evil, Gunnar. It is unnatural."

"Duric," Gunnar began, his voice thick with emotion, "if I had used my magic today, we would not be mourning a fallen comrade. My magic is not a curse—it's a gift that can save lives."

Duric's eyes flashed with anger, and he clenched his fists at his sides. "How can we ever trust you, Gunnar, when you think like that? Magic is dark and dangerous. It corrupts and destroys. We have seen it time and again. How can you not see that?"

Gunnar stood his ground, his expression earnest. "I understand your fears, but you must believe me when I say that my magic can be used for good. Today, it could have saved a life. If we are to face the threats of the Drogo and Nergai, we must use every tool at our disposal."

Duric shook his head, his face a mask of frustration. "It proves impossible for me to trust you, Gunnar. Your magic is a threat, not a solution. I cannot risk the safety of my people on the hope that your intentions are pure."

Gunnar felt a wave of despair wash over him. He had failed to convince Duric, and the loss weighed heavily on his heart. "I respect your decision, Duric, but please know that my offer stands. I seek only to protect and unite our people."

Duric's expression softened slightly, though his resolve remained firm. "I appreciate your efforts, Gunnar, but I must ask you to leave. However, your resolve and dedication have not gone unnoticed. Perhaps not all is lost."

Gunnar nodded, accepting the inevitable. "Thank you, Duric. I will continue my mission and hope that one day, you might see things differently."

With a heavy heart, Gunnar left the hall, the weight of his failure pressing down on him. Yet, Duric's final words offered a sliver of hope. Not all was lost.

Kemp

Kemp stepped out of Thraxos's chamber, the heavy door closing behind him with a resonant thud. The corridor, dimly lit by flickering torches, seemed to swallow sound, each shadow an echo of the ancient fortress's storied past. He took a deep breath, steadying himself. The weight of his mission pressed upon him, heavy as the stone walls around him, but he knew he couldn't face it alone.

He navigated the winding halls with purpose, his mind replaying the conversation he had just had. Memories of fire and ash stirred at the mention of Ruiha and Dakarai—companions who had become his family through trials by sword and sorcery. They had been through so much, and now he needed them more than ever. The thought of asking them to return to the lands of their tormentors filled him with dread, but there was no other choice.

In the training yard, he found them. Ruiha's movements were a dance of lethal grace, her blade a silvery blur as she parried and struck with practiced ease. Dakarai, larger and more imposing, moved with surprising agility, his powerful swings controlled and precise.

Kemp waited until they finished their bout, his heart pounding in his chest. Ruiha was the first to notice him, sheathing her sword as a smile lit her face. "Kemp," she greeted, her voice a lilting melody over the clang of metal. "You look like a man haunted by ghosts. What brings you to the training yards today?"

Dakarai turned, his expression more guarded. "Trouble stirs, doesn't it?" he said, reading Kemp's tense posture as if it were one of his opponent's predictable moves.

Kemp took a deep breath. "I need to talk to both of you. It's important." They exchanged a glance, then nodded. Ruiha motioned for him to continue, her expression curious and concerned. "I've just come from a council with Thraxos and Thalirion," Kemp began, his voice steady despite the storm raging inside him. "They've divined a path to harnessing the Shadowfire that could control the Dragon Crown. But the journey—it's fraught with peril beyond our darkest reckonings."

Ruiha's eyes sparked with intrigue and a touch of fear. "And what role do we play in this harrowing quest?" Kemp met Dakarai's intense gaze. "I need you both to venture with me to the Forgotten Realm. To reach it, we must traverse the southern expanse of the Scorched Mountains, deep in Drogo Mulik territory."

Dakarai paused, his eyes briefly losing focus as if glimpsing a distant, dark memory. His voice, when he spoke, carried a quiet intensity. "Kemp, you're not suggesting we head back through—that place again, are you?" His gaze shifted away, unwilling or unable to hold Kemp's eye.

Kemp nodded, his voice unwavering. "Yes, and I ask not out of desire but of necessity. Your intimate knowledge of Drogo Mulik's lands is crucial, Dakarai. And Ruiha, your swordsmanship and counsel have never been more vital. Only together can we undertake this."

Ruiha stepped forward, her eyes blazing with a fierce determination that matched the flame of her hair. "For you, Kemp, for this cause, I would brave even the darkest abyss."

Kemp felt a surge of gratitude, but his gaze shifted to Dakarai, who still seemed conflicted. "Dakarai, your reluctance is warranted, and your decision is yours to make alone. But remember, in unity there is strength—strength we will need to harness the shadows."

Dakarai was silent for a long moment, his expression troubled. Finally, he let out a sigh, his shoulders slumping as if under an immense weight. "Very well. For the bond that ties us, for the hope of peace, I will walk this path with you. But, Kemp, let it be worth more than the price we may yet pay."

Kemp nodded, relief washing over him. "Thank you. We shall gather at dawn."

Ruiha clapped Kemp on the shoulder, her smile encouraging. "Then let us prepare, for the morrow brings not just a journey, but a destiny."

Dakarai nodded, his expression still grim but resolute. "We'll ready ourselves for whatever awaits. Our fates are now as one, entwined by shared threads of destiny."

As he made his way back to his quarters to prepare, Kemp felt a renewed sense of hope. The whispers in his mind still lingered, but they seemed quieter, overshadowed by the determination and support of his friends. Together, they would face the challenges ahead and emerge victorious.

Ruiha

Ruiha studied Dakarai with an eagle's focus, her gaze dissecting his every subtlety as they sparred in the dusty training yard. His anxiety about their impending journey through the perilous Drogo lands was etched into the very sinews of his movements, a silent scream of fear that she, too, began to feel echoing within her bones.

The muscles in his shoulders told their own story, tensed to stone, a fortress attempting to hold back his dread. His eyes, usually sharp as flint, now skittered from shadow to shadow, as though expecting the ghostly figure of Junak to emerge and claim them both. The specter of their past encounters in those cursed lands haunted him visibly.

As Ruiha watched, a wave of empathy washed over her. She saw the threads of his fear woven tightly around him, a cloak invisible yet palpable. The clang of steel and the grunts of their fellow warriors faded to a distant murmur, drowned out by the loud hammering of Dakarai's fears. His usual veneer of confidence was now subsumed by a tide of anxiety so tangible she could almost reach out and grasp it.

"Dak," she said softly, drawing his gaze to her own. His eyes, limpid pools reflecting back his dread, flickered with the light of a caged creature. "Are you sure we should be heading through Drogo lands again?" he murmured, his voice a brittle shell laced with unease.

Her answer was a solid rock in a swirling sea. "We don't have much of a choice, Dak. Kemp said it's the only route to where we need to go."

Dakarai sighed, a hand rubbing the protruding bones at the back of his neck, each a testament to the burdens he carried. "I know, but what if we are captured again? I can't rid myself of this dread that claws at me."

Crossing the distance between them with a few short steps, Ruiha clasped his hand. Her grip was both an anchor and a promise. "We'll be cautious. We're better armed, better prepared this time. And remember, we have each other. We'll get through it, just as we have before."

Her words, meant to soothe, were also a cloak for her own simmering intentions. Not just to aid Kemp, but a chance to settle scores that burned hot within her heart. The slow pace of Dwarven politics was intolerable; this journey was her chance to strike back at those who had wronged her.

As they turned from the training grounds, Dakarai's concern was still written across his features in lines deep as furrows. "Just promise me you'll be careful, Ruiha. I couldn't bear to lose you."

With a smile soft as dawn, she met his worried gaze. "I promise, Dak. We'll watch each other's backs."

6

A Fragile Alliance: The Cost of Unity

"Unity is the shield that guards against defeat, but it must be tempered by loyalty and sacrifice."

Kemp

Kemp gathered his companions in Thalirion's chamber, the high ceilings and ancient tapestries adding a solemn weight to their meeting. The dim light from the chandeliers flickered, casting shadows that danced across the room, merging with whispers of history etched into every stone. The cold stone floor beneath Kemp's boots grounded him in the gravity of the moment.

Thalirion, an ancient figure of wisdom and authority, stood at the head of the table. His piercing gaze swept over the group, lingering on each face as if assessing their readiness. Despite his short and lean stature, his presence filled the room, commanding respect effortlessly. Kemp couldn't help but feel a shiver of both fear and admiration for the old Sage.

Thraxos, with his imposing frame, leaned against a stone pillar, arms crossed and expression stern. The tension was palpable, the gravity of their mission heavy on everyone's shoulders, pressing down like a physical weight.

"Before you set off, we must discuss your route," Thalirion began, his voice cutting through the silence with precision. His words echoed in the vast chamber, filled with an authority that left no room for doubt. "You must travel southward to the city of Hammer, nestled in the southern expanse of the Scorched Mountains. From there, you must brave the Cimmerian Strait—a tumultuous sea draped in ceaseless mist, veiling indescribable ocean monsters—and make your way to the mountainous Forgotten Realm in the southwestern reaches of Sandarah. Once there, we must uncover the hidden valley where Chronos dwells and implore him for his aid."

Ruiha's face tightened at the mention of Sandarah, her homeland. Her eyes flickered with memories—painful, proud—etched deep within her. Kemp knew those memories, the scars they left behind. He saw the flicker of emotions cross her features but pressed forward. There was no other choice.

Dakarai's voice rumbled with concern, a deep, resonant sound that filled the chamber. "The Cimmerian Strait is notorious for its dangers. Many have tried to cross it and failed." His brow furrowed, shadows of old fears playing across his face, the weight of lost comrades and ancient tales evident in his eyes.

Thalirion nodded, his expression solemn. "The Forgotten Realm itself is equally dangerous. The mountains are treacherous, and the creatures that inhabit them are unimaginable." His voice remained steady, though tinged with unease. Kemp took a deep breath. He understood that this mission carried more weight than just mastering his Shadowfire; Anwyn's life and the fate of Vellhor hung in the balance. A wave of nausea washed over him, the enormity of their task settling in like a dark, heavy fog.

"Why can't we use the Endless Bridge?" Kemp asked, a note of hope clinging to his words like a drowning man to driftwood.

Thraxos snorted before straightening. "We can only create a limited number of Endless Bridges in Vellhor," he replied flatly.

Thalirion nodded in agreement. "As you know, the aura here is much weaker than in Nexus, and despite being Sages, our power diminishes daily. Creating another Endless Bridge would drain us too much."

Ruiha stepped forward, her resolve firm, her eyes meeting those of each of her companions. "We've faced dangers before and emerged victorious. We can do this. We have to." Her voice carried a note of determination that was almost infectious, igniting a spark of hope in the hearts of those around her. She glanced at Dakarai, her eyes softening as she saw the worry in his. "We'll need to be vigilant, but we're stronger together. We've faced worse."

Dakarai took a deep breath, his eyes meeting Kemp's with a mix of resolve and trepidation. "All right. If we're doing this, we need to be prepared for anything." His words were a pledge of loyalty and a reminder of the challenges that lay ahead, a silent promise of steadfastness and courage.

Thalirion spread a map across the table, its ancient parchment crackling under his touch. He traced their route with a steady hand, pointing out key landmarks and potential hazards. "You'll need provisions and a reliable ship to cross the Strait. Once we reach the mountains, it will be a test of endurance and skill to find the hidden valley." His eyes gleamed with a mix of wisdom and concern, the weight of his years and the burden of his knowledge heavy in every line on his face.

Thraxos stepped forward, his gaze intense, his voice a low growl. "You will need to charter a ship and crew once you arrive at the Cimmerian. You'll likely struggle to find someone, owing to the proximity of the Drogo in that area. Not many people there are willing to take the risk of being situated so close to them." Kemp noticed Thraxos's eyes shift uncomfortably towards Dakarai as he spoke, more than likely worried he would offend the Drogo.

Kemp nodded. "Thank you for the advice, Thraxos. And thank you, all of you, for standing by me. We have a long journey ahead, but together, we'll succeed." His words were a beacon of hope, a reminder that they were united in purpose and resolve.

Ruiha's eyes shone with determination, a flicker of that old fire igniting within her. "We'll make it through. For you and Anwyn." Dakarai placed a reassuring hand on her shoulder, his strength a silent promise of protection.

"We will." His words were simple but filled with a depth of emotion, a vow to stand by his friends no matter the cost.

As they finalized their plans and prepared for departure, Kemp felt the weight of their mission pressing upon him. Yet, with his friends by his side, he also felt a glimmer of hope. The path to mastering the Shadowfire and controlling the Dragon Crown was fraught with peril, but they were ready to face it, no matter the cost. Their journey behind enemy lines would mark the beginning of an epic quest, one that would test their courage, their resolve, and their bonds.

Gunnar

Faint morning light seeped through the narrow crevices high in the cavern walls of Gunnar's chamber in Uglich, casting a soft, eerie glow on the rough stone surroundings. The chill in the air was a stark reminder of the unyielding stone and the cold ambitions that thrived within its confines. The memories of Hornbaek's betrayal, the cold rejection from once-trusted allies, made the air feel even icier. He stirred beneath his heavy blankets, the weight of recent events pressing heavily on his mind.

The rejection in Hornbaek gnawed at his confidence, leaving him in a state of turmoil. Betrayal had come from unexpected quarters, friends turning foes in the blink of an eye. Mistrust shadowed his thoughts, whispering doubts into the corners of his mind. His thoughts drifted to Ilara, the fierce warrior he once fought beside. Her absence now a wound that refused to heal, her betrayal a sharp blade twisted in his gut.

As he prepared to meet Gadrin, the shrewd and calculating leader of the Uglich Clan, Gunnar's resolve hardened. The smell of burning coals and molten metal permeated the air, a constant reminder of the industrious heart of Uglich. The subterranean city buzzed with the distant sounds of industry and life, the clang of hammers on anvils a symphony of survival. He knew he needed a different approach, one that would appeal to Gadrin's pragmatism and ambition.

He couldn't afford another failure; the fate of Dreynas depended on it. With a deep breath, he pushed the blankets aside and rose, the cold stone floor beneath his feet grounding him in the reality of the challenge ahead. Gunnar reached out with his mind to Havoc, his trusted Stonesprite companion.

"*Havoc,*" Gunnar thought, their telepathic bond thrumming with a familiar warmth. "*This is my last chance to unite the clans, but Gadrin is a different challenge. He's focused on his own gain. How do I convince him?*"

The Stonesprite's voice resonated in his mind, calm and steady. "*Gunnar, you must understand what Gadrin values most. He's a pragmatist. Show him how a united Dreynas benefits him and his clan directly."*

Gunnar nodded, feeling a renewed sense of determination. "*Y*ou're right, Havoc. *It's not just about the greater good. I need to speak to his interests.*" He donned his armor, the metal cool against his skin, each piece bearing the marks of past battles. He hesitated over his sword, memories of battles fought side by side with Ilara flashing before him. Strapped his battle axe to his back, the weight of it was a familiar comfort, a reminder of battles fought and battles yet to come.

As he moved toward the door, Havoc's voice echoed in his mind. "*Remember, Gunnar, Gadrin's ambitious. He cares more for personal gain than he does for bettering Dreynas. Use that to connect with him.*"

Gunnar left his chamber, the sounds of the bustling forge and the murmur of voices filling the air. Uglich was a place of constant activity, its people industrious and driven. The central hall was no different, filled with the hum of conversation and the clink of metal. Each sound, each movement, reminded Gunnar of the stakes. Every glance from the passing Dwarves seemed to challenge him, to remind him of the thin ice he tread upon. Gadrin stood at the head of the hall, his coppery skin gleaming in the firelight, his eyes sharp and calculating. His robes, adorned with intricate patterns and symbols of power, reflected his status among the clan. As Gunnar approached, the hall fell silent, all eyes turning to the newcomer.

"Gadrin," Gunnar began, his voice steady and clear. "Thank you for meeting with me. I come with a proposition that I believe will benefit Uglich greatly."

Gadrin's eyes narrowed, a hint of a smile playing at the corners of his mouth. "Speak, Gunnar. I am curious to hear what you have to offer."

Gunnar stepped forward, his gaze unwavering. "The threat

of the Drogo and Nergai looms over all of Dreynas. A united front is our best chance of survival. But I understand that unity must offer tangible benefits to each clan. For Uglich, it means trade, protection, and influence."

Gadrin raised an eyebrow, his interest piqued. "Go on."

"Uglich's forges are renowned across Dreynas," Gunnar continued. "But with the support of the other clans, your reach can expand even further. Imagine your goods traded in every corner of Vellhor, your influence growing with each new alliance. Your weapons could arm legions, your tools could build empires. We could build trading partnerships with the Elves and the Humans. Your personal wealth, and the wealth of your clan, would be unparalleled."

A murmur of approval swept through the hall, whispers of ambition and profit dancing in the firelight. Gadrin's avaricious eyes sparkled with intrigue, yet Gunnar discerned a wary glint in his gaze. Dwarves like Gadrin were not easily fooled; offers that appeared too favorable were typically met with skepticism.

"And what do you ask in return, Gunnar? What price must Uglich pay for this alliance?" he inquired.

Gunnar took a deep breath, choosing his words carefully. He knew that this moment could shape the future of Dreynas, and his mind raced with the weight of the implications. His heart pounded as he felt the eyes of every Dwarf in the hall upon him, the stakes higher than ever. "I ask for your support in uniting the clans under one ruler. In return, Uglich will have a seat at the table, a voice in shaping the future of Dreynas. Together, we can build a kingdom where each clan thrives." His voice carried the weight of his vision, each word a brick in the foundation of a new order. His heart pounded with the hope that Gadrin could see the vision he was painting, the promise of a unified and prosperous realm. Gadrin's expression remained inscrutable, but Gunnar sensed a shift.

The leader of Uglich was considering his words, weighing the potential benefits against the risks. "The Drogo and Nergai are a formidable threat," Gadrin said slowly. "A united Dreynas could indeed offer greater protection. But how do I know you can lead us, Gunnar? How do I know you won't use your magic to impose your will?"

Gunnar met Gadrin's gaze with unwavering conviction. "My magic is a tool, but it is not the essence of who I am. I have proven my dedication through hard work and sacrifice. I seek not to impose my will, but to build a future where all our people can prosper." A tense silence followed, the air thick with unspoken fears and ambitions.

Gadrin scoffed, "that's not what Duric seems to think!"

Gunnar's gaze remained fixed on Gadrin, his voice steady and resolute. "Duric is blinded by fear. He cannot see the potential for greatness that lies in unity." Inside, he battled a whirlwind of frustration and sadness, memories of distrust and rejection gnawing at him.

"Duric and the Hornbaek Clan are steeped in superstition. I used my magic to save them, yet they did not trust me. When I refrained from using it and someone perished, they celebrated!" His eyes mirrored the sorrow he felt for the lost dwarf, a pain that lingered in his heart.

"They fail to grasp the true potential of my magic to aid them," he said, his words deliberate and heartfelt, each syllable a plea for understanding and acceptance. Gadrin studied him for a long moment, his eyes narrowing as if weighing Gunnar's very soul. Finally, he nodded slowly.

"Very well, Gunnar. I will consider your proposal. But know this: if you falter or betray our trust, Uglich will not hesitate to defend its interests." Gunnar nodded, a wave of relief washing over him, easing the tension in his shoulders. "Thank you, Gadrin. I will not let you down," he replied, his voice firm with determination and a newfound sense of hope.

As the meeting drew to a close and Gunnar exited the hall, a sense of accomplishment settled over him. He had sown the seeds of unity in Uglich, aware that the journey ahead would be laden with challenges. Yet, he recognized this moment as a pivotal step toward a united Dreynas. The path to unity would be long and arduous, but with Gadrin and Bojan now aligned, his hopes for the future were high and resolute. Outside the hall, the cold air bit at his skin, but he welcomed the sting, letting it fuel his determination. He would not let Ilara's betrayal, nor the doubts of others, deter him from his path.

Ruiha

Ruiha stood at the edge of the courtyard, her sharp eyes scanning the bustling marketplace of Draegoor. The city thrived around her, merchants hawking their wares with enthusiastic cries while stocky Dwarven children darted between stalls, laughter and shouts mingling in the air. She could almost taste the tang of exotic roots and fungi and hear the clink of frosteel coins exchanging hands. Yet, despite the vibrant life around her, Ruiha's mind was anchored to the task ahead. The weight of responsibility pressed on her shoulders, a familiar yet unwelcome companion.

She took a deep breath, feeling the cool stone of the courtyard under her feet, a stark contrast to the chaotic warmth of the market. Dakarai stood to her right, his muscular frame a solid wall of strength and determination. She glanced at him, noting the way his eyes never stopped moving, ever vigilant. On her left, Kemp fidgeted slightly, his Shadowfire flickering around his fingers in a rhythmic pattern that betrayed his anticipation. Their presence was more than just a comfort; it was a reminder of their unity, a silent vow that they would face whatever came together.

Ruiha's thoughts flickered to the challenges they would face, the dangers lurking in the Scorched Mountains. But as she looked at her companions, she felt a surge of resolve. They had come too far, sacrificed too much, to falter now. The marketplace around her seemed to fade into the background, its noises and colors dulling as her focus sharpened. This moment, this courtyard, was merely the beginning. With Dakarai and Kemp by her side, she felt a flicker of hope amidst the uncertainty.

"We need Magnus," Kemp stated, his voice resolute. "He's a formidable warrior, and his skills could tip the scales in our favor."

Ruiha nodded, her thoughts already racing ahead to the confrontation she knew awaited them. "Agreed. But convincing his father will be a challenge."

They navigated through the throng, weaving between animated merchants and spirited children, the lively sounds of the marketplace gradually fading behind them. The path to Magnus's family estate led deeper into the underground Dwarven citadel, the air growing cooler and the light dimmer. Massive stone pillars, intricately carved with ancient runes and Dwarven symbols, lined their route, each one telling a story of the city's storied past.

The walls of the tunnel were a stark contrast to the bustling city above, their surfaces smooth and worn by centuries of careful craftsmanship. Torches flickered in iron sconces, casting a warm, dancing light that illuminated the detailed engravings and brought the carvings to life. The faint sound of dripping water echoed through the cavernous space, a reminder of the subterranean rivers that nourished the citadel.

As they approached the estate, the imposing figure of Erik, Magnus's father, came into view. Erik stood with his back to them, his broad shoulders framed by the heavy fur cloak he always wore. The cloak, rich and dark, seemed almost to meld with the shadowy recesses of the tunnel. His presence exuded a formidable aura, one that spoke of years of battle and unyielding strength.

Ruiha's steps slowed as they neared, her eyes narrowing as she studied Erik. Dakarai's hand brushed against the cool stone of the wall, his senses attuned to any sign of movement. Kemp, ever the diplomat, cleared his throat, but his eyes were fixed on Erik, a mix of respect and caution in his gaze.

Magnus stood beside his father, his eyes narrowed and hands gesturing animatedly. The furrowed brow and tight jawline of Erik matched Magnus' intensity. Though Ruiha couldn't hear their words, the rapid exchange and stiff posture spoke volumes.

"Magnus," Kemp called, drawing the Dwarf's attention.

Magnus turned. "Kemp, Ruiha, Dakarai," he greeted, his voice tense.

Erik's frown deepened as he evaluated them each in turn.

Ruiha stepped forward, her voice calm and steady. "Magnus, Erik," she began. "Thalirion and Thraxos require us to go on a mission, and we want Magnus to come with us."

Magnus took a deep breath, his interest piqued. Erik's jaw set in a stubborn line, but the conflict in his eyes was evident.

"Anwyn's life hangs in the balance," Ruiha continued. "If we can help Kemp master his Shadowfire and control the Dragon Crown, we can save her."

Erik's eyes narrowed in concern. "And who will lead the Snow Wolves? What of our clan? What of uniting the clans?"

Ruiha could see the turmoil within Erik, a father's love clashing with the responsibility of his clan and kingdom. She met his gaze steadily. "Erik, we understand that you have concerns. But Magnus's presence could make the difference between success and failure. This mission is bigger than uniting the clans of Dreynas. It's about the future of Vellhor!"

Erik looked at each of them in turn, his gaze lingering on Magnus. The silence stretched, heavy with unspoken emotions. Finally, Erik sighed, a deep, resigned sound. "If you must go, then so be it. But I will not send you unprotected."

He gestured to a figure standing in the shadows of the courtyard, who stepped forward into the light. Arvi, clad in armor that gleamed with a silvery sheen, his eyes sharp and determined.

"Arvi will accompany you," Erik declared. "He will ensure Magnus's safety and aid you in your quest."

Magnus's expression was a mix of relief and gratitude. "Thank you, Father. We won't fail."

Erik's stern facade softened for a moment, a father's love breaking through. "Return safely, all of you. Draegoor will be waiting."

With their group now complete, Ruiha felt a renewed sense of purpose. She glanced at Magnus and Arvi, then back to her companions. The path ahead was fraught with danger, but together, they had a chance.

As they made their way back through the marketplace, the weight of their mission settled on Ruiha's shoulders once more. But alongside the burden of duty, there was also a flicker of hope. They were stronger now, united in their resolve. And with Magnus and Arvi by their side, they were ready to face whatever challenges lay ahead.

7

BONDS OF BLOOD AND FIRE: A PATH FORGED IN SHADOWS

"To lead with magic is to walk the line between fear and acceptance, where only courage can guide the way."

GUNNAR

Gunnar's journey back to Draegoor was fraught with a mixture of anticipation and dread. The landscape around him, rugged and familiar, did little to calm the storm within his mind. He knew he had to face his father, to relay his recent successes and, with a heavy heart, his failure in Braemeer. His stomach churned at the thought of revealing his affinity to magic. He couldn't help but feel a deep-seated fear and shame about his abilities, emotions that had haunted him since the rejection in Braemeer.

As he approached the towering gates of Draegoor, the sentries acknowledged him with respectful nods, a stark contrast to the turmoil he felt inside. The gates themselves were a marvel—tall and wrought with dark iron, adorned with the intricate sigils of his house. Above the gate, perched on the stone battlements, gargoyles watched with unblinking eyes, as if they were guardians from the old tales. The walls of the ancient fortress rose high, a testament to the craftsmanship of generations past, each stone laid with the purpose of withstanding both time and siege.

Beyond the gates, Draegoor unfolded into a bustling expanse. The courtyards were alive with activity—blacksmiths hammering out the weapons of war, merchants peddling their wares from colorful stalls, and the clatter of warriors training in the practice yards. The air was thick with the mingling scents of sweat, hot metal, and the occasional whiff of spiced meat roasting on a spit. Yet, despite the lively atmosphere, a sense of order and discipline prevailed, like the measured steps of a well-rehearsed dance.

Everywhere, banners of white and gray fluttered in the breeze, bearing the crest of Clan Draegoor—a snow wolf howling at a huge mountain. They were symbols of the house's dual nature: the fierce strength of the snow wolf and the immovability of a mountain. The ancient fortress was a living relic of history, its halls echoing with the footsteps of his ancestors, its stones bearing silent witness to countless stories of valor, sacrifice, and, more recently, betrayal.

But today, Draegoor seemed both welcoming and foreboding to him. The familiar sounds and sights did little to ease the turmoil within his heart. He knew his father awaited him, the unyielding figure of Erik the Blood. Yet, before he could face that reckoning, he had another stop to make. One that weighed just as heavily on his heart. One that would take him to where Anwyn lay at rest. There, in the quiet of her chamber, he hoped to find the courage he needed to face the challenges that lay ahead.

Gunnar made his way through the familiar corridors to Anwyn's chambers. Her room was dimly lit, the air heavy with the scent of herbs and the soft glow of a single candle casting shadows on the walls. Anwyn lay still, her breathing shallow but steady. Her once vibrant eyes were closed, the usual spark of life absent as she slept.

Gunnar approached her bedside, his chest tightening at the sight of Anwyn lying so frail and vulnerable. Her once-rosy cheeks were now pale, and her breathing was barely audible. The coolness of her skin sent a shiver through him as he gently took her hand, his thumb tracing the delicate veins beneath.

Lorelei lay curled on Anwyn's chest, her tiny form rising and falling with each labored breath that escaped Anwyn's lips. The Fae's shimmering body reflected the pale light filtering through the canopy above, a comforting, rhythmic glow. Gunnar ached to wake Lorelei, to ask her how Anwyn had been during his absence. But he knew better. Lorelei spoke to no one but Anwyn, and even then, in whispers that were more feeling than words. He watched her now, so still and peaceful, her small eyelids flickering in some quiet dream.

"Anwyn," he whispered, his voice raw, the word catching like a splinter in his throat. He took a shaky breath, the name trembling on his lips, a plea and a promise wrapped in one. "I'm back."

He leaned closer, searching her face for any sign of improvement. Her eyelids fluttered, the faintest movement, a barely-there flicker that sent a surge of hope rushing through him like a lightning bolt. For one heart-stopping moment, he was sure she would open her eyes, that she would look at him and he would see her there, truly there, behind the fog that had clouded her eyes for so long. He could almost hear her voice, clear and strong, cutting through the silence that had settled over their lives.

But the moment passed. Her eyelids stilled, and she slipped back into the deep, unresponsive slumber that had held her captive. Gunnar's hope, so fiercely kindled, guttered and died like a candle in the wind. His breath left him in a ragged sigh, the sound echoing through the stillness of the room. The brief light that had flared in his heart was replaced by a familiar, crushing despair.

He lowered his head, pressing his forehead against the cool skin of her hand. He wanted to scream, to rage against the injustice of it all. Thalirion and Thraxos, wise and powerful in the arcane arts, had bent all their knowledge toward saving her. Yet here she lay, fragile as a winter leaf, trapped in a place where neither he nor any magic could reach her.

The helplessness was a weight, pressing down on him, grinding his hope into the dirt beneath his feet. He was a warrior, trained to fight, to take action, but against this, he was powerless. All he could do was wait, sit by her side, and hope that one day, when he spoke her name, she would wake and look at him with clear eyes. Until then, his words felt like echoes, fading into the void.

Desperation continued to claw at him as he knelt there, gripping her hand tighter as if willing his strength into her. He had promised to find a way to help her, and the thought of failing that promise gnawed at his soul.

As Gunnar turned to leave, a faint whisper brushed against his ears, barely audible yet unmistakable. His heart leaped, hope fluttering like a trapped bird in his chest. He spun back to Anwyn, eyes scanning her still form for any sign of movement. Her eyelids remained shut, her breathing steady but shallow. He leaned in closer, willing her to speak again, to give him any sign that she was aware of his presence. The silence stretched, heavy and unbroken, dashing his brief moment of hope.

Disheartened, Gunnar's hand lingered on the edge of her bed, reluctant to break the fragile connection. With a heavy sigh, he straightened, feeling the weight of responsibility settle back onto his shoulders. He had to face his father, confess his failures and the truth about his magic. The thought sent a shiver through him, but he steeled himself, drawing on a reserve of courage he wasn't sure he possessed.

The corridors of Draegoor twisted and turned, each step echoing his turmoil. The stone walls, usually a source of comfort, felt oppressive now, closing in around him. His mind raced with memories of his father's stern face, the expectations and unspoken disappointments. Every footfall seemed louder, a drumbeat heralding his impending confrontation. He clenched his fists, trying to steady his breath and his resolve. The path to his father's chambers had never felt so long or so daunting.

When he entered the room, his father and his brother Magnus were deep in conversation. They turned to greet him, their expressions a mix of curiosity and concern.

"Gunnar," Erik said, his voice resonating with authority and warmth. "It's good to see you back. Tell us, how did your mission fare?"

Gunnar took a deep breath, forcing himself to remain steady. "Father, Magnus, I have news from Uglich and Hornbaek. In Uglich, I managed to gain Gadrin's consideration for an alliance. He is pragmatic and sees the benefits of uniting the clans. In Hornbaek, though it was challenging, I made some headway. But... there's more."

Magnus leaned in, his brows furrowing. "What happened in Braemeer?"

Gunnar hesitated, his mind racing to find a way to avoid the full truth. "Braemeer was... difficult. They were not as receptive to our cause."

Erik's gaze sharpened. "Gunnar, there's more to this, isn't there? What aren't you telling us?"

Gunnar's heart pounded, a mix of fear and shame tightening his throat. He glanced at the floor, unable to meet their eyes. "I tried to avoid using my magic, to show them I could lead without it, but... they discovered it."

Silence filled the room, heavy and oppressive. Erik's eyes widened with disbelief. "Magic? You've been practicing magic?"

Gunnar hesitated, before finally whispering, "yes," his voice barely audible. His heart felt like a stone in his chest. "I tried to hide it, but when it was discovered, Duric couldn't accept me after that."

Erik's face turned a deep shade of red, his eyes widening with disbelief. His expression twisted, a storm of anger and confusion brewing in his gaze. "Magic? Why didn't you tell us, Gunnar? How long have you been hiding this from your own family?"

Gunnar's throat tightened as memories of his training in Nexus surged—hearing the whisper of incantations in the dead of night, feeling the surge of power course through him in moments of peril. "It first manifested when we were attacked by the golem in Fort Berg," he said, his voice raw. "It saved my life."

Erik's brow furrowed, his confusion deepening. "Golem? What are you talking about? There are no golems in Dreynas. They require dark magic and sacrifices in order to summon. Not even the Shadowforged would summon a golem!"

Gunnar clenched his fists, knuckles whitening. The image of the massive, lumbering creature flashed in his mind, the terror of that night still vivid. "We later discovered it was the Drogo, working with information Wilfrid passed on."

Erik's face contorted with rage, his fists trembling at his sides. "That treacherous bastard... If I hadn't already killed him..." His voice trailed off, the anger in his eyes slowly giving way to a softer, more pained look. He took a step closer to Gunnar, his gaze searching. "Why didn't you tell me, Gunnar?" he implored, an edge of desperation in his voice.

Gunnar swallowed hard, the weight of his father's disappointment pressing down on him. "Father, I didn't want to disappoint you. I thought you'd be ashamed of me."

Erik's expression softened further, his anger melting into a look of understanding. He placed a hand on Gunnar's shoulder, his grip firm yet gentle. "Gunnar, you are my son. Nothing could ever make me ashamed of you. Your magic is a part of you, and if it saved your life, then it is a gift. We will find a way to use it for the good of our kingdom."

Gunnar felt a wave of relief wash over him, his father's acceptance lifting a heavy burden from his heart. For the first time in a long while, he felt a sense of belonging and hope. With his father's support and the power within him, Gunnar knew he could face whatever challenges lay ahead.

Erik took another deep breath. "Gunnar, magic or not, you are still my son. Your courage and determination are what define you. Magic is but a tool, one that can aid us during these dark times."

At that moment, Havoc emerged from behind Gunnar, his stony form glinting in the dim light. The Stonesprite, now almost the size of Gunnar's entire arm, moved with surprising grace despite his rocky exterior. He landed on the ground with a solid thud, his purple eyes glowing with curiosity and mischief.

Erik and Magnus stared in awe. "What...?" Magnus began.

"This is Havoc," Gunnar said, a hint of pride threading through his voice. "He's been my companion, my guide. And he's grown... significantly."

Gunnar looked Havoc up and down, his eyes widening with genuine surprise at the Stonesprite's impressive size. "I can hardly believe how much you've grown, Havoc," he added, marveling at the transformation of his steadfast companion.

Havoc's voice resonated in Gunnar's mind, playful and

light. "Gunnar, I'm glad to finally be free and not your prisoner any longer."

Gunnar chuckled, translating Havoc's message for his father and brother. "He says he's glad to be free and not my prisoner any longer."

Erik laughed, a warm, hearty sound. "Havoc, you are most welcome here. Any friend of Gunnar's is of course, a friend of ours."

A sudden knock on the door interrupted the moment. Gunnar turned to see Thalirion standing in the doorway. His eyes were somber but determined. "Gunnar, we need to discuss Anwyn's condition. I believe there may be a way to save her, but it will require great risk and cooperation."

Gunnar's heart raced. "Tell me what I need to do."

For the first time in a long while, Gunnar felt a sense of belonging and acceptance. The heavy weight of his fears and doubts began to lift. Surrounded by family and his bonded companion, he felt a renewed sense of hope and determination. The path ahead was still fraught with challenges, but with his father's support and Havoc by his side, Gunnar knew he could face whatever came next. His resolve to unite the clans and save Anwyn had never been stronger.

Kemp

Kemp felt the weight of the mission settle over him like a heavy cloak as they made their way through Draegoor. The bustling sounds of the marketplace surged back into his awareness, a stark contrast to the solemnity of their previous conversations. He glanced at Ruiha, her jaw set with fierce determination, and at Dakarai, whose vigilant eyes missed nothing. Magnus and Arvi had stayed with Erik, making their own preparations for their eventual departure.

Before they could begin gathering supplies, a messenger rushed up to them, breathless and urgent. "Gunnar summons you to his hall immediately," he gasped, looking at each of them with wide, anxious eyes.

Kemp exchanged glances with his companions and nodded. They followed the messenger through the winding streets of Draegoor, the vibrant life around them a fleeting distraction from the daunting path ahead. Soon, they reached Gunnar's hall, its imposing stone structure a testament to the Dwarven Prince's newfound power and authority.

Inside, the hall was alive with the whispers of servants and the flickering light of torches, casting dancing shadows on the stone walls. The usual grandeur of the place was overshadowed by a palpable tension that clung to the air. Kemp's eyes swept over the room, noting the undercurrent of anxiety that seemed to ripple through everyone present.

In Kemp's mind, Gunnar had always been the epitome of calm and control, a pillar of unwavering strength. But today, the Dwarven Prince looked anything but composed. Desperation etched deep lines into his face, his eyes filled with a silent plea that seemed so unlike the formidable ruler. Kemp's heart tightened at the sight, the weight of their mission crashing down on him with renewed intensity. The urgency of their task, the stakes they faced, all crystallized in that moment.

"Thank you for coming," Gunnar began, his voice strained. "Anwyn's spirit weakens by the day. I have been informed she needs your Shadowfire and the Dragon Crown to survive. I know this journey is perilous, but I beg of you, bring back something that can help her."

Kemp felt the weight of Gunnar's words settle heavily on his shoulders. He glanced at his companions, seeing the determination mirrored in their eyes. A silent understanding passed between them—each knew the gravity of their task. "We will do everything in our power, Gunnar," Kemp vowed, his voice firm.

Gunnar's expression softened, relief flickering in his eyes, but it was overshadowed by a lingering desperation. He moved to a nearby chest with a measured grace that belied the urgency in his demeanor. With a nod, he gestured for Kemp and the others to come closer.

"I desperately wish I could go with you. But I have to continue my work in allying the clans. I also fear to leave Anwyn's side for too long. Instead, I ask that you take these," Gunnar said, his voice thick with unspoken emotion as he lifted the lid. Inside, an array of frosteel weapons gleamed under the torchlight, each one a masterpiece of unparalleled craftsmanship. Kemp's breath caught at the sight—the finest weapons in all of Draegoor, perhaps the entire kingdom of Dreynas.

Gunnar's gaze swept over them, lingering on each face. "Take them to Karl before you leave. He will ensure that they are even more formidable for you. I am certain these will aid you on your journey. May they keep you safe."

Ruiha and Dakarai stepped forward eagerly, their eyes wide with amazement. Ruiha selected a pair of elegantly curved daggers, their blades singing as she tested their weight and balance. Dakarai chose a massive axe, his grin widening as he felt its perfect heft in his hands.

Kemp's hand trembled as it hovered over the sword, fingers brushing the air just shy of the hilt before retreating. Memories of his past failures in swordplay flooded his mind—every clumsy swing, every missed opportunity. The polished blade shimmered under the light, a masterwork of craftsmanship, and he couldn't help but marvel at the intricate designs etched into the steel. His chest constricted with the familiar sting of inadequacy, a dull ache that had haunted him for years. He had always been his own worst enemy, crippled by the fear of failure. But something was different this time. Beneath the crushing doubt, a spark of fierce determination ignited. He lifted his gaze, locking eyes with Gunnar. The prince's steady, encouraging nod and warm smile were an unspoken promise of support. Kemp nodded back, silently vowing to meet the challenge ahead without taking the sword, grateful for Gunnar's understanding and unwavering faith in him.

Ruiha and Dakarai's joy was palpable, their excitement a beacon of hope in the midst of their daunting mission. Kemp watched them, a quiet resolve hardening within him. They were stronger now, armed with the best Draegoor had to offer. Whatever lay ahead, they would face it together, united and prepared.

"Good luck," Gunnar said, his voice choked with emotion. "May Dreyna and her sons watch over you."

With that, they left the hall, the weight of their mission even more pronounced. As they stepped back into the marketplace, the lively sounds and bustling energy contrasted sharply with the gravity of their quest, amplifying Kemp's sense of urgency.

They made their way to Karl's workshop, their weapons wrapped in protective oiled cloth. Karl greeted them with a nod, his sharp eyes immediately assessing the bundles in their arms. As they unwrapped their weapons, Karl's gaze grew more focused, his fingers brushing lightly over the blades and handles.

"These are fine weapons," he said, his voice tinged with admiration. "I can add enchantments, but without the foundry in Nexus and Sage Thadwick's guidance, they won't be as formidable as Gunnar's axe."

Ruiha and Dakarai exchanged a glance, their faces reflecting a shared determination. "That's fine," Ruiha replied, her tone resolute. "We're just happy to have an upgrade."

Karl nodded, his expression softening slightly. "Very well. Leave them with me, and I'll do what I can. Come back at dawn and they'll be ready for you."

As they handed over their weapons, Ruiha turned to Dakarai, her voice cutting through the noise around them. "We'll need to gather supplies for the journey." Her words were precise, each one a command.

Dakarai nodded, a sense of purpose in his stride. "Let's get to it, then. We have a lot to prepare." With their weapons in good hands, they set off with renewed determination.

They split up to cover more ground. Kemp found himself navigating through the market stalls, the vibrant life around him now a temporary distraction from the daunting path ahead. He spotted a vendor peddling an array of dried meats and fruits, essentials that would sustain them on their arduous journey. With a purposeful stride, he approached the stall, his keen eye assessing the wares as he engaged in a brief but skillful haggle. The vendor, swayed by his persistence, handed over enough provisions to last several weeks, a triumphant acquisition that lightened his burden of worry.

Turning away, his gaze fell upon Dakarai, who was deep in negotiation with a burly blacksmith. The clang of metal and the murmur of voices mingled in the air as the blacksmith presented a formidable hammer. Dakarai's eyes sparkled with satisfaction as he accepted the weapon, a symbol of their readiness for the trials ahead.

Amidst the bustling market, he noted with a flicker of relief that Dakarai and the few Drogo slaves accompanying Ruiha were being treated with an unexpected kindness. Despite their heritage as ancient foes of the Dwarves, the Drogo were met with a surprising respect. This glimpse of harmony kindled a fragile hope within him—a hope that their mission might forge not just survival, but a unity that transcended old hatreds.

As the market buzzed around him, he held onto that glimmer of hope, a beacon guiding them through the shadows of their quest. The path ahead would be dangerous, but for the first time, it seemed a brighter future was within reach.

Ruiha

Even at dawn, the fire of Karl's forge blazed, sending waves of heat into the cool morning air. The rich scent of molten metal mingled with the sharp tang of burning coals, filling the foundry with an aroma that clung to the skin and clothes of anyone who entered. It was a scent both comforting and harsh, a reminder of creation and destruction interwoven. The forge's light cast an ethereal glow over the stone walls, making them glisten as if they were coated in liquid gold. Shadows flickered and danced, moving with a life of their own, twisting in time with the flames that fed them.

Outside, Ruiha, Kemp, Dakarai, Magnus, and Arvi gathered, their breath turning to mist in the cool morning air. The anticipation was palpable, sparking in their eyes as they waited for their newly enchanted weapons. Each of them wore a mix of armor and travel-worn gear, their readiness for the journey ahead evident in their stances and the way their hands hovered near the hilts of their current weapons.

Inside the foundry, the rhythmic clang of metal on metal was a steady heartbeat, echoing through the underground city.

It was a sound that carried with it a sense of purpose, each strike of Karl's hammer resonating with the promise of strength and protection. The hiss of steam, sharp and sudden, punctuated the air, as if the forge itself were exhaling, adding to the symphony of creation. The heat radiating from the forge was intense, washing over them like a wave, and for a moment, the outside world seemed distant, replaced by the primal forces of fire and metal that thrived in Karl's domain.

The foundry itself was a marvel, with intricate designs etched into the stone, runes glowing faintly from the enchantments Karl had woven into the very structure of the forge. Overhead, massive iron pipes and gears turned slowly, feeding the bellows that kept the forge's fire alive.

Ruiha tightened the straps on her worn leather bracers, her mind racing with thoughts of the battles ahead. Her heart pounded in her chest, each beat a reminder of the stakes they faced. She exchanged a glance with Dakarai, who nodded reassuringly, his presence a steady anchor amidst her swirling emotions.

Karl emerged from the foundry, his wild red hair and beard framing a broad grin that split his sweaty, dirt-streaked face. "Come in, all of you," he called, his voice resonant with the heat and magic of the forge. "Your weapons are ready."

They exchanged eager glances, their hearts pounding with a mixture of excitement and trepidation. Ruiha felt a flutter of nerves in her stomach as they followed Karl inside, the foundry's heat embracing them like an old friend.

Karl led them to a large stone table where their weapons lay, gleaming with an almost mystical light. Each weapon seemed to hum with latent power, a testament to Karl's skill and the powerful enchantments he had wrought.

Ruiha was the first to step forward, awe reflecting in her

eyes as she picked up her daggers. The blades, now etched with intricate runes, shimmered with an otherworldly green glow. Memories of past battles flashed through her mind as she traced the runes with her fingertips, feeling a connection to the magic within. She could almost hear the whispers of the enchantment, promising speed and lethality.

Karl explained, "I've imbued your daggers with a swiftstrike enchantment. They will move faster than the eye can see and pierce through nearly any armor. Additionally, the runes will cause any wound inflicted to burn with a fire that cannot be quenched by water or wind."

A fierce smile graced Ruiha's lips, her fingers caressing the blades with reverence. "These are incredible, Karl. Thank you," she said, her voice filled with gratitude and determination. She could feel the power thrumming through the daggers, an extension of her own resolve.

Next, Dakarai reached for his axe, his hands trembling with anticipation. The axe head also glowed faintly with a greenish hue, and the handle was reinforced with bands of frosteel. "Your axe," Karl said, "has been enchanted with thunderclap. Each strike will release a shockwave, stunning your enemies and shattering shields. The frosteel will ensure it remains unbreakable, even against the hardest foes."

Dakarai's grin was broad, his eyes shining with gratitude and a hint of ferocity. "This will serve me well. Thank you, Karl," he replied, his voice carrying the weight of promises made and battles yet to come. He could almost hear the echoes of future victories in the hum of the enchanted axe.

Karl then turned to Kemp, a thoughtful expression on his face. "And for you, Kemp, I've created something special." He stepped aside, revealing a staff made from the rare frosteel, its surface polished to a mirror-like sheen. At its top was a massive gemstone, shimmering with latent energy. "Inspired by Thalirion's staff, I crafted this from frosteel. It's designed to channel and amplify your Shadowfire."

Kemp's eyes widened with delight as he took the staff, feeling its power thrumming beneath his fingers. "How does it work?" he asked, excitement and a hint of nervousness evident in his voice.

"You need to trickle your aura into the weapon to activate it," Karl explained. "Go ahead, give it a try."

Kemp closed his eyes and focused, letting a trickle of his aura flow into the staff. The gemstone at the top flared to life, glowing a brilliant purple. Karl's eyebrows shot up in surprise. "When I tested it, it glowed green, like all my other enchantments do."

Kemp nodded, his gaze lingering on the radiant gemstone, eyes flickering with a mixture of longing and apprehension. His shadow hand twitched involuntarily, releasing wisps of dark purple flames, as if yearning to grasp the power within yet held back by an invisible force. "Could it be because of my Shadowfire?"

Karl nodded thoughtfully. "It's possible. Your unique power might be enhancing the staff's capabilities beyond what I anticipated."

Karl continued, "I spent countless hours crafting this staff, imbuing it with the essence of frosteel. It's known for its unparalleled durability and magical conductivity. The gemstone at its apex isn't merely decorative; it's a reservoir for Shadowfire, designed to store and amplify your unique energy."

Kemp's eyes sparkled with interest. "So, what exactly can it do?"

Karl smiled. "By channeling your aura into the staff, you can unleash devastating bursts of Shadowfire, manipulate shadows to form protective barriers, or even shroud yourself in darkness, becoming nearly invisible. Each feature is carefully calibrated to resonate with your abilities, making the staff a perfect extension of your power."

Kemp's face tightened, a mix of longing and determination clashing with the uncertainty gnawing at the edges of his mind. Memories of his struggles to control Shadowfire surged, but he took a deep breath, steadying himself. "Thank you, Karl. This will make a huge difference."

With their weapons now enhanced, the weight of their mission settled over them like a heavy cloak. The urgency to control Kemp's Shadowfire and save Anwyn loomed large, pressing on their minds. They stepped out of the foundry, the dim light of the cavern casting long, foreboding shadows on the ground.

Kemp felt a renewed sense of purpose course through him as they navigated the winding passages of the underground city. Ruiha and Dakarai walked beside him, their new weapons a testament to their strength and unity. Magnus and Arvi flanked them, silent but vigilant, their eyes scanning every shadow for threats. Magnus's hand rested on the hilt of his sword, a silent promise of protection, while Arvi's keen gaze flickered around, ever watchful and ready.

The underground city pulsed with its own life, a testament to the resilience and ingenuity of the Dwarves who lived there. The tunnels were a labyrinth of wonder and danger, filled with the echoes of ancient battles and the whispers of forgotten magic.

As they reached the city's edge, the entrance to the labyrinthine tunnels that would lead them to the surface, Kemp paused. He turned to his companions, drawing strength from their unwavering presence. "We have our weapons and our mission. Now, let's control my Shadowfire and save Anwyn."

A chorus of affirmations met his words, their resolve solidifying like steel tempered in the forge. With one last glance at the city that had given them the tools to fight, they plunged into the tunnels, their hearts set on the battles and trials that awaited them above. The journey would be fraught with danger, but together, they were ready to face whatever came their way.

8

Bonds Forged in Battle

"Trust is not given but earned, forged by sweat, blood, and shared struggle."

Gunnar

Gunnar wiped the sweat from his brow as the forge's intense heat beat down on him. He had spent the last few days laboring alongside the smiths and miners of the Braemeer Clan, once again hoping to earn their trust through sheer determination and hard work. His muscles ached from the exertion, but he found solace in the rhythmic clang of hammer on metal, the steady pulse of life within the forge.

Duric had been watching him closely, his skepticism ever-present. Gunnar knew that earning the trust of the Braemeer Clan's leader would be no easy feat. Each night, he returned to his quarters exhausted but resolute, finding brief moments of comfort in his telepathic conversations with Havoc.

Gunnar slumped onto a stone bench outside the forge, the heat still clinging to his skin even as the cool air seeped in. The forge fires flickered against the cavern walls, throwing long, jagged shadows that danced like ghosts. He rubbed at his eyes, the day's work wearing him down to the bone. Hard labor was a welcome distraction, but it didn't last. Not against the thoughts that clawed at him the moment he stopped moving.

Anwyn. Still as death, trapped in that cursed coma. Every day felt like another handful of sand slipping through the hourglass, and he was helpless to stop it. The mission to save her pressed on his chest like a weight he couldn't shake. Each day here in Braemeer felt like a gamble—one that time was winning.

He chewed the inside of his cheek, thinking over the latest round of talks, the endless back-and-forth, the schemes, the promises. Control Kemp's Shadowfire. Convince Chronos to help. It was all dangerous and desperate. Especially the path through Drogo lands—that was practically suicide. But what other choice was there? No one else had a better idea.

He let his head drop back against the rough stone wall, staring up at the jagged ceiling of the cavern. Leadership. Always such a fine word when others wore it, always sounding so damned noble. Now it just tasted bitter. Doubts gnawed at his insides like hungry wolves. Was he leading them to their deaths? Would he ever unite these stubborn, prideful Dwarves in time to make a difference? And even if he did—what then? What if their combined strength wasn't enough to stop what was coming?

Gunnar clenched his fists, feeling his frustration surge. He wasn't some legend, wasn't some hero from the stories. He was just a Dwarf trying to stop everything from falling apart, one day at a time. And some days—most days, recently—it felt like he was losing.

He was sat there, the cool air soothing his heated skin as he brooded, when the presence of someone beside him suddenly pulled him back to the present. Turning, he saw Duric, his expression as unreadable as ever.

"You work hard, Gunnar," Duric said, his voice gruff. "Harder than most would in your position."

Gunnar nodded, unsure of what to say. He sensed that Duric's words, though simple, carried weight.

"I have to," Gunnar replied. "Our future depends on it."

Duric grunted, his eyes scanning the horizon. "Maybe so. But hard work alone won't earn my trust. There's something I need to show you."

Intrigued, Gunnar followed Duric through the winding tunnels of the Braemeer stronghold. They walked in silence, the only sound the soft echo of their footsteps against the stone floor. Eventually, they arrived at a heavy wooden door, reinforced with frosteel bands. Duric produced a key from his belt and unlocked it, pushing the door open with a creak.

Inside was a chamber unlike any Gunnar had seen before. Shelves lined the walls, filled with ancient tomes and artifacts. In the center of the room stood a pedestal, upon which lay a large, ornate box. Duric approached the pedestal and opened the box, revealing a sword of exquisite craftsmanship. Its blade shimmered with an ethereal light, and runes were etched along its length.

"This is the Sword of Eldrin," Duric said, his voice a whisper of reverence that echoed through the ancient hall. The blade glinted under the torchlight, its edges sharp and gleaming, as if forged only yesterday. "Crafted millenia ago by our finest smiths, and infused with enchantments so potent, its power has become legend. It stands as a testament to our clan's strength and legacy."

Gunnar stepped forward, drawn by the weapon's ethereal beauty. The intricate runes etched along the blade seemed to pulse with a life of their own. "Why show this to me?" he asked, his voice barely above a whisper, eyes locked on the mesmerizing artifact.

Duric's gaze hardened, meeting Gunnar's with an intensity

that made the air around them crackle. "Because," he began, each word deliberate and heavy with meaning, "I believe you are destined to play a crucial role in our future. But first, you must prove your worth."

Gunnar's heart pounded. "Prove my worth? How?"

Duric paused, considering his words. "There is a trial. A test that has been passed down through generations. Only the rightful heir to Dreynas can wield the Sword of Eldrin."

Gunnar's eyes shot up and he stared at Duric, frowning. "Why am I not aware of this sword?" he asked, suspicion creeping into his voice.

"This sword has been guarded by Braemeer for centuries," Duric said, his tone low, almost reverent. "Only those deemed worthy are even told of its existence. The time has come for the sword to find its true heir, and I'm beginning to believe that heir is you."

Gunnar opened his mouth to respond, but the words died in his throat as the ground beneath them gave a violent shudder, like the whole mountain had stirred from an ancient sleep. A deep, guttural rumble rolled through the hall, shaking the walls and sending dust cascading from the stone ceiling in thick clouds. The sound was low, primal, something from the bones of the earth itself.

He staggered, arms flailing, catching himself on the edge of the pedestal. His fingers brushed against the cold metal of the sword, but the thing vibrated beneath his touch as if it was alive, as if the very earth had awakened it. The feeling crawled up his arm like a thousand ants biting at his skin.

The floor kept shaking. Worse now. Loose stones rattled, the creak of ancient beams above them sending Gunnar's pulse racing. One more tremor and the whole place felt like it might come crashing down.

He glanced at Duric, whose face had gone pale, his usual calm stripped away. The clan chief stood frozen, wide-eyed, like he was staring into the maw of something he couldn't name.

"An earthquake?" Gunnar asked, though he already knew the answer.

Duric didn't answer right away. His mouth moved, but no sound came. His eyes flicked from the sword to the ceiling, and back to the sword, something dark and fearful twisting in them. He swallowed, hard.

"No," he muttered, barely more than a breath. "No—it's something worse."

Gunnar's skin prickled, the sword humming louder beneath his hand. Something worse than an earthquake? His grip tightened. What in all the hells could that mean? The rumbling hadn't stopped, not completely. A threat, a warning—whatever it was, it wasn't over. Not yet.

And that's when Gunnar felt it: the unmistakable pull of magic, raw and ancient, surging through the stone beneath his feet like blood through veins.

As the tremors finally subsided, a deep, resonant voice echoed through the chamber, sending chills down Gunnar's spine. "So, the Dwarves seek unity?" In the center of the room, a hole tore through the fabric of reality, a swirling vortex of chaotic energy that seemed to defy the very laws of nature. The air crackled with an otherworldly charge, and the boundaries between realms wavered precariously.

Gunnar and Duric turned, their breaths hitching as a figure emerged from the shimmering portal. It was a Drogo Gunnar had never encountered before, yet his commanding presence was undeniable. He could feel the weight of this Drogo's authority pressing against his chest. The figure stepped forward, his reptilian eyes gleaming with malevolent intent. "I am Junak" the stranger declared—the tyrant who had plagued them for so long. He was flanked by several shamans and warriors, each exuding an aura of menace that set Gunnar and Duric on edge. The air seemed to thicken with tension as Junak's gaze bore into them, promising no mercy.

"Junak!" Duric snarled, drawing his weapon. His heart pounded with fury, each beat echoing the image of Anwyn lying comatose, a victim of Junak's evil plan. "I'm glad you showed up. It saves us the trouble of hunting you down!"

Gunnar stood in front of him, a dark smile playing on his lips. The weight of anticipated revenge bolstering him, filling him with a grim confidence.

Junak laughed, the sound cold and devoid of humor, echoing through the tension-laden air. "I've come to deliver a message," he said, his voice dripping with contempt. "Your efforts at unification are futile. The clans will never stand together, and I will see to it that they fall apart."

Gunnar felt a surge of anger and determination rise within him. He stepped forward, the weight of his resolve grounding him. "We won't let you succeed, Junak. We will unite the clans and stand against you."

As he gripped his axe, the runes on the enchanted blade glowed a fierce green, casting a protective aura around him. He could feel the enchantments of his weapon thrumming with ancient power, a stark contrast to the chaotic malevolence of Junak's axe. The ground beneath Gunnar's feet felt steadier, the air clearer, as if the axe itself was cleansing the dark energy around him.

A realization sparked within him—Junak's power, though

menacing, lacked the pure, enduring strength of his act, crafted out of loyalty by his friend. He caught a glimpse of uncertainty flickering in Junak's eyes, a brief but telling moment that revealed a crack in his dark facade.

This small but significant observation filled Gunnar with a fierce hope. He straightened, the weight of the axe comforting in his hands, a belief taking root that they could indeed turn the tide against this tyrant. The glow of the axe's runes grew brighter, illuminating the chamber with a light that seemed to push back the shadows, and Gunnar's heart surged with determination.

The portal's light continued to cast an eerie glow, battling against the luminescence from Gunnar's axe. Shadows danced around them in a macabre ballet as the warriors and shamans flanking Junak moved with a sinister grace, their eyes glinting with dark purpose. The air hummed with ancient magic, the kind that whispered of forgotten legends and buried secrets. Each step the warriors took seemed to reverberate through the chamber, a chilling counterpoint to the throbbing pulse of the portal.

Gunnar saw Duric's grip tighten on his hammer—a simple tool in the smithy, but here, in the thick of battle, it promised blood. Gunnar felt a flicker of relief. At least the old bastard wasn't backing down. He turned his attention back to Junak, whose grin only seemed to grow wider, nastier, with each second that ticked by. The kind of grin that said he knew something you didn't, and it was going to hurt when you found out.

The air between them felt like it was holding its breath. Waiting.

And then it broke. Junak's warriors surged forward on his signal, teeth bared and blades gleaming. Gunnar barely had time to shout before Duric was lost in the throng, hammer swinging. The chamber exploded into noise—screams, the clang of steel, the crackle of spells. A symphony of chaos.

Gunnar parried a strike from one of Junak's brutes, the impact rattling up his arm. Already his muscles burned from days of toil, days of holding back his magic. He avoided using it, even now. Relying on steel and strength, but every second that passed felt like the fight was draining out of him, dragging him down. Sweat dripped into his eyes, and he blinked it away just in time to dodge another swing aimed at his head.

Somewhere in the melee, Duric fought like a Dwarf possessed, his hammer smashing bones and sending warriors sprawling. But they were getting separated, the press of enemies forcing them apart. Gunnar didn't have time to think about it—didn't have time for anything but keeping himself alive. His mind reacted on instinct, but his strength was waning with every swing.

A blast of magic hit him square in the chest like a runaway boulder, knocking the breath out of him. He hit the ground hard, stars exploding behind his eyes, gasping for air that wouldn't come.

Then he saw it—the Sword of Eldrin, still untouched on its pedestal, glowing faintly in the dim light. It was all he could think about. If he could just reach it... if he could just crawl...

With a growl, Gunnar dragged himself towards the sword, every inch a battle against the weight in his chest and the pounding in his skull. His fingers closed around the hilt, and the world seemed to tilt. Power surged through him like cold fire, snapping his senses back into focus. The runes along the blade flared to life, casting the room in an eerie green glow.

Duric, barely holding his own against Junak, turned, momentarily blinded by the light. It was a moment too long. Junak's axe came down with a brutal crash, sending Duric flying into a stone pillar. For a second, Gunnar thought that was it—Duric done for, skull crushed, blood pooling on the floor. But the stubborn old chief got back up, wobbling on unsteady legs, eyes locking onto Gunnar with a look somewhere between awe and desperation.

"Take it!" Gunnar shouted, and hurled the sword.

The blade cut through the air, runes pulsing with each rotation, and Duric caught it cleanly. For a heartbeat, everything stopped. Then Duric grinned, like a wolf scenting blood. He moved fast—faster than a Dwarf his age had any right to. The Sword of Eldrin carved through Junak's warriors like they were nothing more than straw dummies. Limbs flew, and blood sprayed across the stone floor as Duric fought with a ferocity Gunnar hadn't thought him capable of.

But there wasn't time to marvel. The battle was far from over.

Junak's howl of rage cut through the chaos. He came for them both, eyes blazing with hate. At the same time, a shaman's spell erupted beneath Duric, tossing him into the wall. Gunnar barely registered the explosion before Junak's axe came crashing down on his armor, sending shockwaves of pain through his chest. He hit the floor, hard, teeth gritted against the agony.

Every breath was a struggle. Duric wasn't faring any better, slumped against the stone, trying to get his legs under him. The pair of them—battered, broken, but somehow still standing. Gunnar spat blood, and with a quick glance, met Duric's eyes. No words were spoken. They didn't need any. They were in this together, for better or worse.

Junak's warriors pressed in, but Gunnar and Duric stood back-to-back, weapons swinging in brutal arcs. No finesse here—just raw, desperate survival. Gunnar's axe connected with flesh and bone, the satisfying crunch lost in the roar of the battle around them.

He couldn't hold back anymore. Magic flared in his veins, pushing him forward. The ground trembled under his feet as he unleashed it, seismic waves buckling the stone floor, knocking warriors off balance. Jagged spears of rock erupted from the ground, skewering Junak's shamans. Gunnar didn't stop to watch—he kept pushing, kept swinging.

Duric seized the moment, launching himself at the stunned Drogo, his sword singing through the air with deadly purpose. Together they carved a bloody path, pushing towards Junak.

But Junak wasn't done. His reptilian eyes blazed, and he came at them like a storm, dark energy swirling around his axe. Each missed blow sent cracks spiderwebbing through the stone, scorching the floor with raw power. Gunnar dodged, barely, his own magic surging to meet the threat.

And then it happened. Junak, desperate, summoned everything he had, shadows coiling around his weapon, preparing one final strike aimed at Duric. Gunnar saw it all in horrible clarity. He could end it here—could finish Junak and his war forever. But Duric... Duric wouldn't survive the hit.

The choice was clear. And it was impossible.

Breath ragged, heart pounding, Gunnar gripped his axe, feeling the weight of the decision like a stone in his chest. The power surged, begged to be released. He could strike Junak down... or save Duric.

Gunnar made his choice. With a roar, he threw himself between Duric and the shadows, his axe blazing with green light. He deflected the dark magic, a clash of energy that lit up the chamber like a second sun. The explosion rocked the room, sending them all reeling.

When the dust settled, Gunnar was on one knee, breathless, but alive. Duric lay behind him, barely conscious but still breathing. Gunnar had done it. He'd saved him. But it wasn't over.

Junak snarled, his plan thwarted. He wasn't going down like that. With a flick of his hand, a swirling portal of shadows opened behind him.

"No!" Gunnar shouted, pushing himself to his feet, but his legs trembled beneath him. There was nothing left. Nothing to give.

Junak sneered, stepping back into the shadows. "Next time, Dwarf. You won't be so lucky."

And just like that, he was gone.

The silence that followed was deafening. Gunnar stumbled to Duric's side, checking his pulse. Weak, but steady. He exhaled a breath he didn't even know he'd been holding.

They'd won this fight, but barely. And it didn't feel like a victory.

He slung Duric over his shoulder and started the long walk back to the city. The chamber was a wreck—fissures cracked through the stone, blood staining the floor—but Gunnar's resolve was intact. This wasn't over. The war was only just beginning.

There would be be more battles, he knew. More blood. More choices. But Gunnar had made his decision today, and he wasn't about to falter now.

9

Trials, Trust, and Triumph

"When the path grows steep and shadows loom, unity becomes the flame that lights the way forward."

Ruiha

As Ruiha emerged from the fissure into the cool mountain breeze above Dreynas, she paused, letting the biting air wash over her. The sharp, crisp scent of snow and stone filled her lungs, each breath a vivid reminder of how far they had come. The Frost Mountains stretched before her, their jagged peaks half-shrouded in mist, as if the very sky clung possessively to their heights. The fine vapor curled lazily around the stone spires, and from somewhere deep within the earth, the low, distant groan of ice shifting echoed, a voice as ancient as the world itself.

She tightened the straps of her pack, her fingers stiff with the cold, and cast a glance at the sun, weak and pale as it filtered through the mist. Light played across the landscape, softening the harsh edges of the mountain, and as her eyes followed the shimmering glow, she caught sight of a rainbow, faint at first but then blooming into a brilliant arc of color. It stretched across the sky, an almost unnatural burst of beauty in this stark, frozen world, its colors trembling like a breath held too long. For a moment, she stood transfixed, the weight of their journey lifting as if she had found some secret moment of peace amidst the chaos.

But the moment passed, and the heaviness returned, pressing down on her chest. This wasn't some casual trek. The mountain had seen more blood than any of them would care to know. Its jagged peaks were indifferent, scarred by battles long forgotten, and it would endure long after they were all dust. The wind howled through the narrow passes, cutting through Ruiha's clothes like knives, a constant reminder of the harshness of the world they'd stepped into. Every step they took up here felt stolen, a trespass on something old and unforgiving.

Now it bore witness to the beginning of something larger than any of them could truly grasp, though it wouldn't care one way or the other who lived or died. The weight of it settled heavy in her chest, a dull pressure that promised nothing but harder days ahead. There would be no glory here, only survival. And even that wasn't guaranteed.

She glanced back as Magnus emerged from the fissure. His calm, steady presence was a comfort, as always, and he gave her a nod as he adjusted the strap of his pack. Close behind, Arvi blinked against the sudden brightness, still unused to the open sky, while Kemp gripped his staff tightly, his expression unreadable. Finally, Dakarai stepped out, squinting up at the sky, his eyes wide with the wonder of it.

"What is that?" Dakarai asked, his voice low, full of awe as he pointed toward the rainbow.

Ruiha chuckled, unable to help herself. "A rainbow, Dakarai. I forgot that you underground folk missed out on such beauty."

He shook his head, still staring up at the vibrant arc. "No, we don't have things like this down there," he muttered.

Ruiha grinned and nudged him playfully. "Consider yourself lucky. Not everyone gets to see their first rainbow with a view like this."

Dakarai's lips twitched, his usual seriousness breaking for just a moment as a rare smile crossed his face. "I suppose it's something to remember," he said softly, his eyes still lingering on the sky.

The group shared a light laugh, a brief respite in their hard journey. The rainbow, vibrant against the gray mountains, seemed to carry with it a moment of peace, a reminder of the world's strange beauty—beauty that waited for those who dared to seek it.

They continued southward toward the Scorched Mountains. The days blended into one another, each step forward marked by the unrelenting challenges of the path. The jagged rocks jutted out from the mountains like the bones of some ancient beast, and the narrow ledges they crossed forced them to move carefully, each footfall calculated to avoid a fatal misstep.

As they descended from the high passes, the terrain shifted to barren, cracked earth that stretched endlessly beneath the unforgiving sun. The heat bore down on them, a relentless force that made the cool breezes of the mountains feel like a distant memory. Their cloaks stuck to their backs, drenched in sweat, and every step felt harder than the last.

They rationed their water carefully, treating each drop as precious. Springs were few, and they were forced to make do with what little they could find in the arid landscape. Each night, they would huddle together around a small fire, passing the waterskin between them, never drinking more than they needed.

Yet, even amidst the heat and exhaustion, their bond grew stronger. They moved as one, each member of the group finding strength in the others. Magnus, always the quiet rock, led them with his calm presence, his steady steps a comfort to them all.

Arvi, blinking against the harsh sun, never wavered, her quiet determination an example for the rest. Kemp's confidence grew with each passing day, his staff now an extension of himself, and Dakarai—though new to the surface world—adapted with surprising ease, his dry humor and awe at the surface world a welcome light in their grueling march.

"Everything up here feels so... open," Dakarai remarked one evening as they rested beneath the stars, his voice tinged with wonder. "You don't realize how small the tunnels make you feel until you're out here."

Ruiha smiled, leaning back on her pack. "I always forget what it must be like for you undergrounders. But you've handled yourself well."

Dakarai grunted, his eyes on the horizon. "I've had to. Can't be looking like a fool in front of you lot."

Ruiha laughed, shaking her head. "Oh, we'd let you know if you were."

Despite the relentless pace and biting wind, there were moments—precious and fleeting—when the tension lifted, if only for a while. Around the fire at night, the group found themselves drawn closer, bound not just by the weight of their mission, but by the simple, human need for connection. Magnus, ever steady, would sit with his back to the fire, his eyes scanning the horizon even as he quietly teased Arvi about his persistent squinting in the sun. He would roll his eyes, smirking, but never failed to return a sharp retort, often a jibe about the Dwarf's bulbous nose. Kemp, his staff resting beside him, would lean in, the flicker of flames casting strange shadows on his face as he shared odd stories from his days as a student mage—a tale about a poorly cast fire spell, perhaps, or the time he accidentally froze an entire room of candles during a lecture.

Dakarai's laughter, deep and rumbling, would join the crackling of the fire, the sound oddly comforting in the desolate wilderness. He'd shake his head at Kemp's stories, muttering something about how surface dwellers complicated the simplest of tasks. It was in these moments—when the cold seemed less biting and the dark less menacing—that they became more than just a group of travelers. They became something more, something unspoken, forged by the fires of shared struggle.

Each night, as the others drifted to sleep, one of them would remain awake, taking up watch. Kemp's turn often came first, the flickering light from the fire dancing in his eyes as he stared out into the night. His fingers would trace the intricate carvings of his staff, the quiet hum of magic pulsing faintly beneath his touch. But there was always a tension in the air when he was on watch, a sense of power held just beneath the surface, like the taut string of a bow, waiting for the release.

Ruiha took her turn next. She'd sit with her back to the fire, her eyes fixed on the horizon, where the jagged silhouettes of the Scorched Mountains loomed like dark sentinels. The others slept soundly, but Ruiha found little comfort in sleep anymore. Her mind wandered far too often these days, thoughts pulled in a hundred directions, none of them comforting. Kemp's Shadowfire flickered in her mind like the flames before her—dangerous, unpredictable, a power that might consume them all if they weren't careful. She'd seen the way it coiled around him, how it flickered with a life of its own, hungry, searching. Kemp, for all his talent, seemed oblivious to the undercurrent of danger that followed him.

Her thoughts shifted, too, to the Dragon Crown. A poisoned chalice, yes it had saved Kemp's life, but at what cost? And now it sat within Kemp's spirit, a silent presence that seemed to grow heavier with each passing day. Ruiha had seen the way Magnus's eyes lingered on Kemp when he thought no one was looking. They all felt its weight, though none of them spoke of it.

The quiet nights amplified the enormity of their mission. Alone, with nothing but the whisper of the wind and the crackling of the fire, Ruiha couldn't help but feel the suffocating weight of it. Success meant facing horrors that lurked in the Forgotten Realm. Failure? That was something she didn't allow herself to dwell on. But it lingered, always, just on the edge of her thoughts, a shadowy specter that threatened to unravel everything.

One night, as Ruiha sat alone, Dakarai stirred in his sleep. His deep, rough breaths shifted, his face contorting as if he were wrestling with something in a dream. She watched him for a moment, a pang of sympathy tugging at her. His world had been underground, confined, and now he found himself above, beneath an endless sky, chasing a prize that none of them fully understood. He had adapted quickly, but she could see the strain in his eyes, in the way he carried himself—a burden that was more than just physical.

Her gaze drifted back to Kemp. He lay on his back, his staff resting across his chest. Even in sleep, his fingers twitched, as if unconsciously drawing power from the staff, pulling at the threads of magic that surrounded them. The air around him always seemed charged, as though reality bent slightly in his presence.

The firelight flickered, casting long shadows across the camp, and Ruiha allowed herself a rare moment of vulnerability. Was she ready for what lay ahead? Could she lead them through this, knowing that not all of them might survive the journey? Could Kemp truly control the power he wielded, or was it only a matter of time before it consumed him—and the rest of them with it?

The wind shifted, cold and sharp, pulling Ruiha from her thoughts. She tightened her cloak around her shoulders and glanced again at the horizon. The mountains seemed closer now, their peaks cutting into the sky like jagged teeth. They would reach them soon, and when they did, there would be no turning back.

As the days dragged on, evidence of the Drogo presence became harder to ignore. Discarded campsites, bones picked clean by scavengers, and strange symbols carved into the stone—each a reminder that they weren't alone in these mountains. It felt as though the shadows themselves were watching, always just beyond the edges of their sight.

"I thought Drogo stayed underground?" Arvi asked one afternoon, stepping over a sun-bleached skull with a frown.

"Most do," Dakarai said, his voice low and steady. "But the warrior class hunts above ground. They've learned to track prey in places like this." He bent down and traced a carving etched into a stone with his finger. "This indicates a recent patrol," Dakarai murmured, his eyes narrowing as he stood and scanned the rocky landscape ahead. "They've been here, passing through. Not long ago, either."

The gravity of Dakarai's words sank in as they pressed forward, the jagged peaks of the mountains looming closer. Every step now felt harder, as if the land itself resisted their progress, testing their endurance with each rocky incline and narrow pass.

That evening, as the group set up camp in a narrow canyon, Ruiha noticed movement—just a flicker at the corner of her eye, but enough to freeze her in place. She raised her hand sharply, signaling for silence. Kemp and Dakarai followed her gaze, their eyes narrowing. Shadows moved among the rocks, large, deliberate shapes that didn't belong to the wind or the shifting light.

"Prepare yourselves," Ruiha whispered, her voice calm, measured, though the tension in the air crackled like a drawn bowstring.

A moment later, a hulking figure lumbered into view. The troll was massive, its thick, knotted skin as gray as the boulders it had hidden behind. Its eyes glowed faintly, a dull red, reflecting a malevolent intelligence. With a deafening roar, the creature charged, the ground trembling beneath its feet.

Ruiha moved first. She darted forward, her daggers flashing like twin streaks of silver as she dodged the troll's massive club, a weapon as thick as a tree trunk. The impact of the troll's swing shattered the rocks where she'd stood moments before, sending dust and debris into the air. She rolled clear, her eyes already scanning for an opening.

Dakarai was next, his axe gleaming in the dim light as he struck the troll's side. The blade hit hard, but the beast's hide was like stone, barely giving way. Dakarai gritted his teeth, preparing for another blow, when Kemp's staff erupted in purple flame. The fire lashed out, wrapping around the troll's arm, and this time, the creature screamed, its roar echoing through the canyon as the fire burned deep into its flesh.

Magnus and Arvi charged in, their weapons a blur of motion. Magnus swung his warhammer low, aiming for the troll's knees, while Arvi's twin axes carved precise, deadly arcs, slicing through the beast's hide wherever it was weakest. Each strike was calculated, their years of battle-hardened experience on full display as they worked in tandem, driving the troll back step by step.

But the creature was relentless, its strength a near-unstoppable force. It lashed out with wild swings, the club smashing into the ground with bone-shattering force. Ruiha danced around it, her movements precise, calculated, her daggers slashing at the beast's legs as she tried to cripple it. Kemp and Dakarai attacked from the flanks, their strikes coordinated and fierce, but the troll was resilient, its fury seemingly endless.

Then, Ruiha saw it—a moment, brief but enough. The troll's next swing left its neck exposed, and without hesitation, she moved. With a burst of speed, she leaped onto the creature's back, her daggers flashing as she drove them deep into the base of its skull. The troll howled, its body thrashing in pain, but Ruiha held firm, her grip unyielding as the beast staggered.

"Kemp! Now!" she shouted, her voice cutting through the chaos.

Kemp's staff blazed with purple fire again, this time wrapping the troll in a swirling vortex of flame. Dakarai's hammer followed, striking with brutal precision. The combined assault forced the troll to its knees, the ground shaking with the weight of its fall.

Magnus and Arvi didn't hesitate. Together, they delivered the final blow—Arvi's axes slicing through the troll's thick neck as Magnus's hammer came crashing down on its skull with a sickening crack. The creature collapsed with a low, shuddering groan, its body twitching once before it stilled.

Ruiha leapt down from the troll's back, her chest heaving with the effort. She wiped the sweat from her brow, glancing at her companions. Kemp's face was set, the glow of his staff slowly fading, while Dakarai rolled his shoulder, grimacing from the exertion. Magnus and Arvi stood over the troll's body, their expressions a mix of exhaustion and grim satisfaction.

For a moment, no one spoke. They were alive. The battle had been fierce, but their unity had carried them through.

"We've earned tonight's rest," Ruiha said, her voice steady, though her limbs trembled with adrenaline.

Magnus gave a weary nod, his warhammer resting against his shoulder. "That we have," he muttered, casting a glance at the troll's lifeless form. "But something tells me it won't be the last time we see danger on this mission."

10

THE PATH FORWARD: ALLIES, ANCIENT POWER, AND NEW TRIALS

"The weight of a crown is heavy, but it is the bonds of trust that give it meaning."

GUNNAR

Gunnar and Duric made their way back to Braemeer, their steps dragging through the stone corridors of the underground city, each one heavier than the last. Duric, still nursing his injuries, leaned heavily on Gunnar. The air was thick with the scent of burnt ozone and the tang of blood, lingering reminders of their brutal encounter with Junak. The distant growl of shifting rock added a sense of foreboding to their already weary trek.

As they approached Duric's stronghold, the towering stone structure loomed above them, a bastion of strength and history within the cavernous depths. The flickering light of bioluminescent fungi cast eerie shadows on the stone walls, and the banners of the Braemeer Clan were illuminated by glowing crystals embedded in the rock. Duric's personal guard, clad in armor and bearing the sigils of the Braemeer Clan, rushed forward to assist their wounded leader. Behind them, Duric's family emerged, their faces etched with concern.

"Duric!" His wife, Thalindra, ran to him, her eyes wide with worry. She gently cupped his face, her fingers tracing the lines of fatigue and pain. "What happened?" she demanded, her voice breaking with fear.

"I'm fine, Thalindra," Duric murmured, though his voice betrayed his exhaustion. He sighed deeply, his body sagging as he allowed himself to be led inside. His legs trembled, and Gunnar tightened his grip to keep him upright. "Junak and his forces ambushed us."

As Duric was tended to by his family and healers, Gunnar found himself alone with Thalindra. She turned to him, her eyes searching his. "What happened out there?" she asked, her voice trembling slightly.

Gunnar took a deep breath, feeling the weight of the Sword of Eldrin in his hand. He unsheathed it, the blade shimmering with an ethereal light that cast dancing shadows on the stone walls. The light from the sword illuminated the worried lines on Thalindra's face. Thalindra's eyes widened in awe.

"The Sword of Eldrin," she whispered, reverence in her tone. "Duric must have great faith in you if he showed you this, let alone allowed you to hold it."

Gunnar shook his head, his expression somber. "He had no choice," he said quietly, his gaze drifting back to Duric, where healers worked frantically over his wounds. The air was filled with the scent of healing herbs and the murmured incantations of the healers. The desperation of their fight still echoed in his mind. "Junak's dark magic was overpowering. Without the sword's protection, we wouldn't have survived."

The Path Forward: Allies, Ancient Power, and New Trials

Thalindra's gaze softened as she regarded the sword. "Do you know its history?"

Gunnar shook his head, so Thalindra continued, her eyes distant as if seeing into the past. "Eldrin was an ancient ancestor of Duric, the ruler of the Dwarves during the migration from the Scorched Mountains to Dreynas. He was betrayed by dark magic, leading to Duric's hesitance and fear of it. When the Dwarves settled in Dreynas, under the instruction of the gods, Eldrin gave up his rights as leader and separated the clans into a democratic council, vowing that one day the rightful heir of Dreynas would emerge and claim the sword."

Gunnar listened intently, feeling the weight of the sword grow heavier in his hand. The flickering light of the blade seemed to carry the shadows of Eldrin's past battles, the ancient struggles that shaped their present. "I plan on giving the sword to Duric," he said, his voice steady.

Thalindra's eyes snapped back to him, shock etched on her features. "You can't do that," she exclaimed. "Duric wouldn't even be able to use it. Only the rightful heir can."

A slow smile spread across Gunnar's face. "I already gave it to Duric," he said softly, a quiet triumph in his voice. "And Duric used it against Junak."

Thalindra's mouth fell open in surprise, her eyes darting to the sword and back to Gunnar. "He—he used it?" she stammered, disbelief and awe mingling in her gaze.

Gunnar nodded, the memory of the battle vivid in his mind. "Yes, he wielded it with the strength and precision of a true warrior," he said, his voice filled with admiration. "Despite his injuries, Duric's determination was unmatched. Junak didn't stand a chance."

Thalindra's eyes shimmered with unshed tears as she glanced back at the doorway where Duric had disappeared. "Maybe he was right about you, Gunnar," she whispered, her voice a fragile thread of hope and fear. "Maybe you are the rightful heir."

The cavern floor trembled ominously, shaking the stone walls and sending a shiver down Gunnar's spine. In the distance, the deep, resonant groan of shifting earth echoed through the tunnels. The approach of another seismic disturbance was a stark reminder of the battles yet to come. Gunnar tightened his grip on the Sword of Eldrin, feeling the heavy mantle of destiny settle over him. *The fight with Junak was just the beginning*, he thought, bracing himself for the challenges ahead.

The next morning, as the sun bathed the ancient stone walls of the castle in a golden glow, Gunnar sat in the grand common room, the smell of fresh bread and roasted meat filling the air. Tapestries depicting legendary battles adorned the walls, and the flicker of candlelight danced across suits of armor. Duric hobbled in, his steps unsteady but his spirit unbroken. He plopped himself down next to Gunnar, a wry smile on his face.

"I've had worse," Duric said, gesturing to his bandaged wounds.

Gunnar chuckled, passing him a mug of ale. "You fought well, Duric. Better than most Dwarves would have."

Gunnar took a long drink, his eyes meeting Duric's. "I've been thinking," he began, his voice thoughtful. "Do you trust me, even though I had to use my magic?"

Duric's expression grew serious. "Magic has always been a double-edged sword in our world."

Duric paused, his gaze lingering on the flickering firelight. A shadow of doubt crossed his features, but he quickly brushed it aside. "I was blind," he confessed, his voice low and raw with emotion. "I see now that magic itself isn't inherently dark. It's the heart of the wielder that determines its nature. And your heart, Gunnar, was made to protect us from the dark. You want what's best for Dreynas. Yes, I trust you."

Gunnar felt a swell of gratitude and a twinge of internal conflict. He, too, had feared the potential of his own power, the burden of leadership, and the darkness that magic could bring. He reached for the Sword of Eldrin, offering it to Duric once more. "This belongs with you," he said firmly.

Duric shook his head, pushing the sword back toward Gunnar. "It is for the heir to Dreynas."

Gunnar's eyes softened. "I have a weapon," he said, his hand resting on the axe at his side. "Crafted and gifted to me by a dear, loyal friend. It is far more powerful and has saved my life several times over."

The axe hummed in his mind, a gentle reminder that it shared a deep bond with him. He could feel its energy, ancient and potent, waiting to be named, to fully awaken. He remembered the legends of weapons bound to their wielders, growing in power as their bond deepened. Gunnar shook the thought away, promising himself he would name it once he had found a cure for Anwyn and united the clans.

Duric finally accepted the sword, his expression one of deep respect. He cradled the hilt in his hand, feeling the weight of the ancient steel, a symbol of his ancestors' sacrifices and honor. The room seemed to hold its breath as he knelt, the firelight casting long shadows across his weathered face. He looked up at Gunnar, his eyes steady and unflinching.

"I pledge my loyalty to you, Gunnar, Prince of Dreynas," Duric said, his voice a deep rumble that resonated through the hall. "You have my word and the word of the Braemeer Clan."

Gunnar nodded, a sense of solemnity settling over him. He felt the gravity of the moment, the significance of Duric's pledge. This was not merely a gesture; it was a binding vow, one that carried the weight of centuries of tradition and honor. He reached down, clasping Duric's forearm in a warrior's grip, their eyes locking in mutual understanding.

"Your word is a bond I will not take lightly," Gunnar replied, his voice firm yet warm. "Together, we shall forge a path that honors our forebears and secures our future."

With Duric's loyalty secured, Gunnar knew it was time to act. He could not afford to delay, for the tides of conflict were already lapping at their borders. Rising to his full height, he turned to his gathered advisors and retainers, his presence commanding their attention.

"Summon the messengers," he ordered, his tone brooking no argument. "The remaining clan chiefs must be called to council in Draegoor immediately. We have much to discuss and little time to prepare."

The room burst into activity, the quiet reverence giving way to urgent whispers and the hurried footsteps of those carrying out Gunnar's commands. He watched as the Dwarves moved swiftly, their expressions mirroring the resolve in his own heart. The future of Dreynas depended on the decisions they would make in the coming days.

As the messengers dispersed into the night, Gunnar allowed himself a brief moment of reflection. He gazed into the flickering flames of the hearth, seeing not just fire, but the the gods themselves guiding him. He wondered whether Eldrin had once had similar visions.

In the stillness of the hall, amidst the echoes of ancient promises and the murmurs of impending duty, Gunnar steeled himself for the trials to come. This was his burden to bear, his legacy to forge, and he would not falter.

11

A Stranger Among Us

"A heart burdened by shadows can only find peace when it dares to share its light with others."

Kemp

The aftermath of the troll attack lay strewn across the desolate landscape, the silence broken only by the labored breaths of Kemp and his companions. The troll, a massive, hulking beast, now lay defeated at their feet, its lifeless eyes staring blankly at the sky. The air was thick with the scent of blood and charred flesh, remnants of Kemp's Shadowfire still smoldering in the cool evening air.

Kemp stood a few paces away from the fallen creature, his staff gripped tightly in his hand. The frosteel was warm, almost hot to the touch, the residual heat of the Shadowfire still palpable. He turned the staff over in his hands, inspecting it with a mix of awe and dread. The power it contained was immense, a force he was still learning to control. But it had saved them tonight, and for that, he was grateful.

Around him, his companions were tending to their wounds, their faces etched with exhaustion and relief. Magnus, ever the stoic warrior, was binding a gash on his forearm with a strip of cloth torn from his tunic. His movements were steady and precise, a testament to his resilience. Arvi, his usually bright eyes dulled with fatigue, was using his limited healing skill to close a wound on Dakarai's leg. The large Drogo winced but said nothing, his focus fixed on Arvi's clumsy movements.

Ruiha moved among them, her presence a calming force. She spoke softly, offering words of encouragement and comfort. Her own injuries were minor, but the toll of the battle was evident in the lines of worry on her face. She caught Kemp's eye and offered him a small, reassuring smile. He nodded in return, drawing strength from her unwavering determination.

The landscape around them was bleak, the ground scarred by their battle. Jagged rocks and sparse vegetation gave the area a forlorn, almost otherworldly feel. The sun had begun its descent, casting long shadows across the ground. Kemp took a deep breath, the cool air a welcome balm to his frayed nerves. They had survived, but the journey was far from over.

Kemp sat down heavily, the weight of the Dragon Crown pressing on his mind. The voices had been quieter during the battle, the adrenaline and focus pushing them to the background. But now, in the stillness, he could feel them creeping back in, whispering dark promises and threats.

Ruiha joined him, her eyes searching his. "Are you alright?" she asked, her voice barely above a whisper.

Kemp nodded, though he wasn't entirely sure of the answer. "I'm fine," he replied, his voice steadier than he felt. "Just... tired."

She nodded, understanding flashing in her eyes. "We all are," she said softly. "But we made it through. That's what matters."

Kemp looked around at his companions, each one of them a testament to resilience and strength. They had faced a formidable foe and emerged victorious. The scars they bore were proof of their determination to see their mission through, no matter the cost.

"We can't stay here—" Ruiha murmured as she looked around. Kemp acknowledged her with a simple nod as she stood and began walking towards Magnus.

Ruiha and Magnus directed the group to set up camp in a nearby grove, sheltered by a cluster of ancient trees. The grove provided a sense of security, the towering trees forming a natural barrier against any further threats. Kemp sat down heavily, the weight of the Dragon Crown continuing to press on his mind and spirit.

Dakarai went around checking on the wounds of the group. Arvi and Magnus gathered firewood, their movements more cautious than usual after the intense battle. The camaraderie among the group was evident as they worked together, sharing quiet words of encouragement and relief. The fire crackled to life, casting warm, flickering light on their weary faces.

They shared a simple meal, the taste of the food a small comfort against the harshness of their journey. Ruiha joined Kemp by the fire, her eyes searching his. "Are you sure you're okay?" she asked.

Kemp was torn, unsure whether he could open up to her. Was now the right time, he wondered to himself, feeling the weight of his secrets pressing heavily on his chest. He nodded, forcing a smile. "Yes, I'm fine," he said instead, the lie tasting bitter on his tongue.

She nodded, understanding flashing in her eyes. "Okay, Kemp. I'm here if you need me, I'm here for you. When you're ready." She reached out and gently squeezed Kemp's hand before turning and making her way to where she had set down her pack.

As the night deepened, the cold pressed in on the camp, a reminder of the distance between them and the safety of anything familiar. Kemp sat apart, slightly removed from the small circle of flickering firelight, though the warmth was there, both in the flame and in the quiet murmur of voices around it. Yet he felt none of it. The weight of the Dragon Crown was not just on his mind; it was on his soul. He had carried it for too long, and now the voices, once a faint irritation, had become an insistent, pulsing presence, clawing at the corners of his consciousness.

They whispered, dark and low, the words serpentine, twisting into his thoughts like threads of shadow. Promising, they hissed, though what they promised seemed impossible, as though pulling him toward something that would unravel everything. His breath came shallow, and he stared into the flames, seeing nothing but the murmur of the voices entwining themselves deeper into him. Around him, his companions were little more than blurred shapes, distant figures lost in their own laughter, their voices like ghosts that failed to penetrate the fog in his mind.

Magnus spoke, his tone steady as always, but Kemp could barely make out the words. Arvi's laughter—deep, almost like rolling thunder—cut through the night, but it might as well have come from another world. All Kemp could hear was the rising chorus of the voices, their tendrils tightening, drawing him further into the abyss of his own mind.

He couldn't take it anymore.

Without a word, without even a glance to his companions, Kemp stood, his movements deliberate but stiff, as though he feared his own body might betray him. The trees beyond the firelight beckoned, a shadowed refuge from the warmth and light that now felt so foreign. The air grew colder with every step, the fire fading behind him as the dark swallowed him whole. The voices, still hissing their poisonous promises, seemed to pulse with the rhythm of his heartbeat. His body ached, and the silence of the woods pressed in, a heavy weight that made it hard to breathe.

Kemp moved further into the forest until the camp was nothing but a faint flicker in the distance. Here, beneath the oppressive canopy of ancient trees, the world seemed smaller, the air sharper. He found a secluded space, hidden between the twisted trunks of trees that seemed to lean in, as if they were watching, waiting. He knew his companions wouldn't hear him here. They wouldn't see his weakness.

The ritual began, slow and methodical, each movement precise despite the tremble in his hands. His fingers traced the symbols in the air, each stroke glowing faintly in the darkness, casting pale light across his face. His lips moved, whispering the words of the Shadowpurge, each syllable a quiet agony, tearing at his throat as they slipped into the night. His voice faltered once, but only for a moment. The pain in the words was nothing compared to what was coming.

The agony, when it arrived, was not a sharp strike but a slow, burning flood. Fire, liquid and searing, coursed through his veins, turning his blood to molten iron. His muscles twisted beneath his skin, convulsing violently, as though something inside him sought escape. His bones cracked under the strain, a feeling so intense it nearly blinded him, and for a moment, he feared they would break entirely. But worse than the physical pain were the voices—screaming now, howling in protest, as if they, too, could feel the purge tearing them apart.

They clawed at his mind, desperate to hold on, each scream a battle he was losing, each whisper a knife in his chest. Kemp's breath came in ragged gasps, his body trembling on the edge of collapse, but still he pressed on. The ritual was unforgiving, merciless, but so was the dark influence it sought to expel. It was a war, fought silently in the shadows of his own soul.

And then, in the midst of the chaos, Kemp felt it: a presence. Watching.

Through the haze of pain, his senses sharpened. A pair of eyes, faintly glowing in the dark, observed him from the edge of the clearing. There was no malice in them, but curiosity, a silent figure bearing witness to his suffering. Fear, irrational and fierce, flared in his chest, but he could not stop now. The pain crescendoed, searing through him, blurring the world into nothing but fire and torment.

Finally, with a shudder that left him gasping, the purge ended. The fire in his veins extinguished as suddenly as it had come, leaving an emptiness that felt worse than the pain. The voices were silent now, their presence stripped from his mind, but they had left behind something broken, hollow. Kemp collapsed, his body drained, his strength sapped by the purge. The earth beneath him was cold, unyielding, but he was too weak to care. He lay there, panting, trembling, his mind struggling to process the deafening silence that now filled him.

But the voices were gone. And for that, at least, he was grateful.

The silence stretched, oppressive in its absence of chaos, and Kemp slowly pulled himself to a sitting position. His staff lay beside him, still clutched in his hand, its magic a faint pulse beneath his grip. He wrapped himself in its power instinctively, feeling the familiar hum of the Shadowfire, though it no longer brought comfort. He was too raw, too exposed.

That's when he saw her.

A young Drogo woman stood at the edge of the clearing, her gaze fixed on him, eyes wide with something between fear and concern. She held a staff of her own, intricately carved, a symbol of something Kemp couldn't place. His breath caught, every muscle in his body tensing, the magic in his staff flaring to life, purple flames licking along its length.

She didn't move. She flinched, yes, but did not retreat. Her hands rose, palms open, a gesture of peace Kemp was not inclined to believe. "I mean no harm," she said, her voice steady, too steady. "My name is Elara. I am a wanderer, exiled from a distant clan."

Kemp's grip tightened on his staff as he forced himself to his feet, his legs shaking beneath him. His eyes narrowed, memories of Harald flickering at the edges of his mind. The betrayal. The loss. The memory of running through the shadows of Nexus. He would not trust so easily again.

"Why are you here?" His voice was rough, the flames on his staff casting long shadows across the clearing. He wasn't about to lower his guard—not for a stranger.

Her reptilian eyes flicked to the staff, taking in the magic that played along its surface. But her gaze did not falter. "I was drawn to the power of your ritual," she said, a note of intrigue in her voice. "I've been watching your group for some time, intrigued by your strength. You're on a dangerous path. And I can help you."

Kemp scoffed, the sound sharp in the cold air. He took a deliberate step back, his gaze hardening as his grip on the staff tightened. "Drawn to the power?" His voice cut through the silence like the crack of a whip. "We're in the middle of nowhere. Now tell me the truth—why are you here?"

The words hung between them, filled with distrust, but his mind raced beyond them, already mapping the worst possibilities. Had she been sent by the Drogo? The thought came unbidden, a sudden, cold certainty that this was a trap. Sabotage, perhaps. His paranoia flared to life, and with it, the Shadowfire coiled beneath his skin, ready to lash out, to destroy her before she could make her move.

But Elara stood her ground, her hands still raised in a gesture of surrender. Slowly, she lowered them, her expression softening.

"I told you already," she said, her voice quieter now, though no less certain. "I'm exiled. My clan has cast me out, and I have nowhere to go. I'm alone."

Kemp's eyes narrowed. His breath came slow and measured, but his distrust was like a palpable force in the air between them. "Convenient," he muttered, his voice a growl. He didn't relax his stance.

Elara hesitated then, a brief flicker in her eyes as she weighed her response. When she spoke again, her voice was quieter, softer, "I understand your reluctance," she said finally. "I don't expect your trust. Not easily."

Her eyes darted around the clearing, taking in the shadows and the silence, as though searching for the right words. When she met his gaze again, there was something else there—something that made Kemp pause, if only for a moment.

"But I know this land," she said, her voice barely more than a whisper. "I know the dangers that lie ahead. You can see them, can't you? The signs of warriors up here searching, hunting?"

Kemp's jaw tightened, the tension in him coiling like a spring. His instincts screamed at him to push her away, to call for the others, to get rid of her before she became a problem. But something about the way she stood—calm, unwavering—held him back. Not trust, not yet, but something else. Curiosity, perhaps. Or a sense that there was more to her than she had revealed.

"You know nothing about us," Kemp said, his voice low, a warning that lingered in the air like a blade hanging between them. "If you're lying, you'll regret it."

Elara didn't waver. Her gaze held his, steady, unflinching. "I understand," she said. "I'll prove myself if I have to. But I swear to you, Kemp, I'm not here to harm anyone."

Kemp didn't respond immediately. His mind churned, turning over the possibilities, calculating the risks, weighing the danger of letting her stay against the uncertainty of her true intentions. But for now, he didn't lower his staff. The Shadowfire flickered, its glow casting long shadows across the clearing, and he made no move to hide it.

"You'll prove it to the others," he said at last, his voice flat, unyielding. "And I'll be watching you. Closely."

He lowered his staff slightly, just enough to show her that she'd earned a sliver of attention, but nothing more. Trust was still far beyond her reach.

Elara took a step closer, her gaze never leaving his. There was something about the way she moved, deliberate and calm, that made Kemp hesitate for just a heartbeat. She smiled then, faint and brief, as though she had seen something in him that even he wasn't aware of.

"The winds carry many secrets," she murmured. "Your struggle, your pain—they are known to those who listen." She knelt beside him then, her movements slow, her hand glowing with a soft, healing light. "And I can offer you relief from the torment you endure."

Kemp's body tensed, and for a moment, he almost pulled away, the Shadowfire pulsing in warning. But something in her words, something in the calm certainty of her gaze, stayed his hand. He allowed her to touch him, hesitantly at first, his heart racing with doubt and suspicion. But as her hand rested against his chest, a warmth spread from her fingertips, not the burning heat of fire but a soothing, quiet glow that eased the pain still lingering from the purge. It was gentle, a whisper of comfort that calmed the remnants of the dark voices that had haunted him.

Kemp's wariness did not fade, but he sensed no immediate threat. For now, he nodded, though his guard remained firmly in place. "We could use all the help we can get," he said, his tone guarded but acknowledging the truth.

Elara rose, her expression serious, the faint glow of her healing magic fading. "I will help you," she said softly. "But be warned—the path ahead is fraught with peril. You must be prepared for the trials that await."

Kemp nodded again, though the weight of her words settled heavily in his mind. "We will be," he said, his resolve hardening, though the future felt more uncertain than ever.

As they walked back to the camp, Kemp felt the quiet presence of Elara beside him, her steps light but deliberate. There was a calmness in her that unsettled him, a sense of something unspoken, something unknown. The voices were silent, for now, but the mistrust lingered, as did the questions that circled his mind like shadows.

They were battered, bruised, and weary. But they were not broken. Not yet. And with Elara's help, perhaps they would continue. Perhaps they would prevail.

But Kemp would be watching.

Kemp led Elara back to the camp, his mind a whirl of thoughts and worries. The flickering firelight cast long shadows on the ancient trees, and the night air was filled with the sounds of distant wildlife. Kemp's heart pounded as they approached the campsite, where the rest of the group awaited.

Magnus was the first to notice their return. His eyes narrowed as he took in the newcomer. "Who is this?" he asked, his voice low and edged with suspicion.

"This is Elara," Kemp replied, striving to steady his voice. "She—she helped me."

Ruiha's sharp gaze fixed on Elara. "Helped you how?" she demanded. "And why were you out there alone, Kemp?"

Elara remained calm, meeting Ruiha's eyes without flinching. Her voice was smooth, with a hint of sadness. "I am a wanderer, exiled from a distant clan," she said smoothly. "I saw Kemp in distress and offered my aid."

Ruiha's eyes narrowed further. "Exiled, you say? And what clan might that be?"

Elara's smile was polite, yet her eyes flickered with a momentary sorrow. "It is a long story, not easily told in a few words. Suffice it to say, my clan and I had irreconcilable differences."

Ruiha's frustration was palpable. "Convenient," she muttered. "And what are you doing here, so far from your clan?"

Elara's gaze did not waver, but her voice softened. "As I said, I am a wanderer. My path crossed yours, and I offer my assistance. Whether you accept it or not is your decision."

Magnus crossed his arms. "And what exactly do you expect in return for this—assistance?"

"Nothing but the opportunity to travel with you," Elara replied. "I seek no reward, only the chance to help."

Ruiha turned back to Kemp. "And you? What were you doing out there alone, Kemp?"

Kemp stuttered, his voice trembling slightly. "I—I needed time to clear my head."

Ruiha's eyes softened slightly, her tone a mix of concern and frustration. "You've been acting strangely, Kemp. We all have our burdens, but isolating yourself won't help. Why didn't you come to us?"

Kemp's shoulders sagged, and he avoided her gaze. "I didn't want to burden anyone," he admitted quietly.

Ruiha sighed, a mixture of concern and exasperation on her face. She stepped closer, her voice gentle but firm. "Come, let's talk privately." She gestured for Kemp to follow her. They moved away from the campfire, their figures soon lost in the darkness.

As they walked, Ruiha's voice softened even further. "Kemp, we're a team. We rely on each other. You don't have to carry your burdens alone."

"I know," Kemp replied, his voice heavy with guilt. "It's just—I've been hearing voices. They were getting louder. I thought I could handle it on my own."

Ruiha stopped, turning to face him. "Voices? What do you mean?"

Kemp took a deep breath, the weight of his secret pressing down on him. "I haven't told anyone else in the group. Only Thraxos and Thalirion know. The Dragon Crown, it—it speaks to me. At first, it was just whispers, but lately, it's been getting worse, louder, more insistent. It's like a constant barrage in my mind."

Ruiha's expression shifted to a mix of confusion, fear, and determination. "Why didn't you tell us? We could have helped you."

"I didn't want to worry you all," Kemp admitted. "And I thought I could manage it. I've developed a ritual called the Shadowpurge. It's incredibly painful, but it can banish the voices for a few days. It's the only thing that's worked so far."

"What is this Shadowpurge?" Ruiha asked, her voice trembling slightly.

"It's a ritual that involves using Shadowfire to burn away the dark influences within me," Kemp explained. "I draw arcane symbols, recite an incantation, and endure immense pain. It feels like my veins are on fire, my muscles contort, and my bones feel like they're being shattered and reformed. But when it's over, the voices are gone, at least for a while."

Ruiha's eyes widened with horror and empathy. "And you've been doing this alone? Enduring this kind of pain without anyone to help you?"

Kemp nodded, feeling shame wash over him. "I didn't want to burden anyone with my problems. Thraxos said there might be a cure, though. He believes that if I can learn to control my Shadowfire, I might be able to control the voices as well."

Ruiha placed a hand on his shoulder, her grip firm and reassuring. Her eyes softened with understanding and resolve. "Kemp, you should have come to us. We're in this together. We face our challenges together. You don't have to go through this alone anymore."

Kemp nodded, feeling a sense of relief and renewed hope. "Understood."

They continued walking in silence for a moment. Ruiha finally broke the silence, her voice full of quiet determination. "We'll figure this out, Kemp. We'll help you control the Shadowfire and silence the voices for good."

Kemp looked at her, gratitude shining in his eyes. "Thank you, Ruiha. I appreciate it more than you know."

As they made their way back to the camp, Kemp felt a newfound sense of camaraderie and support. For the first time in a long while, he felt like he wasn't alone in his struggle. With Ruiha and the rest of the group by his side, he believed they could face whatever challenges lay ahead.

Back at the camp, the atmosphere was tense. Magnus kept a wary eye on Elara, while Arvi, sensing the tension, tried to lighten the mood. "Well, if Elara's here to help, then we should give her a chance," he said, offering her a friendly smile.

Elara returned the smile graciously. "Thank you, Arvi. I assure you, I only wish to assist."

Dakarai, who had been silent throughout the exchange,

finally spoke. "Your presence is... intriguing, Elara. I hope you understand our caution."

Elara nodded. "Of course. Caution is wise in these times."

As the night deepened, the group settled into an uneasy truce. Kemp and Ruiha returned, their conversation having brought some clarity, though the air was still thick with unspoken questions.

Elara's presence had stirred the camp, her calm demeanor both a balm and a source of suspicion. But as the fire crackled and the night wore on, one thing became clear: the path ahead would require all their strength and trust, and Elara's role in their journey was only beginning.

As the group settled for the night, Kemp found a spot near the fire, his thoughts still heavy with the revelations he had shared with Ruiha. Elara sat across from him, her eyes reflecting the dancing flames.

Elara spoke softly, her voice a soothing presence amidst his turmoil. "Kemp, how do you feel? It's not easy to admit one's struggles."

Kemp glanced at her, his expression a mix of guarded curiosity and tentative trust. "It's not easy to trust a stranger, either. Why did you help me?"

Elara's gaze was steady, her words thoughtful. "Because I saw someone in need. In my exile, I've learned that kindness is a rare currency. It's worth offering when one can."

Magnus, who had been quietly sharpening his blade nearby, looked up. "Kindness is a luxury we can't always afford," he interjected. "Especially when trust is in short supply."

Elara nodded in understanding. "I know I have much to

prove. All I ask is a chance to do so."

Arvi, ever the peacemaker, leaned forward. "We all have something to prove, Elara. It's why we're out here in the first place. Let's give her a fair chance."

Ruiha, who had been listening quietly, spoke up. "For now, we move forward together. We'll need every bit of help we can get, especially with what lies ahead."

Dakarai's eyes flicked to Kemp. "And what exactly does lie ahead, Kemp? Do you have a plan for controlling the voices?"

Kemp sighed, running a hand through his hair, his voice weary but determined. "Thraxos believes there's a way. In the Forgotten Realm, I should be able to find a way to control my power."

Magnus sheathed his blade with a decisive click. "Then our mission remains. We go to this place, and we find a way to help Kemp."

Ruiha nodded in agreement. "Agreed. We stand together in this."

The group exchanged glances, a silent pact forming among them. Despite their differences and the shadows of doubt, they were united by a common purpose.

As the night deepened, they took turns keeping watch, the fire a small beacon of warmth and light in the vast darkness. Kemp, his heart lighter than it had been in weeks, drifted into a restless sleep, the murmur of the Dragon Crown's whispers silenced.

In the early hours of the morning, the group broke camp, readying themselves for the journey ahead. Elara moved with quiet efficiency, her presence a blend of mystery and reassurance.

Ruiha approached Kemp as he adjusted his pack. "We'll get through this, Kemp. Together."

Kemp nodded, gratitude in his eyes. "Thank you, Ruiha. I believe we will."

As they set off, the forest around them seemed to hold its

breath, the path ahead shrouded in uncertainty. But with each step, their resolve grew stronger. They were more than a group of wanderers and exiles; they were a team, bound by shared challenges and newfound trust.

And as the first light of dawn pierced through the trees, it brought with it a glimmer of hope. For the first time in a long while, Kemp felt that they were on the right path, and with his friends beside him, he believed they could conquer whatever lay ahead.

Elara walked beside him, a quiet reminder that exile doesn't come with a warm welcome, but you can carve out a place with kindness, and will. The unknown stretched before them like a beast waiting to be tamed. Together, they were ready to face the unknown, not afraid of what lay ahead. They weren't just survivors of their past—they were ready to rewrite their future. In the end, it was not the world that defined them—but how they chose to defy it.

12

WHISPERS OF BETRAYAL

"Trust is a delicate thread, easily severed by the greedy hands of those who seek power without honor."

GUNNAR

Gunnar's return to Draegoor was a grueling ordeal. It was faster for him to travel overground, rather than through the twisting turning tunnels between the cities. Each step through the jagged landscape echoing the burden on his shoulders. The mountains loomed like ancient guardians, their peaks piercing the sky, while the dense forests whispered secrets of old. After five relentless days, the grim silhouette of Draegoor Mountain finally emerged from the mist. Relief and dread coiled within him at the sight.

As he approached his underground home, the runes along the fortress walls shimmered faintly, remnants of ancient magic still vigilant. Within those stone walls, preparations for a crucial council were underway. The chiefs would be gathering: Erik of Draegoor, his father; Bojan of Hornbaek; Durik of Braemeer; and Gadrin of Uglich.

Gunnar took his time after arriving, allowing himself a

moment of respite. The journey had been arduous, and he needed to gather his strength and composure. He spent the evening in quiet contemplation, finding solace in the silent presence of Anwyn as she lay in her magically induced coma.

Two days passed, and Gunnar found himself at her bedside for most of each day. He prayed to the gods for her recovery, for the unity of the clans, and for an end to the war with the Drogo and Nergai. Although they tirelessly searched for a cure, progress was slow. Gunnar held her hand, whispering words of hope and love, his heart heavy with the fear of losing her. He vowed to stay strong for her, drawing comfort from the steady rhythm of her breath.

Finally, the summons arrived. Gunnar paused at the entrance of the grand council chamber, drawing a deep breath to steady himself. The hall was thick with tension, every murmur a potential spark. As he entered, silence fell, all eyes turning to him. The animosity between Erik and the other chiefs was an undeniable force pressing against him. Instinctively, he touched his enchanted battle axe, the cool frosteel a reminder of the power that flowed through him.

Erik's gaze was locked on the clan chiefs, a silent exchange of resolve. "You allowed Wilfrid to usurp me," he accused, his voice sharp and cold, fury blazing in his eyes. "The very brother I trusted. You stood by and let it happen."

Bojan and Durik shifted uncomfortably, but Gadrin met Erik's ire with steady indifference. "The Drogo threat demanded our attention," Gadrin replied, his voice even, unrepentant. "We had no troops to spare for your squabbles."

Gunnar watched Gadrin closely, his eyes narrowing as he studied every subtle shift in the Dwarf's expression. A twitch at the corner of Gadrin's mouth, the slightest tightening of his brow—each could be a clue, a crack in the mask of calm he wore.

Was it genuine, or was he hiding something deeper? Gunnar wasn't sure, but his instincts told him to stay wary. Across from him, Erik stood rigid, fists clenched so tightly that his knuckles had gone white.

Gunnar could sense the fury radiating off his father, the tension in the room thickening with every word. Erik's voice, low and trembling with barely controlled rage, cut through the silence.

"And what of the loyalty I've shown you? The aid I've given your clans? The Dwarves who bled and died under my banner?"

Gadrin's response was a dismissive wave, a gesture that seemed designed to provoke. Gunnar saw Erik's body stiffen even more, the insult landing like a blow.

"We needed Draegoor's help against the Drogo," Gadrin said, his voice cold, detached. "Wilfrid promised us that. We acted in the best interests of Dreynas."

Gunnar felt the shift before Erik moved. His father's breath grew heavier, more ragged, his chest rising and falling with barely contained rage. The air in the chamber seemed to contract, the voices of the others fading as if muffled by the roaring fury within Erik. Gunnar tensed, watching his father closely now, feeling the danger in every breath Erik took. It was as if the world around them had narrowed, leaving only Erik and Gadrin in its wake, like two predators circling.

Gunnar gripped the haft of his axe tighter, the familiar weight of it steadying him. But the usual calming aura it gave off felt weaker, as if even the magic within it struggled to soothe the tempest building in his father. A faint green light flickered from the axe's edge, but it was a dim, uncertain glow.

Before Gunnar could act, Erik moved. His hand lashed out with brutal speed, backhanding Gadrin across the face. The crack of impact echoed through the hall, and Gunnar saw the blood and spittle fly from Gadrin's mouth. For a moment, Gadrin staggered, eyes wide with shock, but Gunnar didn't miss the way that shock turned to rage almost immediately.

Chaos erupted. Voices rose in anger, the room devolving into a cacophony of shouts and accusations. Gunnar felt the weight of it all bearing down on him—the fragile peace they'd fought so hard to maintain threatening to crumble in an instant. Erik stood over Gadrin, trembling with the effort of holding himself back from doing worse.

Gunnar stepped forward, his grip tightening on the axe. He drew deeply on its calming magic, feeling the warmth of the green light as it flared brighter, more steady now. The light spread around him, a soothing balm to the fraying tempers in the room. He took a breath, the tension in his chest loosening as the light flowed outward.

"Enough!" Gunnar's voice cut through the din, filled with the force of command, backed by the magic in his veins. The sound reverberated through the hall, causing the bones of every Dwarf present to vibrate. Slowly, the room quieted, all eyes turning to him. Erik was still panting, his chest heaving, but he didn't move.

Gunnar stood tall, his presence filling the space, and when he spoke again, his tone was calm, but filled with the gravity of the moment. "We stand on the brink of annihilation. We cannot afford to be divided, to weaken ourselves with these grievances. The Drogo threat isn't just steel and claw; they wield dark magic that could unravel everything we've built. Our strength lies in unity, or we will fall."

The weight of his words settled over the room, the anger and hostility among the chiefs giving way to reluctant silence. Gunnar didn't relax. He could feel the tension still thrumming in the air, but at least, for now, it was contained.

Erik glared down at Gadrin, his voice still thick with contempt.

"This isn't over," he spat, venom dripping from every word. "One day, you'll pay for your cowardice."

Gunnar watched as Gadrin wiped the blood from his mouth, his eyes burning with unspoken rage, but he remained silent. For now, at least, the threat had passed.

Durik was the first to step forward, his movements deliberate as he knelt before Gunnar. Erik joined him, their allegiance already pledged, their heads bowed in solemn respect.

"We recognize Gunnar as the Dwarven Prince," Erik declared, his voice filled with pride and conviction. But even as the words were spoken, Gunnar's eyes drifted to Bojan, who had remained silent, his gaze sharp and skeptical.

"What measures will you take against the Drogo?" Bojan asked, his voice cutting through the stillness. Gunnar felt the challenge in his words, the weight of his doubt pressing against him. "What of their dark magic?"

The question hung in the air like a gauntlet thrown, and Gunnar met Bojan's gaze, knowing this was only the beginning of what lay ahead.

Gunnar drew a deep breath, steadying himself. "We will harness the power of the Shadowforged," he began, his voice steady but edged with the urgency of their plight. "Their magic is potent. We also have Kemp, Thraxos, Thalirion, and myself. Our combined magical power is unrivaled on Vellhor." His gaze momentarily flickered as his thoughts drifted to Anwyn, still comatose, her formidable powers locked away in an unresponsive body. Her absence gnawed at him. He vowed silently, once again, that he would save her.

He turned his focus back to Bojan, locking eyes with him. "We've faced dire threats before," Gunnar continued, his voice gaining strength. "And each time, we've found a way to persevere. This time is no different. The Shadowforged's magic, combined with our own, gives us a fighting chance. We will study their sorcery, counter it, and adapt."

A murmur rippled through the hall, chiefs exchanging glances. Gunnar's heart pounded, but he pressed on, his voice growing more passionate. "We will not fight them on their terms alone. We will out-think them, out-maneuver them. Every clan's strength will be our shield, every warrior's heart our weapon."

He paused, looking directly into Bojan's eyes. "I have walked the jagged paths of this land, felt the weight of our ancestors' expectations. I know the fear that grips us all, the uncertainty. But I also know our potential. United, we are a force greater than any dark magic."

Bojan's gaze flickered, a crack in his steely demeanor. He saw not just the prince before him, but the weight of leadership that had settled on Gunnar's shoulders, the sincerity in his eyes. Bojan could see the young prince's hands were steady, his voice unwavering, but there was more—a depth of emotion that spoke of personal sacrifice and unwavering commitment.

Bojan took a step forward, his posture softening. "You speak with conviction, Gunnar," he said slowly, almost reluctantly. "But conviction alone won't win this war."

Gunnar nodded, his eyes never leaving Bojan's. "No, it won't. But it's a start. With your help, with the unity of all clans, we will forge a path to victory."

Bojan hesitated for a heartbeat, then slowly, he knelt before Gunnar, the movement deliberate and filled with significance. "I pledge my service to you, Dwarven Prince," he declared, his voice firm, the echo of his words a promise that resonated through the hall.

Gunnar's breath caught in his throat, relief mixing uneasily with a familiar sense of impending doom. A small victory, nothing more. The first step, sure, but they had a mountain to climb and all it took was one bad misstep to tumble into the abyss. He reached out, his hand resting on Bojan's shoulder. "Together, we'll save our land and our future," he said, the words sounding more hollow than they should've.

The room settled, all eyes eventually falling on Gadrin who sat in stony silence. His fingers, thick and calloused, steepled before him, the faintest smirk twisting his bloody lips. He didn't rush, taking his sweet time, his sharp gaze cutting across the chamber like a blade, weighing everyone in it. Gunnar knew that look all too well—calculating, opportunistic. The kind of Dwarf who smelled blood in the water.

Gadrin finally spoke, his voice slow, deliberate, each word dripping with greed. "And what benefit do we gain?" he asked, eyes glittering with calculation. "Uglich is wealthy. What more can you offer us?"

Gunnar could feel Erik bristle beside him, his father's barely-restrained anger flaring like a blacksmith's bellows. He didn't bother to hide the venom in his voice. "Uglich has everything it needs. What more could you possibly want, Gadrin? What else would satisfy that insatiable greed of yours?" Erik spat. "Are the lives of every Dwarf in Dreynas not enough reward for you?"

Gadrin smiled, the kind of smile that made Gunnar want to reach for his axe. The old Dwarf turned his gaze to Durik, who still held the Sword of Eldrin, the blade gleaming with power. His voice turned smooth, oily. "I see other leaders have received certain... *gifts* from young Gunnar." His tone mocked, prodded. "Erik's son named ruler of Dreynas? That's quite the prize, isn't it? How do we know this isn't just Draegoor lining its coffers with more power? What guarantees do we have that this isn't a ploy?"

Gunnar stepped forward before his father could explode again, the frustration bubbling under his skin. "I'll treat all clans equally," he said, each word tight, controlled, though his patience was fraying. "No one clan gets special treatment. Not Uglich. Not Draegoor. My only concern is Dreynas."

Gadrin's eyes turned cold, his smile fading as quickly as it had come. "Mere words, Prince," he said, dismissing Gunnar with a flick of his hand. "And I do not believe them."

Gunnar's fists clenched at his sides, every muscle in his body tensing as Gadrin's words struck home. The nerve of the bastard. Gunnar could see it in Gadrin's eyes—that cold, calculating gleam, the look of a Dwarf who'd already sold his soul for a better offer. The kind of Dwarf who'd trade loyalty for a shiny coin, honor for a sharper blade. In that moment, Gunnar thought of Wilfrid. Of his uncles betrayal. His anger flared, hot and fast, but he clamped it down. Barely.

Gadrin stood with a heavy sigh, dismissive as ever, his cloak trailing behind him like a shadow. He gave a final, arrogant glance at the assembled chiefs, and something dark flickered in his eyes—something more than greed. Gunnar's heart sank further. He had a sickening thought. *What had the Drogo promised him?* Power? Riches? Land? Whatever it was, it had turned Gadrin, and that meant the Drogo—or someone worse—were already here, their poison spreading through the very heart of Dreynas.

As Gadrin swept from the room, Gunnar's mind raced, the weight of the situation bearing down on him like a stone slab. If Gadrin had made deals with the Drogo or another dark force, then the council's alliances were weaker than he'd feared. The whole thing could crumble with one more push, and the Drogo wouldn't even need to draw a sword to bring Dreynas down.

His father stood seething, fists trembling with the urge to act, to follow Gadrin and finish what had begun. Durik wasn't much better, his face dark with barely controlled fury. Gunnar knew he had to stay calm, had to keep his wits about him. The stakes were too high, the future too fragile. One wrong move and everything would shatter.

The familiar hum of his axe tugged at his thoughts, a subtle reminder of the dangers lurking outside the room, beyond the council's squabbles. There were bigger threats, darker enemies waiting in the shadows. Gunnar swallowed hard, his resolve hardening. There wasn't time for anger or petty disputes. There wasn't time for anything but cold, hard decisions. He clenched his fists tighter, letting the pain sharpen his focus.

The road ahead would be long, brutal, but Gunnar knew there was no other choice. He would see it through. He had to. For Dreynas. For his people. Whatever the cost.

Gunnar had finally managed to arrange another council meeting, hoping it would fare better than the last. But as he watched the chiefs engage in their hushed yet heated discussions, each word a strategic move on a chessboard, he wasn't confident this one would go any smoother.

The air was thick with tension, and Gunnar could almost feel the weight of their scrutiny pressing down on him. He knew that the unity of the clans hung by a thread, and that thread was fraying with every passing second. His heart pounded not only with the fear of failure but also with the knowledge that failure could lead to the decimation of Dreynas, perhaps even all of Vellhor.

Erik's jaw was tight, the muscles in his neck twitching, as if the slightest word might send them snapping. His breath came slow, deliberate—controlled—but the fire in his eyes flickered, flared, then dimmed, like a forge struggling to contain its heat. Durik's unease was clear, his fingers drumming nervously on the table, and Bojan's skepticism was a constant thorn, his eyes narrowing with every suggestion.

But it was Gadrin—his eyes always measuring, lips twitching with unspoken schemes—that unsettled Gunnar the most. There was something hidden in every glance, every pause, like a shadow just out of reach. Gunnar knew the whispered rumors about Gadrin's ambitions, how his gaze seemed to pierce through pretenses, always searching for an advantage. Gadrin's demeanor was a mask of calm, but Gunnar sensed the storm beneath.

"We cannot delay any longer," Erik said, his voice a low growl. "Our enemies are at the gates."

"And rushing into this could fracture us beyond repair," Bojan countered, his tone icy. "We need more than just bold claims."

Durik's voice wavered as he spoke. "Is there no way to ensure everyone's loyalty? Can we trust anyone completely?"

Gadrin's voice cut through the murmurs like a knife, "trust is a fragile thing, easily shattered. We must be certain that allowing a single ruler is the correct path to tread."

The meeting adjourned for the evening, and Gunnar took the opportunity to follow a hunch. Something about Gadrin's demeanor had struck him as odd. A gnawing suspicion took root in Gunnar's mind. It was more than just instinct; it was a gut feeling born of years of experience in reading people. Gunnar knew he had to dig deeper, to trust his intuition that Gadrin was hiding something.

His heart raced as he slipped away quietly, his steps as light as a thief's. Each shadow seemed to whisper secrets, and every creak of the floorboards sent a chill down his spine. The fortress, once a symbol of safety, now felt like a labyrinth of deceit. His mind raced, replaying every interaction with Gadrin, every hint of deceit that he had dismissed too easily before. Gadrin's dismissive wave and the dark aura that trailed him had not gone unnoticed. Gunnar was determined to uncover the truth.

Gunnar's footsteps echoed softly as he approached the private chambers where Gadrin had retired. He pressed his ear to the door, listening intently. The cold wood was rough against his bearded cheek, the murmured voices within like the whispers of ghosts. The tension in the air was palpable, each breath feeling like a weight on Gunnar's chest. Gunnar's heart pounded as he recognized the harsh, guttural tones of the Drogo. His pulse quickened with both fear and determination, knowing that this moment could change everything.

Carefully, Gunnar edged closer, catching snippets of their conversation. Promises of power, wealth, and dominion flowed from the Drogo envoy's lips like venom, each word dripping with the poison of temptation. Gadrin's responses were filled with greed and ambition, confirming Gunnar's worst fears. The betrayal in Gadrin's voice was a dagger to Gunnar's heart, each word a twist of the blade. Gunnar clenched his fists, his nails digging into his palms as he heard Gadrin's treacherous words. Memories of his uncle, who had betrayed his clan flooded his thoughts, fueling a surge of righteous anger. The Drogo had indeed made their offer, one too tempting for Gadrin to refuse.

Gunnar's blood boiled, his fists clenching at his sides like iron. He knew that confronting Gadrin openly would only lead to more chaos. He needed to act swiftly and decisively. His mind raced, formulating a plan that would expose Gadrin's betrayal without plunging the clans into civil war. Slipping away as silently as he had come, Gunnar returned to the council chamber, where Erik and the other chiefs were still gathered. Their faces were etched with worry and determination, a reflection of the storm brewing within Gunnar's own soul.

13

THE CAPTIVE AND THE FALLEN

"The hardest fight is not with the sword, but with the fear of losing those beside you."

RUIHA

Ruiha's breath frosted in the cool morning air as she watched the camp stir to life, a scene both familiar and eternally comforting. The dawn cast a golden glow, illuminating the dewy grass and the embers of last night's fire. She inhaled deeply, the crispness of the morning invigorating her senses, a welcome balm to the lingering worry from the night before.

Across the clearing, her eyes fell upon Elara, the young Drogo woman who had joined them the previous night. Elara stood apart from the others, her presence a stark reminder of the mysteries yet to unfold. Her wooden staff, adorned with intricate carvings, was clutched tightly in her hand. Ruiha's gaze lingered on the staff, noting the ancient runes etched into the wood, symbols of power that seemed to pulse with a life of their own.

Ruiha couldn't help but feel a twinge of unease. The runes were unlike any she had seen before, and their unfamiliarity gnawed at her curiosity and caution alike. She wondered what secrets Elara held and whether she was friend or foe.

Elara's eyes met Ruiha's, and for a moment, the world seemed to narrow to just the two of them. In Elara's gaze, Ruiha saw both vulnerability and a guarded strength. She felt a pang of empathy—Elara was alone in the world, much as Ruiha had once been.

The camp continued to wake around them, with the exchange of quiet greetings and preparing for the day's journey. The scent of brewing tea mingled with the crisp morning air, adding a sense of normalcy to the scene.

Ruiha stepped toward Elara, her heart pounding slightly with the effort to bridge the distance between them. 'Good morning, Elara,' she said softly, her voice carrying both warmth and a subtle invitation for connection.

Elara's grip on her staff relaxed slightly, and she offered a small, tentative smile. 'Good morning,' she replied, her voice as soft as the morning light.

For a moment, they stood in silence, the golden light wrapping around them like a protective cloak. Ruiha knew that trust wouldn't come easily, but she felt a flicker of hope. The day held promise, not just for their journey but for the bonds they might forge along the way.

As they turned to join the others, Ruiha couldn't shake the feeling that the runes on Elara's staff would play a crucial role in the trials ahead. She silently vowed to unravel their mystery, for she sensed that understanding them would be key to the path that lay before them all.

"We need to move out," Magnus called, his voice slicing through the camp's early morning chatter, a sharp reminder of the day's impending challenges. "The Forgotten Realm awaits, and we have no time to waste."

Ruiha nodded, gathering her belongings with swift, practiced movements. Her heart beat in time with the urgency of Magnus's words. She cast a quick glance at the horizon, where the mountains in the distance were shrouded in mist, marking the end of the Scorched Mountains. The mist seemed almost alive, a shifting veil that hid untold dangers and secrets. As the group began to assemble, she noticed Dakarai standing near Elara. His dark eyes flicked toward her with an unreadable expression, his stance tense, the slight tightening of his jaw betraying his inner turmoil. Ruiha's lips pressed into a thin line. Dakarai seemed to have a growing interest in the Drogo woman and it was a potential complication they didn't need.

The journey was arduous, the path winding through dense forests and rocky terrain. Every step was a test of endurance, the forest a labyrinth of hidden perils. Each crunch of leaves and snap of twigs set Ruiha's nerves on edge. She stayed vigilant, her senses attuned to any sign of danger. Elara walked a few paces behind Kemp, her presence a constant reminder of the uncertainties they faced. Despite her suspicions, Ruiha couldn't help but notice the ease with which Elara navigated the treacherous landscape, her steps light and sure, as if guided by some unseen force.

Ruiha stole a glance at Elara, wondering at the secrets the Drogo woman carried. What power lay in those light steps, what knowledge behind those watchful eyes? The runes on Elara's staff seemed to glow faintly in the dim forest light.

Seeing the way Dakarai kept glancing over at Elara continued to gnaw at her thoughts. She recalled the many battles they had fought side by side, his loyalty unwavering. The way he watched Elara, the silent communication in his eyes, made Ruiha uneasy. She knew Dakarai well enough to see the conflict within him, torn between duty and a fascination he seemed to barely understand himself.

As the day wore on, Ruiha found herself walking alongside Magnus. His presence was a steadying force, a reminder of their shared purpose. "What do you make of Elara?" she asked quietly, her eyes fixed ahead.

Magnus's expression was thoughtful. "She's an enigma, true enough. But we need her. There's something about her—I feel she's meant to be part of this journey, whether for good or ill."

Ruiha nodded, her thoughts heavy with the implications. The path ahead was fraught with danger, but she sensed that Elara's role in their quest was far from insignificant.

During a brief rest, Ruiha found herself next to Elara. The silence between them stretched, heavy with unspoken questions. Finally, Ruiha broke it.

"What brought you to our camp last night?" Ruiha asked, trying to keep her tone neutral.

Elara met her gaze, her eyes steady. "I was exiled from my clan for being a hedgewitch," she said simply. "The shamans felt threatened by my power."

Ruiha raised an eyebrow. "Exiled?" The word hung heavily between them. "You're a hedgewitch?"

Elara nodded. "Born with the gift, but my clan's leaders saw it as a threat rather than a blessing."

Ruiha's expression softened slightly. She knew the sting of rejection, the loneliness of being seen as different. "What kind of magic do you wield?"

"Herbal and elemental," Elara replied. "I can draw power from the earth and the plants. It's how I survived after my exile."

Ruiha's breath caught. The raw sincerity in Elara's voice, the vulnerability laced with strength—it stirred something deep inside her. "It must have been difficult," Ruiha said quietly. "Being cast out."

Elara's eyes shimmered with a mix of pain and determination. "It was. But it also made me stronger."

Ruiha nodded slowly, a thread of understanding weaving between them. Strength came in many forms, she had always believed, and here was a living testament to that belief. "Strength comes in many forms," she murmured.

As they continued their journey, Ruiha couldn't help but notice the subtle interactions between Elara and Dakarai. The way his hand would brush against hers in passing, the secret smiles they shared. There was an undeniable chemistry between them, an unspoken connection that seemed to grow with each passing hour. Ruiha wondered if Dakarai saw in Elara what she was beginning to see—a resilient spirit forged in adversity.

The chasm yawned before them, a black void that seemed to swallow the world. The mist within it moved like something alive, coiling and writhing as if it had purpose. Elara stood at the edge, her eyes narrowed as she studied the swirling depths. "This is the boundary," she said, her voice low, barely audible over the wind that whistled through the rocks. "Ancient tales say it was meant to keep intruders out, a barrier between the world we know and what lies beyond."

Ruiha's gaze flicked to the bridge, a thread of ancient stone stretching across the abyss. Narrow, weathered, the kind of bridge that looked like it would hold right until the moment it didn't. She felt a twist of unease in her stomach.

Magnus stepped forward, testing the stone with a cautious foot. It creaked but didn't give way. "It's old," he said, voice tight. "But it should hold." There was no confidence in his words, just the grim acceptance of someone who knew they had no choice.

Behind him, Kemp looked at the bridge like it was his own grave. His foot barely touched the stone before one of the cobbles crumbled beneath him. Unbalanced, he teetered on the edge, arms flailing wildly, eyes wide with panic. Ruiha's heart lurched into her throat. For a split second, she saw the end of their journey in Kemp's desperate scrabble for balance—the bridge, their mission, their lives, all hanging by a thread.

But then Elara was there, moving fast. Too fast for someone so composed. Her hand shot out, grabbing Kemp's arm with a strength that belied her size. The runes on her staff flared to life, glowing faintly, and Kemp jerked back onto solid ground, pale as a ghost.

"Careful," Elara warned, her voice steady, unnervingly calm. "This bridge is more fragile than it looks."

Kemp nodded, but his face was still drained of color, his breath coming in short, sharp bursts. "You saved my life."

Elara said nothing, but Ruiha noticed her fingers tighten around her staff, the glow of the runes fading, as if they were holding something back. Power, maybe. Or fear. The air felt heavy with something unsaid, something ancient, and Ruiha couldn't shake the feeling that the bridge wasn't the only thing on the verge of breaking.

They crossed one by one, every step slow, deliberate. Every creak and groan of the stone felt like a warning, and Ruiha's heart pounded in her chest with each step. Her eyes scanned the mist, watching for... what? She wasn't sure. But she knew something was out there, waiting.

When they reached the other side, the relief was short-lived. They set up camp, but the chasm loomed behind them, the mist shifting as if it was watching, waiting for another chance. The fire crackled weakly, barely holding back the cold.

Ruiha sat next to Elara, her eyes drawn to the runes on her

staff. They seemed quieter now, their glow dim but constant, like the pulse of a distant heartbeat.

"Those runes," Ruiha began, her voice low. She wasn't sure she wanted to know the answer, but curiosity gnawed at her. "They reacted to the bridge. What do they mean?"

Elara's eyes flicked to the staff, then back to the fire, as if she was considering how much to reveal. "They're old," she said finally, her voice soft. "Symbols of protection, guidance. My mentor believed they connected us to the land, to the past. On that bridge…" She hesitated, her brow furrowing. "They recognized something."

"Something?" Ruiha echoed, a frown tugging at her lips. She didn't like where this was going.

Elara met her gaze, and for the first time, Ruiha saw something in her eyes—something dark, unspoken. "The land remembers," Elara said, her voice barely above a whisper. "And so do the stones."

A cold knot of dread formed in Ruiha's stomach. The land wasn't just a place; it was alive, watching. Waiting. And their path was written in its bones.

Arvi, who had been silent until now, stirred beside the fire. His eyes gleamed in the dim light. "The Forgotten Realm," he muttered. "It's not just a place. It's a story. And we are a part of it, whether we want to be or not."

Ruiha glanced at the bridge again, at the chasm and the mist that writhed within it. She had the sinking feeling they hadn't just crossed into a new land. They had stepped into something far older, far more dangerous.

The evening dragged on, the fire's flickering warmth creating a small cocoon of light in the vast, oppressive darkness. It made the forest seem distant, a place that couldn't touch them, but Ruiha knew better. She always knew better. There was no real safety out here, just the illusion of it, and illusions could shatter with the smallest breath of wind.

Conversations dwindled, replaced by the comforting crackle of burning wood, though even that sound felt thin and hollow tonight. The usual night's symphony—rustling leaves, distant animal cries—was conspicuously absent. Instead, there was only silence, thick and suffocating, as though the forest itself were holding its breath, waiting.

Ruiha felt her instincts flare, sharp as a blade. She shifted her weight, eyes narrowing as they scanned the shadows. Something was wrong. The stillness wasn't natural. It was the kind of quiet that came before a predator struck. Every fiber of her being screamed at her to move, to act, but she stayed still, watching, listening.

Then, it happened. A subtle shift in the shadows, the faintest hint of movement, barely there, but enough to set her heart pounding. She strained to see through the gloom, and then, like ghosts emerging from the night itself, Drogo warriors appeared. Their scaled skin blended into the dark, like part of the forest, as if the very earth had spawned them.

The first sound was a chilling series of metallic scrapes. Weapons being drawn. A cold, mechanical sound that cut through the night like the promise of death.

Ruiha's stomach dropped. These warriors hadn't stumbled upon them by accident. They had been hunted. Like prey caught in a trap, every step leading them closer to their doom, and they hadn't even realized it.

The Drogo moved with a terrifying grace, materializing from the dark with a ghostly whisper, their approach almost soundless, like death creeping ever closer. The fire flickered in response, casting long shadows that danced against the forest floor. Ruiha knew, in that moment, that they were surrounded.

She reached for her weapons, every nerve alight, her breath coming faster now. She glanced around the camp. The others hadn't noticed yet, their gazes still lulled by the fire's false sense of warmth and safety. They were about to wake to a nightmare.

Elara was the first to notice. Her hand tightened on her staff, the runes etched into it flaring with a dull, warning light, as if the ancient magic within it sensed the danger before any of them did. Her eyes met Ruiha's, a brief exchange of understanding passing between them.

Then the Drogo attacked. They didn't charge—they didn't need to. They moved like shadows, silent, deadly. Ruiha had a fleeting thought: There would be no battle cries here. Only death, swift and quiet.

Ruiha sprang to her feet, her enchanted daggers flashing as she engaged the nearest attacker. The blades, etched with intricate runes, shimmered with an otherworldly green glow.

The clang of steel against steel rang out, shattering the oppressive silence. Ruiha parried a blow aimed at her head, twisting with the fluidity of long-practiced combat. Sparks flew from their clashing blades, illuminating the fierce determination in her eyes. Her movements were a blur of deadly precision, each strike aimed with lethal intent.

Around her, the chaos intensified. Magnus wielded his massive hammer with brutal efficiency, each swing a bone-crushing testament to his strength.

Elara's staff glowed with an eerie light as she summoned her magic, her face a mask of concentration. Dakarai was at Elara's side, his enchanted axe releasing concussive shockwaves that staggered his opponents and shattered their defenses.

Kemp's frosteel staff unleashed bursts of dark shadowy flames, incinerating anything in their path. In the thick of battle, Ruiha spotted Arvi fighting valiantly, his sword dancing through the air with relentless power. But even his immense skill couldn't save him from the Drogo. As he fought off two attackers, a third approached from behind, spear poised for a lethal strike.

"Arvi, behind you!" Ruiha cried out, but her warning came too late. Arvi turned just as the spear pierced his side, a look of surprise in his eyes. With his last ounce of strength, Arvi lunged forward, driving his sword into the Drogo attacking him, killing him instantly. He fell to his knees, blood pouring from his wound, a hero's death in the midst of chaos.

Ruiha's anguish fueled her fury. She fought with renewed ferocity, her enchanted daggers cutting through the Drogo warriors with lethal efficiency. The runes flared, each wound she inflicted burning with unquenchable fire. The Drogo she faced was relentless, his attacks swift and merciless. Ruiha blocked a series of rapid strikes, the jarring impact traveling up her arm. She countered with a swift slash, her blade cutting through the air with a whistle. The warrior dodged, but not quickly enough—her dagger grazed his arm. The runes blazed, and the Drogo screamed in agony, the unbearable heat and pain overwhelming him.

Ruiha's heart pounded, adrenaline surging through her veins. Every move was instinctual, honed by years of training and countless battles. She could see the determination in her opponent's eyes, the unwavering resolve to defeat her. The fire cast grotesque shadows on the surrounding trees, the flickering light creating a surreal battlefield. The scent of sweat and blood filled the air, mingling with the earthy aroma of the forest. The distinct clinks and clashes of weapons, the grunts and shouts of exertion filled her ears.

In the midst of the fray, she saw Elara standing her ground, her staff glowing as she cast spells to protect their comrades. Dakarai fought with fierce intensity, his eyes never straying far from Elara. Their synergy was a beacon of hope amidst the turmoil, a testament to their growing bond.

A sudden, sharp pain exploded at the back of Ruiha's head, stars bursting before her eyes. She staggered, vision blurring as she struggled to stay upright. The battle became a distant roar, fading into the background. As she fell to her knees, Ruiha's vision swam with the blur of battle and the sting of sweat in her eyes. Her grip on her daggers slackened, the once-reliable blades now feeling like lead in her hands.

Through the chaos, she caught sight of Kemp, his usually calm eyes now filled with terror. He struggled, his frosteel staff clutched tightly but rendered useless against the overwhelming force. Two Drogo warriors, their scaled hands like iron clamps, dragged him backward. Kemp's panicked gaze met hers for a fleeting moment, a silent cry for help that pierced her heart.

Desperation clawed at her, but her body refused to respond. Darkness crept closer, a suffocating shroud threatening to consume her. She watched helplessly as Kemp was pulled further into the shadows, his form fading into the encroaching night.

A cold, all-encompassing void swallowed her consciousness, the sounds of battle dimming to a distant murmur as she slipped into oblivion.

14

The Price of Treachery

"Betrayal cuts deep, but the strength of a leader is shown in how they wield truth to heal the wound."

Gunnar

The weight of the room pressed down on Gunnar as he stood before the gathered chiefs. He could feel the tension, thick as smoke, as their eyes followed him, waiting. Taking a deep breath, he steadied himself, knowing that what he was about to say would change everything.

With steely resolve, his voice low but urgent, Gunnar began. "Gadrin has betrayed us," he said, his gaze sharp as it met each chief's in turn. "He's made a deal with the Drogo. We have no time to waste—we must act before it's too late." The words were bitter on his tongue, but he knew they were the only truth that could save them.

Erik's eyes blazed with fury, but it was Durik who spoke first. "What do you propose we do?"

Gunnar's mind raced, formulating a plan. "We must turn Gadrin's own warriors against him. They are loyal to Uglich, to Dreynas, not the Drogo. If we can reveal his treachery, they will not stand by his side." He thought of the warriors who had stood by his side in countless battles, who deserved to know the truth. The image of their betrayed faces steeled his determination further.

Bojan nodded slowly, his skepticism giving way to a grudging respect. "How do we reveal his betrayal without causing a rift?" he asked, the weight of responsibility heavy in his voice.

"We need evidence," Gunnar replied. "Something undeniable. And we need to act swiftly." He glanced around the room, reading the expressions of his fellow chiefs—each a mixture of anger, fear, and determination. They needed a clear path, a beacon in the murk of treachery.

Erik stepped forward, his voice a calm contrast to the storm in his eyes. "I have contacts who can infiltrate Gadrin's quarters. If there's anything incriminating, they'll find it."

Durik nodded, his initial shock giving way to a fierce resolve. "And once we have the proof, we'll need to rally the warriors. Make them see that Gadrin's actions are a betrayal not just of us but of everything we stand for."

Gunnar felt a spark of hope kindling within him. "Agreed. We must be swift and precise. This cannot turn into a bloodbath." He paused, letting his gaze sweep across the assembled chiefs.

The chiefs exchanged determined nods, the gravity of their mission settling over them like a shroud. Each knew the risks, but their shared purpose was a powerful force. Gunnar could see the flicker of belief reigniting in their eyes—a belief in their unity and in their collective strength to overcome the darkness that threatened to consume them.

Plans were laid, and messages sent to trusted members of Gadrin's guard. Gunnar spent the night strategizing with his closest allies, ensuring every detail was meticulously planned. By dawn, they had gathered enough support to confront Gadrin.

The air was thick with anticipation and tension as they marched toward the citadel. Gunnar felt a grim satisfaction, knowing that justice was within their grasp, but also a heavy weight of responsibility. This was not just about Gadrin; it was about the future of Dreynas.

The confrontation was swift and decisive. Gunnar stood at the forefront, his voice steady as he presented the evidence.

He produced a series of parchments, each marked with Gadrin's distinctive seal. The first parchment was a trade agreement, ostensibly for simple goods, but the quantities and items listed were suspicious. "Two hundred barrels of saltpeter," Gunnar read aloud, his voice echoing in the silent chamber. The gathered crowd murmured, understanding the implication of such a large amount of an essential ingredient for explosive powder.

Next, Gunnar displayed a map. At first glance, it seemed like a standard regional chart, but subtle marks in the corners revealed hidden meeting spots. "These locations," Gunnar pointed, "correspond to recent Drogo raids."

The final piece of evidence was the most damning. Gunnar unfurled a worn, leather-bound ledger. "Here," he said, tapping a page. "Payments received, from the Drogo." The entries were meticulous, detailing dates and amounts. Gunnar's finger traced the columns, each line a testament to his greed.

Gadrin's warriors, presented with irrefutable proof of his dealings with the Drogo, turned on him without hesitation. Expressions of shock and anger played across their faces as they absorbed the truth. Their faces, etched with betrayal, spoke volumes. The treachery cut deep. In the tense silence that followed, whispers of outrage and dismay rippled through the ranks. As Gadrin was dragged away, screaming curses and denials, Gunnar felt a cold, hard knot of resolve in his chest. He glanced at his comrades, each nodding in silent agreement—this was just the beginning. This was a victory, but the war was far from over. Gunnar knew the path ahead would be fraught with challenges, but for the sake of their people, he was ready to face them.

Gunnar watched as Gadrin was stripped of his power, the once formidable leader now a shadow of his former self. Uglich's new leader, chosen from among the ranks of warriors, stepped forward with a fierce loyalty to Gunnar and the alliance of clans. Their eyes met, a silent promise of unity and strength against the looming threats.

As the torchlight flickered across the vast caverns of Draegoor, Gunnar felt a sense of relief wash over him. The immediate threat had been neutralized, but Gadrin's treason lingered, a stark reminder of the dangers that still lay ahead.

The clans now stood united, their resolve as unyielding as the stone that surrounded them. The path ahead was still fraught with peril, but Gunnar's determination was unwavering. Together, they would face the darkness, reclaim their land, and forge a future beneath the earth.

He stood at the edge of the fortress, the subterranean winds whispering through his hair, and gazed out across the city of Draegoor. This was just the beginning. The real test of their unity and strength lay ahead, and he would be ready.

Gunnar stood before the council, the weight of the moment pressing down on his broad shoulders. The chamber was dimly lit, flickering torches casting long shadows across the stone walls. Chiefs from all the clans of Dreynas sat in a semi-circle, their faces stern and weathered, eyes flicking between Gunnar and the figure standing at the far end of the hall—Gadrin.

The Price of Treachery

"Your accusations are grave, Gunnar," Chief Bojan said, his voice rough but controlled. "But Gadrin has served this council for decades. To claim betrayal without absolute proof—"

"I bring proof," Gunnar interrupted, stepping forward, his eyes blazing with resolve. His heart pounded, but he kept his voice steady. "Gadrin has sold us to the Drogo. He has brokered a deal with our enemies, a deal that will see Dreynas in flames."

Gadrin, tall and gaunt, smiled coldly. "Proof?" His voice was a snake's hiss, low and slippery. "You claim much, but offer little. I wonder how much of this is desperation, Gunnar. Perhaps the burden of leadership weighs too heavily on your shoulders."

There was a murmur from the council, and Gunnar's gut clenched. Gadrin was a master of the game, and already, doubt was creeping into the minds of the chiefs. Gadrin's eyes flickered to Erik, who stood silently beside Gunnar, fists clenched. "Ah, Erik," Gadrin sneered. "Does he not whisper in your ear, Gunnar? Feeding you stories of betrayal? Perhaps you've been played by your own blood."

Erik took a step forward, anger flashing across his face, but Gunnar stopped him with a hand. The council had to see Gadrin for what he was—a manipulator, a betrayer.

"Show them," Gunnar said, tossing a series of parchments onto the council table. "Gadrin's seal is on every one of these trade agreements. Look closer, and you'll see they are not for trade, but for weapons, supplies, and gunpowder—all destined for the Drogo."

Chief Durik picked up one of the parchments, squinting at the fine print. "Gunpowder..." he murmured, and whispers spread through the chamber.

But Gadrin didn't flinch. His laugh was sharp, echoing off the walls. "Trade agreements? Is that all you have, Gunnar?" He stepped forward, his presence commanding. "This is nothing but a smear campaign, an attempt to weaken me, so you can take my place on this council. You want to break us apart, not the Drogo."

A few Dwarves nodded slowly. Gunnar could feel the ground shifting beneath him. Gadrin was twisting the narrative, turning the Dwarves fear against him. Doubt was settling in.

And then, with a cold smile, Gadrin struck. "Even if I were guilty of such treachery—" He turned to face the council, his voice rising in confidence, "—what would it change? Look at the state of Dreynas. The Drogo are at our gates, our people suffer, and what has our *prince* done? Nothing! Other than poison us with his unnatural dark *magic!*" Gadrin spat the words as if they were bitter in his mouth.

Gunnar's jaw tightened, but before he could speak, Gadrin continued, his voice dripping with venom. "But let's talk about the real secret, Gunnar. Does the council know the truth of your uncle? How many bodies did Wilfrid leave behind in the name of Draegoor?" He smirked as Erik's face paled. "And how much blood have you shed to hide those sins?"

The chiefs exchanged uneasy glances, and Erik took another step forward, fury blazing in his eyes. But Gunnar knew Gadrin's game. The longer this dragged out, the more the council would fracture. This wasn't just about exposing Gadrin's betrayal anymore—it was about keeping the clans united.

Gadrin's smirk twisted wider, all teeth and malice. "You think you've won?" His voice oozed like oil over stone. "Even if you cut me down right now, it won't make a difference. Dreynas is already rotting, Gunnar. It's crumbling from the inside, and I'm just the sharp end of the blade. Cut me down, and there'll be ten more just like me, eager to finish the job."

Before anyone could blink, his hand flashed to his sleeve. A blade, sharp and gleaming, appeared as if by magic. In one fluid motion, Gadrin lunged at Chief Bojan, steel aimed for the Dwarf's throat. Chaos erupted. Warriors surged forward, clashing like storm-tossed waves, weapons drawn, shouts echoing through the hall.

But Gadrin was faster than them all, a slip of smoke in the melee. He darted through the throng, boots barely touching the ground, eyes wild with desperation and triumph. His laughter—sharp, mocking—rippled through the hall as he neared the door.

Gunnar spat a curse under his breath. Of course, the bastard would try to run. If Gadrin slipped away now, it would only make his poison words stick in the chiefs' minds. They'd wonder, they'd doubt—maybe he was telling the truth. Maybe the Drogo would swoop in amidst the confusion. Or maybe Gadrin was just full of shit.

"Let him run!" Gunnar's voice rang out like a hammer on iron, stopping warriors mid-step. The chiefs turned to him, eyes wide with confusion, disbelief. "He's already lost!" Gunnar's lips curled into something between a grin and a snarl. "There's nowhere for him to hide now."

The heavy doors slammed shut behind Gadrin, the sound reverberating through the chamber. But Gunnar didn't budge, didn't even glance toward the exit. His gaze was locked on the chiefs, the real battle still to be fought.

"Gadrin's words?" He jabbed a finger toward the table, toward the crumpled parchments. "Lies. Every last one of them." Gunnar stepped forward, his eyes hard as frosteel. "And this evidence—this is the truth. But the final proof? You all saw it with your own eyes. Does someone innocent flee like a rat when cornered?"

The room fell into a heavy silence, thick as the weight in Gunnar's gut. Chiefs exchanged looks, the tension thick enough to choke on.

Chief Durik was the first to rise, his face a mask of grim

resolve. "Gunnar's right. Gadrin's actions speak louder than any words, any documents. He's betrayed us, and now he'll face the consequences."

A murmur of agreement followed. But as Gunnar stood there, the cold, unshakable certainty in his chest was a lie. Gadrin was gone, and his parting words echoed in the back of Gunnar's mind like a poison. Ten more blades, Gadrin had said. Ten more ready to cut them down. And the worst part?

Gunnar knew it wasn't just talk.

Gunnar stood at the center of the council chamber, the echo of his words still hanging in the stale air. The chiefs—each one a lord of their own hold—sat in a tight semi-circle, their eyes not full of the doubt Gunnar had feared but steely with grim understanding. Gadrin had fled, and that had said more than any scrap of parchment ever could. He was guilty, and every Dwarf in the room knew it. But that didn't stop the tension from thickening, the cracks in their unity threatening to split wide open.

He could feel it in the air, like the distant rumble of an avalanche. Gadrin's betrayal wasn't just about one cowardly Dwarf. The rot in Dreynas went deep, deeper than anyone wanted to admit. And now it was up to Gunnar to make sure the whole thing didn't collapse in on itself.

Durik, his hand resting on the pommel of his sword, broke the silence first. "Gadrin's proven his treachery by running. But there's more to this, Gunnar. You and I both know it."

Gunnar grunted, his jaw clenched tight. He knew it, alright. The bastard's words still echoed in his mind, gnawing at him. *I'm just the tip of the blade...* Gadrin had been right about one thing—there were others. There had to be. And that made this moment all the more precarious.

"Doesn't matter how deep his scheme runs," Bojan said, his voice low but firm. "He's done for. Fled like a coward, proven everything we needed to know. Now it's just a matter of dragging him back here and ending him. The Drogo can't negotiate with a dead Dwarf."

"Aye," Gunnar agreed, his voice rough with frustration. "But Gadrin's not the problem anymore. We all saw the same thing. He ran because he knew he was caught, and he won't go far, not with our warriors after him. But it's what comes after that's going to be our real fight. Gadrin wasn't working alone."

"Gunnar's right," Durik said, his voice gravelly. "We can cut Gadrin down, but that won't solve the problem. There's more going on here than just one Dwarf's treachery. The Drogo aren't stupid enough to rely on one Dwarf. There's more to this."

Bojan slammed his fist on the table, rattling the empty tankards. "Then we hunt them down, all of them. Every last one. If Gadrin's the tip of the blade, we'll break the damn sword."

Easier said than done, Gunnar thought. His frustration was like a knot in his chest, tightening with every passing second. He needed to keep the chiefs together, to keep Dreynas from falling apart at the seams, but it felt like he was trying to hold back a mountain with his bare hands.

Just then, the chamber doors slammed open, and in marched Erik, his face flushed, his breath ragged. Gunnar's gut twisted. Erik only ever looked like that when things had taken a turn, and rarely for the better.

"They've caught him," Erik said, eyes darting between the chiefs. "Gadrin's been found."

A ripple of acknowledgment passed through the room. No surprise, no shock—just grim satisfaction. Of course they'd caught him. There was no escaping the consequences now.

"Where?" Gunnar asked, already striding toward Erik.

"Near the old quarry. He's hurt, but he's still breathing. Says he'll talk if we spare him."

Bojan spat on the stone floor. "Talk? He's done talking."

"And so are we," Gunnar growled, his patience at an end. "We'll get what we need out of him, and then we'll finish this."

They found Gadrin where Erik had said—slumped against the cold stone wall of a building on the outskirts of the city, blood seeping from a ragged wound in his leg. He looked smaller now, diminished, though the same twisted smirk clung to his face, stubborn as rot.

"Took you long enough," Gadrin rasped, voice hollow but still brimming with spite. "Thought you'd just let me bleed out here."

Gunnar crouched before him, eyes cold, his broad hand resting on the hilt of his blade. "You'll die, alright. But not until I know how deep this runs."

Gadrin's chuckle came out more like a cough, wet and weak. "You still think it matters, don't you? Kill me, Gunnar, and Dreynas still rots. It's too late. The Drogo have all they need. They don't need me anymore."

"They don't need a corpse, either," Gunnar said, pressing the tip of his knife under Gadrin's chin, just enough to draw a bead of blood. "Tell me who else is in on this, and maybe I'll make it quick."

Gadrin's smirk remained, though the blood bubbling at the corner of his lips made him look more pitiful than menacing. "You think I'm the only one?" he rasped, his voice a broken whisper, yet still laced with bitterness. "You really believe that?

More blades in the shadows, Gunnar. Kill me, and others will rise to finish what I started. You can't stop it."

Gunnar's grip tightened around the hilt of his blade, the cold steel pressed into his palm. He could end it right here—one swift motion, and Gadrin would be gone. The traitor's words would mean nothing, his lies silenced by death. But something held Gunnar back. Gadrin had always been clever, too clever for his own good. And there was something in his eyes now—something not quite defiant but desperate, like a cornered animal trying to claw its way out.

Gunnar's lips curled into a grimace. He'd dealt with enough liars in his time to know the truth when he saw it. And this—this felt wrong. He stepped closer, leaning in until his face was mere inches from Gadrin's. "Enough of your games," he growled, his voice low and dangerous. "Tell me the truth. Who else is involved? How deep does this rot go?"

Gadrin's breath hitched, and for a moment, Gunnar saw the faintest flicker of fear in the traitor's eyes. The smirk faltered, and his shoulders slumped as though the weight of his deceit was finally too much to carry. He coughed again, spitting a mouthful of blood onto the dirt between them.

"Alright," Gadrin muttered, his voice cracking, no longer holding the cocky sneer it had moments before. "I'll tell you the truth, but only if you swear on Dreyna herself that you won't kill me."

Gunnar froze, the weight of the moment pressing down on him. His instincts screamed at him to end it here, to rid the world of Gadrin once and for all. He could imagine it now—driving his blade through the traitor's throat, watching the life drain from his eyes. It would be justice, and justice would taste sweet.

But a promise weighed heavier still. Gunnar had made a vow, not to himself, but to Dreynas—to his people. He had sworn to put their needs, their survival, before any personal desire for vengeance. His grip tightened around the haft of his axe, his teeth grinding together, but slowly, with a long exhale, he nodded.

"I swear on Dreyna herself," Gunnar said, his voice cold, steady. "If you tell me the truth, you will live." He stepped closer, his eyes narrowing as they locked onto Gadrin's. "But know this—if I find out you've lied to me, you'll wish I'd killed you here and now. I'll make sure of it."

The threat hung in the air like a sharpened axe, and for the first time, Gunnar saw genuine fear flicker in Gadrin's eyes.

"Alright, Gunnar, you win." His gaze dropped, eyes clouded with something Gunnar hadn't expected—resignation. "There's no one else. Just me."

Gunnar's brow furrowed, the anger in his chest tightening into something colder, sharper. *Just him?* No great conspiracy, no hidden blades lurking in the dark? He had expected more, but instead, it was just Gadrin's greed that had nearly brought Dreynas to its knees. The coward had played them all. Gunnar's jaw clenched. "You're lying."

Gadrin shook his head, the motion weak and pathetic. "No, I'm not. I knew that if I convinced you—if I made you think there were more—you'd have to spare me. You'd be too afraid to kill me. I knew it was the only way I'd live through this."

His voice trailed off, and Gunnar could feel the bitter truth settling between them like a weight. Gadrin had hoped to outsmart him, to sow just enough doubt to save his own skin. And he had bloody managed it.

Gunnar felt a slow burn of anger rise in his chest. He'd been played, just as Gadrin had hoped. The Dwarf had been sowing doubt, turning their focus outward, buying himself time, all while the truth was simpler. And uglier.

"So you were working alone?" Gunnar asked, the words slow

and deliberate, his knife still hovering at Gadrin's throat.

"Aye," Gadrin said, his voice barely a whisper now. "Just me. No one else. But I've made sure you'll have to spare me. Your honor won't let you break a bargain, and I've given you what you wanted."

Gunnar's eyes narrowed. Gadrin was right. He couldn't kill him now. Not without breaking his word in front of the chiefs, not without showing the council that their leader was no better than the traitor bleeding in the dirt. His honor held him, just as Gadrin had counted on.

Gunnar stood, withdrawing the knife, though every instinct screamed to end this here and now. "You're right," he muttered, his voice like stone scraping over stone. "I won't kill you."

For a moment, Gadrin's face flickered with triumph, like a Dwarf who's crawled out of the grave only to taste victory. But that moment passed as Gunnar's next words cut through the air.

"Father," Gunnar called, not taking his eyes off Gadrin. "Incarcerate him. He'll stand trial before the council."

Erik moved forward, his hand already gripping Gadrin by the collar, hauling him to his feet. Gadrin coughed, but the smirk was back, weak but there. He'd played his hand and won. Or so it seemed.

But as Gadrin was dragged away, the chiefs exchanged glances—resolute, grim. Gunnar had played his hand too, and it had worked. The clans were no longer divided, no longer squabbling over doubts and fears. Gadrin's flight had proven his guilt to everyone, and Gunnar's restraint had solidified his leadership. There would be no fractures in the council, no questioning his honor or his decisions. The clans were united.

And Gadrin's plan to sow chaos? Dead in the water.

"We'll need a new chief for Uglich," Durik said, his voice rough but steady. "Someone loyal."

"Aye," Bojan added. "Someone who knows what loyalty to the council really means."

Gunnar nodded, his face still a mask of iron. "Uglich will appoint a new chief, and we'll make sure they know where their loyalties lie. And as for Gadrin—he'll rot in a cell, alive, just as he wanted. But the clans are united. That's all that matters."

As Gadrin was dragged out of sight, his laughter faded into the wind, but it held none of the triumph it had before. He may have avoided the blade, but Gunnar had won the real fight. The clans were whole again, and Gadrin's name would become a curse whispered in the darkest corners of Dreynas.

Gunnar turned to the chiefs, his eyes as hard as the mountain. "We're done here. The Drogo are still out there, and now that we're whole, it's time we made them feel the weight of our hammers."

And with that, the chiefs nodded, united once more behind their leader.

15

Lost and Found

"A true friend's strength is measured not by their presence, but by their relentless pursuit when all seems lost."

Kemp

Kemp watched in horror as Ruiha fell to her knees, the fight draining from her body. Her daggers clattered to the ground, their runes flickering weakly. He strained against the iron grips of the Drogo warriors dragging him away, but their hold was unyielding. The roughness of their scaled hands bit into his arms, sending jolts of pain through his body with each step they took.

His heart hammered in his chest, a wild, erratic beat that echoed his mounting fear. He wanted to scream, to call out to Ruiha, but his voice caught in his throat, choked by a wave of helplessness. He could still hear the distant sounds of battle—the clash of steel, the cries of his companions—but they felt muffled, as if coming from another world.

"Ruiha!" The name tore from his lips in a desperate cry, but she didn't respond. Her form was becoming a distant shadow, swallowed by the chaos and darkness. Kemp's vision blurred, a mix of tears and frustration clouding his sight. "No!" he shouted, his voice raw with despair. *This can't be happening. Why had they been ambushed? Why was he being taken?*

The Drogo were relentless, their movements precise and mechanical. Kemp struggled against them, his muscles straining, but it was futile. They were too strong, too many. He could feel his hope slipping away, replaced by a cold dread that settled deep in his bones.

"Where are you taking me?" Kemp demanded, trying to glean any information from the warriors. His voice echoed back at him, met only with silence.

A rough sack was shoved over his head, plunging him into darkness. The fabric was coarse and smelled of sweat and earth, its fibers scratching against his skin. He gasped for breath, the air inside the sack stifling and hot. Panic flared, a fierce, wild thing that clawed at his mind. He couldn't see, couldn't breathe properly. Each inhale was a struggle, a battle against the suffocating confines of the sack.

His mind raced, searching for a way out, a way to fight back. *Magic.* He had his magic. But how could he use it when he couldn't see? He focused, trying to summon the familiar warmth of his power, but the fear and disorientation made it hard to concentrate. He muttered an incantation, his voice shaking, and felt a brief surge of energy.

Screams echoed around him, followed by a harsh, guttural dialect he could barely understand. The Drogo shouted in anger and pain, their grips momentarily loosening. Kemp felt a spark of hope. He had hurt them, had managed to break through their defenses. But the victory was short-lived.

A blunt force slammed into the back of his head with a sickening thud. Pain exploded through his skull, a hot, searing agony that consumed his senses. The ground beneath him seemed to tilt and spin, his equilibrium shattered.

His legs buckled, and he crumpled to the ground, his knees striking the hard surface with a jolt that sent another wave of pain through his body. He tried to raise his hands to his head, to cradle the source of the agony, but his arms felt like lead, unresponsive and heavy. The rough sack over his head scraped against his face, the fabric pressing tightly, amplifying the disorientation.

Sounds around him blurred into a chaotic cacophony. The shouts of the Drogo and the distant clashing of steel all melded together into a distorted, muffled roar. He could taste blood in his mouth, metallic and bitter, as his senses began to fade.

The world around him became a whirl of darkness and confusion. He could feel the cold, hard ground against his body, the texture of the earth beneath him pressing into his skin. Darkness crept in from the edges of his consciousness, a suffocating blackness that swallowed everything.

His body gave one last shudder, muscles twitching uncontrollably before everything went still. The last sensation he registered was the relentless, pounding ache in his head, then all was black.

When Kemp woke, the world was a blur of pain and confusion. His head throbbed, each pulse sending fresh waves of agony through his body. He was no longer being dragged but lay on a cold, hard surface. The sack was gone, but darkness still surrounded him, broken only by the faint, flickering light of torches in the distance.

The sound of footsteps approached, and Kemp tried to focus. A Drogo warrior loomed over him, inspecting him with cold, reptilian eyes. "Why are you doing this?" Kemp croaked, his voice barely more than a whisper. The Drogo remained silent.

Kemp tried to move, but his limbs felt heavy, unresponsive. His thoughts were sluggish, muddled by the pain and disorientation. Why had they taken him? What did they want? Questions swirled in his mind, unanswered and relentless.

He thought of Ruiha, of her determined eyes and fierce spirit. Had she survived? Were the others still fighting? He hoped, with a desperation that burned through the fog of pain, that they were safe. That they would come for him.

But for now, he was alone. Captured. And the Drogo had plans for him—plans that twisted in the shadows, far beyond anything he could yet imagine. The darkness pressed in, thick and suffocating, but Kemp clung to a single truth: he had to stay strong. He had to survive. For Ruiha. For all of them.

Failure wasn't an option.

Because if he didn't find a way out, the Drogo would break him—and they wouldn't stop with just him.

Ruiha

Ruiha's world came back into focus with a throbbing headache and the acrid taste of blood in her mouth. The last thing she remembered was the sharp pain at the back of her head and Kemp's panicked cry. Now, the battle was over, and silence hung heavy in the air, broken only by the soft crackling of the dying campfire.

She pushed herself up, her muscles protesting, and her vision swam for a moment. Blinking away the haze, she looked around and saw Magnus, Elara, and Dakarai standing nearby, their faces etched with concern. Her eyes widened, darting frantically as she scanned the chaotic scene. Panic gripped her chest, squeezing tighter with each heartbeat. A few paces away, Arvi lay still, his lifeless form stark against the cold ground. Kemp was nowhere to be seen. A cold dread seeped into her bones, her heart plummeting into the pit of her stomach.

"Kemp!" she shouted, her voice raw and desperate. She staggered to her feet, ignoring the sharp protests from her body. "Where is Kemp?"

Elara stepped forward, her face pale. "Ruiha, please. You need to calm down."

"Calm down?" Ruiha spat, fury rising in her chest like a storm. "They took him! We were ambushed, and they took him!"

Magnus reached out a hand, trying to steady her. "We need to think this through. Charging after them recklessly won't help Kemp or us."

Ruiha shrugged off his hand, her eyes blazing. "He's out there, Magnus! He's out there, and we're standing here doing nothing!"

Her mind was a storm of memories, images she had tried to bury, but that now rose to the surface with brutal clarity. The cold iron chains around her wrists, the jeering crowds, the suffocating smell of blood and sweat in the pit. She remembered the unrelenting fight for survival. Each moment in that hellish arena had been a battle, not just against her opponents, but against the creeping despair that threatened to consume her.

Dakarai's deep voice cut through the tension. "Ruiha, we understand your anger. Kemp is our friend, too. But we have to be smart about this."

The words did little to soothe her rage. She felt like a failure, guilt gnawing at her insides. She had let Kemp down, had failed to protect him when he needed her the most. The memory of his terrified, stormy eyes haunted her, fueling her need to act.

"Smart?" she snapped, her frustration boiling over. "You think this is smart? We're wasting time! We need to find him before it's too late."

Elara stepped in, her voice calm but firm. "We're not suggesting we abandon him, Ruiha. But we need to plan our next move carefully. Running into an unknown situation could get us all killed."

The argument simmered, voices rising with urgency and raw emotion. Magnus finally held up his hands, demanding silence. "Enough! We can't afford to fall apart now. I will return to Draegoor and inform Gunnar about the situation. We need reinforcements and a revised plan."

Dakarai nodded, his agreement evident in the firm set of his jaw. "Gunnar needs to know what happened. If the mission has failed, we must regroup and determine our next steps."

Ruiha's jaw clenched, the sense in their words gnawing at her resolve. She couldn't shake the feeling they were losing precious time. "Fine. You go to Draegoor. But I'm not leaving Kemp. Dakarai, Elara, and I will go after him. We can't wait for reinforcements that might come too late."

Dakarai placed a steadying hand on her shoulder, his touch a silent promise of support. "We'll find him, Ruiha. And we'll ensure the mission continues. Kemp needs us."

Elara's eyes were resolute, a quiet strength in her gaze. "We're with you."

With their minds made, the group divided. Ruiha watched as Magnus gathered his gear, a pang of guilt twisting in her chest. She knew he was right, but the urgency within her refused to be quelled.

"Be careful," Magnus said, his voice gruff but sincere. "I'll get help and meet you as soon as we can."

Ruiha nodded, swallowing the lump in her throat. "And you. Make sure Gunnar understands what's at stake."

Final words exchanged, the two groups parted ways. Magnus headed back toward Draegoor, his form soon swallowed by the forest's embrace. Ruiha, Dakarai, and Elara turned in the opposite direction, their steps quickening with each heartbeat as they set off in pursuit of Kemp.

Ruiha's thoughts churned with worry and determination. The forest around them seemed to close in, shadows deepening as they moved further from the camp. Every rustle of leaves, every snap of a twig set her nerves on edge. She couldn't afford to lose anyone else. Not now.

Dakarai walked beside her, his presence a steady anchor. Elara followed closely, her staff held at the ready, the faint glow of her magic casting eerie shadows on the forest floor. Together, they pushed forward, driven by a shared purpose and the silent hope that they would find Kemp before it was too late.

The journey through the mountains was grueling, the rugged terrain unforgiving as Ruiha, Dakarai, and Elara pressed on. The thin, biting air of the high altitudes stung their lungs, each breath a testament to their determination. The sun barely penetrated the dense canopy of trees and jagged rock formations, casting long, eerie shadows across their path.

Ruiha led the way, her keen eyes constantly darting to every shadow and crevice, seeking any hint of the Drogo warriors' passage. Each snapped twig and disturbed patch of earth became a clue, her senses heightened by the urgency of their mission. Dakarai moved with a silent grace behind her, his footfalls barely a whisper on the rocky path. His broad shoulders and imposing frame were a steadying presence, a silent guardian in the treacherous landscape.

Elara, though visibly weary, maintained her resolve. Her steps were slower, but her knowledge of these mountains was their lifeline. She pointed out hidden pitfalls and secret trails, her fingers tracing routes only she could see in the dense foliage and craggy rocks.

The path wound higher and steeper, the air growing thin and cold. The sound of their breathing, harsh and labored, was the only thing that broke the silence. Finally, they reached the mouth of a cavern concealed behind a curtain of ivy and moss. Ruiha's hand moved to the foliage, pulling it aside to reveal a dark entrance, the smell of damp earth and ancient stone wafting out.

She turned to Elara, her eyes questioning. Elara stepped forward, examining the opening, then nodded. "This is the way," she confirmed, her voice steady despite the tremor of exhaustion.

Ruiha took a deep breath, the cold air filling her lungs, and stepped into the darkness, the weight of their mission pressing heavily on her shoulders.

As they descended into the depths, the air grew colder and damper, the sound of dripping water echoing around them. The light from their torches flickered against the walls, illuminating ancient carvings and strange markings. The tunnel twisted and turned, a labyrinthine network that seemed to go on forever.

After hours of traversing the underground passage, the tunnel opened up into a vast, cavernous space. Ruiha's breath caught in her throat as she beheld the sight before her. The city of Hammer lay sprawled out beneath them, an underground metropolis illuminated by a stunning mixture of light shafts, bioluminescent fungi, and glowing crystals embedded in the walls. The buildings, carved directly into the rock, were a blend of natural formations and skilled masonry, their architecture both awe-inspiring and alien.

Elara stepped forward, her eyes filled with a mix of nostalgia and sorrow. "This is the city of Hammer," she said softly. "My former home."

Ruiha could sense the weight of Elara's words, the history and memories tied to this place. She placed a hand on Elara's shoulder, offering silent support. Dakarai, ever vigilant, scanned the area for any signs of danger.

"We need a plan," Ruiha said, breaking the silence. "If Kemp is here, we must find him and get him out without drawing too much attention."

Elara nodded, her expression hardening with determination. "They will have him in the central fortress," she explained. "It's the most fortified area, heavily guarded. But there are old tunnels and passages that will not be monitored."

Ruiha's mind raced, piecing together a strategy. "We'll need a distraction," she said, thinking aloud. "Something to draw their attention away from the fortress while we infiltrate."

Dakarai's eyes gleamed with a fierce light. "I can handle that," he said, a hint of a grin playing on his lips. "A few well-placed landslides should do the trick."

Ruiha nodded, appreciating Dakarai's confidence. "Elara, you'll lead us through the tunnels. We'll need to move quickly and quietly."

Elara's gaze sharpened with resolve. "I can do that. But once we're inside, we'll need to be prepared for anything. The Drogo warriors are ruthless."

"I know," Ruiha mumbled in response.

The plan was set. As they moved deeper into the city, Ruiha

marveled at the intricate details of Hammer. The walls were adorned with murals depicting the city's Dwarven history—battles, celebrations, and the rise and fall of leaders. Statues of long-forgotten heroes stood vigil in alcoves, their stone eyes seeming to follow the intruders with silent judgment.

"The Dwarves once inhabited the Scorched Mountains." Dakarai began. "They built these cities a millennia ago."

They reached the outskirts of the central fortress, its looming presence carved from the very bones of the mountain itself. Jagged stone walls towered above them, dark and imposing, as if the mountain had birthed the fortress in defiance of time itself. The air around it felt heavier, charged with a quiet, ancient power that seemed to hum in the rock.

Elara moved ahead, her steps silent, her eyes scanning the surroundings with the caution of someone who knew this place far too well. She led them toward the shimmering veil of a waterfall, the water glowing with a soft, ethereal light that cast rippling shadows across the rocky ground. It wasn't just any water—it pulsed with magic, a natural barrier meant to deter anyone unworthy from finding the hidden path.

Elara knelt, her hands brushing over the stone beside the waterfall. She murmured something too quiet to catch, and the magic in the air seemed to shift, like the very mountain was responding to her. A crack in the rock face, barely noticeable before, widened, revealing a narrow entrance concealed behind the cascade.

"Here," she whispered, motioning them forward. "This way."

They slipped inside, the cool spray of the waterfall trailing after them. The roar of the falling water filled the space, its sound echoing off the stone walls, masking any trace of their movement. Inside, the narrow passage was dark and damp, but Elara moved with the confidence of someone who had walked this path many times before.

Ruiha glanced back, the weight of the mountain pressing down on them. The waterfall's glowing curtain shimmered behind him, sealing them inside. The fortress awaited—silent, cold, and unknowable. Whatever lay ahead, they were now deep within its grasp, with only the shadows and the sound of the waterfall hiding them from the dangers that lurked within.

The tunnel beyond was tight and claustrophobic, twisting through the heart of the mountain like an ancient, forgotten vein. The walls closed in on them, jagged rock brushing their shoulders as they moved single file, the rough stone cold beneath their fingertips. The air grew thick, filled with the scent of damp earth, old stone, and the faint, musty tang of something that had been sealed off for far too long.

Every step felt heavier, the oppressive weight of the mountain pressing down as they pushed deeper into its core. The distant sounds of Drogo warriors echoed through the rock—harsh, guttural voices carried on the stale air, accompanied by the clang of metal and the rhythmic thud of boots on stone. It was impossible to tell how far off they were, or how much time they had left before they might be discovered.

At last, the tunnel widened, and they stepped into a vast chamber that stretched out before them, like stepping into the belly of some ancient beast. The underground courtyard was immense, the ceiling arching high above, barely visible in the dim, eerie light. Bioluminescent fungi clung to the walls and crevices, casting an otherworldly glow over the space. The pale, ghostly light flickered across the weathered stone, illuminating the worn carvings and long-forgotten symbols etched into the walls, relics of a time long past.

Elara moved ahead, her gaze sharp as she scanned the far side of the chamber. She pointed toward a series of narrow, shadowed passages, barely discernible in the faint glow of the fungi.

"Those passages," she whispered, her voice barely more than a breath, "lead to the holding cells. Kemp should be there."

The air around them felt colder, and a sense of urgency settled over the group as they exchanged glances. Ruiha's heart pounded in her chest. They were close, so close. She turned to Dakarai. "Are you ready?"

Dakarai grinned. "Always."

With a final nod, they split up. Dakarai moved stealthily toward the main gates, his every step calculated to avoid detection, while Ruiha and Elara slipped into the shadows, making their way toward the passages.

The ground trembled beneath their feet as Dakarai used his axe to dislodge a supporting wall. Its collapse reverberated through the underground city, the sound like thunder. Shouts of alarm and the hurried footsteps of Drogo warriors filled the air. Ruiha and Elara moved quickly, the chaos providing the perfect cover.

They reached the holding cells, a series of iron-barred doors lining a dimly lit corridor. Ruiha peered into each cell, her heart sinking with every empty one. The flickering torchlight cast long shadows, making the place feel like a tomb. Anxiety gnawed at her; time was slipping away.

"Empty," Ruiha muttered, her frustration mounting. She clenched her fists, forcing herself to stay calm. Elara touched her arm, offering silent support.

They moved deeper into the maze of cells, each door revealing only emptiness or prisoners who were not Kemp. The sense of urgency intensified with each step, the sounds of Drogo warriors echoing closer.

Just as despair threatened to overwhelm her, Ruiha spotted something—a glint of metal through the bars of a cell deeper within. Hope surged, but as they approached, it became clear: the cell was empty, save for the remnants of what might have been a struggle. Scorch marks on the stone floor, a broken chain, but no Kemp.

"We need to keep moving," Elara urged, her voice a strained whisper. "He has to be here somewhere."

Ruiha nodded, swallowing her disappointment. "Let's go," she said, determination hardening her voice.

They retraced their steps, slipping through the shadows as they continued their search. The labyrinthine corridors seemed endless, each turn leading to more uncertainty. The city of Hammer, once Elara's home, now felt like an impenetrable fortress.

As they reached another junction, the ground trembled again—Dakarai's work was relentless, each disruption buying them precious moments. But how long could he keep it up?

Ruiha glanced at Elara, who was scanning the walls with a furrowed brow. "There's another way," Elara said suddenly, her eyes lighting up. "A hidden passage that leads to the deeper cells. It's a long shot, but—"

"Lead the way," Ruiha urged.

Elara led them through a narrow passage, almost invisible behind a tapestry of hanging moss. They moved quickly, the corridor sloping downward. The air grew colder, the dampness more pronounced.

At the end of the passage, a heavy door stood ajar. Ruiha's heart raced as they stepped inside, but her hope faltered when the room was revealed to be empty, save for a few scattered belongings.

"Kemp!" Ruiha called softly, but there was no response.

Elara touched a wall, her fingers finding an inscription. "This is it," she said, her voice filled with both sorrow and resolve. "We'll find him. I know it."

With renewed determination, they continued their search, the underground city of Hammer a maze of despair and fleeting hope. Though they hadn't found Kemp yet, Ruiha refused to give up. The journey was far from over, but she clung to the belief that they would find him, reclaim their friend, and escape the darkness that sought to consume them all.

Kemp

Kemp awoke to the same oppressive darkness that had surrounded him since his imprisonment. He lay on the cold, damp floor of the underground cell, the rough stone digging into his skin. The collar around his neck was a constant, heavy reminder of his powerlessness. It had been placed there by the Drogo shamans, its enchanted metal suppressing his abilities, rendering him unable to carry out any magic. Preventing him from performing the Shadowpurge that was his only defense against the dark voices.

His stomach growled weakly, reminding him that he was fed sporadically. Time had lost all meaning in this place. Days, weeks, possibly months—it all blended into an unending nightmare. The darkness from the Dragon Crown, once a whisper, now roared in his mind, a cacophony of malevolent voices that threatened to consume him.

"You are nothing," the voices hissed. "A tool, a vessel for our master. Nergai will rise, and you will be his puppet."

Kemp shivered, not just from the cold but from the fear gnawing at his soul. He curled into himself, trying to block out the voices, but they were relentless. The darkness was winning. He could feel it creeping into his thoughts, his emotions, tainting everything with its foul presence. He had once been strong, confident in his abilities, but now he was reduced to this—a broken man, clinging to the last shreds of his sanity.

Memories of his arrival played over and over in his mind. The shamans' cruel faces, their muttered incantations, the agony as the collar snapped into place. He had fought, oh how he had fought, but it was all in vain. The power of the Crown, the very thing that had once saved them all, was now his curse.

In the suffocating darkness, Kemp's thoughts turned to his friends. Ruiha, Dakarai, Magnus, Gunnar, Thalirion, Thraxos—were they searching for him? Did they even know he was alive? The uncertainty was another dagger in his heart. He had to believe they were coming. He had to hold on to that hope, fragile though it was.

A soft clink of chains broke the silence, each motion sending a jolt of pain through his battered body. The Drogo were not gentle captors. They took pleasure in his suffering, each blow another step toward breaking him completely.

He remembered their reptilian faces—the sadistic glee, the chants that echoed in his mind. But he also remembered Ruiha. Her determination, her courage, her fierceness. He used her memory as his anchor, his guiding light, his source of strength, his sanity in this hell.

Kemp forced himself to breathe slowly, deeply, trying to center his mind. The collar burned against his skin, a constant reminder of his captivity, but he focused past it. He envisaged the Shadowpurge even the memory of the excruciating pain it caused felt like a slight relief from this torture.

The darkness roiled, sensing his defiance. The voices grew louder, angrier, but Kemp shut them out. He would endure. He had to. His friends were out there, somewhere, and they would come for him. Until then, he would hold on to the hope that he could withstand the darkness, that he could keep his spirit intact.

He heard a faint sound—a whisper of movement beyond the cell door. His heart leaped. Was it his captors returning for another round of torment, or could it be—?

No, he wouldn't entertain false hopes. But the possibility, however slim, was enough to reignite a spark within him. Kemp lay motionless, every muscle tense, listening intently.

"You will serve Nergai," the voices whispered, almost soothingly now. "Embrace the darkness. It is inevitable."

"No," Kemp murmured, his voice barely audible. "I will not."

But even as he spoke the words, he felt the weight of them, the hollowness. Resistance felt futile, yet he clung to it, the last vestige of his former self.

His mind drifted to a distant memory—Ruiha's laughter, the way her alluring eyes sparkled with determination. He had to believe in that light, had to hold onto the hope that he could still make a difference. For her, for his friends, for himself.

He shifted again, the chains clinking softly, and focused on the faint sound beyond the door. It grew louder, more distinct. Footsteps. The lock rattling. He thought he heard his name being called, but the voices in his head were so loud he could easily have imagined it.

His heart raced. Was this the moment? Rescue or torment?

The door crashed open, and Kemp squinted against the sudden sliver of light. His eyes adjusted, revealing a shadowy figure. He braced himself, ready for whatever came next.

16

A Call to Arms

"True leadership is knowing when to wield the sword and when to guide with wisdom."

Gunnar

Gunnar sat by Anwyn's bedside, the room filled with her rhythmic breathing and the soft glow of the enchanted lamps. His fingers intertwined with hers, feeling the faint pulse of life that still lingered within her comatose body. His voice was a gentle murmur, a stream of words meant more for himself than for the silent figure on the bed.

"I did it, Anwyn," he whispered, his eyes glistening with unspoken emotions. "I unified the clans. We stand together once more. It was not easy, but the thought of you gave me strength. I hope you can hear me, wherever you are."

Across the room, Havoc and Lorelei engaged in a playful exchange, their flirtatious banter barely registering with Gunnar. Havoc's purple eyes sparkled with mischief as he leaned closer to Lorelei, who responded with a soft, tinkling laugh, her cheeks tinged with a hint of color. Their light-hearted interaction contrasted sharply with the heavy atmosphere surrounding

Gunnar and Anwyn. The room, divided by the weight of concern and the levity of budding romance, seemed to pulse with unspoken tension.

Gunnar's thoughts drifted momentarily from the weight of his own worries. He felt a pang of envy for their carefree flirtation, something he hadn't experienced in what felt like a lifetime. He squeezed Anwyn's hand, wishing she could share in their joy, but the reality of her comatose state pulled him back into the depths of his anxiety.

Then, the sound of hurried footsteps approached. The door burst open, slamming against the wall with a resounding thud. All heads turned. Magnus strode in, his face a mask of urgency.

Gunnar's heart skipped a beat, a jolt of shock running through him. Magnus was supposed to be in the Scorched Mountains, searching for a cure for Anwyn. His unexpected appearance here, now, could only mean something had gone terribly wrong.

"Magnus?" Gunnar's voice was a mix of confusion and concern. "What are you doing here? You were meant to be on the mission."

Magnus didn't waste a moment. "Gunnar, the mission to the Forgotten Realms has failed. Kemp has been kidnapped."

The words hit Gunnar like a physical blow. His mind struggled to process the information. Magnus being here meant he had abandoned the search for Anwyn's cure—a search that was their last hope. Despair mingled with a burgeoning panic. How could they save Anwyn now?

"By the gods," Gunnar muttered, his grip on Anwyn's hand tightening as if to anchor himself to the present. "How can we save her now?"

Magnus moved closer, his expression grave, but his eyes flickered with a hint of his own turmoil. "We need to act quickly. Kemp's abduction changes everything."

Gunnar took a deep breath, forcing himself to remain calm despite the storm of emotions raging within him. "We need Thalirion and Thraxos. Now."

Minutes later, the room filled with a shimmering light as Thalirion and Thraxos appeared. Their faces were etched with concern, their presence commanding.

"What has happened?" Thalirion asked, his voice a soothing balm to Gunnar's frayed nerves.

Gunnar recounted the dire news, his voice laced with worry. "Kemp has been taken by the Drogo. He was our only hope to save Anwyn. We don't know why they've taken him, but it can't be good."

Thalirion's brows furrowed, his hand instinctively moving to the haft of his staff. "The Drogo would not take him without reason. They must know about the Crown's power."

Thraxos nodded, his curved horns glinting in the torchlight. "If Kemp is struggling to control the power of the Crown, the Drogo might believe he is the key to resurrecting Nergai. They could use him to harness the Crown's energy for their dark purposes."

The room fell silent, the weight of Thraxos' words sinking in. Gunnar's mind churned, the urgency of the situation becoming painfully clear. "We cannot let that happen. Kemp must be retrieved, and soon."

Thalirion stepped forward, his hand warm and steady on Gunnar's shoulder. "We must send a force to rescue him immediately. The longer Kemp remains in their hands, the graver the danger."

Thraxos nodded, his agreement a low, rumbling grunt. "Time is of the essence. We cannot afford delay."

Gunnar surveyed the room, meeting the eyes of each of his companions. The weight of their shared resolve settled over him, hardening his own determination. "Agreed. We will dispatch our finest warriors at once. Kemp's rescue is our utmost priority. Once he is safe, we will proceed with our mission to the Forgotten Realms and find a way to save Anwyn."

As they laid out their plans, Gunnar felt a renewed sense of purpose. The road ahead would be perilous, but he would not waver. For Anwyn, for Kemp, and for the future of their world, he would confront whatever trials lay before them. The threads of fate were being spun, and Gunnar was resolute in his commitment to see them through to the end.

Gunnar stood at the balcony, overlooking the vast expanse of Draegoor. Moonlight shone through light shafts in the cavern ceiling, casting a silver glow over the rugged landscape, highlighting his homeland's strength and resilience. The land seemed to pulse with life, a living testament to its people's endurance. His heart ached with fierce love for Dreynas, tempered by the gnawing fear of the impending war. The weight of his responsibilities pressed down, making his shoulders feel leaden.

Gunnar traced the stone railing with his fingers, imagining the countless ancestors who had stood here before him. Their whispers seemed to mix with the wind, a murmur of judgment and encouragement. Would they approve of his choices? Every decision felt monumental, each step a path toward salvation or ruin. His mind wandered to a memory of his childhood, standing in the same spot, dreaming of adventures far less daunting than leading his people into war.

His father joined him, his presence a steadying force. Erik's face, etched with the lines of countless battles and decisions, was a comforting sight. Gunnar had always admired his father's unwavering strength, his ability to remain calm in the face of chaos. But now, looking at him, Gunnar also saw the toll that leadership had taken. The burden of command was a heavy one, and it showed in the stoop of Erik's shoulders, the deep lines around his eyes.

"Father," Gunnar began, his voice low but firm, "we need Magnus to lead the Army as General." His words fell like stones into a still pond, sending ripples through the night's silence.

Erik turned to him, his gaze searching. Gunnar could feel his father's eyes boring into him, probing the depths of his soul. It was as if Erik was weighing not just the words, but the Dwarf who spoke them. Gunnar resisted the urge to shift uncomfortably under that scrutiny. He needed his father to see his resolve, to understand the conviction behind his words.

"Magnus," Erik repeated, the name a question in itself. Gunnar could see the flicker of doubt in his father's eyes, quickly masked by the practiced neutrality of a seasoned leader. "You believe he is ready?"

Gunnar took a deep breath, steadying himself. "Yes, Father. He is the only one who can inspire the warriors. They will follow him into the abyss if need be." He paused, his gaze returning to the moonlit plains. "And I trust him."

Erik's face fell, lines deepening with sudden sorrow. He turned away, looking out over the land as if searching for something lost. "I, too, trusted my brother," he murmured, his voice barely a whisper, the weight of the words almost too much to bear.

The silence stretched between them, a tangible thing filled with the weight of the past and the uncertainty of the future.

"Magnus is not like Wilfrid, Father. You must realize that?"

Erik sighed, a deep, weary sound. "Aye, son. I know. Magnus is a good Dwarf. A good soldier."

Gunnar straightened, his gaze locking onto his father's. "No,

Father. Magnus is a good leader. Look at how he led the Snow Wolves out of the Drogo lands."

Erik's lips twitched into a brief smile. "I always thought it'd be you who I'd be appointing as General. Every past Clan Chief of Draegoor has served as General for a time."

Gunnar chuckled softly. "I never wanted to be Clan Chief, Father. Did you know that?"

Erik put his arm around his son. "Aye, Gunnar, I knew. I could always tell, but you would've made a formidable chief you know." He let out a soft chuckle. "And look at you now, hey. You're not leading a clan anymore! You're leading all of us!"

Gunnar shook his head in disbelief. "I wanted this even less."

His father's expression turned serious as he looked into Gunnar's piercing blue eyes. "And that, my son, is why you are the perfect Dwarf to lead us."

Gunnar sighed, "What if I fail?" he asked.

"Courage lies in the attempt, for even failure is more honorable than never trying."

Gunnar let out a low laugh. "I never took you as a philosopher, Father."

Erik looked sheepish before muttering, "Aye, well, your grandfather taught me a thing or two before he passed."

Gunnar nodded, the memory of his grandfather providing him some determination and encouragement.

After a long period of contemplation, Gunnar broke the silence. "Are you in agreement about making Magnus General, Father?"

Erik's eyes softened slightly, and Gunnar saw a flicker of something that might have been pride. "Very well," Erik said, at last, his voice gruff. "We will summon Magnus. But remember, Gunnar, leadership is not just about strength. It is about wisdom, about knowing when to fight and when to seek peace."

Gunnar nodded, absorbing his father's words. Relief mingled with a deeper resolve. He knew Magnus was worthy, ready to lead Draegoor through the coming storm. The path ahead was perilous, but a fierce determination burned within him. He would honor his forefathers' legacy and carve out a future for his people, no matter the cost.

The two Dwarves made their way back into the fortress, their steps clanging softly against the ancient stone walls. Shadows danced in the flickering torchlight as they approached the central chamber, where Magnus was engaged in conversation with several Dwarves Gunnar did not recognize. The air was thick with the scent of burning wood and the faint murmur of distant voices.

As they drew near, Magnus turned to face them, his expression one of polite curiosity tinged with the perpetual weight of leadership. The lines on his face, etched by countless battles and hard decisions, softened slightly at the sight of his father and Gunnar.

"Magnus," Erik began, his voice steady and imbued with the authority of a seasoned leader, each word carrying the weight of unspoken years of wisdom and hardship, "we have a matter of great importance to discuss with you."

Magnus straightened, his attention laser-focused on Erik, the respect for his father evident in his every movement. "Of course, Father," he replied, his voice a low rumble in the stillness.

Erik glanced at Gunnar, a silent exchange passing between them, an unspoken understanding forged in the fires of shared experiences. Gunnar stepped forward, his brow furrowed with the gravity of their mission.

"Magnus," Gunnar said, his voice both firm and gentle, "we would like you to assume the role of General of the Draegoor Army. Your leadership and expertise are invaluable, and we believe you are the best choice to guide our forces in the battles to come."

Magnus's eyes widened briefly, a flash of surprise quickly replaced by a deep sense of responsibility. He bowed his head, the gesture heavy with emotion and the solemnity of the moment. "It would be the greatest honor, Prince Gunnar, Father. I pledge to serve with all my strength and wisdom."

Erik placed a hand on Magnus's shoulder, the touch a blend of fatherly pride and the burdens of command. "We have full confidence in you, Magnus. Lead our warriors to victory."

Magnus straightened once more, his chest swelling with a renewed sense of purpose and pride. "I will not let you down."

As they stood together in that ancient fortress, the weight of their ancestors watching over them, Gunnar felt a surge of hope. With Magnus at the helm of the Draegoor army, their chances against the Drogo seemed not just possible, but within their grasp.

Gunnar paced back and forth across the stone floor of the council chamber, his mind a whirlwind of thoughts and strategies. The fires crackled in the hearths, casting long shadows against the rugged walls adorned with ancient tapestries depicting the glory of Dwarven past. His steel-blue eyes scanned the faces of the assembled chiefs and generals, each bearing the weight of their clan's honor and future on their shoulders.

Erik was the first to speak, his deep voice resonating through the chamber. "Prince Gunnar, we must know the last known position of Kemp. Magnus, you have the latest report."

Magnus stepped forward. "Kemp was last seen near the outskirts of Hammer. Ruiha, Dakarai, and a Drogo Hedgewitch named Elara are currently scouring the area. Their intelligence suggests that Kemp is being held within the city, likely in one of the fortified keeps."

The murmurs of concern from the gathered leaders filled the room. Gunnar raised a hand, silencing them. "We must rally our forces and prepare for an assault on Hammer. The Drogo cannot be allowed to use the Dragon Crown to resurrect Nergai."

Chief Durik spoke next, his voice steady but laced with worry. "Gunnar, we will need time to gather our warriors. An assault of this magnitude requires careful preparation."

A general from the Braemeer Clan nodded in agreement. "Our forces are ready to fight, but we must ensure we are fully equipped and organized. Ten days would be sufficient."

Gunnar's eyes flashed with impatience. "We do not have ten days. Every moment we delay, Kemp's life hangs in the balance, and the Drogo draw closer to their dark goal."

Chief Bojan leaned forward, his weathered face etched with concern. "Gunnar, while your urgency is understood, we must be realistic. We need to ensure our warriors are ready for the battle ahead. Five days for the first wave, seven for the second, and ten for the support units. This way, we can maintain a steady flow of reinforcements."

Another one of the clan generals added, "We will send our best with the first wave. It will be the vanguard of our assault."

Gunnar clenched his fists, but he knew they were right. "Very well. The first wave of infantry will depart in five days. The second wave follows in seven, and the support units in ten. I will lead the first wave personally."

This declaration caused a ripple of unease among the chiefs and generals. The newly appointed Chief Henrik of the Uglich Clan spoke, his voice measured. "Traditionally, our generals report to their chiefs."

The general of the Uglich Clan nodded. "It is a matter of

protocol and honor."

Gunnar stood tall, his voice firm and resolute. "In this war, we cannot afford division. As your prince, I will lead this army. The generals will report directly to me. Our unity is our strength, and we must present a united front against the Drogo."

After a tense moment, Erik broke the silence. "Gunnar is right. We stand together, or we fall divided. Let us put aside tradition for the greater good."

There were nods of agreement, albeit some begrudging, from the other chiefs and generals. Gunnar felt a weight lift from his shoulders. The hardest part of this council was over.

Magnus raised another concern. "What of the Snow Wolves? Their numbers are decimated Only fifteen to twenty remain."

Gunnar nodded. "Karl will lead the Snow Wolves. Each clan will provide ten of their best warriors to join this elite unit. They will leave immediately, separate from the main army, to strike ahead and gather intelligence."

The chiefs exchanged glances, but there was no dissent. The Snow Wolves were legendary, and their reputation alone would bolster morale.

With the plan set, Gunnar felt a sense of grim determination settle over him. The path ahead was fraught with danger, but the clans were united, and their cause was just. The rescue of Kemp and the prevention of Nergai's resurrection depended on their strength and unity.

The council adjourned, and as the chiefs and generals filed out, Gunnar lingered by the fire, staring into the flames. The journey ahead would test them all, but he knew that together, they could overcome any obstacle. The fate of their world depended on it.

17

The Edge of Despair

"In the darkest moments, it is not the battle we lose that defines us, but the will to rise and fight again."

Ruiha

The corridors twisted and turned, a labyrinth of shadowed passages that seemed to mock Ruiha with every step. Each echo of their footsteps felt like a countdown, a reminder of the precious time slipping away. She cast a glance at Elara, whose eyes burned with the same fierce determination. Kemp's face haunted her thoughts, the memory of his gentle nature now a painful reminder of what they stood to lose.

Every door they passed, every darkened corner was a potential to find Kemp or run into the Drogo. Ruiha's heart pounded louder with each minute, the urgency of their mission driving her forward.

They had maneuvered their way around the guards, each close encounter leaving them more desperate and weary. But Ruiha refused to let exhaustion slow her down. Kemp was counting on them.

Finally, they reached a heavy, iron-bound door at the end

of the passage. Ruiha's hand trembled as she reached for the handle, hope and fear warring within her. She pushed the door open, and her breath hitched.

The room was empty.

As Ruiha scanned the empty room, the weight of their mission pressed heavily on her shoulders. She clenched her jaw, refusing to let the creeping despair take hold. "We need to keep moving," she urged, her voice a tense whisper. "He can't be far."

Elara nodded, her face set in grim determination. They slipped back into the narrow passage, every step calculated and cautious. The distant sounds of the Drogo warriors grew louder, a constant reminder of the imminent danger.

The tunnel ahead seemed to stretch on endlessly, its narrow walls pressing in as if trying to suffocate their resolve. The air grew colder with each step, an icy chill that seeped into her bones while the darkness threatened to swallow her whole. Ruiha's breaths came shallow and rapid, echoing eerily in the confined space, a constant reminder of their dire situation.

Finally, the passage opened into another chamber; smaller than the previous ones. In the dim light, Ruiha could make out the outlines of more cells, these ones appearing even older and more decrepit. She hurried forward, peering into each one, her anxiety mounting with each empty cell.

"Here!" Elara's voice was a hiss, barely audible above the noise of their pursuers. Ruiha rushed to her side, hope flaring within her. Elara was kneeling by a cell door, her fingers working frantically at the lock.

Inside, Ruiha could just make out a figure slumped against the wall, chains binding their wrists. "Kemp," she breathed, relief washing over her. But as Elara struggled with the lock, the sounds of the Drogo warriors grew dangerously close.

"Hurry," Ruiha urged, her eyes darting to the corridor they had come from. The ground trembled once more, Dakarai's relentless efforts continuing to provide a fragile cover. But they were running out of time.

Elara cursed under her breath as the lock resisted her efforts. Ruiha glanced back, her heart racing. The shadows in the corridor seemed to move, and she could hear the unmistakable clanking of armor and weapons. "They're coming," she said, a note of panic in her voice.

With a grim snarl, Ruiha hacked at the last chain holding the cell door. It clanged open, the noise echoing like a death knell through the dank corridors. She slipped inside, her eyes locking onto Kemp. He was barely recognizable, a shadow of the man she knew, slumped and broken.

"Elara, get him up," Ruiha hissed, her voice taut with urgency. She watched as Elara knelt beside Kemp, lifting his gaunt face. His eyes fluttered, recognition flickering weakly.

"Kemp, it's us," Elara murmured, her voice trembling as she hauled him to his feet. Ruiha felt a fleeting relief as they steadied him. They had to move fast.

He swayed, legs buckling, but Ruiha and Elara each took an arm, dragging him toward freedom. The corridors stretched out, a grim maze of stone and shadows. Every step was a struggle, each twist and turn of the path seared into their memories from countless nights of preparation.

A guttural shout echoed behind them as they rounded a corner. Ruiha's heart plummeted. Drogo warriors, clad in dark iron, were closing in, their faces twisted with anticipation. There was no time, no escape.

"Go!" Ruiha barked, pushing Kemp toward Elara. "I'll draw

them off. Get him to the tunnel."

Elara's eyes widened, filled with fear and a fierce determination. "Stay alive, Ruiha," she whispered, her grip tightening on Kemp.

"Just go," Ruiha growled, already turning to face the advancing Drogo. She drew her daggers, the blades gleaming malevolently. The first warrior lunged, and Ruiha sidestepped, slashing across his arm. Blood sprayed as he let out a guttural scream of pain, but more warriors surged forward, relentless in their advance.

Ruiha heard Elara dragging Kemp through the winding passages. Every step was a struggle for them, she knew, but she couldn't look back. She focused on the fight, each movement precise and lethal. Her blades danced in her hands, blurs of steel cutting through the air. The Drogo warriors pressed on, their attacks fierce and unrelenting.

The tunnel entrance loomed ahead, and Ruiha's heart clenched as she imagined Elara hesitating, glancing back at her. She couldn't afford to falter. Not now. "Go, Elara," she whispered to herself, fighting back tears.

As Elara pushed Kemp through the tunnel entrance, Ruiha could almost feel the brutal yank on Elara's hair, hear the scream that followed. She saw it in the corner of her eye even as she fought, a Drogo warrior with a cruel grin.

"No!" Ruiha's voice, raw with desperation, cut through the chaos. She fought her way toward them, but the Drogo warriors closed in, overwhelming her. She was forced back, her eyes wide with helpless fury as they dragged Kemp away.

Ruiha stumbled, her body screaming in protest, but she couldn't stop. She had to find another way. Another plan. She ran through the corridors, each step a knife in her side until she found a hidden alcove. There, she collapsed, her breath ragged, tears streaming down her face.

They had failed. Kemp was still a prisoner, and Elara more

than likely dead. But Ruiha was alive, and that meant there was still hope. She clenched her fists, resolve hardening like iron. The fire of determination flared within her, burning away the despair.

This wasn't the end. It was just the beginning. She would find a way to save them, no matter the cost. The Drogo warriors had no idea what they had unleashed.

The passage opened into another chamber, smaller, darker, a suffocating pit of ancient stone and iron. Ruiha's eyes darted, scanning the shadows that clung to the walls like death. Cells lined the chamber, their rusted bars crumbling in places, their doors hanging like the jaws of forgotten beasts. She moved faster, heart pounding against her ribs, each empty cell tightening the knot of dread in her stomach.

"Here," Elara hissed, her voice barely a breath above the distant echo of their pursuers' boots. Ruiha lunged to her side, hope surging. Elara crouched by a cell door, her hands shaking as they fumbled with the lock.

Inside, a figure slumped against the wall, chains glinting in the faint light. "Kemp," Ruiha whispered, relief flooding her veins, if only for a moment.

The lock held fast, and Elara cursed, sweat beading her horned brow. Behind them, the metallic clank of Drogo armor grew louder, closer. The ground trembled, Dakarai's distant efforts a faint reminder that their time was running out.

"Hurry," Ruiha snapped, casting a frantic glance down the corridor. The shadows seemed to crawl toward them, alive with menace. The Drogo were coming. Her gut twisted with the bitter taste of panic, every instinct screaming to fight, to run, to do something.

Elara's hands worked faster, the lock clinking under her desperate fingers, but it wasn't enough. Ruiha growled, drew her dagger, and swung at the chain with all the fury boiling inside her. Frosteel met iron with a harsh screech, sparks flying. The chain shattered. The cell door slammed open with a metallic wail that echoed through the dank corridors like a death knell.

Kemp was barely alive—skin pale, eyes sunken, body limp. A shadow of the man who'd once wielded magic with strength and grace. Elara knelt by him, lifting his head, her voice shaking as she murmured his name. His eyes fluttered, recognition flickering like a dying flame.

"We need to move," Ruiha barked, her voice raw, every nerve on edge. She grabbed Kemp's arm, pulling him to his feet. He staggered, knees buckling like a puppet with its strings cut, but they dragged him forward, every step slow, agonizing.

A shout rang out behind them, deep and guttural. Ruiha's stomach dropped. She turned, catching a glimpse of the Drogo warriors in their dark iron, their faces twisted with bloodlust. No escape now. No time for hesitation.

"Go," Ruiha growled, shoving Kemp into Elara's arms. "Get him to the tunnel. I'll hold them."

Elara's eyes flashed with fear, but she didn't argue. She hauled Kemp forward, desperation lending her strength. "Stay alive, Ruiha," she hissed, and then they were gone, disappearing into the labyrinth of stone and shadow.

Ruiha turned to face the oncoming horde, daggers drawn, the cold weight of them familiar in her hands. She planted her feet, her heart a drumbeat in her ears, the tremor of the ground beneath her matching it. The first Drogo lunged, a hulking brute with murder in his eyes. Ruiha stepped aside, her blade flashing, slicing deep into his arm. Blood sprayed hot and thick, but there was no time to savor the scream. Another came at her, faster, meaner, and she barely deflected the blow aimed at her throat.

They were everywhere—shadows, steel, snarling faces. Each swing of her blades felt heavier, each step harder. Blood spattered the floor, hers and theirs. Pain bit into her shoulder, her side, but she pushed it down, pushed it away, her mind a razor focus on survival.

Behind her, the tunnel entrance loomed, a promise of escape. Ruiha's chest tightened, imagining Elara and Kemp struggling through. She couldn't afford to think about them, couldn't afford to falter.

The Drogo pressed closer, and then she saw it—a cruel hand yanking Elara back, the scream tearing from her throat like something out of Ruiha's worst nightmares.

"No!" Ruiha's roar was raw, a howl of desperation as she fought her way toward them. Blades clashed, bodies fell, but there were too many. Too fast. Too brutal. A blow struck her across the face, and she staggered, her vision swimming, blood hot in her mouth. Kemp, limp, was being dragged back into the shadows.

Ruiha's knees buckled, and she barely caught herself before she fell. The air was thick with the stink of sweat and iron, her breath coming in ragged gasps. The Drogo had him. They had Kemp.

She forced herself to move, legs screaming, the walls spinning around her. She stumbled into a hidden alcove, collapsing against the cold stone. Her hands shook as she pressed them to her side, blood soaking through her fingers. Every breath burned.

They had failed. Kemp was gone, and Elara... Elara was probably dead. Ruiha pressed her forehead to the stone, the taste of failure bitter and cold.

But she wasn't dead. Not yet. And that meant there was still a chance, still hope. She clenched her fists, the pain grounding her, a flicker of rage kindling in her chest. She would find them. She would save them.

The Drogo had no idea what they had just unleashed.

Ruiha emerged into the main corridor. The fortress was eerily silent, the tremors that had rocked it now stilled. Her breath came in ragged bursts as she scanned her surroundings, eyes searching for any sign of Dakarai. She felt a heavy weight of failure pressing on her chest, each step echoing her inner turmoil.

Suddenly, a hand grabbed her shoulder. Ruiha whirled around, daggers raised, only to see Dakarai's familiar face. Relief washed over her, but it was fleeting. "Where's Elara? Kemp?" he asked, desperation leaking into his voice.

Ruiha shook her head, her voice choked with emotion. "They're still back there. I couldn't get him out."

Dakarai's face paled, his dark eyes clouding with worry. He pulled back slightly, searching Ruiha's face for any sign of hope. "Elara?" he asked, his voice barely a whisper, the concern for her evident. His hand trembled as he placed it on her shoulder, a rare crack in his usual stoic demeanor.

Ruiha's shoulders slumped, the weight of their failure pressing down on her. "I couldn't save her. She stayed behind to try to help Kemp. I'm sorry, Dakarai. I…" Her voice broke, and she couldn't finish the sentence, her eyes welling up with tears. Memories of past failures surged up, making her doubt her abilities.

Dakarai took a deep breath, his jaw tightening. He placed a comforting hand on Ruiha's shoulder, trying to steady himself as much as her. "We'll find them. We have to." His voice was firm, but the crack in it betrayed his fear. She saw the same guilt in his eyes that gnawed at her.

Ruiha nodded, wiping away the tears that threatened to fall. "We can't leave them. Not like this."

They moved quickly but cautiously through the dimly lit corridors, every shadow a potential threat. The fortress, with its ancient stone walls, seemed to close in around them, each step echoing ominously. The air was thick with the scent of damp stone and the faint, lingering smell of smoke.

Suddenly, they heard a faint noise – a pained gasp. Ruiha's heart leaped into her throat.

"Elara?" Dakarai called out softly, his voice trembling.

"Here," came a weak reply.

They rushed toward the sound, rounding a corner to find Elara slumped against the wall, clutching her side. Blood stained her tunic, and her scaled face was pale, but her eyes were sharp and determined.

"Elara!" Dakarai dropped to his knees beside her, gently inspecting her wounds. Ruiha's stomach churned at the sight of Elara's injuries. "Are you okay?" His voice was a mix of fear and hope, his hands shaking as he checked her.

Elara's face twisted, her lips pulling back as she drew in a sharp breath, but she gave a quick nod, teeth clenched. "I'll live." Her voice was ragged, more a scrape than a sound. She wiped at her split lip with the back of her hand, smearing blood across her chin. "Kemp…"

Her eyes darted away, finding something in the shadows to focus on, as if staring into the dark would make it easier to say. "They dragged him off." Her jaw tightened, knuckles white around the hilt of her blade. "I tried."

The pause stretched, heavy. She let out a slow breath, one that trembled with more than just exhaustion. "But I wasn't enough." Her words hung there, hollow, like an apology to no one.

Ruiha knelt beside them, her face a mask of guilt and determination. "We'll get him back. We'll regroup and figure out a plan. We won't leave him behind."

Elara reached out, gripping Ruiha's hand. "It's going to be much harder now. They know we're coming."

Dakarai's eyes hardened with resolve. "Then we'll just have to be smarter and stronger. We don't abandon our own. Not now, not ever." His voice carried the weight of countless battles.

They helped Elara to her feet, moving as one, their unity a silent testament to their unbreakable bond. This failure, though painful, was not their defeat. It was a harsh lesson, a trial through which they would forge their resilience and resolve. Each setback was a step on the arduous path to their ultimate victory, shaping them into the warriors they were destined to become.

Kemp

Kemp had been beaten senseless more times than he could count since Ruiha and that Drogo woman had bungled their rescue attempt. Now, his head was crammed inside a rough, scratchy sack that reeked of sweat and despair, and he was being hauled off to who-knew-where.

Time had lost all meaning, swallowed by the suffocating darkness. The sack felt like it had been glued to his face for days, maybe weeks. Hunger gnawed at his belly, his throat was dry as sand, and the voices in his head were a relentless, maddening drone.

Every breath was a battle. He felt himself slipping away with each wheeze, fragments of his mind scattering like leaves in a storm.

In a rare moment of lucidity, he realized he was on a wagon. The bone-jarring bumps and ruts of the road were unmistakable.

He tried to grasp how long he'd been riding this hellish cart, but the thought evaporated as the darkness closed in again.

The next time he came to, the pain was worse. His body screamed with every jolt of the wagon, every slam of wood against his bruised flesh. He tried to focus, to hold onto something solid, but there was nothing. Just the endless black, the stench of the sack, and the voices whispering his doom.

With a final, desperate thought, Kemp wondered if he'd ever see daylight again before the merciful oblivion took him.

18

Forged in Duty

"The fire of duty never dies, especially in those who seek peace"

Gunnar

The glow of molten forges bathed the grand cavern in a ruddy light, casting flickering shadows on the ancient rock walls as Gunnar made his way toward Karl's foundry, deep within the mountain's heart. The rhythmic clang of hammer on metal and the hiss of steam filled the air, sounds so familiar they felt like a heartbeat to any Dwarf. Each step Gunnar took echoed softly on the stone floor, mingling with the rich scent of burning coal and hot iron.

Inside the forge, Karl was deeply engrossed in Spiritsmithing, the arcane process of infusing weapons and armor with the essence of spirits, a skill he had mastered in Nexus. His movements were a symphony of precision, each strike of his hammer a note in a complex melody. Nearby, a young Dwarf, barely twenty years old, watched in awe, his eyes wide with admiration and reverence.

Gunnar's arrival broke the spell, catching the apprentice's attention. He nearly dropped the tongs he was holding, his voice trembling with excitement as he stammered, "Your Highness!"

Karl glanced up from his work, a broad grin spreading across his face. "Gunnar! What brings the Dwarven Prince to my humble forge?" He clapped a sooty hand on the apprentice's shoulder, causing the lad to jump. "Steady, lad. Gunnar's just another Dwarf, same as you and me. Now, why don't you fetch more coals for the furnace? Then you can work that sword into shape."

The apprentice nodded vigorously, casting one last, star-struck glance at Gunnar before hurrying off to his task.

Gunnar chuckled softly. "I see you've taken on an apprentice."

"Aye, he's a good lad," Karl replied, watching the apprentice bustle about. "Strong work ethic. Reminds me of a younger before the gray began overtaking the red in my beard."

The two Dwarves found a quiet corner of the foundry and settled onto a couple of stone stools. For a moment, they sat in companionable silence, the sounds of the forge weaving a familiar tapestry around them. Gunnar's gaze wandered over the well-worn tools and the glowing embers, memories of their shared past surfacing like long-lost treasures.

"Do you ever miss our time with the Snow Wolves?" Gunnar asked, his voice tinged with nostalgia.

Karl laughed, a deep, hearty sound that echoed off the cavern walls. "How could I not? Escaping General Wilfrid and Fort Bjerg was a feat worthy of song."

Gunnar smiled, the warmth of old camaraderie filling his chest. "And our time in Nexus."

Karl's expression grew more serious, his eyes reflecting the forge's glow like twin embers. "Aye, we've had our share of adventures. But I suspect you didn't come here just to reminisce."

Gunnar's demeanor shifted, his shoulders tensing slightly. "You're right, old friend. I need your help."

Karl raised an eyebrow, curiosity piqued. "What kind of help?"

Gunnar hesitated, the weight of his words heavy on his tongue. Then, with a deep breath, he plunged ahead. "I need you to lead the Snow Wolves."

Karl's reaction was immediate, a firm shake of his head. "No, Gunnar. My army days are over. I'm a Spiritsmith now, not a soldier."

Gunnar leaned forward, his voice urgent and low. "Karl, Kemp has been kidnapped. Without him, we cannot save Anwyn. The unit is scattered, leaderless. They'll follow you. Together, we can rebuild them."

Karl's eyes flickered with a complex mix of emotions, old wounds, and past glories warring within him. "Gunnar, you know why I left—I've found my peace here."

"I understand, Karl. But this isn't just about us. Anwyn's fate hangs in the balance. Not only do the Snow Wolves need you. I need you."

Karl looked away, his jaw tightening as the weight of Gunnar's plea settled upon him. The apprentice, busy at the furnace, glanced over, his eyes filled with a glimmer of hope.

Gunnar's voice softened, threading through the forge's heat like a quiet promise. "Think of the lives we can save, the difference we can make. You're more than a Spiritsmith. You're a leader, a hero. The Snow Wolves need a commander."

Karl shook his head slowly, his red hair and beard swaying hypnotically in the torchlight. He took a deep breath, the weight of his words heavy in the air. "Gunnar, I am already helping. Who do you think is arming the soldiers? Who is providing them with the enchantments for their armor? Who do you think will continue doing that if I lead the Snow Wolves?"

Gunnar's gaze drifted across the room, lingering on Karl's apprentice for a moment, the young Dwarf struggling to hammer a particularly stubborn piece of metal.

Karl scoffed, the sound harsh against the backdrop of the forge. "Jurgen? Bah, he barely knows how to light the forge!"

Gunnar met Karl's eyes, his voice steady and persuasive. "You said yourself that he's got a strong work ethic. Most of the weapons and armor are already made. Surely, he can manage the forge for one mission! Once we have rescued Kemp, you can select a new leader and return to your work here."

A tense silence fell between them, broken only by the crackle of the furnace and the steady rhythm of metal striking metal. The heat of the forge seemed to press in on them, the weight of unspoken thoughts hanging heavy in the air. Karl stared into the dancing flames, the light casting sharp shadows across his face.

Finally, Karl sighed deeply, the sound resonating with the finality of a man making peace with his fate. He looked back at Gunnar, a flicker of resolve in his eyes. "Alright, Gunnar. For Anwyn. For Kemp and for the Snow Wolves. I'll do it."

Gunnar placed a hand on Karl's shoulder, a gesture of gratitude and camaraderie. "Thank you, old friend. Together, we'll bring Kemp back and save Anwyn."

Karl nodded, the firelight catching in his eyes, reflecting a determined gleam. The Snow Wolves would rise again, their path illuminated by the strength and courage of a Spiritsmith who was more than he seemed.

The council chamber echoed with the murmurs of the gathered chiefs and generals. Each banner, adorned with the sigils of their respective clans, hung proudly from the high rafters. The stone walls, worn by centuries of counsel and conflict, bore witness to the weighty decisions that had been made within this chamber.

Today, rather than a joint council, it was Gunnar who would lead them through the storm that threatened to engulf their world.

Gunnar stood at the head of the great stone table, his presence commanding and somber. He felt the weight of history pressing down upon him, a mantle of responsibility that both humbled and invigorated him. His eyes scanned the faces of those who had answered his summons, each one bearing the marks of their respective battles and the burdens of their clans. He raised his hand, and silence fell over the assembly.

"Welcome to the Council of Dreynas," Gunnar began, his voice steady and resolute. "This council replaces the old Dwarven Council, for we now face a threat that requires the unity of all our peoples."

As he spoke, Gunnar's mind flickered with memories of the past councils—moments of unity and discord, victories and losses. He remembered the endless debates that often seemed to go in circles, with each clan passionately defending their own views and interests. Decisions were hard to come by, and often, crucial time was lost in the process. Important matters that required immediate action were delayed by the need for consensus, and the cost of these delays was sometimes measured in lives.

But now, with a single leader, a decisive decision-maker, the landscape had changed. The era of prolonged discussions and stalemates was over. Gunnar understood the value of swift, resolute action, especially in times of crisis. No longer would they be paralyzed by debate. With clear leadership, they could respond to the Drogo threat with speed and efficiency.

Gunnar looked around the chamber, meeting each Dwarf's eye. "We meet here today, not because we want to fight, but because we have no choice. We're on the edge of war, driven by the need to protect our homes, our kin, and everything we hold dear.

"We face an enemy hell-bent on destruction. Indecision is

deadly. Now, with one purpose, we rise to meet the storm head-on.

"This war isn't about glory or conquest. It's about survival—about making sure our children, and their children, live free and in peace.

"We'll face hardship and loss, no doubt. But in our unity, we'll find strength. We don't fight as individual clans, but as one force, bound by a common cause.

"As we march into the unknown, remember: our cause is just. We fight to defend our land, our people, and our way of life. Together, we'll stand victorious, proof of our unbreakable spirit.

"So, let our courage and unity be our guide. For today, I summon us to war."

Chief Erik and General Magnus of the Draegoor Clan nodded gravely. Beside them, Karl, Commander of the Snow Wolves, leaned forward, his eyes sharp and attentive. Gunnar noted the fire in Karl's gaze, a readiness that bordered on impatience. Chief Durik and General Andrik of the Braemeer Clan exchanged a glance, their expressions unreadable. Gunnar sensed a shared understanding between them, a silent communication honed by years of partnership. Chief Bojan and General Bjorn of the Hornbaek Clan listened intently, their features carved with determination. Chief Henrik and General Stannor of the Uglich stood in stoic silence, their posture a testament to their unyielding resolve. Thalirion and Thraxos observed with measured calm, the Sages's composure a stark contrast to the turbulent emotions that swirled through the room.

Gunnar turned to Magnus, who rose to address the council. "The mission to the Forgotten Realms has failed," Magnus announced, his voice heavy with the weight of the news. "Kemp has been kidnapped. Ruiha stayed behind, hoping to rescue him, but we have received no word since."

A murmur of concern rippled through the council. Thalirion

stepped forward, his eyes narrowing with concern. "Kemp's kidnapping could have dire consequences. I fear the Drogo have taken him, knowing he has harmonized with the Dragon Crown. They may seek to use it to resurrect Nergai."

The room fell into a tense silence. Gunnar's heart pounded in his chest. Nergai was a name that haunted their darkest nightmares, a specter of destruction that threatened to unravel everything they fought to protect. Chief Bojan broke it first. "Is there any way this could truly happen?"

Thalirion hesitated, then answered, "Theoretically, it is possible. The Dragon Crown holds immense power, and if the Drogo have the means to harness it, they could indeed bring Nergai back. But in all honesty, I do not know for certain."

Gunnar's mind raced. Uncertainty was their greatest enemy, feeding the fear and doubt that threatened to undermine their resolve. Thraxos, who had been silent until now, nodded in agreement. "There is a possibility. And that possibility is too great a risk to ignore."

Gunnar's eyes hardened as he addressed the council. "If the Drogo resurrect Nergai, we would face an enemy nearly impossible to defeat. We cannot afford to delay."

A heated debate ensued, voices overlapping as the chiefs and generals weighed the urgency against the need for preparation. Gunnar watched them, his mind a tempest of strategy and emotion. Finally, Chief Henrik and General Stannor stood. "We require at least ten days to prepare our troops."

Karl's voice sliced through the noise, sharp and clear. "Ten days to prepare is too long. The Snow Wolves can move immediately. We will strike first, and the Draegoorian Army can follow within three days."

Gunnar admired Karl's decisiveness but knew the wisdom of restraint. General Magnus shook his head, raising his hand for silence. "No, Karl. The Snow Wolves will not mount an attack just yet. Your role is more critical than a mere assault. You are to scout the area, identify vulnerabilities, and set up a suitable camp for the armies that will follow."

Karl frowned but nodded, understanding the strategic necessity. Gunnar saw the conflict in Karl's eyes—the desire to act clashing with the need for caution. "We will need to move swiftly and with caution then. Our scouts will cover the terrain and ensure we know every inch of it before the main force arrives."

Chief Bojan leaned forward, his voice gruff but steady. "It is a sound plan. The Snow Wolves are known for their stealth and endurance. They can gather the intelligence we need without alerting the Drogo to our presence."

General Andrik added, "This reconnaissance will be invaluable. Knowing the land will give us the advantage we need when the time comes to strike."

Chief Duric spoke up, his voice carrying the weight of his years. "Agreed. The Snow Wolves will pave the way for the rest of our forces."

Gunnar nodded, satisfied with the consensus. He felt a surge of pride at their resolve but knew the road ahead was fraught with peril. The faces around him reflected his own determination and fear—a mirrored tapestry of their shared destiny. "Karl, your mission is clear. Scout the area, identify the enemy's weaknesses and establish a secure camp for our troops. Magnus, your army will mobilize within three days to support the Snow Wolves. The rest of the clans will join within the week."

The council reluctantly agreed, each chief and general understanding the gravity of the decision. Gunnar felt the weight of their trust and the burden of leadership settle more heavily on his shoulders. He took a deep breath, steeling himself for the trials to come. "Then it is settled," Gunnar declared. "We march to Hammer, and we will not stop until the Drogo city is under our control and Kemp is freed."

As the council disbanded, Gunnar caught Thalirion's eye. The Elf's gaze was filled with unspoken concerns, and Gunnar knew their battle was only just beginning. The flicker of doubt in Thalirion's eyes mirrored his own, but he pushed it aside. They had a plan, and that was more than they had moments ago.

The council of Dreynas had spoken, and their united front would be the beacon of hope against the encroaching darkness. Gunnar stood for a moment longer, watching his allies depart, each step echoing the promise of their resolve. The path ahead was uncertain, but together, they would face whatever came. He allowed himself a rare moment of hope, clinging to the belief that unity and courage would see them through the storm.

19

THE WOLVES OF WAR: MARCH TO HAMMER

"In every shadow lies a choice: to fight for what is lost or to seek what can still be saved."

KARL

Karl stood on the snowy ridge, his breath clouding the air in front of him. He adjusted the new insignia on his cloak—three silver wolves howling at a crescent moon. Commander of the Snow Wolves. It sounded impressive, but right now, it felt more like being the chief herder of particularly unruly sheep.

"Are you sure about this, Karl?" asked Torain, his second-in-command, scratching his beard, which seemed to have a life of its own under the layers of frost.

"Absolutely, Torain," Karl replied, trying to muster the confidence that was expected of a commander. "We're heading to Hammer to gather intelligence. The Drogo City won't know what hit them."

"I hope you mean that metaphorically," mumbled Uleg.

Karl ignored him and turned to face the remnants of his

once-proud unit. The Snow Wolves had seen better days. More precisely, they had seen better commanders. Both Gunnar and Magnus were far better suited for this malarkey than he was. But Karl was determined to change that, even if it meant dragging every one of them to Hammer.

"Listen up, lads!" Karl shouted, his voice echoing across the frozen landscape. "We've been given a second chance. We march to Hammer at dawn. It's a reconnaissance mission, not an invasion, so pack light and stay sharp."

"What exactly are we looking for, Commander?" asked Andrin, the unit's scout, who had a knack for finding trouble even when he wasn't looking for it.

"Information," Karl replied. "Anything and everything. The Drogo have kidnapped Kemp, for reasons known only to the gods—and possibly their pet goat, but let's not speculate. The powers that be have ordered us to head there, find out what's going on, and pave the way to rescue the Human. So, pack your wits and your warm socks, because we're in for a cold, long trek."

The unit grumbled but began to prepare with the practiced efficiency of seasoned warriors. Equipment was gathered and rations were packed with the kind of camaraderie that only comes from years of shared battles.

As predicted, the journey to Hammer was long and cold, filled with the kind of small talk that soldiers used to keep their minds off frostbite and boredom. Karl tried to instill a sense of purpose, regaling them with tales of past glories and emphasizing the importance of their mission. He spoke of Laslo's epic last stand against the golem, and the unit was awestruck, their breaths visible in the cold night air as they listened. Determined to honor the mighty Dwarven warrior, the group began crafting a cadence, their voices rising in unison:

> "*Laslo fought with axe in hand,*
> *Stood his ground to make a stand.*
> *Golem came, all stone and might,*
> *Laslo charged without a fright.*
>
> "*Swingin' steel, he carved the air,*
> *Bravery beyond compare.*
> *Stone and shadow, clash and roar,*
> *Laslo fell and rose no more.*
>
> "*Mighty Laslo, brave and bold,*
> *In our hearts, his tale is told.*
> *For his kin, he gave his all,*
> *Laslo stands where legends call!*"

The words echoed through the mountains as their boots crunched in the snow, each step harder, but somehow lighter with the memory of Laslo's bravery fueling them. Karl might have exaggerated the tale a bit, making Laslo's deeds grander with every retelling, but morale was important, after all.

One evening, as they set up camp beneath the icy stars, Uleg approached Karl with a thoughtful look on his weathered face. "You know, Karl, you're doing alright for a new commander."

In the background, the soldiers continued their cadence, voices steady as they readied the camp.

"Thanks, Uleg," Karl said, surprised. "I appreciate that."

"Don't get too comfortable," Uleg added with a grin. "We're still a pack of unruly wolves, and you're the one who has to keep us from biting."

Karl laughed, feeling a bit of the weight lift from his shoulders. "I'll keep that in mind."

As they neared Hammer, the mood grew more serious. The temperature had risen dramatically, the frosty and snow-laden days of their journey replaced by an almost unbearable heat. Layers of clothing and armor were shed, some pieces abandoned along the way, deemed too burdensome in the scorching environment.

The Drogo City loomed ahead, its imposing walls stark against the shimmering sky. The Snow Wolves fell into a tense silence, each member acutely aware of the gravity of their mission. The weight of what lay ahead pressed down on them, more oppressive than the heat.

Karl gathered them one last time before they reached the city's outskirts. His voice was low but commanding, carrying the weight of their shared purpose. "Remember, we're here for information. Stay hidden, stay safe, and above all, stay together. Let's show the Drogo that the Snow Wolves are back."

With that, they slipped into the shadows, a pack of wolves on the hunt once more. Their movements were silent and synchronized, a testament to their training and unity. The city's walls seemed to pulse with a dark energy, but the Snow Wolves moved with purpose, their determination a shield against the unknown dangers that awaited them.

Ruiha

Ruiha crouched by a small stream, filling their water flasks while Dakarai and Elara scoured the nearby underbrush for firewood and edible plants. The forest was dense, the thick canopy filtering the sunlight into a soft, green glow that made the place feel almost otherworldly. The three of them had been on edge since escaping Hammer, but the peaceful sounds of nature managed to ease their tension somewhat.

Ruiha's ears perked up when she heard the distinct crunch of boots on snow and the jingle of metal. She stood up, eyes narrowing as she spotted a large group of figures moving through the trees. "Dakarai, Elara," she called softly, "over here."

The two Drogo joined her, eyes fixed on the distant figures. "Dwarves," Dakarai whispered, hope flickering in his voice. "They must be. Look at the armor."

"Should we approach?" Elara asked, her hand instinctively resting on the haft of her staff.

Before Ruiha could respond, a crossbow bolt thudded into the ground just inches from Elara's foot. All three froze as a Dwarf emerged from the shadows, crossbow aimed steadily at them. "Don't move," he growled, his eyes widening in confusion as he took in the sight of a Human with two Drogo.

Ruiha raised her hands slowly, trying to appear non-threatening. "We're friendly," she said, her voice calm but firm. "We mean you no harm."

The Dwarf's eyes narrowed. "Friendly, you say? Unlikely story, considering your company. I'm not interested in your tales. You'll come with me to Karl. He'll decide what to do with you."

Ruiha's jaw tightened, her fingers drumming a sharp rhythm against the hilt of her dagger. She took a step forward, eyes narrowed into slits. "We don't have time for this," she cut in, voice like iron, the words snapping off her tongue before anyone could protest. "We need to—"

The Dwarf fired another bolt, this one embedding itself in the tree behind her. "One more step and the next one goes through you," he warned.

Before anyone could react, a blur of white fur and fangs launched itself at the Dwarf. Ghost appeared from the underbrush, knocking the crossbow from the Dwarf's hands and sending it skittering across the forest floor. The dwarf yelped in shock, clutching his bleeding hand as Ghost stood over him, growling menacingly.

Elara's eyes widened. "What in the—"

"Where in the void did he come from?" Dakarai exclaimed, stepping back in awe.

Ruiha shrugged, a smirk tugging at her lips. "He must've followed us."

The Dwarf, still in shock, managed to sit up, holding his hands up in surrender. "All right, all right! No need for the wolf! I'll take you to Karl."

Ruiha, Dakarai, and Elara exchanged glances, then moved to restrain the Dwarf. Ruiha bound his hands with a strip of leather. "What's your name?" she asked.

"Andrin," he muttered, glaring at Ghost, who had settled back on his haunches, watching him intently.

"Well, Andrin," Ruiha said, hauling him to his feet, "you're going to take us to Karl and explain everything. Let's go."

They marched Andrin through the forest, Ghost trailing behind them like a silent sentinel. As they approached the camp of the Snow Wolves, Ruiha felt a mix of anxiety and anticipation. They needed allies, and she hoped Karl and his unit would be the answer to their prayers.

Karl

The Snow Wolves' camp came into view, the Dwarves standing at attention as they noticed the newcomers. Karl, recognizable by the insignia on his cloak, stepped forward, his eyes narrowing as he took in the sight of Ruiha and her companions.

"Andrin," Karl called out, his voice stern, "what's the meaning of this?"

Andrin looked down, still nursing his hand. "Found them in the forest, Commander. I thought it best to bring them to you."

Glancing at the restraints around Andrin's wrists, Karl chuckled. "Bring *them* to us you say?"

Sheepishly, Andrin nodded. "They say they're friendly, boss."

Karl raised an eyebrow. "Friendly, you say? Friendly like a hungry bear in a berry patch, or friendly like a bard in a tavern?"

Before Andrin could respond, Ruiha strode forward, pulling back her hood with a sly grin. "More like the second one, Commander. We don't bite—much."

Karl's laugh boomed through the air, eyes widening with recognition. "Ruiha! Magnus said you stayed to help Kemp!" His surprise gave way to relief, a grin spreading across his weathered face as he took in the familiar faces before him.

Ruiha's face dropped with sorrow. "We tried and we failed."

Karl gave a half-smile despite himself. "Alright, well, let's see what kind of trouble you've brought to my doorstep. Welcome to the Snow Wolves' camp—"

Uleg and Torain walked over, their faces lighting up in recognition when they noticed Ruiha and Dakarai. "Shadowhawk! Dak! What in Vellhor are you two doing here?" The two Dwarfs turned to Andrin, eyebrows raised in surprise. "How in Draeg's stony ball sack did you not recognize them?"

Andrin coughed, the embarrassment clear in his demeanor.

"Well—all these Drogo and Humans look the same for Dreynas' sake! How am I supposed to know the difference?"

Karl sighed, then his gaze shifted to Ruiha, Dakarai, and Elara. "So, tell me. What's happened?"

Ruiha stepped forward, meeting his gaze evenly. "We need your help, Karl."

Karl studied them for a moment, then nodded. "Very well. Let's hear what you have to say."

As Ruiha began to explain their situation, she couldn't help but feel a glimmer of hope. Perhaps, with the Snow Wolves by their side, they could finally turn the tide in their favor.

Gunnar

Gunnar marched at the head of the Draegoorian army, the rhythmic thud of boots and the clanking of armor a reassuring backdrop to his roiling thoughts. Each step forward was a beat of certainty in an uncertain world. Beside him, his brother Magnus, the general of their forces, moved with an effortless confidence that Gunnar both envied and relied upon.

Gunnar cast a sideways glance at Magnus, hoping he had made the right decision in appointing him. Magnus had always been steady, but leading an army was a different beast altogether. Could his brother truly handle the weight of this responsibility? Gunnar's mind churned with doubt, but seeing Magnus stride forward with such natural authority, those doubts began to melt away.

Magnus, although new to the role of General, exuded a calm and strategic mind that Gunnar knew they needed. Perhaps this appointment had been a gamble, but as he watched his brother lead, Gunnar realized Magnus was, indeed, the best Dwarf to guide them to victory. Magnus's ability to inspire confidence and his knack for anticipating enemy movements were invaluable assets. Gunnar clung to that belief like a lifeline.

Behind them, Thalirion and Thraxos moved with a quiet grace, their presence a palpable reminder of the arcane power they commanded. The air seemed to hum around them, charged with the latent magic that could turn the tide of any battle.

The Sympathetic Link Systems had been invaluable, allowing Gunnar to stay in contact with Karl and the Snow Wolves. He knew that Ruiha and Dakarai were with them now, their skills and knowledge crucial for the task ahead.

As they neared the forest, the ancient trees standing like silent sentinels, Gunnar felt the weight of responsibility settle heavier on his shoulders. The forest loomed, a place of shadows and secrets.

Karl

The Snow Wolves slipped from the shadows, led by Karl, their steps silent as ghosts in the night. Gunnar's heart clenched at the sight of them—familiar faces, familiar strength—but the relief was fleeting. There were no smiles, no greetings, just grim nods. Warriors, all of them, with eyes that held the weight of the battles yet to come. Ruiha and Dakarai were among them, their stances like coiled springs, ready to strike. The flicker of resolve in their eyes mirrored his own.

Gunnar's mind drifted for a heartbeat, back to fireside laughter and the simpler days when they were bound by camaraderie rather than duty. But those days were distant now, buried beneath the looming shadow of war. The scent of smoke and steel had replaced the warmth of those memories.

He called for a meeting, the command sharp, and they gathered inside his tent. The canvas walls seemed to close in, the air thick with the weight of what lay ahead. It wasn't just the space that felt small; it was the burden on Gunnar's shoulders, pressing down like the iron chains of responsibility. His eyes scanned the faces around him—trusted, weathered, and worn—but it was the silence that spoke louder than any words.

Karl seated himself first, his movements slow, deliberate, as though each step was weighed with thought. Gunnar caught the flicker of something in his eyes—worry, perhaps, or just the understanding of how close they stood to the edge. He didn't need to speak; the tension in his jaw said it all. Ruiha and Dakarai followed, their eyes not on him, but on the map, their focus sharp, like wolves scenting prey. A Drogo woman stood beside them—Elara, Magnus had called her—and though Gunnar had his doubts, he trusted the judgment of those who vouched for her.

As they settled in, the lanterns cast long, wavering shadows across the room. Gunnar's hand hovered over the map, his fingers tracing the familiar routes and landmarks. It felt like handling a loaded blade, one wrong move and everything would unravel. His heart hammered in his chest, every beat a reminder of the weight he carried. He had led before, but this was different. Every decision here would mean lives—his people's lives.

He exhaled slowly, steadying his mind. The faces of the fallen lingered in his thoughts, a constant reminder of what was at stake. He couldn't afford to lose more. Not now. Not when they were this close.

"The terrain is our lifeline," he began, voice low and steady, though his mind churned like a storm. His eyes flicked to the others, reading the hardened resolve in their expressions. "We need to know it better than our enemy. Every hill, every shadowed pass. If we misstep, there's no turning back."

The silence stretched, heavy and thick, as the reality of his words settled in. This wasn't just a plan—they were gambling with everything they had.

The silence was broken only by the rustling of the map and the distant sounds of the army preparing outside. Each of them carried their own burdens, their own fears and hopes, but in this moment, they were united by a common purpose. The stakes had never been higher, and Gunnar knew that failure was not an option. He looked around at his comrades, drawing strength from their presence. Together, they would face whatever came their way, driven by the shared belief in their cause and the unyielding determination to see it through.

Elara stepped forward, her keen eyes scanning the map with a practiced ease that Gunnar found both reassuring and unsettling. "I know this area well," she said, pointing out various landmarks and potential ambush sites. "Here, near the river, the ground is soft and could hinder heavy troops. And this forest path is narrow and easily defended."

Thalirion's gaze lingered on Elara's staff, a gleam of curiosity in his eyes. "You have an impressive knowledge of the terrain, Elara. May I ask, what kind of magic do you wield?"

Elara hesitated, then replied, "I am a hedgewitch. My magic is elemental and herbal."

Thalirion's interest deepened, his focus unwavering. "Elemental and herbal, you say? Fascinating. Your staff—it seems more than just a tool for walking."

Elara nodded, a hint of pride in her eyes. "It channels my

magic, aiding me in both combat and healing."

The strategic discussions continued, but Ruiha's question cut through the planning like a knife. "How is Anwyn?" she asked softly.

Gunnar's expression darkened, the weight of his personal sorrow almost too much to bear. "Her spirit is still damaged. She remains in a magically induced coma. We've tried everything, but nothing has worked."

Elara's interest was piqued, and Thalirion and Thraxos exchanged glances. "Have you tried any elixirs?" she asked, hesitantly.

Gunnar looked up, a spark of hope flickering in his eyes. "Elixirs? What's elixirs do you speak of?"

Elara stepped closer, her earlier hesitation gone, replaced with knowledge and earnestness. "Elixir of Elysian Blossoms. It's an ancient remedy known to heal the spirit.

Skepticism flashed across Thalirion's face, but Gunnar seized the opportunity, his voice firm. "If there's even a chance this elixir can save Anwyn, we must try."

Thraxos, his deep monotone vibrating through the tent, spoke, "I have never heard of this elixir? How do you know of this?"

"When I was studying under the shamans, there were many tomes in the library. Most Drogo cannot read, but I learned. I must have read every tome in that library." A faint smile appeared on her face as she reminisced about her past. "One of those tomes spoke of remedies which would strengthen the spirit. One in particular was designed to heal the spirit."

"And you remember the ingredients and preparation methods for this elixir?" Thraxos interrupted."

She shook her head slowly. "Unfortunately not. I know that it requires rare and dangerous herbs and materials to prepare. It might be our only hope."

Gunnar was brimming with energy and excitement. "Then we must leave immediately to gather these ingredients!"

Elara nodded, determination in her eyes. "I can guide us to the necessary ingredients, but I do not remember the preparation method."

Gunnar's heart sank. "Then we are no better off than before."

"Not necessarily," Elara said. "The library is in the city of Hammer. I have no doubt in my mind that the tome will still be there."

"Then we must retrieve it!" Gunnar exclaimed.

"Yes," Ruiha added. "However, our primary concern must be rescuing Kemp!"

"Agreed," Magnus interjected. "Kemp must be rescued as a matter of priority. I suggest that Ruiha, Dakarai go with Karl and the Snow wolves to rescue Kemp. Whilst a separate force led by Elara, Thalirion and Thraxos seek the tome."

"No," Gunnar said thoughtfully. "Whilst I agree with Karl and Ruiha leading the Snow Wolves to rescue Kemp." He turned to Thraxos, his gaze steady. "You will stay with the army and provide magical assistance. Once you are inside the city, you will lead a force to find the tome. Thalirion, Elara, and I will gather the ingredients. If they are truly that rare we will need as much time as possible."

With the plan set, Gunnar, Thalirion, and Elara prepared to venture into the wilderness. The path ahead was uncertain, but Gunnar felt a glimmer of hope. He gripped the hilt of his axe, ready for whatever challenges lay ahead. With Elara's guidance and Thalirion's magic, they would find the Elixir of Elysian Blossoms and bring Anwyn back.

20

THROUGH BLOOD AND FLAME

"Every warrior bears scars, but it is the unyielding heart that rises, time and again, to lead the charge toward victory."

RUIHA

Ruiha's heart pounded as the war drums began their steady, ominous beat. The underground city of Hammer lay before them, its entrance a gaping maw that promised nothing but darkness and danger. The Draegoorian army stood in grim formation, Magnus at the forefront, his presence a beacon of resolve and authority.

Beside him, Karl and the Snow Wolves, smaller but elite, prepared for the assault. Ruiha, her grip tight on her daggers, felt the weight of the mission bearing down on her shoulders. Dakarai stood at her side, his eyes scanning the entrance with a mix of anticipation and dread.

Magnus raised his warhammer, the steel glinting in the dim light. "Today, we bring the fight to the Drogo! For too long, they have hidden in their underground sanctuaries, thinking themselves safe. For too long, they have launched relentless assaults on Dreynas, leaving devastation in their wake. Today, we show them that nowhere is safe from the Draegoorian might!"

The army responded with a thunderous roar, the sound reverberating through the air and into the very bones of those who heard it. Ruiha felt the surge of adrenaline, her fears momentarily eclipsed by the collective resolve of her comrades. She glanced at Karl, who nodded, a silent acknowledgment of the battle ahead.

"Snow Wolves," Karl barked, his voice cutting through the noise. "We move in fast and hard. Our objective is to find Kemp and extract him. Leave no Drogo standing in our path."

Ruiha took a deep breath as the Snow Wolves moved to the side entrance, a hidden passage known only to a few. The Draegoorian army would create the main diversion, drawing the bulk of the Drogo forces while they infiltrated from the side. The entrance loomed before them, a dark, narrow tunnel leading into the bowels of the city. Karl led the way, his movements silent and purposeful, the Snow Wolves following in his wake.

The tunnel was cold and damp, the air thick with the scent of earth and decay. They moved swiftly, their footsteps barely making a sound. Ruiha's senses were on high alert, every shadow a potential threat. The tunnel opened into a larger cavern, and they paused, taking in their surroundings. The cavern was lit by glowing crystals embedded in the walls, casting an eerie light that played tricks on the eyes.

Karl raised a hand, signaling them to halt. "Scouts ahead. Take them out silently."

Ruiha's heart quickened, the familiar rush of adrenaline coursing through her veins. She exchanged a quick glance with Dakarai, who nodded, his eyes steely with resolve. The weight of the mission pressed heavily on her shoulders, but she pushed it aside, focusing on the task at hand.

Moving forward with cat-like stealth, Ruiha felt every muscle in her body tense and relax in perfect harmony. Each step was measured, her senses honed to the faintest sounds. The tunnel walls seemed to close in around her, the darkness pressing in, but she remained undeterred. Ahead, the Drogo scouts were positioned at strategic points, their eyes scanning the shadows for any sign of intrusion.

Ruiha crept up behind one, her breath steady and controlled. She could hear the scout's shallow breathing, see the slight rise and fall of his chest. Her movements were fluid and precise, a deadly dance of life and death. With a swift, silent motion, she drove her dagger into the scout's back, the blade slipping between his ribs with a sickening ease. The scout stiffened, a strangled gasp escaping his lips before he crumpled to the ground.

Dakarai moved in tandem, his axe a whisper in the darkness. He approached his target with the same deadly grace, his movements a blur of efficiency. The axe flashed in the dim light, and the second scout fell, his lifeless body hitting the ground with a soft thud.

They pushed deeper into the tunnels, where the air grew colder, pressing against their skin like a tangible force. Each step forward was met with resistance—the Drogo, fierce and unrelenting, ambushed them at every turn. Their attacks were swift, deadly, but the Snow Wolves countered with precision and ferocity honed by years of blood and steel.

Ruiha was in the thick of it, her blades moving like extensions of her arms, slicing through the air with a fierce, practiced grace. A spear shot toward her face, and she barely dodged, the tip grazing her cheek as she spun away, heart pounding. Without thinking, she lashed out, her blade catching the Drogo across the chest. He crumpled, but there was no time to breathe, no time to savor the victory.

Another Drogo charged—tall, broad, and radiating pure, savage intent. His rusty sword came down, aiming for her heart.

Ruiha lifted her blade, the impact sending shockwaves up her arm, rattling her bones. She winced but held firm, her feet sliding backward on the slick, blood-stained stone. His eyes locked with hers, filled with a dark, relentless determination.

Her pulse raced, the tension between them electric, but she wouldn't let him see her falter. Not now. Not when every second counted.

The Drogo smirked, confident in his size and strength, certain that victory was within his grasp. He pressed harder, his sheer bulk driving her back step by step. Ruiha's muscles screamed in protest, but she wasn't about to give him the satisfaction. She gritted her teeth, feeling the burn of fatigue, and twisted sharply, letting his overconfidence work against him. In one fluid motion, she sidestepped, slipping out of his reach and using his own momentum to unbalance him. Her blade flashed, catching the back of his knee. He dropped with a howl, and before he could recover, she spun again, her heart hammering in her chest as she drove her dagger into his side.

She could feel the impact reverberate through her body, the blade sinking deep, and for a moment, everything slowed. The Drogo's eyes widened in shock, his hand grasping for his sword, but he was already lost. His body slumped against her, heavy and still. Blood pooled around them, warm against the cold stone.

Ruiha's breath came in sharp gasps, her chest heaving as she stepped back, her hands trembling from the adrenaline and the strain of the fight. She wiped the sweat and blood from her brow, but there wasn't time to process what had just happened. In a fight, there was never time.

Beside her, Dakarai's hammer cleaved through another Drogo, his movements raw and powerful, as if the weight of battle didn't touch him the way it did her. Together, they moved like they were one, each anticipating the other's next step, their training making the chaos around them feel almost like choreography.

But it wasn't choreographed. It was brutal and bloody and real. Every slash of her blades, every dodge, every breath she took was earned with grit and determination. And as the faces of the fallen flickered in her mind, ghosts of the past she couldn't forget, she pushed harder, fought fiercer.

This fight wasn't just about survival. It was about everything she had lost and everything she refused to lose again.

As they pressed deeper into the tunnels, the resistance intensified, each clash more brutal than the last. The Drogo fought with everything they had, their desperation to protect their home evident in every strike, but the Snow Wolves? They were unstoppable. They weren't just fighting for survival; they were fighting for their home, for each other, and for Kemp. That fire burned hotter than any pain. It drove them forward, fueled them when their muscles screamed in agony and their lungs begged for air. Every ragged breath was a reminder of what was at stake, and they weren't about to give up now.

Ruiha could feel the shift, a subtle change in the rhythm of battle. They were gaining ground. With each swing of her daggers, with every Drogo that fell before her, they moved closer to their goal. The weight of the mission pressed heavily on her, but it was that very pressure that pushed her forward, that made her keep fighting when her body begged for rest.

The path ahead was littered with danger, shadows shifting with unseen threats, but turning back wasn't an option. Not now. Not ever. They wouldn't stop until the Drogo were crushed beneath their boots and Kemp was free. Hammer was within their grasp, and Ruiha wouldn't let it slip away. Not this time. The Drogo would pay, and they would fall. One way or another, victory was coming.

Magnus

Magnus gripped his warhammer tightly, feeling the familiar weight and balance in his hands. He stood at the head of the Draegoorian army, his eyes fixed on the entrance to the underground city of Hammer. The air was thick with anticipation and the acrid smell of torch smoke. He could sense the tension in his troops, the silent determination etched into their faces. They were ready to fight, ready to avenge the relentless Drogo assaults on Dreynas.

He raised his warhammer high, the steel glinting in the dim light. "Today, we bring the fight to the Drogo! For too long, they have hidden in their underground sanctuaries, thinking themselves safe. For too long, they have launched relentless assaults on Dreynas, leaving devastation in their wake. Today, we show them that nowhere is safe from the Draegoorian might!"

Magnus felt a surge of pride and determination. He nodded to Karl and the Snow Wolves, signaling them to move to their side entrance. Their elite unit would infiltrate the cells while the main force mounted the main attack on the city.

"Draegoorian army, with me!" Magnus bellowed, his voice carrying over the clamor. "We make our stand here, we fight for Dreynas!"

The main entrance to Hammer was a formidable structure carved into the rock and reinforced with heavy doors. Magnus led the charge, his warhammer swinging with brutal force. The doors shuddered under the impact, splintering and cracking. His troops surged forward, weapons drawn, eyes blazing with the fire of retribution.

Thraxos stood by his side, muttering incantations and launching spells at the gates of the city. Each spell causing the doors to crack further.

As they breached the entrance, the Drogo were ready. The initial clash was a cacophony of steel and cries of pain. Magnus's warhammer was a blur of motion, smashing through Drogo armor and bone. He fought with a fierce intensity, every strike driven by the memory of his recent imprisonment by the Drogo.

A Drogo warrior lunged at him, spear aimed for his heart. Magnus parried with his warhammer, the spearhead skidding off the metal with a screech. He swung his weapon in a wide arc, catching the Drogo in the side. The warrior crumpled, and Magnus pressed forward, his troops following in his wake.

"Hold the line!" he shouted, rallying his soldiers. "Push them back!"

The Drogo fought with a savage desperation, their defenses formidable. They knew the tunnels and used the terrain to their advantage, launching ambushes from hidden alcoves and side passages. But the Draegoorian army was relentless, their drive to avenge Dreynas giving them strength.

Magnus spotted a group of Drogo archers taking aim from a ledge above. He pointed with his warhammer. "Crossbow team, take them down!"

A volley of bolts flew overhead, striking the Drogo archers before they could release their deadly barrage. The ledge was cleared, and Magnus pressed on, his warhammer leading the charge like a battering ram. The tunnels echoed with the sounds of battle, the clash of steel on steel, the guttural cries of the wounded and dying. Every step was a step closer to vengeance.

Magnus's warhammer was an extension of his will, a deadly instrument of retribution. He swung with brutal efficiency, the weight of the weapon crushing armor and bone alike. Each blow was fueled by the memory of his imprisonment, of friends and comrades falling beneath the barbaric Drogo. The rage burned hot and fierce in his chest, driving him forward.

A Drogo warrior lunged at him from the shadows, spear aimed at his heart. Magnus twisted, the spear grazing his side, and brought his warhammer down with bone-crushing force. The Drogo fell, his skull shattered, and Magnus pushed on, a juggernaut of fury. Around him, his troops fought with equal ferocity, their resolve steeled by the presence of their indomitable leader.

The tunnels were a maze of twisting passages, each turn revealing new horrors. Drogo warriors poured from hidden alcoves, their attacks swift and deadly. But the Draegoorian army was unstoppable, a relentless tide of steel and fury. Magnus could feel the weight of their determination, the collective drive to avenge the atrocities committed against their homeland.

"Keep moving!" Magnus bellowed, his voice a roar above the din of battle. "We take this city, we avenge Dreynas!"

They pushed deeper into the city, the resistance growing fiercer with every step. The Drogo were cornered, their desperation evident in their wild, frenzied attacks. They fought with the ferocity of the doomed, knowing that this was their last stand. But Magnus was a force of nature, his warhammer a blur of deadly motion. He broke through their lines with crushing blows, his troops following with unwavering determination.

The final push was brutal, the Drogo fighting with the ferocity of cornered beasts. Magnus's warhammer cleaved through their ranks, each swing leaving a trail of broken bodies in its wake. The Draegoorian army pressed forward, their momentum unstoppable. The Drogo defenses crumbled under the relentless assault, their once formidable lines shattered.

Magnus could see the fear in their eyes, the dawning realization that they were beaten. The Drogo fell back, their desperation giving way to panic. Magnus seized the moment, driving forward with renewed ferocity. He smashed through their last defenses, his warhammer crashing down with a final, decisive blow.

When the last of the Drogo fell, a heavy silence settled over the tunnels, broken only by the labored breathing of the victorious. Magnus stood amidst the carnage, his armor slick with blood. He raised his weapon high, his voice echoing through the cavernous tunnels. "The city of Hammer is ours!"

A cheer went up from the Draegoorian forces, the sound reverberating off the stone walls. They had done it. They had taken the city, avenged Dreynas, and secured a foothold in the Drogo's underground stronghold. Magnus sheathed his warhammer, exhaustion washing over him like a wave. But there was no time to rest.

"We've secured the city," he said, his voice steady despite the weariness in his bones. "Now we find Kemp and the tome. Anwyn's fate, and perhaps the fate of us all, depends on it."

His words hung in the air, a reminder of the larger mission at hand. The battle for Hammer was won, but the war was far from over. With grim determination, Magnus led his troops deeper into the heart of the city, ready to face whatever challenges lay ahead. The path was fraught with danger, but they would not falter. They had come too far to turn back now. The Drogo would pay for their crimes, and Dreynas would be avenged.

Gunnar

Gunnar trudged through the barren landscape of the Scorched Mountains, the unforgiving sun beating down upon him. The air was thick with heat and dust, each breath a reminder of the harsh environment they were traversing. He cast a glance at Thalirion, whose eyes were fixed ahead, and then at Elara, who led the way with a determined stride. Her knowledge of the Elixir of Elysian Blossoms was their only hope, but the journey was proving to be as arduous as he had feared.

The mountains stretched endlessly before them, a desolate expanse of jagged rocks and parched earth. Gunnar wiped the sweat from his brow, his thoughts drifting to Anwyn. Her pale face, still and silent, haunted his dreams. This quest was for her. To bring her back from the edge of death. The weight of it pressed heavily on his shoulders, but it also fueled his resolve.

"Elara, how much further?" he called out, his voice barely carrying over the wind that whipped through the mountains.

"Not far now," she replied without turning, her tone unwavering. "The first ingredient, the Firebloom, should be near the peak of this ridge."

Gunnar nodded, though he felt no comfort in her words. The Firebloom was said to grow only in the most inhospitable of places, its petals vibrant against the stark, rocky landscape. It was a plant born of fire and ash, much like the mountains themselves. Dangerous to harvest but essential for the elixir.

Thalirion, ever the silent companion, moved with a grace that belied his strength. His magic had been a boon on this journey, shielding them from the worst of the elements. Yet even he seemed affected by the relentless heat, his steps slowing as they ascended the ridge.

As they climbed, Gunnar's mind wandered to the stories he had heard of the Scorched Mountains. Tales of ancient Dragons and forgotten battles. He shook his head, dispelling the ghosts of the past. Now was not the time for legends. They had a mission to complete.

Elara paused at the top of the ridge, her eyes scanning the

horizon. Gunnar and Thalirion joined her, the sight that greeted them both awe-inspiring and daunting. The peak was a jagged, rocky outcrop, and there, nestled in a crevice, were the fiery petals of the Firebloom. It glowed with an ethereal light, a beacon in the desolation.

"There it is," Elara said softly, a note of reverence in her voice. "The Firebloom."

Gunnar approached the plant cautiously. The heat radiating from it was intense, and he could feel the burn even from a distance. "How do we harvest it without getting scorched?"

Elara knelt beside the plant, her hands moving with practiced precision. "Carefully," she replied, pulling out a small knife. "The petals must be cut at the base, and we must avoid touching the stem."

Gunnar watched as she worked, her hands steady despite the danger. The petals came away easily, and she placed them in a small pouch, sealing it tightly. "One down," she said, standing and brushing the dust from her knees. "We have what we need here. Now, for the next ingredient."

They trudged down the ridge, the burden of their task still heavy, though maybe just a touch lighter after their small win. Gunnar let a flicker of hope slip through the cracks. It wasn't much, but a victory was a victory, however small. They'd stared death in the eye and walked away without so much as a scratch. But the hard part wasn't behind them—not by a long shot. The road ahead wasn't just long; it was the kind that didn't break you all at once, but chipped away at you, bit by bloody bit, until hope was a memory, and all that was left was the fight to survive.

Gunnar

As they continued through the mountains, Gunnar found himself drawn to Elara's quiet strength. She bore the knowledge of the elixir with a grace that was both humbling and inspiring. He marveled at her determination, her unwavering focus. In her, he saw a reflection of his own resolve, a mirror to his inner turmoil.

"Tell me, Elara," he said as they walked, the harsh landscape stretching endlessly around them. "What drives you to know so much about the elixir? What fuels your quest for knowledge?"

Elara glanced at him, her eyes thoughtful. "Knowledge is a means to an end, Gunnar. It is a way to heal what is broken. Much like you, I have seen too much suffering. If my knowledge can bring about even a small measure of peace, then it is worth every hardship."

Her words resonated deeply with Gunnar. They were kindred spirits, each driven by a desire to mend the wounds of the past. As they ventured further into the Scorched Mountains, he felt a renewed sense of purpose. The path ahead was fraught with danger, but they were not alone. Together, they would find the ingredients, brew the elixir, and bring Anwyn back. The mountains had tested them, but their spirit remained unbroken.

The journey pressed on, each step a testament to their unbreakable will. Gunnar tightened his grip on his axe, bracing for the trials that awaited. With Elara's knowledge and Thalirion's magic, they would carve their way through the Scorched Mountains. The elixir was close—close enough to taste. Failure wasn't an option. Not now. Not ever.

Victory, or nothing.

21

A Race Against Time

"A sword in the hand's worth more than a thousand promises, but don't be surprised when both fail you in the end."

Gunnar

The oppressive heat of the Scorched Mountains weighed heavily on Gunnar, each step a testament to his determination. The jagged rocks and parched earth stretched endlessly around them, a desolate expanse that mirrored the exhaustion in his bones. As they moved, the memory of Anwyn's pale, lifeless face spurred him onward. This perilous journey was for her, to bring her back from the brink of death.

Elara led the way, her stride firm and purposeful, each step imbued with an unwavering resolve that Gunnar found both reassuring and daunting. She moved as though the weight of the Scorched Mountains themselves could not deter her, driven by the knowledge she carried of the Elixir of Elysian Blossoms. This knowledge was their beacon in this forsaken land, a fragile thread of hope that kept them pressing forward despite the odds.

Beside Gunnar, Thalirion moved with a grace that seemed almost unnatural, his every motion fluid and silent. There was a serenity to him, a calm that belied the harsh environment and their grueling journey. The recent success in harvesting the Firebloom had kindled a small flame of hope within their hearts, but Gunnar, ever cautious, knew better than to let his guard down.

The mountains, imposing and relentless, seemed to close in around them as they descended from the ridge. Each jagged rock and parched crevice whispered of ancient dangers and hidden perils. Gunnar's instincts prickled with unease, a familiar sensation that had kept him alive through countless battles. With every step, the sense of impending danger grew, tightening like a noose around his chest.

He glanced at Elara, her face set in a mask of determination, her eyes scanning the path ahead with a hawk's intensity. When she met his gaze, there was a slight nod, a silent confirmation that she, too, felt the weight of unseen eyes upon them. Her expression mirrored his own wariness, a shared understanding that they were being watched.

Thalirion, the silent sentinel, was ever vigilant. His eyes, deep pools of ancient wisdom, flickered with a faint blue light as he extended his magical senses. Gunnar had come to trust this unspoken language between them, the way Thalirion could sense what lay beyond the visible.

A sudden rumble, like distant thunder, reverberated through the mountains. Gunnar's head snapped up, his eyes narrowing as he scanned the horizon, muscles tensing in readiness. The sound was out of place in the still, hot air, sending a shiver down his spine.

"We are not alone," Thalirion said, his voice a low growl that seemed to vibrate with the earth beneath their feet. His eyes glowed brighter, confirming what Gunnar already suspected. "A patrol of Drogo soldiers approaches."

Elara's face hardened, her lips pressing into a thin line. "We need to move. Now." There was no fear in her voice, only a steely determination that Gunnar found infectious. He tightened his grip on his axe, readying himself for the confrontation that seemed inevitable.

They turned to descend the ridge, urgency propelling their steps, but it was as if the mountains themselves conspired against them. From behind the rocks, heavily armored Drogo emerged, their scales gleaming malevolently in the harsh sunlight. The leader, a towering figure with scales the color of molten gold, stepped forward, his eyes burning with an almost palpable malice.

"Seize them!" he barked, his voice echoing off the rocky crags, and the soldiers surged forward, weapons drawn and intent clear.

Gunnar's heart pounded, adrenaline surging through his veins. He drew his axe, the familiar weight a comfort amidst the chaos. "Elara, stay behind us. Thalirion, can you hold them off?"

Thalirion nodded, his hands already weaving intricate patterns in the air. A barrier of shimmering light formed between them and the advancing soldiers, but Gunnar knew it wouldn't hold for long. He could see the strain on Thalirion's face, the beads of sweat forming on his brow. He was getting visibly weaker here with the weak aura in Vellhor.

The Drogo crashed against the barrier, their claws and weapons sparking off the magical shield. Thalirion's concentration was absolute, but even he had limits. "I can't maintain this for long," he warned, his voice strained.

Gunnar tightened his grip on his axe, his muscles coiling in anticipation. "On my signal, drop the barrier."

Thalirion nodded again, his eyes never leaving the enemy. Gunnar took a deep breath, his heart thundering in his chest. "Now!"

The barrier flickered, sputtering like a dying flame, and

then vanished, leaving them bare to the storm. Gunnar's roar tore through the chaos, primal, fueled by a mixture of rage and desperation. He surged forward, axe raised, the weight of it familiar in his grip, as if it was an extension of himself. The first Drogo came at him, but Gunnar's axe met him with savage force, splitting armor and bone in a brutal arc. The impact jolted through his body, his muscles screaming, but there was no room for pain. Not now. Not when so much was at stake.

He felt the battle magic coil around him, slowing the world to a crawl. Every heartbeat stretched into eternity, each movement of the enemy telegraphed before it even began. It was a gift, this clarity, but a curse too—because it never lasted long enough.

The Drogo pressed in, but Gunnar saw them coming. He swung his axe with precision, cleaving through another soldier, feeling the sickening crunch of bone beneath the weight of his strike. Blood sprayed, hot and thick, covering his face and hands, but it was the faces of his comrades that grounded him. Thalirion, magic crackling at his fingertips, sent bolts of energy tearing through the enemy ranks with deadly accuracy. Elara, all grace and fury, danced among the Drogo like a whirlwind, her staff slamming into the ground, sending tremors through the earth. The Drogo stumbled, and she moved in for the kill.

But even as he fought, it was Anwyn who filled his mind. Her pale face, always just out of reach. A ghost that haunted his every swing, his every breath. She was why he was here. She was the reason none of this could go wrong.

Gunnar's magic kept him ahead of the fight—until it didn't. Time, once his ally, began to speed up again, and the Drogo came faster, more desperate. His muscles burned, the weight of his axe growing heavier with each strike. One enemy swung a sword at him, faster than expected. Gunnar blocked, barely, the clash of steel reverberating through his arm. His grip faltered for a split second. The Drogo pressed in, their ferocity unmatched, their sheer numbers overwhelming. Gunnar grunted, forcing his blade back into play, carving through another foe, but the exhaustion was creeping in, the cracks in his armor growing wider with every breath.

He spared a glance at Thalirion, his magic flickering, fading. The mage was pushing too hard, trying to hold the line. Gunnar's heart pounded—if Thalirion fell, they all did. He gritted his teeth, slamming his axe down onto the shoulder of a charging Drogo, the impact jarring, a reminder that his own strength was ebbing. They were running out of time.

But they couldn't stop. Not with the elixir so close. Not with Anwyn's life hanging by a thread. Not when everything he loved could slip through his fingers if he let up for even a second.

His movements became more desperate, each swing of his axe fueled by something rawer than determination. Fear. It gnawed at him, whispered in his ear, made every miss feel like a failure that would cost him everything. His breath came in ragged gasps, his body aching, but he fought on, because there was no other choice.

Thalirion, face pale and drenched in sweat, gathered what remained of his strength and unleashed a final burst of magic. The wave of force rippled through the battlefield, sending the remaining Drogo flying, their bodies hitting the ground with sickening thuds.

Gunnar seized the moment, raising his axe one last time. It came down heavy, cleaving through the last attacker, the impact shaking him to his core. Then, silence. The battlefield lay still, the only sound their labored breathing, the weight of what they had just survived hanging in the air like a fog.

Gunnar's chest heaved as he wiped the blood from his axe. His eyes swept over the carnage, searching for any sign of lingering danger, but finding none. His legs trembled beneath him, the exhaustion finally settling in, but he forced himself to stay upright. They had survived—barely.

He couldn't help but glance at Thalirion, at Elara—they were alive and he was grateful. But in his mind, it was Anwyn's face that lingered, always reminding him of what was still at risk.

"Is everyone alright?" His voice was rough, strained.

Elara nodded, though her face was pale. "We need to move. More could be coming."

Thalirion, his magic spent, leaned heavily on his staff. "Agreed. We can't stay here."

They resumed their journey, the weight of their task pressing down on them more heavily than before. Gunnar's thoughts drifted back to Anwyn, and his resolve hardened. They had overcome this obstacle, but many more lay ahead. They would need every ounce of strength and determination to succeed.

Ruiha

In the grim aftermath of the assault on Hammer, the halls reeked of blood and burnt flesh. Shadows flickered in the dim light, casting eerie patterns on the cold stone walls. Ruiha, her eyes sharp and determined, stalked through the desolate cells. Each creak of metal and each muffled groan from the wounded fueled her urgency, her heart pounding like a drum in her chest.

"Kemp!" she called, her voice echoing off the damp stone. The silence that answered her only intensified the dread gnawing at her insides. The Snow Wolves, fierce and unyielding, had taken many hostages, but Kemp was nowhere to be found. Her mind raced, each second heightening her desperation. She had to find him—had to save him.

Dakarai moved silently beside her. His reptilian eyes scanned the cells, his presence a steadying force amidst the chaos. "Ruiha, over here," he rumbled, his voice low and gravelly.

She hurried over, her boots splashing in the puddles of blood and grime. A group of prisoners huddled in the corner of a dingy cell, their eyes wide with fear and exhaustion. Ruiha's gaze hardened. They would talk. They had to.

"Where is he?" she demanded, her voice a blade cutting through the air. The prisoners exchanged terrified glances, their reluctance evident.

Dakarai stepped forward, his massive frame casting a shadow over them. "You heard her. Speak."

One of the prisoners, a scrawny Drogo with a bloodied face, whimpered. "They took him—the shamans—we don't know where!"

Ruiha's patience snapped. She grabbed the Drogo by his collar. "You're lying," she hissed, her eyes blazing with fury. "Tell me where, or you'll wish you had."

The man trembled, his resolve crumbling under her intense gaze. "I swear, I don't know!" he cried. "Please, don't—"

Dakarai placed his hand on Ruiha's back, his touch a grounding force against the storm of her rage. She exhaled, the breath shuddering through her, and released her grip on the prisoner. Her hands trembled, a mix of anger and frustration coursing through her veins like poison.

"These prisoners know nothing, Ruiha. We're better off interrogating the guards the Snow Wolves took hostage," Dakarai said quietly.

Ruiha nodded, her eyes cold and resolute. She turned and marched toward the cells holding the Drogo hostages. Each step echoed with purpose, the sound bouncing off the stone walls like the tolling of a death knell.

As she approached, Torain held out his hand hesitantly. "Ruiha," he began, his voice steady but betraying a flicker of unease in his eyes. "You can't just come here; you need to speak to the commander first."

Before she could retort with a sharp comment or worse, Uleg intervened, his hand lowering Torain's arm. Relief flashed across Torain's eyes.

"Lad, let her pass. She's on our side," Uleg said softly.

"Aye, Uleg, I know. Just doing my job, is all."

"I know, lad. Now, let her through."

With a nod of thanks, Ruiha marched past the two Dwarven soldiers. She moved with the grace of a predator, her eyes fixed on her prey.

The first hostage she approached was slumped in the corner, his eyes narrowing into a sneer as she neared. Without hesitation, she kicked him in the jaw, the sound of bone against boot echoing through the cell. He sprawled onto the floor, groaning in pain. Ruiha leaned down, gripping his collar and yanking him up until they were eye to eye.

"You think this is a game?" she hissed, her voice dripping with venom. Her grip tightened, the prisoner's breath coming in ragged gasps.

"Dakarai, hold him," she commanded.

Dakarai's massive hands clamped onto the prisoner, holding him immobile like a vice. Ruiha drew her daggers, the blades catching the dim light and glinting wickedly.

"You'll talk," Ruiha said, her voice cold and merciless, "or you'll bleed."

The other hostages watched in mounting terror as Ruiha set to her grim task. Their eyes widened, breaths hitching in collective dread, the flickering torchlight casting long, twisted shadows on the walls. Ruiha's hands moved with practiced precision, the gleaming daggers slicing through flesh and muscle with sickening ease. Each cut, each deliberate slice, elicited screams that echoed through the dungeon, bouncing off the cold stone walls and reverberating into the dark recesses beyond.

The prisoner's pleas for mercy fell on deaf ears. Ruiha's determination hardened with every pained cry that tore from his throat. Her face was a mask of cold resolve, each stroke of her blade an assertion of her unyielding will. Blood flowed freely, a crimson river that pooled on the floor, soaking into the cracks between the stones. She felt the warmth of it on her hands, the metallic scent mingling with the damp, musty air, but her heart remained as cold and unfeeling as the steel she wielded.

"Please—no more," the prisoner whimpered, his voice raw and broken. "I'll tell you—anything—just—stop."

Ruiha paused, her dagger poised above the Drogo's trembling form. She leaned in close, her breath hot against his ear. "You should have thought of that before," she hissed, her voice dripping with disdain. "But it's too late for mercy now."

She drove the blade into his shoulder, the wet crunch of muscle and bone eliciting another guttural scream. The hostages recoiled, some turning their heads away, others transfixed by the brutal spectacle. Ruiha's eyes never left the prisoner's face, watching the pain twist his features, the fear dilate his pupils.

"Now... where is he?" she snarled, her voice a growl that cut through the prisoner's wails. She twisted the dagger, and his scream turned into a choked sob.

"The Tomb—the Tomb of Nergai!" he finally broke, his resolve crumbling under the relentless agony. Tears mingled with the blood on his face, his voice a broken whisper. "They said they were taking him to the Tomb of Nergai!"

Ruiha stepped back, her breathing steady and controlled, the adrenaline still surging through her veins. She wiped the blood from her daggers with a cold efficiency, the motion almost ritualistic. The blades gleamed once more, a symbol of her unwavering purpose.

She looked down at the broken Drogo before her, his body trembling with the aftershocks of pain. A malicious smile curled her lips, a dark satisfaction gleaming in her eyes. "See? That wasn't so hard."

For a moment, she allowed herself to feel the victory, the sense of control. But it was fleeting. The path ahead was still fraught with danger, and the thought of Kemp suffering in the hands of their enemies gnawed at her. She turned to Dakarai, her resolve solidified, her heart a fortress against the horrors she had just inflicted. "We need to move. Now."

As they left the cells, the sounds of the prisoners' cries faded behind them, but the memory of their grim work lingered. Ruiha felt no remorse, only a relentless drive to find Kemp and make their enemies pay. The darkness of the Tomb of Nergai awaited them, but Ruiha was ready to face it head-on, her heart steeled for the brutality to come.

They found Karl in the war room, hunched over the table that bore the scars of countless strategies. Maps and plans lay scattered across its surface, a testament to the chaos of their recent assault. Ruiha strode in, her urgency palpable.

"Karl, we need to get to the Tomb of Nergai. Kemp is there."

Karl's eyes, a deep well of contemplation, met hers. "Are you certain?"

"Certain enough to risk it," Ruiha replied, her voice steady despite the turmoil within. "We can't leave him in their hands."

Karl's gaze lingered on her, weighing the gravity of her words. "I'll need to discuss this with Magnus first."

"Karl," Ruiha's voice trembled, a mix of frustration and desperation. "We can't delay!"

Karl raised a calming hand, his bushy red beard swaying slightly with the movement. "I agree, Ruiha," he said softly, his voice a soothing balm. "But Magnus is the general. Ultimately, it's his call."

Ruiha's fists clenched and she gritted her teeth ready for a harsh retort. Dakarai stepped forward, placing a hand on her shoulder, a silent plea for patience. She let out a deep sigh, her shoulders sagging with frustration. With a curt nod, she turned on her heel, her movements sharp and precise, and stormed off. She dropped onto a stone bench, yanking out her daggers and furiously picking at the grime under her nails, each scrape a testament to her simmering anger.

Minutes stretched into what felt like hours before Magnus finally arrived. His presence filled the room, his face a mask of unyielding determination. He surveyed the room, his eyes lingering on the maps before fixing on Karl.

Ruiha stood and immediately informed Magnus of Kemp's whereabouts.

"If Kemp is at the Tomb of Nergai, we have no choice but to go after him," Magnus said, his voice a low rumble that brooked no argument. "We can't let the shamans keep him."

Ruiha looked up, her eyes flashing. "Then let's move. Every moment we waste, Kemp suffers."

Magnus nodded, his expression serious, the weight of the

situation evident in his tired eyes. "Prepare a small team."

As they discussed the logistics of their plan, Thraxos entered the room, his imposing figure nearly filling the doorway. His horns caught the torchlight, casting intricate shadows, and his eyes held a mix of wisdom and urgency. He waited patiently at the side, his attention focused on their conversation, clearly eager for any update regarding Kemp. Ruiha knew that Thraxos had been Kemp's mentor in Nexus. Without Thraxos's help, Kemp would have surely perished. She felt a surge of gratitude toward him.

When their plans were finally laid out, Thraxos stepped forward, his presence seeming to grow even larger. "I found the tome Elara spoke of," he said, raising a weathered book. "The Elixir of Elysian Blossoms."

Magnus nodded. "I'll keep it safe until I can deliver it to Gunnar. We can't afford to lose it now."

Thraxos's gaze shifted to Ruiha. "I'll go with you to find Kemp. My magic will help."

Ruiha felt a surge of relief. With Thraxos by their side, their chances of success increased. "Thank you, Thraxos."

Ruiha watched as the departure plans took shape. Karl, understanding the gravity of the situation, rallied a small team of Snow Wolves. She admired his swift efficiency, knowing the journey to the Tomb of Nergai would be treacherous, filled with unknown dangers and dark magic. But they were determined. Kemp needed them, and Ruiha felt a resolute determination settle over her. They would not fail him.

22

Broken Bones, Unbroken Will

"You might be broken, but in every piece lies the courage to keep going."

Kemp

Kemp's cell door groaned open, a sickly echo reverberating through the chamber as pale light sliced into the oppressive darkness. The silhouette that filled the doorway was tall and gaunt, cloaked in furs and bone trinkets that clinked with every movement. The shaman's eyes glinted with a feral intelligence, the fire of madness dancing within them. Kemp squinted against the sudden brightness, his mind a battlefield of swirling darkness and fractured hope.

With deliberate steps, the shaman approached, the collar around Kemp's neck thrumming in response. He could feel the malicious energy of the Dragon Crown intertwining with his thoughts, whispering insidious promises of power and ruin. Kemp clenched his fists, fingernails digging into his palms, the pain a lifeline to sanity.

"You resist," the shaman's voice was a rasp, as dry and cold as the grave. "But resistance is futile. The Crown speaks to you, does it not? It beckons you to surrender."

Kemp's throat was parched, his voice a mere croak. "You'll get nothing from me."

The shaman's lips curled into a sneer. "We shall see."

Two Drogo guards emerged from the shadows, seizing Kemp's arms and hauling him to his feet. His shadow hand was extinguished and limp, the collar having drained its power. His legs buckled, muscles atrophied from disuse, but they dragged him forward through the doorway and into a corridor lined with flickering torches. The heat was oppressive, the air thick with the scent of burnt herbs and blood.

They led him to a chamber deep within the bowels of the earth, where a circle of Drogo shamans awaited, their faces painted with gruesome designs, eyes glimmering with malice. In the center of the room was a slab of stone etched with runes that pulsed with a sickly purple light. Kemp was thrown onto the slab, his limbs bound with leather straps. The stone was cold against his skin, a chilling contrast to the feverish heat of the chamber.

The lead shaman stepped forward, the jagged obsidian blade in his hand catching the dim torchlight. His smile was thin, predatory. "We will extract the knowledge you hide," he said, voice dripping with cruel certainty. "The Crown has marked you, bound itself to your soul. Its secrets are in you now, and we will have them."

Kemp's heart thudded in his chest, each beat a hammer against his ribs. His pulse felt like it was trying to escape his body, but there was nowhere to go. The room was too small, too suffocating, the air thick with the copper tang of blood and the musty scent of damp stone. The coldness of the slab beneath him seeped through his bones, its rough surface biting into his back as the leather restraints pulled tight against his wrists and ankles.

The shaman began to chant, a low, guttural rumble that crawled under Kemp's skin, making every hair on his body stand on end. Kemp watched as his lips twitched in a twisted mockery of a smile, as if the anticipation was the sweetest part of it all. The blade wasn't meant to cut, not yet. Instead, the shaman pressed the knife's cold edge to Kemp's bare chest, teasing along the surface of his skin with unbearable slowness.

It wasn't the pain that hit first. No, it was the waiting, the knowing. Kemp's breath caught in his throat as the cold tip of the obsidian traced delicate patterns across his chest, a cruel caress that promised agony. He could almost imagine the blade sinking into him, ripping him open, but the shaman was toying with him. Dragging it out. Making him beg for the pain, because the waiting—Gods, the waiting was worse.

Then it came. Sharp, brutal. His body jerked instinctively, a gasp ripping from his throat, but the restraints held firm.

This was just the beginning.

They forced a vile concoction down his throat, the thick liquid burning as it slid down into his stomach. It felt like fire, a slow, corrosive burn that started deep within and spread outward, lighting every nerve on fire. Kemp gagged, his body convulsing as the foul brew took hold. It was as if his insides had been doused in acid, his throat raw and burning. His vision swam, the room spinning as he tried to blink away the pain.

But the shamans didn't blink. They watched him, unblinking, their eyes alight with a sadistic curiosity, like they were watching a fascinating insect squirming under a magnifying glass. The convulsions wracked his body, his muscles straining against the leather straps. They hadn't even started properly, and already Kemp could feel his mind teetering on the edge.

The Crown. It pulsed within him now, an ugly presence that throbbed in time with his heartbeat. Dark, twisted visions unfurled in his mind, ripping through his thoughts like a tornado. He saw the Dragon Crown, wreathed in flames so dark they seemed to consume the light. It sat upon a throne of skulls—Human, Dwarven and Elven skulls—its voice a thousand whispers merging into one. *Give in. Surrender.*

Kemp grit his teeth, his jaw clenched so tight it felt like it might shatter. He couldn't give in. He wouldn't. He thought of Ruiha, of her fierce defiance, her determination burning hotter than any fire. If she could keep fighting, so could he.

The shamans smeared his skin with oils, slick and viscous, their touch burning like acid. The air was thick with smoke, the pungent smell of the oils choking him. His skin sizzled where they touched, the heat unbearable, but worse was the sound—the quiet, insidious crackle of his own flesh burning.

"Tell us," the lead shaman hissed, his voice a razor slicing through the haze of pain. "Tell us the secrets of the Crown."

Kemp blinked through the blood and sweat dripping into his eyes. "Fuck. You."

The shaman's eyes blazed with fury. "Then you will break."

The needle came next—thin, sharp, made of bone. It pierced his skin with a soft, sickening *pop*, and Kemp's entire body seized. Pain shot through him like lightning, a jolt that left his vision white for a moment before fading to a dull roar. But the worst part was how precise it was. The needle dug into the exact nerve that sent pain arcing through his limbs, lighting him up like a storm in his own skin.

"Feel that?" The shaman's voice was almost tender, a lover's whisper in the dark. "That's where it begins."

More needles, each one worse than the last, each one finding a new way to tear him apart from the inside. He could barely breathe, the air sucked from his lungs as each fresh stab sent shockwaves of agony through his body. The Crown's darkness roared in his mind, louder and louder, pushing him toward the edge.

But Kemp clung to the image of Ruiha, her face clear and strong, her voice the only anchor in the storm. She would find him. She always did. And she would kill anyone in her way.

Then the creatures came—nightmarish, twisted things that clawed at the edges of his sanity. They weren't real. Not fully. But that didn't stop the fear from gnawing at his mind as they circled him, their grotesque forms flickering in and out of focus. They whispered to him, their voices soft and seductive, promising release, promising power.

But Kemp wasn't ready to break. Not yet. His body screamed, his soul teetered on the brink, but somewhere deep inside, that stubborn spark still burned. *The shamans couldn't have that. Not that.*

They might strip him of his strength, his sanity, but they would never have his soul.

The shaman's voice slithered through the fog of pain. "Tell us."

Kemp spat blood, his grin feral. "I—said—fuck y—."

The shaman sneered. "Then suffer."

And suffer he did. But in the darkest depths of agony, Kemp found something else: hope. The memory of Ruiha, of Dakarai, of his mentor Thraxos and their unwavering strength, became his lifeline, the only thing holding him together. He imagined Ruiha charging through the doors, knives flashing, her rage a storm.

She was coming. He knew it. The shamans could do their worst, but they wouldn't break him. Not while that hope burned within him.

He would not surrender. Not to the shamans. Not to the Crown. And especially not to the darkness. As long as he could still draw breath, he would fight.

23

Of Shadows and Sacrifice

"In the end, it's not the fight that wears you down, but the love that makes you keep fighting long after the blood's dried."

Gunnar

The heat of the Scorched Mountains continued to weigh heavily on Gunnar, Elara, and Thalirion as they moved with a renewed urgency. They had collected the final ingredient for the Elixir of Elysian Blossoms, and now it was time to contact Magnus and ensure the next step of their journey.

Elara led the way, her steps unwavering despite the harsh conditions. Gunnar followed closely, his axe at the ready, while Thalirion, despite his exhaustion, maintained a vigilant watch. The path before them was treacherous, but their determination was unshakeable.

When they reached a relatively sheltered spot among the rocks, Gunnar stopped and pulled out the SLS. Holding it carefully, he activated the power within. Magnus's voice crackled through.

"Gunnar, is that you?"

"Aye, Magnus," Gunnar replied. "We have all the elements for the elixir. Are you ready on your end?"

Magnus's voice held a mix of relief and urgency. "Yes, we've found the tome."

Gunnar's heart lifted at the news. "We're on our way," he said, glancing at Elara and Thalirion. "Let's move."

The journey back to Hammer was a grueling race against time, each step filled with the knowledge that Anwyn's life hung in the balance. Despite their weariness, they pressed on, driven by the flicker of hope Magnus's message had ignited.

Upon their arrival in Hammer, the town felt like a vision from a nightmare. Smoke billowed from burning buildings, and the air was thick with the scent of ash and blood. Drogo peasants scurried through the streets, their faces etched with fear and despair.

As Gunnar, Elara, and Thalirion approached, they saw Magnus waiting for them at the entrance to the Guild. He was flanked by heavily armed guards, their weapons drawn and eyes surveying their surroundings.

"Magnus." Gunnar nodded. His voice was filled with pride at his little brothers achievements.

Magnus's lips curled into a smile. "Welcome," he said. "Hammer is under new management now."

Elara stepped forward. "Magnus," she began, "we must head straight to the Apothecary's Laboratory."

Elara

The Apothecary's lab was lined with jars of exotic herbs and vials of mysterious liquids surrounding a central stone table where the tome lay open.

Elara hovered over the ancient tome, her fingertips barely grazing its worn pages. The weight of the world pressed down on her shoulders, and for a moment, she let herself feel it—the crushing responsibility of everything that lay ahead. She closed her eyes, drew in a sharp breath, then snapped them open. There was no time for fear.

"Alright," she said, her voice steady but low, the kind of calm that held panic beneath the surface. "We need to be extremely careful. This process is more than just delicate—it's dangerous. One wrong move..." She didn't need to finish. The consequences were written in the tension between them all.

Thalirion stepped forward, close enough that his presence grounded her, a steady force against the rising tide of her nerves. His gaze held hers, unwavering. "I'm here, Elara. What do you need me to do?"

She swallowed, her heart hammering against her chest, and gestured toward the vibrant red petals laid out before her. "First, the Firebloom. Grind them to a fine powder. No coarser than dust." Her voice cracked with the pressure of time slipping away, but she pushed the emotion down, buried it deep.

Thalirion's hands moved with purpose as he picked up the mortar and pestle, his jaw set in that determined way of his. The sound of the petals breaking apart echoed in the chamber, too loud in the thick silence. Gunnar stood on the edge of the room, his body tense, as if ready for battle, even though the fight ahead was far more dangerous than blades and blood.

"The potency fades quickly," Elara murmured, her eyes on Thalirion's hands as they worked with deliberate care. "We need to move fast, but..." her breath caught, "not too fast."

Thalirion gave her a small, firm nod, his brow furrowed in concentration. She watched him, and for a fleeting moment, she wasn't focused on the elixir, the ritual, or the stakes. It was him—his steady breathing, the way he trusted her without question. And gods, did she need that right now.

The scent of the herbs thickened the air, sharp and almost bitter, like the weight of their situation. Her fingers twitched, anxious to finish the task, to save Anwyn, but Thalirion's calm steadied her once more.

"Next," Elara said, pushing through the swell of emotions. Her voice dropped, almost too quiet. "The essence of Nightshade. Just a single drop."

The vial was heavier in her hand than it had any right to be, its dark liquid shifting ominously inside. She hesitated for the briefest second—if her hand slipped, if they miscalculated even a little, this would end in death, not salvation.

She handed it to Thalirion, their fingers brushing for the smallest of moments. He took it carefully, his eyes locked on hers before carefully tipping the vial. The single drop fell like the weight of their mission, landing with a soft hiss as the elixir bubbled, blue smoke curling upward.

Elara's breath caught, her heart thudding in her chest. "No more," she warned, the words tight. "Anything more, and we'll have failed."

The room was silent except for the low gurgling of the elixir, and every second felt like a heartbeat too loud in her ears. Gunnar's eyes darted around, tension radiating off him in waves. Elara knew that he could feel it too—that tightening pressure, as if their time was running out faster than they could keep up.

"Lastly," Elara whispered, her throat dry, "the scales of the Moon Serpent. Grind them to dust. Add them slowly."

Thalirion moved with the grace of a seasoned alchemist, and Elara couldn't help but watch the way his hands worked—how calm he remained despite the storm raging around them. The scales shimmered as they crushed beneath his touch, a strange, ethereal glow lighting the chamber.

Her hands shook as she stirred the mixture, her movements slower now, measured. The elixir began to glow, pulsing softly with each stir. It was beautiful and terrifying all at once, like the fragility of hope wrapped in the thinnest of glass.

"It's ready," she whispered, her voice a thin thread of relief mixed with fear. But there was no triumph, no joy. Only the harsh reminder that this was just the beginning.

Thalirion let out a long breath beside her. "We need to leave now," he said, his voice low, edged with urgency. His eyes caught hers again, and in them, she saw the unspoken truth: Anwyn was running out of time.

Gunnar's voice broke the silence, rough but steady. "Gather your things. The journey to Draegoor is difficult. We'll need all the strength we can muster."

Elara felt a weight settle in her chest, heavier than before. This was more than just a mission now. It was everything. Thalirion met her gaze one last time before they turned to prepare, she saw it in his eyes. The pressure, the fear, the hope—they were all tied to this one moment, and the bond between them had never felt more fragile or more powerful.

As they dispersed, Elara took a moment, her eyes lingering on the glowing elixir. Her hands shook as she released the spoon. This was it. The fate of Anwyn—of all of them—hung in the balance. There was no room for failure.

But in the quiet stillness of the room, as the shadows lengthened and the glow of the elixir faded, she allowed herself a single thought: We will make it. Because they had to.

Gunnar

The journey back to Draegoor was a harrowing trek through hostile territory, but the stakes left no room for hesitation. The landscape grew more treacherous with every step, the air thick with the oppressive heat and sulfurous fumes from the Scorched Mountains.

As they approached Anwyn's bedchamber, the weight of their task pressed down upon them like an iron cloak. The city bustled with life around them, a stark contrast to Gunnar's somber mood.

Inside the chamber, Anwyn lay motionless in her bed, encircled by runes. Her skin was pale, and her breaths came shallow and infrequent.

Elara stepped forward, holding the elixir carefully. "We must begin the ritual," she said, her voice steady despite the tension.

Gunnar nodded, and Elara opened the tome, reading the incantation aloud. The air around them crackled with energy, the runes glowing in response to the ancient words. Elara knelt beside Anwyn, her hands steady as she dripped the elixir onto Anwyn's lips, each drop infused with their hopes and fears.

As the elixir touched Anwyn's lips, the runes flared brightly, casting an intense glow. Gunnar and Thalirion exchanged frantic glances as the heat seemed to intensify, the air thick with the acrid scent of burning wood.

"Gunnar, you must drink the remainder of the elixir," Elara said, her voice firm yet gentle.

Gunnar's eyes locked onto the vial, his hand reaching out. But before he could grasp it, Elara's voice cut through the chaos.

"I must warn you," she said, her gaze steady. "This will only work if you truly love Anwyn. If not—"

Without a moment's hesitation, Gunnar seized the glowing elixir and drank it in one gulp. As the warmth spread through him, he looked up to find Elara watching him with a soft, empathetic smile.

"Now reach out to her with your spirit," Elara instructed. "Try to make a connection with her spirit."

Doubt flickered in Gunnar's mind. Flashes of his failed attempts to bond with Havoc and connect to the aura in Nexus overwhelmed him. Panic surged, and he glanced at Thalirion, seeking reassurance.

The old Elf stepped forward, placing a steadying hand on Gunnar's shoulder. "You can do this, Gunnar," Thalirion intoned, his voice a calm anchor in the storm. "Relax and connect to the aura. Your love for her will make it easier than you think."

Thalirion's calm smile bolstered Gunnar's resolve. He closed his eyes, banishing thoughts of past failures, and instead focused on the challenges he had overcome. Reaching out to the aura, he felt the familiar surge of euphoria.

Minutes passed as he grappled with how to project his spirit from his core. Then, it dawned on him—it was simpler than he'd imagined. His was trying to control his spirit, contain it almost, but he realized, it felt bound to Anwyn, eager to reunite with her kindred essence. He simply released it, and it enveloped her.

A warm light surrounded Anwyn, and for a brief moment, everything was still. Then, with a final, thunderous crash, the light faded, leaving Anwyn lying motionless, her skin now a healthy color.

"Anwyn?" Gunnar whispered, hope and fear battling in his chest.

Slowly, Anwyn's eyes fluttered open, a spark of life rekindling within them. She looked up at Gunnar, her voice weak but unmistakably hers. "Gunnar…"

Relief washed over Gunnar, his knees buckling as he knelt beside her. "You're back," he murmured, tears streaming down his cheeks and disappearing into his beard.

Anwyn's hand reached up, touching his face gently. "I never left," she whispered, her voice gaining strength.

Elara stepped forward, her expression a mix of exhaustion and triumph. "The bond is true," she said softly. "You've done it."

Gunnar's heart swelled with gratitude and relief, but he knew this was only the beginning. There were questions to answer, threats to face, and a kingdom still in peril. But for now, in this fleeting moment of victory, he allowed himself to simply feel.

Thalirion placed a hand on Gunnar's shoulder, his eyes filled with a quiet pride. "Rest now, both of you. There will be time for battles and quests. Tonight, you have earned your peace."

As the room settled into a serene quiet, Gunnar held Anwyn close, feeling the steady rhythm of her breath. He knew that whatever came next, they would face it together.

And for the first time in a long while, the future didn't seem quite so daunting.

Ruiha

Ruiha tightened the straps on her gear as their small team prepared to leave the relative safety of Hammer. The subterranean air was cold and damp, the weight of the earth pressing down on them from all sides. She glanced at the faces of her companions: Dakarai, silent but determined; Thraxos, his imposing form a reassuring presence; Karl, whose leadership had never been more crucial; Uleg, the old Dwarf with eyes still as sharp as a hawk's;

and Torain, the young warrior whose loyalty was unquestionable.

Ruiha's mind churned with worry and self-doubt. The responsibility of her decisions weighed heavily on her, the stakes higher than they had ever been. She had to save Kemp, but fear of failure gnawed at her confidence. What if she led them all to their deaths and could not save Kemp? She shook the thoughts away, reminding herself that worry only darkens the light of hope.

"Everyone ready?" Karl's voice cut through her thoughts, firm and commanding.

"Ready," Ruiha replied, trying to sound more confident than she felt.

Their journey began with a swift march through the labyrinthine tunnels that stretched beneath the Scorched Mountains. The path was lit by flickering torches, casting long, eerie shadows on the rough-hewn walls. Every sound echoed off the stone, amplifying the crunch of their footsteps and the occasional drip of water from above.

Ruiha kept her senses alert, every rustle in the darkened corners setting her on edge. They moved in a tight formation, with Uleg and Torain scouting ahead, their keen eyes scanning for any signs of danger. It wasn't long before Uleg raised a hand, signaling them to halt.

"What is it?" Ruiha whispered, moving up to his position.

Uleg pointed to a set of tracks in the dust. "These aren't natural," he said, his voice low. "Something's been following us."

A chill ran down Ruiha's spine. She had to stay strong, but the constant pressure gnawed at her resolve. "Keep moving," she ordered. "But stay alert."

As they pressed on, the terrain grew more challenging. Narrow tunnels forced them to squeeze through tight spaces, while underground rivers blocked their path, requiring them to wade through icy water. The air grew thicker with every step, laden with the musty scent of earth and the faint tang of sulfur.

Thraxos moved to the front, his eyes glowing faintly as he muttered incantations under his breath. The ground before them shimmered, revealing hidden traps and ancient wards designed to deter intruders. With a wave of his hand, Thraxos dispelled the dangers, clearing a path for the group.

"Without Thraxos, we wouldn't stand a chance," Ruiha thought, her gratitude for the Sage growing with each passing obstacle. She marveled at his magical prowess, a testament to countless years of study and practice.

Hours turned into days, and the journey took its toll on the group. They navigated perilous drops where a single misstep could mean falling into an abyss. They climbed jagged rock faces that tore at their hands and feet. All the while, the sense of being watched never left them.

One night, as they made camp in a small cavern, Dakarai approached Ruiha. "I don't like this," he said, his voice barely above a whisper. "We're being herded."

Ruiha frowned. "Herded? By what?"

"I'm not sure," Dakarai admitted, "but something wants us to follow this path."

Ruiha remained silent, giving his words some thought. She couldn't pinpoint anything in particular that was wrong about the journey, but she'd also had an imposing sense of dread since they left Hammer. Her instincts, honed as they were, were rarely wrong.

The next morning confirmed Dakarai's fears. They found themselves at the entrance of a vast underground chasm, the only feasible route forward. The ceiling loomed high above, disappearing into darkness. As they entered, the temperature dropped, and an eerie silence settled over them.

Halfway through the chasm, a sudden rumble echoed off the walls. Before they could react, the ground beneath them gave way, and they fell into a hidden chamber below.

Ruiha hit the ground hard, the wind knocked out of her. She scrambled to her feet, taking stock of their situation. They were in a vast subterranean hall, its walls lined with ancient runes that glowed faintly in the dim light.

Thraxos stood, brushing off the dust. "This is no accident," he said grimly. "We've been led here."

Karl unsheathed his axe, the intricate runes etched along the blade gleaming with a soft green light. "Stay together. We don't know what's down here." His voice was steady and authoritative.

As they moved deeper into the massive hall, the air grew thick with an oppressive energy. Strange whispers echoed off the walls, and shadows seemed to move just beyond the edge of their vision.

Suddenly, a figure stepped out from the darkness, clad in dark robes and carrying a staff that crackled with arcane power. "Welcome," he said, his rasping voice grating on Ruiha's ears like nails on slate. "I've traveled far to find you." He smiled, and Ruiha saw his skeletal face, skin stretched thin like parchment over jagged bone. His eye sockets were deep, hollow pits, glowing with a cold, unsettling light. Teeth, yellowed and sharp, grinned back at her, a grotesque parody of a living face.

Ruiha drew her daggers, her eyes narrowing. "Who are you?"

The figure cackled. "I am Chronos, Keeper of Crystals from the Forgotten Realm. I bring a warning."

The group tensed, but Ruiha gestured for them to listen. "What warning?" she asked, suspicion and curiosity warring in her voice.

"Nergai seeks to consume the Human you know as Kemp,"

Chronos said, his voice echoing with the weight of his message. "Kemp is the perfect sacrifice to resurrect Nergai. You must act quickly."

Dakarai, his hammer poised and ready, asked suspiciously, "Why are you telling us this? What do you have to gain?"

Chronos let out a harsh, rasping laugh that made Ruiha wince. She had to visibly restrain herself from covering her ears. "I do not wish for Nergai to walk this realm. It would be—inconvenient for me," he replied cryptically, his voice echoing with an otherworldly resonance.

Karl stepped forward, his expression stern and unyielding. "Then, how do we stop this?"

Chronos reached into his robes and produced a shimmering crystal, its surface swirling with mystical energy. "This crystal will transport you directly to the Tomb of Nergai. Use it wisely. Time is of the essence."

Thraxos took the crystal, examining it with trepidation. His fingers traced the intricate runes, understanding the powerful magic within.

Chronos nodded, his gaze settling on each of them. "Good luck," he said before fading back into the shadows.

Ruiha turned to her companions, her determination renewed. "Everyone, gather around. It's time to end this."

The group huddled close as Thraxos activated the crystal. A bright light enveloped them, and the world around them shifted, the walls of the cavern dissolving into a whirl of colors and energy.

When the light faded, they stood at the entrance of the Tomb of Nergai. The air was heavy with an oppressive energy that pressed down on them, thick with foreboding.

Gasping for breath, Ruiha took in their surroundings. This was the place where she had first been separated from Kemp, the memory still a raw wound in her mind. She tightened her grip on her daggers, determination hardening her resolve.

"Kemp is waiting. We can't stop now," she said, her voice steady despite the tumultuous memories.

With a collective nod, the group pressed on, their resolve like steel. They would face whatever came next together.

24

Bound by Shadow, Freed by Love

"In the face of ancient evil, it's not the blade that wins the day, but the hearts that refuse to break under the weight of sacrifice."

Ruiha

The air inside the Tomb of Nergai clung to Ruiha's lungs like a shroud, thick with the choking incense and the acrid stench of fresh blood. She struggled to keep her breath steady, each inhale a conscious effort. Shadows, cast by flickering torches, danced malevolently over the black dragon-shaped stone coffin etched with countless runes. The sight of Kemp hanging suspended over it, chains clinking softly as he swayed in and out of consciousness, gnawed at her insides. She couldn't let her fear show; her team depended on her resolve. Below him, several Drogo shaman chanted in their guttural language, a hypnotic rise and fall that seemed to reverberate through her bones.

Junak stood to the side, a dark figure with eyes as cold as frosteel, his lips twisted into a cruel smile. He watched the ritual with a predator's patience, knowing the moment was near. The head shaman approached the coffin, raising a ceremonial dagger high above his head. Ruiha's muscles tensed; the anticipation hung thick in the air, ready to snap. Kemp's blood would awaken Nergai, the ancient Dragon, and the world would tremble beneath its fury.

Ruiha's heart pounded in her chest, each beat a thunderous drum in the tense silence. The oppressive atmosphere seemed to press down on her, thick with the weight of ancient power. She glanced at her team, their faces set in grim determination, each a pillar of strength in the shadowed tomb. They were already in position, hidden behind stone pillars and alcoves, waiting for her signal.

She signaled to Karl with a subtle nod. In response, he swiftly pulled a small, spherical device from his belt. He whispered an incantation, and a faint rune glowed a dim green as he activated it. Then, a blinding flash of light erupted, searing through the darkness. The shamans' chant faltered, voices breaking into cries of shock and pain as they were momentarily blinded.

"Now!" Ruiha's voice was a sharp command, slicing through the chaos. She leaped from her hiding place, leading her team with weapons drawn.

Junak spun around, his eyes narrowing in fury as he saw them. "Stop them!" he shouted, drawing his huge axe. "Or do you need an invitation?"

Dakarai and Thraxos moved in sync, their strikes precise and deadly. Karl's axe cleaved through the first line of shamans, sending blood and bone splattering across the cold stone floor. Uleg's blade flickered in the dim light, a whirlwind of steel that cut down anyone who dared to approach.

At Ruiha's side, Torain fought with the ferocity of a cornered beast, his eyes sharp and clear despite the overwhelming odds.

Each of his movements was pure aggression, a testament to his strength. The clash of steel, the cries of the dying, and the unending chant of the shamans filled her ears, a cacophony of despair and defiance.

"Stay focused, Torain," Ruiha muttered, her voice steady despite the chaos around her. "We can't afford mistakes."

"Worry about your own blade, Ruiha," Torain shot back, gritting his teeth. "I'm fighting for Brenn."

Ruiha slashed through an attacking shaman and pressed forward, her goal clear in her mind. She fought her way toward Kemp, her daggers a blur of silver in the torchlight. The weight of her mission pressed down on her. Each slash of her daggers, each step forward, was a defiance against the darkness threatening to engulf them all.

She could feel the ancient power stirring within the tomb, a malevolent force awakening from its slumber, and she knew they had precious moments to stop it.

The ritual would not be completed. Not if she had anything to say about it.

The clang of steel against steel filled the tomb, the sound sharp and deafening as weapons collided with desperate fury. Ruiha barely had time to think, her muscles screaming as she parried a blow, the weight of the battle pressing down on her. Sweat dripped from her brow, stinging her eyes, but she couldn't afford to blink. Not now.

Thraxos was already moving, his lips forming the words of an incantation, magic sparking from his fingertips. The chains binding Kemp shuddered before shattering in a violent burst of light. Kemp dropped, his body limp from the strain, but Thraxos was there, catching him with a soft whisper of magic, lowering him before he hit the ground.

Junak's figure loomed out of the darkness, weapon raised.

But Dakarai was faster. With a bellow that echoed through the chamber, he threw himself into the fray, hammer meeting axe in a brutal clash. The force of their blows sent sparks flying, illuminating the grim determination etched on Dakarai's face.

"You won't stop us, Junak!" Dakarai's voice was a growl, his muscles straining as he pushed back, eyes flashing with raw fury.

Junak grinned, wild and feral, shoving Dakarai off with a grunt. "I'll do more than stop you. I'll make you beg for death." He lunged, his axe a blur, but Dakarai was ready, meeting it with a bone-jarring strike of his hammer. The two warriors locked in a brutal dance, each hit reverberating through the tomb.

Above them, the head shaman's voice reached a fever pitch, the guttural chant rising with the thick, choking smoke. The ritual was slipping from his grasp, and the desperation in his voice was palpable. His eyes, wild with rage, locked on Kemp. The ceremonial dagger gleamed as he lunged, intent on finishing the job.

Ruiha's breath froze in her throat as the dagger sliced through the air, a flash of steel in the dim light. Her body reacted before her mind did, muscles coiling to move, but time felt like it slowed, every heartbeat dragging out as if the universe itself was holding its breath.

Uleg moved faster. His body slammed into the shaman's path, blocking the dagger's deadly arc. The blade sank into his chest with a sickening crunch. He let out a guttural gasp, the sound mingling with Ruiha's scream, sharp and raw.

"No!" The word ripped from Ruiha's throat as she fell to Uleg's side, her hands trembling as they pressed against the wound. Blood, hot and thick, poured over her fingers. "Uleg, stay with me," she begged, her voice barely more than a whisper. His eyes, usually so sharp, were already losing focus, the life draining from them.

Uleg coughed, a faint smile tugging at his lips despite the blood bubbling from them. "Finish it," he rasped, his breath shallow. "Without me."

Ruiha's chest tightened with despair, but there was no time to mourn. The ground beneath them shuddered violently, and her eyes snapped up to the dragon-shaped coffin, where Nergai's spirit was rising—an ominous mass of darkness, boiling with hatred and power.

"Dakarai!" Ruiha shouted, her voice cutting through the chaos. "We need to do something!"

Dakarai was already locked in battle with Junak, their blows shaking the very walls. "Easy to say!" he bellowed, blocking a savage swing with a grunt. "Harder to do!"

Nergai roared, the sound a deep, bone-rattling tremor that tore through the chamber. Several shamans were caught in its path, their screams silenced as they disintegrated into nothingness, obliterated by the sheer force of Nergai's fury.

Ruiha's mind raced. Her body ached with exhaustion, the weight of Uleg's sacrifice crushing her resolve, but she forced herself to push forward. Her blade was a blur as she slashed through a shaman, blood spraying in an arc. The tomb was a whirlwind of violence—steel flashing, magic crackling, bodies colliding in brutal, desperate strikes.

Nergai's spirit, a looming mass of darkness, coiled and twisted, searching for its true target. It found him: Kemp. Ruiha's heart leaped into her throat as the dark form lunged, wrapping around Kemp like a serpent, squeezing the life from him.

Dakarai, still battling Junak, snarled as he saw the dark mist closing in. With a roar that shook the tomb, Dakarai hurled Junak across the chamber, sending him crashing into Nergai's path. "Handle this, Junak!" Dakarai growled, his voice savage. "Let's see what you're made of!"

Junak barely had time to react before Nergai's spirit engulfed him, the mist swirling around his body. His screams echoed through the chamber, his form twisting and contorting as Nergai's essence tore through him.

"Now!" Ruiha shouted, her voice sharp as a blade. Thraxos raised his hands, chanting a spell that filled the air with a blinding light. The energy enveloped Junak, trapping Nergai's spirit within. The tomb trembled as the ritual's magic rebounded, cracks splitting the walls.

Junak's body collapsed, his form crumpling to the ground, unmoving. The chamber seemed to sigh with relief as the spirit dissipated, the dragon-shaped coffin settling once more. The runes along its surface flickered weakly before fading into darkness, but something lingered in the air—a subtle, unsettling stillness, as if the tomb itself was waiting for what might come next.

Ruiha's chest heaved with the effort, her heart still pounding in her ears. The immediate threat was gone, but the air was heavy with the price they had paid. Uleg's body lay still beside her, and the cost of their victory weighed on her like an anchor, dragging her down into the cold realization that this was far from over.

Dakarai's voice broke the silence. "Gather your strength," he said, his voice rough but steady. "This isn't the end."

Ruiha knelt beside Uleg's still form. "He gave his life for us," she whispered, her voice choked with grief.

She glanced up as Kemp staggered to his feet, his face pale and drawn. There was something unsettling in his eyes, a glint she hadn't seen before. "It's not over yet," he muttered, his voice oddly hollow.

Karl placed a reassuring hand on Kemp's shoulder, his grip firm. "We'll finish it together," he said.

"Together," Kemp echoed, his tone flat. His stormy eyes met Ruiha's, and for a brief moment, she saw a flicker of something dark.

Ruiha stepped closer, her voice low. "Are you alright, Kemp? You look—different."

"Different?" Kemp's lips twisted into a smile that didn't reach his eyes. "Perhaps that's what it takes to survive in a place like this."

Ruiha frowned, unease gnawing at her. "We need to stay focused. The fight isn't over."

"Oh, I'm focused," Kemp replied, his voice eerily calm. "More than ever."

The team gathered around, their resolve hardening. They had prevented the sacrifice, but the battle was far from over. With Nergai's spirit still lingering in the air, they knew a greater fight awaited them. But for now, they would prepare for the challenges ahead.

As they left the tomb, Ruiha glanced back at Kemp, unease gnawing at her. The storm swirling in his eyes flickered with a menacing light, and for a brief moment, his lips curled into a sinister smile. She wondered how much the Dragon Crown's ancient power, awakened by Nergai's proximity, had latched onto him, whispering dark promises and old secrets.

Gunnar

Gunnar had been worried that Anwyn had slipped into a coma again, but Thalirion had to keep reassuring him that she was simply resting. Every slight movement or sound had made his heart lurch with fear, but now, finally, Anwyn's eyelashes fluttered as she emerged from the depths of her sleep.

The room was dim, but the soft glow of candlelight gently

illuminated her delicate features. Gunnar sat beside her, his heart pounding in his chest, the overwhelming relief nearly bringing him to tears.

He had spent countless hours at her bedside, whispering words of love and encouragement, praying she would return to him. The fear of losing her had been a constant shadow, a weight pressing down on his soul.

As her eyes began to open, he felt a profound sense of gratitude. She was his light, his anchor, and seeing her awaken was like witnessing a miracle. He had held onto hope with a grip so tight it had hurt, refusing to let despair take root. And now, here she was, stirring, a testament to his unyielding love.

"Anwyn?" he whispered, his voice trembling with hope and love. He gently brushed a strand of hair away from her face, his touch tender and reverent.

Her eyes slowly opened, the familiar spark of life rekindling in their honeyed depths. She looked up at him, confusion giving way to recognition. "Gunnar," she murmured, her voice weak.

"You're awake," Gunnar breathed, his voice thick with emotion. He took her hand in his, holding it tightly as if afraid she might slip away again.

Anwyn's fingers curled around his, her grip strengthening with each passing moment. "I heard you," she whispered, her eyes locking onto his with a fierce intensity. "All those times you spoke to me, I heard every word."

Gunnar's heart swelled with emotion. He leaned in closer, his forehead resting against hers. "I was so scared, Anwyn. I didn't know if you'd ever wake up. But I couldn't give up on you. I love you too much."

Anwyn's eyes filled with tears, her heart aching with the depth of his love. "You saved me," she whispered, her voice breaking. "You brought me back."

For a moment, they simply held each other, the world outside their small sanctuary fading away. Gunnar's love for Anwyn was a tangible thing, a force that had guided him through the darkest of times. His every thought, every action, had been driven by his need to see her well again.

"Tell me everything," she said, her voice gaining strength. "I remember some things, but I need to know what's happened."

Gunnar nodded, his expression turning serious. "The clans have united, Anwyn. It wasn't easy, but we did it. The threat of the Drogo brought us together. But there's more...Kemp has been taken."

Anwyn's eyes widened, shock and sadness mingling in her gaze. "Kemp...taken?" She shook her head, struggling to comprehend. "How could this happen?"

"It's a long story," Gunnar said gently. "But we will get him back. We'll do whatever it takes."

Anwyn nodded, her resolve hardening. "I believe in you, Gunnar. I always have."

They spent the next few hours in tender conversation, sharing the burdens of their hearts and the joys of their reunion. Gunnar's fingers traced patterns on Anwyn's hand, their touch grounding him in the reality of her presence. He spoke of the challenges he had faced, the alliances forged, and the hope that had kept him going.

Anwyn listened intently, her eyes never leaving his face. She could see the weariness in his eyes, the lines of worry etched into his brow, but she could also see the unwavering strength and love that had driven him to succeed.

"Gunnar," she said softly, reaching up to touch his cheek, "I am so proud of you."

Gunnar's heart soared at her words, his love for her filling every corner of his being. "I couldn't have done it without you, Anwyn. Even when you were unconscious, you were my guiding star."

Their moment was interrupted by the gentle knock on the door. Thalirion entered, his expression one of quiet authority. "Anwyn needs rest, Gunnar," he said softly. "She's been through a lot."

Gunnar nodded, though it pained him to leave her side. "Of course," he said, his voice tinged with reluctance. "She needs to recover."

Anwyn smiled up at him, her eyes filled with love and gratitude. "I'll be here when you return," she whispered.

Gunnar leaned down, pressing a tender kiss to her forehead. "Rest well, my love," he murmured. "We have much to do, but for now, let's just cherish this moment."

As Thalirion helped Anwyn settle back into bed, Gunnar watched her with a heart full of hope and love. Whatever challenges lay ahead, he knew they would face them together. For now, he was content to see her safe and on the road to recovery.

As the room grew quiet once more, Gunnar left, feeling a profound sense of peace. The future still held many uncertainties, but with Anwyn by his side, he felt ready to face them all.

25

A Sword Raised, A Crown Bound in Darkness

"In the clash of blades and the roar of war, honor is the only shield that holds firm against the tide of darkness."

Gunnar

Gunnar closed the door softly behind him as he left Anwyn's chamber, his heart still swelling with the joy of her recovery. The corridors of the fortress were dimly lit, the soft flicker of torches casting elongated shadows on the stone walls. His footsteps echoed softly as he made his way to his own chamber, a brief respite from the relentless demands of his role. He pushed open the heavy oak door, and what he saw stopped him in his tracks.

There, in the center of the room, stood Draeg, the god himself, in the image of Hansen. Draeg's eyes, a piercing blue, seemed to hold the weight of the ages. In his hands, he held Havoc, who bounced playfully, emitting low, rumbling noises of delight.

"Draeg," Gunnar breathed, his voice barely above a whisper, his mind struggling to reconcile the surreal image before him.

Draeg's gaze met Gunnar's, and he smiled, an infectious gesture that spoke of ancient knowledge and just a hint of pride, like a teacher whose student had finally grasped the basics of adding one and one together. "Gunnar, my prince," he said with an exaggerated bow, so low his beard brushed the stone floor, collecting a fine layer of dust. As he straightened, he boomed out a laugh that seemed to vibrate through the very stones of the room and probably gave the nearby servants heart palpitations. "You have come far, my boy. Farther than I thought possible, frankly. But now, your journey must take a new turn. The Drogo threat looms larger than ever. Yet, in a stroke of luck that can only be described as cosmically improbable, they are currently *disorganized*. You must deliver the decisive blow immediately or risk losing this once-in-a-lifetime opportunity."

Gunnar blinked, trying to process the rapid shift from profound wisdom to urgent action. "Disorganized, you say?"

Draeg nodded, his eyes twinkling. "Yes, apparently their leader decided it was a good time to be eaten by an ancient deceased Dragon. Can you imagine?"

Gunnar couldn't, but he tried anyway, picturing Junak being torn to pieces in the mouth of a huge black Dragon. It was, admittedly, difficult to envisage. "So, we strike now?"

"Yes, now!" Draeg said, clapping his hands together in a way that made it sound like thunder had entered the room uninvited. "Before they can reorganize themselves, you will lead an assault on them!" He gestured for Gunnar to come into the room. "But first. Tell me of your time in Nexus!"

Gunnar stepped further into the room, his eyes never leaving Draeg. "I faced many trials," he said, his voice steady but laced with the weariness of his recent ordeals. "I trained to be a Battle Mage. It was grueling. We nearly died, all of us. But I succeeded. I am now a Battle Mage." Images of his time in the Corpselands, of Commander Aelric, of Urlok flashed through his mind, and he shook them away. Distant memories, he thought.

Draeg nodded, setting Havoc gently on the ground. The Stonesprite ran over to Gunnar, hopped up and settled on his shoulder. "I have watched your journey, Gunnar. Nexus forged you in the fires of hardship and honed your skills. But what you face now is beyond individual prowess. It is a battle for the future of Dreynas."

Gunnar squared his shoulders, the weight of responsibility settling upon him. "What must I do?" he asked his voice firm with resolve.

Draeg's expression grew serious. "You must strike at the heart of the Drogo."

Gunnar looked thoughtful for a moment. He decided to ask Havoc for his opinion on the matter. Havoc responded telepathically, as usual. "Simultaneous attacks will divide their forces and sow chaos."

Gunnar nodded in agreement before turning back to Draeg. "Magnus will lead an assault from Hammer to Fang while I lead another force from Braemeer to Claw."

Gunnar's mind raced, already envisioning the strategy, the movements of troops, the timing of the attacks. "It will take careful planning," he said, more to himself than to Draeg.

Draeg stepped forward, placing a hand on Gunnar's shoulder. The touch was warm, grounding him. "You are not alone in this. Havoc is your bond, your strength. Together, you will lead us to victory."

As Draeg spoke, Gunnar felt a surge of energy, a renewal of purpose. "Thank you, Draeg," he said, his voice thick with emotion. "For your guidance and for believing in me."

Draeg's form began to shimmer, the edges blurring. "You have always had the strength within you, Gunnar. Now, it is time to unleash it." With that, Draeg faded, leaving behind a sense of warmth and a faint scent of pine and earth.

Gunnar stood in silence for a moment, letting the reality of the encounter sink in. Then, he turned to Havoc, who looked up at him with glittering purple eyes. "We have much to do, my friend," he said, his voice resolute. "We need to plan our attacks on Fang and Claw."

Havoc nodded in agreement, his eyes reflecting the same fierce determination that burned within Gunnar. Together, they moved with a sense of purpose to the table in the center of the dimly lit room, spreading out maps and charts with meticulous precision. The air was thick with anticipation, and the flickering candlelight cast shadows that danced across their faces, mirroring the intensity of the moment.

Gunnar's mind, a finely tuned instrument honed by years of rigorous training with the Snow Wolves and further sharpened by his time in Nexus, worked relentlessly. He delved into the maps, his fingers tracing the contours of the land, his eyes scanning for every possible advantage. Each move and counter-move played out in his mind like a complex game of chess, with lives hanging in the balance.

Hours passed, the world outside fading into insignificance as Gunnar considered every possible angle and outcome. His thoughts were a whirlwind of strategies, each plan crafted to balance the boldness required for victory with the prudence needed to safeguard his soldiers.

The first attack would launch from Hammer, striking at Fang with the full might of the clans already positioned there, leaving behind a small enough contingent to defend the city in the unlikely event of an attack. Meanwhile, a covert force from Braemeer would move to Claw, using the element of surprise to their advantage. The goal was to disrupt the Drogo's command structure, forcing them to fight on multiple fronts and weakening their resolve.

As dawn approached, Gunnar leaned back, his eyes heavy but his heart steadfast. He looked at Havoc, who snored softly, a rumbling sound that brought Gunnar a sense of calm. "We're ready," Gunnar sighed to himself, his voice filled with a quiet confidence.

The room was silent, save for the crackle of the dying fire. Gunnar knew that the path ahead was fraught with danger, but with Draeg's blessing, he felt prepared to face whatever lay ahead. The future of his people depended on the outcome of this pincer attack, and he was determined to see it through.

Ruiha

As they exited the tomb, Ruiha couldn't shake the feeling of dread that clung to her like a second skin. The air outside was cool and crisp, a stark contrast to the oppressive atmosphere they had just escaped. The night seemed to swallow the light of their torches, amplifying the sense of foreboding. The team gathered around her, their faces etched with exhaustion and determination.

"We need to regroup and plan our next move," Ruiha said, her voice steady despite the turmoil inside her. "Nergai's spirit is contained for now, but we can't assume it will stay that way. We need to be prepared for anything."

Kemp nodded, though his eyes remained distant. "I need some time to process everything," he said quietly. "The Dragon Crown—it's more powerful than we realized. I can feel its influence, and I need to learn to control it."

Karl stepped forward, his expression one of concern. "We'll help you, lad. You're not alone in this. We'll find a way to manage the Crown's power and use it to our advantage."

Ruiha studied Kemp for a moment longer, her worry deepening. "We'll support you, Kemp," she agreed, "but we also need to be cautious. The Crown's power is ancient and dangerous. We can't let it consume you."

Kemp's lips tightened into a thin line, but he nodded again. "I understand. I'll do my best to keep it in check."

They set up camp a short distance from the tomb, using the time to rest and tend to their wounds. Ruiha glanced at the distant horizon, where the last vestiges of twilight were swallowed by night, mirroring the encroaching darkness they faced. As the night deepened, Ruiha found herself unable to sleep. She wandered a short distance from the camp, her thoughts heavy with the events of the day. The stars overhead provided a cold, distant light, and she felt the vastness of the world pressing down on her.

"You're troubled," a voice said softly behind her. She turned to see Dakarai approaching, his expression one of quiet understanding.

"I can't shake the feeling that we're missing something," Ruiha admitted. "Nergai's spirit may be contained, but the danger hasn't passed. And Kemp—I'm worried about him."

Dakarai nodded, his gaze thoughtful. "Artifacts like the Dragon Crown," he began, his voice a soft rumble, "were forged with intentions beyond mortal understanding. Its power seeks dominion, and its will is insidious. But Kemp is strong. He has us to help him, and we won't let him face this alone."

"I know," Ruiha said, her voice barely above a whisper. "But it's hard not to worry. We've already lost so much."

Dakarai placed a reassuring hand on her shoulder. "We'll get through this, Ruiha. Together. We've faced impossible odds before, and we've come out stronger. We'll do it again."

Ruiha nodded, drawing strength from Dakarai's words. "You're right. We'll face whatever comes next together."

The following morning, the team was ready to move. They had discussed their next steps and were determined to find a way to deal with the lingering threat of Nergai's spirit and the influence of the Dragon Crown. Kemp seemed more focused, though the haunted look in his eyes remained.

As they were about to depart, Thraxos approached Ruiha with a worried expression. "I am concerned for Kemp," he admitted in a low rumbly voice.

Ruiha sighed. "I am too, Thraxos. But I'm not sure what we can do to help."

Thraxos stared past Ruiha toward where Kemp was sitting alone. The morning mist curled around Kemp's shadow hand, making the purple flames seem even more otherworldly. When Ruiha looked over, he was examining his shadow hand, flexing it and producing small purple flames from his fingertips. He glanced up and saw Ruiha staring at him. He offered a smile, and Ruiha returned it with a weak smile of her own.

"Why hasn't he attempted a Shadowpurge yet?" Thraxos inquired. "The shaman's restraints are gone, yet he hesitates."

Ruiha's brow furrowed in thought. "Perhaps he isn't ready to carry it out yet. He admitted to us, it was an extremely painful experience. He might not have the strength to survive it."

Thraxos grunted and continued staring at Kemp for a while longer. Eventually, he muttered something which sounded to

Ruiha like, 'maybe' before fixing his gaze back on her.

"We need to go through the old texts," Thraxos said. "There might be something in the ancient Drogo tomes I came across in Hammer that can help us understand the Crown better and how to neutralize Nergai's spirit permanently."

Ruiha nodded. "Then that's where we'll go. We'll find the answers we need and put an end to this threat once and for all."

With a renewed sense of purpose, the team made their way back to Hammer. The journey felt like a battle itself, each step a testament to their resolve. The landscape changed from barren rock to the familiar, weathered paths leading to the city. The journey was long and arduous, but they were driven by the knowledge that they were racing against time. The closer they got to the city, the more Ruiha's resolve hardened. She wouldn't let Nergai's spirit or the Dragon Crown destroy everything they had fought for.

The air in Hammer weighed heavily on Ruiha, thick with the scent of dust and ancient stone, a stark contrast to the crisp, biting wind of the mountains above. This place, carved deep into the mountain's heart, seemed to exhale memories from the very rock, the weight of centuries pressing down on her. Every cavern, every intricate tunnel felt alive, like the mountain itself was a witness to the changes being forced upon it. The footsteps of its new occupants reverberated through the hollowed halls, blending the old and the new, a strange harmony of invasion and history. Flickering torchlight danced against the rough-hewn walls, throwing long shadows that traced the marks of ancient craftsmanship, once a testament to dwarven pride, now an eerie reminder of what had been. The mountain had a heartbeat, and

Ruiha could feel it beneath her boots.

Karl led the way through the winding passages, his keen senses attuned to every subtle shift in the atmosphere. Dakarai followed with the fluid grace of one born to the subterranean world, his eyes flickering with quiet determination. Ruiha stayed close to Kemp, her senses on high alert as they maneuvered through the newly occupied city. Behind her, Torain trudged along with a grim expression, his stoic endurance evident in every step. Thraxos towered above them all, his imposing presence a bulwark of strength and resolve.

As they neared their destination, the group split. Karl and Torain made their way to the citadel, where Magnus was likely orchestrating the aftermath of Hammer's occupation. Ruiha, Dakarai, Kemp, and Thraxos headed to the library, intent on gathering information.

The scent of old parchment and leather-bound books greeted them as they approached the library. Dust and aged wood lingered in the air. The expansive chamber, though modest compared to Dwarven or Human libraries, was filled with shelves of ancient tomes, scrolls, and curious instruments. In the center of the room stood a lone figure, poring over a dusty manuscript.

The Drogo researcher looked up as they entered, his sharp, dark eyes gleaming with intelligence. He appeared younger than Ruiha had expected, his face still carrying the softness of youth. Unlike Dakarai, this Drogo's demeanor was that of someone studious. He bowed slightly, a gesture of respect and greeting.

"Welcome," he said, his voice steady despite the tension that lingered in the air. "How can I assist you?"

Ruiha and Dakarai exchanged a glance, both slightly taken aback by the youthfulness of the researcher. Ruiha stepped forward, her curiosity piqued. "We are searching for information on the Dragon Crown and Nergai's spirit," she explained.

"Are there any tomes or scrolls here that might contain such knowledge?"

The young Drogo's eyes widened slightly at the mention of the Dragon Crown. He hesitated, glancing at the shelves filled with ancient texts. "The Dragon Crown—that is a subject of immense power and danger. I wish Corgan were here; he would know exactly where to look."

Ruiha's heart skipped a beat. "Corgan?" she repeated, a mixture of surprise and regret in her voice. "You knew him?"

The researcher nodded, a shadow of sadness crossing his features. "Yes, Corgan was my mentor. I am Aelan, his apprentice. He was a great Drogo, knowledgeable and wise."

Dakarai's eyes flickered with recognition and grief. "Corgan was a friend and ally to us," he said quietly. "He never mentioned having an apprentice."

Aelan chuckled softly. "Why would he have need to mention his apprentice?"

Ruiha felt a pang of sorrow. She had not anticipated encountering someone so closely connected to Corgan. "Corgan—died in the pit," she said softly, her voice tinged with sadness. "It was a brutal loss for all of us."

Aelan's eyes filled with grief. "I had hoped—"

Ruiha stepped closer, placing a reassuring hand on Aelan's shoulder. "I avenged his death," she said quietly, her eyes distant as she recalled the moment. She remembered the intensity of Rainok's gaze, the treachery in his eyes. The memory of her sword sliding through his heart was vivid, a mix of justice and sorrow. She had looked into his eyes, seeing the life drain from them, feeling a grim satisfaction as she avenged her fallen friend.

Aelan's expression softened, a mix of gratitude and sadness. "Thank you," he whispered. "Corgan meant a great deal to me. He taught me everything I know."

"We owe him our lives; perhaps he can help us once more from the afterlife," Ruiha said, her resolve firm. "We need to understand the Dragon Crown and Nergai's spirit. His teachings might guide us."

At the mention of the Dragon Crown, Kemp winced, his stormy eyes darting around the library as though expecting an attack. Ruiha noticed his unease and placed a reassuring hand on his arm.

Aelan nodded, determination in his eyes mirroring her own. "Follow me," he said, his voice steadier now. "There are many ancient tomes here. Together, we will find the answers you seek."

He led them to a secluded alcove at the back of the library, where ancient texts lay spread out on a large stone table. The tomes were bound in leather, their pages yellowed with age. Symbols and runes, etched in a language long forgotten by many, adorned the covers.

Dakarai leaned in, his fingers brushing lightly over the runes. "These are from the earliest days of the Drogo. They hold secrets that even the shamans have yet to uncover."

Aelan nodded. "Corgan believed the Dragon Crown was created by our ancestors to channel divine magic. He was studying ways to harness its power without succumbing to its corruption."

Thraxos grunted, his deep voice rumbling through the chamber. "And how do we find these ways?"

Aelan opened one of the tomes, revealing pages filled with intricate diagrams and flowing script. "Corgan was close to a breakthrough. He believed that combining the arcane arts with ancient Drogo rites could neutralize the Crown's influence. It requires a balance of power and will, something only a few can achieve."

Kemp frowned, the storm clouds in his eyes a flurry. "And do you know how to perform these rites?"

Aelan hesitated, his hand clenching briefly at his side. "I have some knowledge, but it's incomplete." His voice was low, edged with the weight of things unsaid. He paused, staring into the distance as if he could still see Corgan's face. "Corgan took many secrets to his grave." The words hung in the air, and then he drew a sharp breath, his gaze hardening with resolve. "But I am willing to try. For him." His jaw tightened, and his voice grew firmer. "For all of us."

Ruiha placed a hand on Aelan's shoulder. "We will do this together. No one faces this alone."

As they delved into the ancient texts, the atmosphere grew thick with concentration and urgency. The flickering torchlight cast an almost ethereal glow on the pages, illuminating secrets long buried. Ruiha felt a surge of determination. They had come this far, faced impossible odds, and survived. They would find a way to harness the Dragon Crown's power without falling to its dark influence. They would honor Corgan's legacy and protect their world from the shadows that threatened to consume it.

26

A Fortress Fallen, A Power Awakened

"In war, it is not the sword alone that wins the day, but the heart that endures when all seems lost,"

Gunnar

Dawn in Hammer was a subtle thing, marked by a shift in the flickering torchlight rather than the rising sun. The city, carved deep into the heart of the mountain, thrummed with the activity of its inhabitants. Gunnar's gaze swept across the horizon, the weight of command pressing hard on his chest. Every choice, every life, rested on his shoulders. But as the banner of Dreynas snapped in the wind above him, its colors bold against the darkening sky, he let himself feel something he rarely allowed—hope. They had fought, bled, and suffered, yet still they stood, unbroken. The path ahead stretched long, riddled with danger, but they were stronger now, forged in fire. As long as breath filled his lungs, Gunnar would lead his men with fierce resolve, his blade ready to carve a future they deserved. He would see them through. He had to. Because if he fell, the dream they fought for would die with him preparing for the challenges ahead. The distant clanking of hammers and the murmurs of conversation filled the vast caverns. Ruiha awoke with renewed determination, her mind focused on the mission ahead.

The previous night's revelations from the ancient Drogo library had been both enlightening and frustrating. They had hints, fragments of knowledge, but no concrete solutions. As she dressed, her thoughts turned to Aelan, the young researcher with bright, inquisitive eyes who had proposed a daring course of action: a journey deeper into the mountain to the fabled Hall of Whispers, where the oldest and most powerful Drogo artifacts were said to be hidden.

Aelan had spoken with an intensity that belied his youth. "Corgan believed the Hall of Whispers was the most likely solution," he had insisted, his voice echoing in the ancient library. "The artifacts there could help us control the Dragon Crown and defeat Nergai's spirit."

Ruiha had felt a flicker of hope then, a spark that had grown into a determined flame by morning. But before they could embark on this perilous journey, they needed to inform Magnus of their plans.

The citadel, bustling with activity after the recent occupation and now brimming with preparations for war, felt like a hive of tension. Soldiers moved with purpose, their faces etched with a mix of resolve and worry. The air was thick with urgency, every footfall and command echoing through the stone corridors.

Magnus stood at the center of it all, his brow furrowed with concern as he surveyed the preparations. His broad shoulders seemed to carry the weight of the entire city.

Ruiha approached him, flanked by Kemp, Thraxos, and Dakarai. "Magnus," she called, her voice cutting through the din.

He turned to face them, his eyes sharp and assessing. "Ruiha, what brings you here so early?" he asked, though the worry in his voice suggested he already knew it wasn't good news.

"We need to leave for the Hall of Whispers," Ruiha began, her voice steady despite the turmoil inside her.

"What is the Hall of Whispers? And why do you need to go there so urgently?" Magnus queried, his brows knitting together in concern.

Thraxos interjected, his baritone booming through the chamber. "It's an ancient Drogo site deep within the mountain, said to hold the oldest and most powerful artifacts. The Dragon Crown's influence is growing rapidly, and if we don't find a way to control it, it could corrupt Kemp entirely. The Hall of Whispers might contain the knowledge or tools we need to neutralize Nergai's spirit and harness the Crown's power safely."

Magnus's eyes darkened, his concern deepening. "Might?" he asked, his voice heavy with doubt. "Gunnar has ordered an attack on Fang. I don't have the troops required for another offensive, nor enough to defend Hammer if you take more with you."

Ruiha stepped forward, her determination unwavering. "Our mission is of the utmost importance. Any chance of controlling the Dragon Crown and stopping Nergai's spirit is crucial to the safety of everyone. If we don't succeed, Dreynas won't stand a chance, no matter how many troops you have."

Magnus sighed, the weight of his responsibilities bearing down on him. He rubbed his temples, clearly torn. "I understand the stakes, but I can't spare any forces to accompany you. You'll be on your own."

"We'll manage," Ruiha said firmly, her resolve like steel. "We have to."

Magnus studied her for a long moment, his eyes filled with both admiration and reluctance. "Very well. May the gods watch over you," he finally said, his voice tinged with resignation.

Ruiha

With Magnus's reluctant blessing, the team set out, descending deeper into the mountain's heart. The narrow tunnels grew darker before opening into vast underground caverns filled with eerie, phosphorescent fungi that cast a ghostly glow. The air grew colder and more oppressive, each step echoing the weight of their mission.

Kemp walked beside Ruiha, his face etched with tension. "Do you really think we can find what we need in the Hall of Whispers?" he asked, his voice low and strained.

Ruiha glanced at him, noting the flicker of doubt in his eyes. "We have to believe it, Kemp," she replied firmly. "It's our best chance."

As they ventured further, the path became increasingly treacherous. The walls closed in, and the air grew colder still. Every sound seemed amplified, the drip of water from stalactites and the distant echo of their footsteps magnifying their sense of isolation. The weight of the mountain pressed down on them, a constant reminder of their perilous journey.

After hours of navigating the twisting tunnels, they finally arrived at a vast chamber. The Hall of Whispers lay beyond a formidable gate, its entrance flanked by two ancient, weathered statues of Dragons. Ruiha could feel the ancient magic thrumming in the air, a palpable force that sent shivers down her spine.

Their first trial awaited them: a series of intricate puzzles woven into the very stone of the ancient gate. Designed to test intellect, magic, and the unity of their team, these puzzles were not mere obstacles—they were a rite of passage, a challenge set to weed out the unworthy. Ruiha took a deep breath, her focus sharpening, her senses attuning to the layers of magic surrounding them.

The first puzzle loomed before them: a massive stone slab etched with elaborate carvings and runes. Kemp stepped forward, his hands trembling slightly as he reached for the Dragon Crown's power. Shadows coiled and writhed at his fingertips, answering his call. With a flick of his wrist, he sent them slithering across the slab, revealing hidden markings that danced in the moonlight. The carvings shifted, telling fragmented stories of battles long forgotten. Each symbol, each swirl of shadow, felt like a whisper of something ancient, something sacred.

Thraxos knelt beside Kemp, his sharp eyes tracing the symbols. "Here," he murmured, his voice barely more than a breath. He pointed to a series of runes carved deep into the stone. "These represent the four elements. Fire, water, air, earth. We must align them in the proper sequence to unlock the gate."

Dakarai stepped closer, his expression thoughtful as he examined the ancient symbols. "The Drogo shamans always revered the elements," he said, his deep voice resonating in the stillness. "We do not control them, but we honor their power."

Kemp's face tightened with concentration, beads of sweat forming along his brow as the shadows twisted under his command, shaping into the elemental symbols. "Earth first, then water," he muttered. Slowly, painstakingly, the shadows shifted, fitting each piece into place. With a low groan, the stone slab shuddered. A deep *thunk* echoed through the chamber as the first lock disengaged.

A moment of silence fell over the group, broken only by the slow exhale of breath. But there was no time for relief. They moved on to the next challenge—a series of rotating columns, each covered in complex patterns that seemed to shift as the light hit them.

Dakarai ran his fingers over the columns, his eyes narrowing. "This... this is a Drogo myth," he said softly, almost reverently. "The tale of the Dragon's Ascent." His voice took on a distant, almost nostalgic quality. "We must reconstruct the journey—each column, a step in the Dragon's rise to the heavens."

Ruiha exchanged a glance with Dakarai. Together, they began rotating the columns, their hands moving with careful precision. It wasn't just the alignment that mattered—each turn had to mirror the mythical steps of the Dragon's ascent. The weight of history pressed down on them with each adjustment.

Sweat dripped down Ruiha's temple as the final column clicked into place. The image of a Dragon, wings unfurled and soaring towards the sky, flickered into view. A loud *clang* reverberated through the stone as the second lock disengaged.

"Careful, Kemp," Ruiha said, her voice low but firm, catching the strain in his eyes. His connection to the Dragon Crown was wearing him thin.

Kemp's hand shook as he wiped the sweat from his forehead. "I'm fine," he whispered, though his voice was heavy with fatigue.

But there was no time to stop. The final puzzle loomed before them: a labyrinth of light and shadow, a test of both magical finesse and teamwork. A beam of light shot from the ceiling, dancing wildly through the maze of mirrors and lenses that lined the walls. Only by bending the light at the perfect angles could they illuminate the hidden rune on the far wall.

Ruiha's mind raced, her gaze flickering over the angles and reflections. "Thraxos, adjust that mirror to the left," she instructed. Thraxos moved swiftly, his hands steady as he tilted the mirror, his magic flowing through the ancient glass, adjusting its angle. The light wavered, reflecting off a lens, barely missing the target.

"More to the left!" Ruiha barked, her voice tightening with

urgency. They were running out of time.

Thraxos adjusted again, the beam slicing through the air in a perfect arc. The light hit the final lens, refracting into a prism of colors before striking the rune squarely. The room trembled, the ground beneath their feet vibrating as ancient gears whirred to life. Slowly, the gate creaked open, stone grinding against stone.

The moment hung heavy in the air as the gate fully opened, revealing the yawning tunnel ahead, bathed in darkness. Ruiha's breath hitched in her throat. This was it—the threshold to the next chapter of their journey. There was no going back now.

Her hand tightened on her blade as she turned to her companions. "We've passed the test. But what comes next... it won't be any easier." The weight of her words settled over them, but no one flinched.

They had faced the ancient trials and won. Now, they would face what lay beyond.

As they stepped through, Ruiha felt a surge of hope tempered by the knowledge of the trials still to come. The Hall of Whispers awaited, a place of ancient power and potential salvation. The journey had only just begun, but the first step had been taken.

Gunnar

As dawn broke, Gunnar stood atop a ridge overlooking his encampment, the faint light of morning casting long shadows across the rugged landscape. His army below bustled with activity, sturdy Dwarven warriors strapping on armor, sharpening blades, and preparing for the day's bloody work. Gunnar took a deep breath, savoring the crisp air tinged with the scent of pine and earth. Today, they would march on Claw.

Gunnar descended from the ridge, his presence commanding immediate attention. The soldiers fell silent as he approached, their eyes filled with a mix of admiration and fierce loyalty. He knew the weight of their expectations rested on his shoulders. His voice was steady, but the fire in his eyes betrayed the urgency of their mission.

"Warriors of Dreynas," he began, his voice carrying over the ranks, "today we strike at the heart of our ancient enemy. The Drogo have long been thorns in our side, harbors of treachery and rebellion. We will show them the might of Dreynas, and we will not falter."

The crowd murmured in agreement, the tension palpable. Gunnar continued, outlining the carefully crafted plan. "We have divided our forces. One army will assault Fang, led by General Magnus. The other, you, will take Claw. We move with stealth and precision, striking swiftly and without mercy."

His words were met with nods and grim smiles. The soldiers were ready. Gunnar knew that their resolve would be tested, but he trusted in their strength and his own strategic acumen.

As they broke camp and began the march, Gunnar felt the weight of command settle on his shoulders like a familiar cloak. Every decision, every order, carried the potential to lead his army to victory or to their deaths. He took a deep breath, the crisp morning air filling his lungs, and steeled himself for the journey ahead.

The force moved out in disciplined silence, the only sounds being the rustle of their gear and the occasional bird flapping its wings or calling to its mate.

Gunnar led them through dense forests, where ancient trees towered above, their branches intertwining to form a canopy that blocked out the sun. The forest floor was a tangle of roots and underbrush, making each step a potential hazard. Gunnar's keen eyes scanned the surroundings constantly, ever vigilant for any sign of movement.

The rocky passes were even more treacherous. Loose stones and narrow ledges tested the soldiers' balance and resolve. Gunnar set a steady pace, his every step purposeful. He knew that one misstep could spell disaster, not just for him but for the entire column. His mind raced with thoughts of strategy and the weight of his responsibility. The terrain was fraught with danger, but it also provided cover and opportunities for ambushes.

Drogo scouts prowled the woods, their keen eyes ever watchful for intruders. Gunnar knew their methods well; he had faced them before. He moved with a blend of caution and confidence, his senses finely tuned to the forest's whispers. The soft crunch of leaves underfoot, the rustle of a branch in the wind—he noticed everything.

He signaled for a halt, raising his hand as he crouched low, peering through the underbrush. His eyes caught the faintest flicker of movement—a shadow slipping between the trees, almost imperceptible. The Drogo scouts were cunning, their camouflage blending seamlessly with the forest. Gunnar's heart pounded, but he remained outwardly calm, his mind racing with possibilities.

He motioned silently to Hakon, his head scout, pointing to a narrow deer trail that veered off their current path. Hakon nodded, understanding Gunnar's unspoken command. They would take the hidden route, a less obvious trail known only to the most seasoned of travelers and woodsmen.

Gunnar moved like a predator, each step deliberate and soundless. His men followed suit, their training evident in their synchronized movements. The forest provided a labyrinth of natural cover: dense thickets, fallen logs, and rocky outcrops.

Gunnar used these to their advantage, weaving through the terrain like a ghost.

The scent of pine and damp earth filled the air, masking their presence. Gunnar's eyes flicked constantly, watching for any signs of the Drogo scouts. He saw them before they saw him—a pair of scouts perched on a rock outcrop, their eyes scanning the horizon. He gestured to his archers, who readied their crossbows and took aim. With a soft thud of bolts being released, the scouts fell silently, their bodies slumping to the ground. Gunnar didn't need to give further orders; they knew what to do. They moved quickly, dragging the bodies into the underbrush, covering their tracks with leaves and branches.

Gunnar felt a grim satisfaction. He had outmaneuvered the scouts, but the journey was far from over. They pressed on, Gunnar's sharp mind and unerring sense of direction guiding them through the forest's maze. The Drogo were relentless, but so was he. His resolve hardened with every step, every breath. He would lead his army to victory, no matter the cost.

As they approached a particularly dense section of forest, Gunnar held up a hand, signaling a halt. The soldiers stopped instantly, their training evident in their disciplined response. Gunnar listened intently, the faint rustle of leaves and distant bird calls filling the silence. He felt a prickle of unease but couldn't pinpoint its source.

He turned to his second-in-command, Hakon, a burly warrior with a fierce loyalty. "Keep the men alert," Gunnar whispered. "The Drogo scouts could be anywhere."

Hakon nodded, his eyes hard. "We'll be ready, Commander."

They pressed on, the air growing cooler as the sun climbed higher. Gunnar's thoughts drifted to Claw and the formidable fortress they were about to face. He had studied its defenses, knew its weaknesses, and had crafted a plan that relied on precision and surprise. But even the best-laid plans could go awry, and he could not shake the nagging doubt that something might go wrong.

The first sign of trouble came as they navigated a narrow ravine. The ground was slick with moss, and the walls of the ravine loomed high, casting long shadows that danced menacingly. Gunnar signaled for silence, his hand raised. The column halted, every soldier tense and alert.

A faint rustling ahead. Gunnar's hand went to his sword, the familiar weight reassuring. "Scouts," he whispered to Hakon. "Prepare the men. We take them quickly and quietly."

Hakon nodded, passing the command down the line. The soldiers readied their weapons, their eyes scanning the ravine for any sign of movement. Gunnar moved forward, his senses sharp. The scouts emerged from the underbrush, unaware of the silent death creeping towards them. Gunnar's blade flashed, and the first scout fell without a sound. His soldiers followed suit, dispatching the rest with practiced efficiency.

As they moved the bodies into the underbrush, Gunnar couldn't help but feel a grim satisfaction. They had overcome the first obstacle, but many more lay ahead. "Move out," he ordered once the bodies were hidden. The column resumed its march, the soldiers' eyes darting nervously. Gunnar felt a surge of pride. They were good Dwarves, loyal and true, but the path ahead would only grow more perilous.

The forest began to thin, the trees giving way to rocky outcroppings and uneven ground. The air grew warmer, the sun beating down on the party as they ventured further into the arid landscape. Gunnar called a halt, surveying the terrain. The entrance to the Scorched Mountains lay ahead, a daunting barrier of rugged peaks. Within these mountains, the subterranean city of Claw awaited. Smoke curled from hidden vents, and the oppressive heat shimmered in the distance, promising a challenging journey ahead.

"We attack at nightfall," Gunnar announced. "Rest now, for the battle will be fierce."

The soldiers settled in, their faces grim but determined. Gunnar walked among them, offering words of encouragement. He knew the value of morale, the power of a leader's presence. Each warrior he spoke to, each clasp on the shoulder, was a reminder that they were not alone in this fight.

As night fell, Gunnar gathered his captains for a final briefing. They huddled around a makeshift table, maps and diagrams spread before them.

"We strike from the north," he said, pointing to a narrow path that wound up the cliffside. "Their defenses are weakest there. We move in silence, take out the guards, and open the gates for the main force."

Captain Ingrid, a seasoned warrior with a scar running down her cheek, nodded. "And if they spot us?"

Gunnar's eyes hardened. "They won't. We've come too far to fail now."

The captains dispersed, and Gunnar was left alone with his thoughts. The weight of command pressed heavily on him, but he welcomed it. This was his duty, his purpose. He would lead them to victory or die trying.

As the moon rose high, casting a pale light over the fortress, Gunnar and his troops moved into position. The night was silent, the air thick with anticipation. Gunnar's heart pounded in his chest, but his hands were steady.

They reached the base of the cliff, and Gunnar began the

descent into the Scorched Mountains, his soldiers following close behind. The path was narrow and treacherous, but they moved with the surefootedness of seasoned warriors. As they entered the mountain, Gunnar signaled for silence. The guards were close.

With a swift, silent motion, Gunnar leaped through a hidden alcove, his axe flashing in the last vestiges of the moonlight. The first guard fell, his throat cut before he could utter a sound. The others followed, dispatched with deadly efficiency. Gunnar wiped his blade clean, his eyes scanning the darkness.

"Move," he whispered, and his soldiers surged forward, slipping into the fortress like shadows.

Inside, chaos erupted as the Dreynas warriors struck with lethal precision. The clash of steel on steel rang out, punctuated by the guttural cries of the dying and the wounded. The scent of blood and sweat mingled with the acrid smell of smoke, filling the air with the unmistakable stench of battle. Gunnar fought at the forefront, his axe a blur of deadly efficiency. Each swing, each thrust, was met with the resistance of flesh and bone, the enemy falling before him in a gruesome dance of death.

Gunnar's eyes were fierce, his movements a symphony of controlled violence. He felt the heat of battle, the adrenaline surging through his veins like liquid fire. This was where he belonged, in the heart of the fight, leading his army to victory. His war cries mixed with the shouts of his comrades, their collective fury an unstoppable force. The enemy, once formidable, crumbled under the relentless assault, their morale shattered by the sheer ferocity of the Dreynas warriors.

The corridors of Claw echoed with the sound of combat, the clash of weapons, and the screams of the fallen reverberating through the subterranean city. Gunnar's blade struck true time and time again, each kill a testament to his skill and determination. He moved with the grace of a predator, his senses honed to a razor's edge, aware of every movement around him. The heat of the subterranean city was stifling, but Gunnar barely noticed, lost in the thrall of battle.

As the hours dragged on, the tide of battle began to turn decisively in favor of the Dwarves. Gunnar's warriors pressed their advantage, driving the enemy back with a relentless barrage of attacks. By dawn, the fortress of Claw was theirs. The once-imposing stronghold now lay in ruins, the bodies of the fallen strewn across the blood-soaked ground. Gunnar stood atop the battlements, surveying the battlefield with a grim sense of satisfaction. The price had been high, but they had won.

He knew the war was far from over, but this victory was a crucial step. "Raise the banner," he ordered, his voice carrying over the silent aftermath of battle. "Let them know that Dreynas stands strong." As the banner of Dreynas unfurled over Claw, Gunnar felt a fierce pride swell within him. They had struck a blow against their enemies, and they would not stop until Fang and every other threat to their land was crushed.

Gunnar's gaze swept across the horizon, the weight of command pressing hard on his chest. Every choice, every life, rested on his shoulders. But as the banner of Dreynas snapped in the wind above him, its colors bold against the darkening sky, he let himself feel something he rarely allowed—hope. They had fought, bled, and suffered, yet still they stood, unbroken. The path ahead stretched long, riddled with danger, but they were stronger now, forged in fire. As long as breath filled his lungs, Gunnar would lead his people with fierce resolve, his blade ready to carve a future they deserved. He would see them through. He had to. Because if he fell, the dream they fought for would die with him.

27

Through Stone and Steel

"War is fought with steel, but it's fear that forges warriors, their hearts tempered by the flame of battle."

Ruiha

Deeper into the mountain, the air grew colder, and the oppressive darkness seemed to close in around them. Ruiha led the team through the twisting tunnels, their footsteps echoing off the ancient stone walls. The faint glow of luminescent moss provided their only light, casting eerie shadows that danced and flickered.

"Just what we need," muttered Thraxos, his breath visible in the chill. "More darkness."

Suddenly, the passage opened into a vast chamber, and before them stood stone golems—ancient protectors of the Hall. Their eyes glowed with malevolent energy as they came to life, stone grinding against stone. These hulking behemoths were guardians of the secrets buried deep within the mountain.

The ground shook beneath their feet as the golems advanced, their stone bodies grinding with every step. Each thud felt like a countdown to disaster. Ruiha's hands tightened around her daggers, her heart a drumbeat in her chest, but her voice remained steady. "Prepare for battle!" she called out, though a knot of fear twisted deep inside her. There was no room for hesitation.

Dakarai swung his hammer, the runes etched into its handle flashing with a violent burst of light. He brought it down with a roar, and the nearest golem's stone limb exploded in a shower of debris. But the creature barely faltered. Its heavy body swayed, turning back toward him, undeterred. "Gonna need more than brute force for these bastards," Dakarai grunted, his breath ragged. Sweat dripped down his temple, exhaustion already pulling at his limbs.

Ruiha darted forward, slipping past the massive stone arms with the fluid grace of a shadow. Her daggers flashed in the dim light, striking at the weak points where joints met stone. Each blow was precise, a calculated cut meant to slow them down—but the golems didn't stop. Every time one crumbled, another took its place, relentless and unforgiving.

"Kemp!" Ruiha shouted over the chaos. "We need you!"

Kemp stood at the back, his eyes already darkening with the flicker of Shadowflame. He raised his hand, the Crown's power coiling through his veins like a poison. Shadows twisted at his command, surging from his palm with a hiss. The dark energy slammed into the nearest golem, consuming it, turning stone to ash in a fiery burst. But with each attack, Kemp's shoulders sagged further. The magic drained him—each surge of power drawing him deeper into the Crown's pull.

Ruiha's breath hitched as she saw him waver, his face pale, eyes haunted. "Kemp, watch out!" she screamed, just as a golem's arm swung toward him with crushing force. She leapt, her dagger catching the stone just in time to deflect the blow. The impact rattled up her arm, bones vibrating from the force. Her teeth clenched against the pain, but she held her ground.

Kemp turned to her, his eyes burning with Shadowfire, dark and dangerous. He unleashed another blast of power, obliterating the golem, but the effort left him trembling. "I'm fine," he muttered, though his voice cracked with the weight of the lie. Ruiha could see the Crown digging its claws deeper into him. One more burst, and she feared he wouldn't come back.

A crash echoed through the chamber as Thraxos stepped forward, his massive form commanding attention. "Enough!" His voice boomed, reverberating off the stone walls. He planted his feet firmly, raising his hands high, the air shimmering with raw energy. His lips moved in a guttural chant, magic crackling around him. The ground beneath the golems trembled, and for a moment, everything seemed to hang in the balance.

Then, with a deafening roar, the ground erupted. Stone and earth exploded upward, engulfing the golems in a storm of arcane power. Lightning arced from Thraxos's fingers, each strike a bolt of raw fury. Stone shattered, limbs crumbled, and the golems fell in heaps of rubble. Thraxos's eyes blazed with power, his chest rising and falling with the exertion. He had torn through them, but the cost was visible in the deep lines of exhaustion creasing his face.

"That should even the odds," Thraxos said, a hint of a smile tugging at the corner of his mouth, though his eyes betrayed the strain he carried. The battle wasn't over, and they all knew it.

Ruiha turned to Kemp, worry flickering in her gaze. His hands still trembled, and there was a distant look in his eyes, as if he were fighting a battle only he could see. The Crown's grip was tightening, and with each passing moment, Ruiha feared it might be too late to pull him back. But they didn't have time to dwell on it. Not yet.

"Let's move," Ruiha ordered, her voice sharp. "This isn't over."

As they pressed on, the weight of the battle hung heavily in the air. Each of them was fraying at the edges, their bodies bruised and battered, their minds teetering on the brink of exhaustion. But there was no choice. The golems were just the beginning.

Nearby, Kemp's voice trembled as the Crown's whispers grew louder. "You don't understand what it's like," he said, his eyes wide with fear. "The Crown... it's inside my head, whispering, pushing me to do things."

Ruiha's heart ached as she watched Kemp struggle. She could see the torment etched in his face, the way his eyes darted as if searching for an escape from the insidious whispers. She felt a fierce protectiveness well up inside her, mixed with a pang of helplessness. Placing a hand on his shoulder, she met his gaze with determination, her eyes filled with concern. "We're here for you, Kemp. We won't let it consume you."

Finally, they reached the Hall of Whispers. The chamber was vast, the walls lined with ancient runes glowing faintly in the dim light. At the center stood an ethereal figure, an ancient spirit shaped like a Dragon, its presence overwhelming, a testament to the power and wisdom of ages past.

"To enter, you must confront your deepest fears," the spirit intoned, its voice echoing through the chamber.

Ruiha stepped forward, heart pounding, feeling as if the weight of her fears could crush her chest. "I fear losing those I care about," she admitted, her voice barely above a whisper. For someone who had never known the warmth of family or the bond of true friendship, who had been raised as an orphan and tricked into joining the Sand Dragons by the cunning Faisal, the fear was all-consuming. Yet, as she stood among the closest people she had ever known, she realized she couldn't bear the thought of losing any of them. "But I won't let that fear stop me," she declared, her voice gaining strength.

The spirit's gaze shifted to Dakarai. Ruiha watched him,

sensing the weight of unspoken torment pressing down on him. His jaw clenched, and she could see the raw memories threatening to tear him apart. She felt a surge of empathy and a fierce protectiveness for the Drogo, who had become a trusted ally.

"My fear—" Dakarai began, his voice a low growl, "is watching my family suffer and being powerless to stop it." He paused, swallowing hard, his hands trembling slightly. "I saw my son tortured before my eyes, his screams echoing in my nightmares. And my wife—raped and murdered, her life stolen while I could do nothing but watch."

Ruiha's heart ached at the pain in Dakarai's voice, the torment and anguish bleeding through every word. "I was a miner, untrained in combat. I was nothing. Useless. Helpless. The faces of those monsters—they haunt me. Every night. Every waking moment. The feeling of failure, of not being able to save them—it's a weight that crushes my soul."

Unable to remain silent, Ruiha stepped closer, her eyes filled with empathy and determination. "Dakarai, you're not alone in this. We all have our demons, our nightmares. But together, we can face them."

Thraxos nodded, his gaze steady. "You've carried this burden for too long, my friend. It's time to let us help you bear it."

Ruiha saw Dakarai look at them, the faces of his new family, the only solace he had found since that dark day. He drew a shaky breath, his resolve hardening. "I won't let that fear control me any longer. I won't let the past define who I am. I'll fight for them, for all of us."

The spirit's gaze turned to Kemp, whose eyes were stormy with inner turmoil. He clenched his shadow fist, his body trembling. "I fear the Crown's power. It is a dark tide threatening to overwhelm me," he confessed. "But I'll fight it with everything I have." He looked at Ruiha, drawing strength from her unwavering support.

The spirit regarded him curiously, its ancient eyes filled with an insatiable hunger. Ruiha felt a sudden wave of nervousness wash over her, the spirit exuding a sinister presence that sent chills down her spine.

The spirit's gaze turned to Thraxos, who hesitated, the weight of his shame practically visible. He swallowed hard, stepping into the light. "I fear what I once was," he began, his voice filled with remorse. "On my home planet of Stepphoros, during the war between the Minotaurs and the Centaurs, I did things. Unspeakable things."

The room grew silent, the air thick with tension. The spirit looked at Thraxos, its expression blank. "You must admit your shame, or you shall not pass," it intoned.

Thraxos took a deep breath, his eyes fixed on the ground. "There was a village, mostly Centaur females and children. We were ordered to take it, to send a message. I led the charge. We didn't just take the village; we destroyed it. Burned their homes, slaughtered those who couldn't fight back. I—I killed innocent people. A mother and her two children begged for mercy. I—I didn't give it to them."

The confession hung in the air, heavy and oppressive. Thraxos's voice trembled as he continued, "I've never spoken of it to anyone. I buried it deep, trying to forget, but those memories haunt me every night."

Dakarai placed a hand on Thraxos's shoulder, his grip reassuring. "The past shapes us, but it doesn't define us."

Ruiha stepped closer. "We all have our demons, Thraxos. The important thing is that you're trying to be better."

The spirit observed the exchange, its eyes glimmering with approval. "You have faced your fears with honesty and courage. You may proceed."

As they moved forward, the bond between them grew

stronger. Each confession, each shared moment of vulnerability, forged them into a tighter, more resilient unit, ready to face whatever challenges lay ahead. The road to redemption and victory would be long and arduous, but together, Ruiha knew they could conquer anything.

Magnus

Magnus surveyed the subterranean battlefield, his eyes cold and calculating. The city of Fang sprawled ahead, a labyrinth of stone and iron deep within the bowels of the mountain. The Drogo forces were arrayed before it, a seething mass of armor and muscle illuminated by the flickering light of torches and phosphorescent fungi. Magnus tightened his grip on his sword, feeling the familiar weight of it in his hand. Today, blood would be spilled.

"Forward," he growled, his voice cutting through the din. The clans surged ahead, a tide of ferocity and resolve. Magnus led the charge, his heart a drumbeat of rage and anticipation.

The Drogo met them with a roar, and the world exploded into chaos. Blades clashed, metal on metal, the sound a cacophony of violence. Magnus swung his sword with deadly precision, each stroke a calculated kill. His tactical mind played out the battle like a brutal game of chess, each move deliberate, each decision a matter of life and death.

A Drogo warrior lunged at him, spear aimed for his heart. Magnus sidestepped, bringing his sword down in a brutal arc. The Drogo's head toppled from his shoulders, blood spraying in a crimson arc. Magnus didn't pause, didn't let himself think about the Drogo he'd just killed. There was no room for hesitation here, no space for mercy.

Around him, the clans fought with a savage determination. They were outnumbered, but Magnus had taught them well. They fought in tight formations, each Dwarf covering his kin, each Dwarf striking with lethal precision. They were a machine of war, relentless and unforgiving.

Magnus saw a gap in the Drogo lines, an opportunity. "There!" he shouted, pointing with his bloodied sword. His warriors followed his lead, pushing through the breach. The Drogo fought back fiercely, but Magnus's tactical brilliance turned their strength against them. He led his men in flanking maneuvers, cutting off the Drogo's retreat, turning their lines into a slaughterhouse.

Suddenly, a horn sounded from within Fang, a deep, resonant note that sent a shiver down Magnus's spine. From the shadows of the cavern emerged a horde of bonebacks—creatures of nightmare, their skeletal forms covered in jagged, bone-like armor. Hundreds of them poured forth, their eyes glowing with a feral light, their growls echoing off the cavern walls.

"Bonebacks!" Magnus shouted, rallying his troops. "Form up! Shields ready!"

The bonebacks crashed into their lines with terrifying force. Magnus fought with all his might, his sword slicing through the air, but the bonebacks were relentless. Their claws raked through armor, their teeth snapping at throats. The air was filled with the sound of snapping bones and dying screams.

Magnus moved with a blend of fury and precision, his sword a blur of deadly steel. He struck down boneback after boneback, but for each one that fell, two more seemed to take its place. He could see his warriors struggling, their formations breaking under the onslaught.

"Hold the line!" Magnus roared, his voice carrying over the

din. "We cannot fall here!"

Karl fought beside him, his axe cleaving through bone and sinew. "We need to take out the pack leaders!" Karl shouted. "They're driving the others!"

Magnus scanned the battlefield, spotting the larger, more vicious bonebacks that led the charge. He signaled to his archers, who loosed a volley of bolts. The pack leaders fell, their howls of rage echoing in the cavern.

With the leaders down, the bonebacks' assault began to falter. Magnus pressed the advantage, rallying his warriors. "Push them back! Drive them into the depths!"

The clans surged forward, their renewed ferocity unstoppable. Magnus led the charge, his sword cutting a path through the remaining bonebacks. The creatures, now leaderless and disoriented, fell beneath the relentless onslaught of the Dwarven warriors.

Finally, the last boneback lay dead, the floor littered with their broken bodies. Magnus stood amidst the carnage, his chest heaving, his sword dripping with blood. He looked around at his soldiers, their faces grim but determined.

"Well fought," he said, his voice carrying the weight of their shared struggle. "But this is only the beginning. Fang awaits."

The clans regrouped, their resolve hardened by the brutal battle. Magnus led them forward. The city loomed ahead, its dark alleys and towering structures promising more bloodshed.

"Prepare for the assault," Magnus commanded. "We take Fang tonight."

As his forces moved into position, Magnus felt a fierce pride. They had overcome the bonebacks, but the true test was still to come. The Drogo would fight to the last, but so would he. The battle for Fang had begun, and Magnus would lead his men through every bloody step of it.

Suddenly, a low rumble echoed through the cavern, followed by a series of bone-chilling howls. Magnus turned, his blood running cold. From the deepest shadows of the cave, a wave of cavern spiders emerged, larger and more vicious than the bonebacks. The Drogo had been holding back their most ferocious beasts.

"To arms!" Magnus shouted, but before the words fully left his lips, the cavern spiders were upon them, tearing through the ranks with terrifying speed.

Magnus fought with every ounce of strength left in him, his sword cutting through bone and sinew. Around him, his warriors were being overwhelmed, their earlier victory turning into a desperate fight for survival.

"Regroup! Regroup!" Magnus ordered, his voice raw with desperation. His soldiers began to fall back, forming a defensive circle near the entrance to Fang. The Drogo, seeing their advantage, pressed the attack, driving the cavern spiders forward with savage glee.

Magnus knew they couldn't hold out much longer. He needed to turn the tide, and fast. With a roar, he charged at the largest of the cavern spiders, a monstrous beast that towered over him. He dodged its snapping jaws, plunging his sword into its side. The creature let out a deafening howl, staggering backward.

Seizing the moment, Magnus rallied his army for one final push. "For Dreynas!" he bellowed, charging into the fray. His warriors followed, their battle cries echoing through the cavern.

With a final, desperate surge, they drove the cavern spiders back, cutting through the Drogo lines. The entrance to Fang lay open before them, and Magnus knew they had to seize the opportunity.

"Into the city!" he commanded. "We take Fang now, or we die trying!"

The clans surged forward, their determination unbreakable. They poured into the city, fighting through the narrow corridors and twisting tunnels. The Drogo defenders fell back, unable to withstand the ferocity of the assault.

As the battle raged on, Magnus found himself standing at the heart of Fang, the city trembling under the weight of their onslaught. The Drogo had been driven to the fortress, their last stronghold, and victory was within reach.

Magnus raised his sword high, his voice a thunderous roar. "Today, Fang falls! For Dreynas!"

The clans echoed his cry, their voices a chorus of defiance and triumph. Looking around at his weary, battered warriors, Magnus knew the fight was far from over, yet he was determined to prevail.

"Raise our banner," Magnus ordered, his voice steady despite the exhaustion that weighed on him. "Let them know that Dreynas stands strong."

As the banner of Dreynas unfurled over Fang, Magnus felt a fierce pride and a grim determination. They had one last battle to claim Fang. He would lead his men through every bloody step until victory was theirs.

28

Lost to the Darkness

"You can fight the dark all you want, but sometimes the hardest fight is keeping hold of those who get lost in it."

Ruiha

The Hall of Whispers was a vast chamber, its walls lined with shelves that climbed toward the vaulted ceiling, each crammed with age-worn books and scrolls. The air was thick with the scent of parchment and ink, a musty, almost sacred aroma that spoke of centuries of accumulated wisdom. Flickering torches cast dancing shadows that seemed to whisper secrets of their own.

Ruiha, Kemp, Dakarai, and Thraxos moved cautiously through the hall, their eyes wide with awe and curiosity. They could feel the weight of history pressing down on them, the echo of countless scholars who had walked these halls before them. It was a place where knowledge was revered, and the silence was profound, broken only by the soft rustle of pages as they began to explore.

"Look at this," Ruiha said, her voice hushed as she carefully pulled a large tome from a shelf. The cover was embossed with an intricate crown, Dragons circling the crown entwined with runes that glowed faintly in the dim light. She opened it, revealing pages filled with detailed illustrations and precise script.

Kemp leaned over her shoulder, his eyes scanning the pages. "It's a chronicle of the Dragon Crown's creation. It speaks of Nergai's spirit, bound to the Crown. But there's more here... something about an ancient pact and a hidden power."

Thraxos, drawn by a faint glimmer in the corner of the hall, approached a pedestal where a delicate artifact rested under a glass dome. It was a small, intricately carved amulet, its surface etched with symbols that seemed to shift and change as he looked at them. "This amulet," he murmured, "it's connected to the Crown. It says here it can channel the Crown's power, but only if the bearer's heart is pure."

Kemp turned a page, his eyes widening as he read. "There's a legend here about an ancient threat. A darkness that predated even Nergai. It's tied to the Crown, a force that can corrupt and consume if not controlled. The spirit of Nergai is just a vessel, a guardian meant to keep this darkness in check."

Dakarai frowned in confusion. "So, the true danger isn't just Nergai's spirit. It's this ancient force waiting to be unleashed. If we're to harness the Crown's power, we need to find a way to contain it, to purify it."

Thraxos nodded, his eyes lingering on the amulet. "The amulet might be the key. But it requires someone with a pure heart. Someone who can resist the temptation of the Crown's power."

Ruiha closed the tome, her expression tinged with a hint of sorrow. "A pure heart? That's something I lost long ago." She reflected on her past; her time as an assassin had stripped any trace of purity from her. But they had come this far together, facing their fears and sharing their darkest secrets. She had to believe they could find a way to harness the Crown's power without succumbing to its corruption.

Taking a deep breath, she said, "We can do this."

Dakarai's eyes met hers, filled with determination. "Then we need to find out how to use the amulet. And we need to be prepared for whatever this ancient darkness might throw at us."

As they prepared to leave, Kemp began to act erratically. His stormy eyes, once filled with curiosity and determination, now glowed with a malevolent light that seemed to dance and writhe like serpents. He staggered backward, clutching at his head with his shadow hand, dark fingers digging into his scalp as if trying to tear away the creeping darkness.

"Kemp!" Ruiha shouted, her voice sharp and edged with panic. She took a step forward, but Thraxos's arm shot out, blocking her path.

"Stay back," Thraxos warned, his voice low and tense. "He's not himself."

Kemp's body convulsed, wracked by spasms that made his limbs jerk and twist unnaturally. He fell to his knees, the dark energy around him swirling faster, an ominous storm gathering strength. His breathing grew ragged, punctuated by guttural growls that sent shivers down their spines.

Dakarai unhooked his hammer from his belt, the steel gleaming in the dim light. "We need to do something. That darkness is consuming him."

Kemp's eyes snapped open, locking onto Dakarai with an intensity that burned. "You don't understand," he rasped, his voice a guttural snarl. "The Crown—it wants me. It wants— *everything.*"

Ruiha's heart pounded in her chest, each beat a drum of impending doom. She had seen men broken by power before, had watched as they succumbed to their own ambitions, greed and fears. But this was different. This was a malevolence that gnawed at the soul, a darkness that sought to devour everything in its path.

Without warning, Kemp let out a scream—a sound so raw and primal it seemed to claw at the very air. Dark energy erupted from him, a violent wave that sent them all sprawling. Ruiha hit the ground hard, the breath knocked from her lungs. She scrambled to her feet, eyes searching the chaos for any sign of Kemp.

"Kemp!" she called again, desperation lacing her voice. But there was no answer, only the lingering echo of his scream and the oppressive silence that followed.

Thraxos staggered upright, his face grim. "He's gone. Transported by the Crown."

Dakarai cursed under his breath. "We need to find him before it's too late."

Ruiha nodded, though her mind was a whirlwind of fear and uncertainty. "He's out there, somewhere. And we're going to get him back."

They moved through the hall with a new urgency, every shadow a potential threat, every whisper of the ancient stone walls a reminder of the peril that now loomed over them. The Crown's influence was spreading, its dark tendrils reaching further into their world, corrupting and consuming.

As they descended deeper into the bowels of the scorched mountains, the reality of their situation settled over them like a shroud. The oppressive weight of the earth above and the suffocating darkness pressed down on them, amplifying their sense of dread. The flickering torchlight barely cut through the blackness, and the air grew colder and more stifling with each step.

Thraxos held up the amulet, its glow faint but steady. "This is our only hope. We need to understand it, to wield it against the darkness."

Ruiha's gaze hardened, her jaw set with resolve. "We will. And we'll save Kemp, no matter the cost."

Dakarai placed a reassuring hand on her shoulder. "We're in this together. We'll find a way."

Their path was now fraught with greater peril than they had ever imagined. Kemp was lost to them, a pawn of the ancient darkness, but he was not beyond reach. They would face the darkness, not as heroes in shining armor, but as survivors, scarred and battered by the trials they had endured.

The road ahead was grim, and the shadows deepened with each step they took. But they pressed on, their resolve steeled by the bonds they shared and the hope that somewhere beneath the cloak of darkness, Kemp was still fighting to break free.

In the silence of the tunnels, their footsteps echoed like the drumbeat of war. Each step was a vow, carved from exhaustion and fury. They would not rest, would not falter, until they had wrenched their friend from the jaws of the Crown's malevolent grip. The shadows clung to the walls, cold and suffocating, but it was not the darkness that threatened to consume them—it was the thought of failure.

Kemp was lost, swallowed by the darkness that clawed at his soul, but he wasn't gone. Not yet. They had seen it in his eyes—the flicker of the man they once knew, buried beneath the weight of the Crown's twisted power. The path ahead was fraught with danger, but it wasn't the monsters or magic that terrified them. It was the fear that they might be too late.

The darkness had claimed Kemp, but it had yet to reckon with the fury of those who had fought beside him, bled beside him. The resolve that burned in their hearts was not just a fleeting hope—it was a storm, a force of nature that would rip through anything standing in their way.

Ruiha's grip tightened around her daggers, her jaw clenched. She'd carve her way through hell itself if that's what it took. There weren't many people who meant something to her—but Kemp was one of them. And that meant he wasn't getting left behind.

In their fierce, unyielding determination, there was more than just a spark of hope. It was a wildfire, blazing through the darkness, relentless and unstoppable. And when the Crown finally met them, it would know one simple truth:

Nothing was more dangerous than loyalty forged in fire.

29

A City Turned to Ash

"When shadows consume and cities fall, it's not the power that's frightening—it's the man who wields it."

Kemp

Kemp's mind was no longer his own. The Crown had consumed him, filling every corner of his consciousness with its dark power. His former self was a distant memory, buried under layers of malevolent influence. Now, he was a vessel for something ancient and unspeakable, a puppet of Nergai's will.

With a sudden, almost violent lurch, he used the Crown to transport himself to the fortress in the city of Fang. The air was thick with tension, the Dwarves outside the walls, their banners raised, ready to storm and take control. Kemp's lips curled into a sickening, evil smile. The anticipation of destruction, the taste of power—it was intoxicating.

He barely noticed the Drogo guards who approached him, their hands hovering near their weapons, eyes filled with suspicion. One of them, a grizzled veteran with a scar running down his face, stepped forward.

"Halt! State your business!"

Kemp didn't bother with words. With a casual flick of his shadow-wreathed hand, the guards disintegrated into ash too quickly for their screams to leave their throats. He stepped over their remains, moving forward with a purpose that was both relentless and horrifying.

The fortress was a hive of activity, with shamans chanting spells and guards rushing to and fro in a desperate attempt to mount a defense. As Kemp entered, they turned their eyes on him, confusion evident on their faces. A few brave souls attempted to intercept him, their voices raised in incantations and commands. He didn't even blink. With another wave of his hand, they were gone—obliterated, their bodies crumbling to dust.

The corridors echoed with the sound of his footsteps, a grim harbinger of the destruction that followed in his wake. He moved through the fortress like a wraith, leaving death and chaos in his path, until he reached the Great Hall.

Inside, the warlord and his advisors were gathered, poring over maps and strategies, their faces lined with worry. As Kemp entered, the warlord looked up, disbelief and anger warring in his eyes.

"Who dares intrude—" he began, but his words were cut short. Kemp raised his hand, and a stream of shadowfire erupted, engulfing the warlord in a blaze of dark energy. His body was incinerated before he could even finish his sentence, leaving nothing but a charred outline on the stone floor.

The remaining guards and advisors stood frozen, confusion and terror etched on their faces. Kemp's evil smile returned, more sinister than ever.

"I am the vessel of Nergai," he said, his voice a cold, echoing whisper. "You will listen to me now."

One of the shamans, a frail old Drogo with a staff, found the courage to speak. "You cannot—"

Kemp didn't let him finish. Another flick of his hand, and the shaman was gone, reduced to a pile of ashes.

"Any other questions?" Kemp asked, his sinister chuckle reverberating through the hall.

The silence that followed was heavy and absolute. The guards and advisors looked at each other, their fear palpable. Slowly, they knelt, their horned heads bowed in submission. Kemp's smile widened.

With the fortress now under his control, Kemp turned his attention to the Dwarven force outside. He climbed the battlements, his eyes scanning the enemy ranks with a predatory glint. With a wave of his hand, dark energy surged forth, ripping through the Dwarven lines, scattering them like leaves before a storm. The ground trembled with the force of his power, and the Dwarves, brave as they were, stood no chance against the onslaught.

In a matter of moments, the battlefield was silent, the dwarven banners lying trampled in the dirt. Kemp stood atop the fortress, the embodiment of dark power, his eyes blazing with unholy light. The city of Fang was his, and with it, the first step in Nergai's grand design.

As the echoes of battle faded, Kemp looked out over the conquered land, his heart—what was left of it—filled with a twisted sense of triumph. The darkness had claimed him, but it had also given him a purpose, a destiny steeped in shadow and blood. And woe to any who dared to stand in his way.

His gaze fell upon the remnants of the Dwarven force, stragglers and wounded who had managed to escape the initial onslaught. Among them, two figures caught his eye: Magnus and Karl, bloodied but unbroken, defiance still burning in their eyes. Kemp could see the hatred, the resolve in their stances.

With a cold, calculated smile, Kemp raised his hand once

more, dark energy crackling at his fingertips. But instead of unleashing another wave of destruction, he let the power dissipate.

"Let them live," he commanded, his voice a low growl that resonated through the ranks of his own forces. "I want them to spread the word of what happened here."

The Drogo hesitated, confusion and fear mingling on their faces. He hadn't shown an ounce of mercy thus far. But they knew better than to question him. With terse nods, they began to pull back, allowing Magnus and Karl to stumble away, dragging their wounded comrades with them.

Kemp watched them go, his eyes never leaving their retreating forms. The darkness inside him purred with satisfaction. Fear was a powerful weapon, and he intended to wield it to its fullest. As long as there were survivors to tell the tale, the legend of his power would grow. And with every whispered word, the shadow of his reign would spread further, deeper, until there was no place left untouched by his dark dominion.

He turned away from the battlements, descending back into the fortress with a sense of grim purpose. The city of Fang was his, but this was only the beginning. There were more battles to fight, more enemies to crush, and with every victory, his power would only grow. The world would learn to fear him, and those who opposed him would find no mercy, only darkness.

30

A Heart Torn Between Love and War

"When love and war collide, it's the heart that bears the heaviest wounds."

Ruiha

Ruiha, Dakarai, and Thraxos made their way back to Hammer. The path was treacherous, but the three moved with a grim determination, the echoes of Kemp's disappearance still haunting their steps. The oppressive weight of the mountain pressed down on them, a constant reminder of the danger that lay ahead.

As they neared the entrance to Hammer, the oppressive weight of the mountain pressed down on them, yet something stirred in Ruiha's heart at the sight of a white blur streaking through the dim light toward them. Ghost, his coat as pristine as freshly fallen snow, bounded up to her. His icy blue eyes, familiar and comforting, held a mix of joy and deep concern, reflecting the gravity of the situation with a clarity that cut through her fatigue.

Ruiha's breath hitched as she dropped to her knees, her fingers tangling in Ghost's thick fur. The warmth of his body against her own felt like a lifeline. She buried her face in his neck, the scent of pine and frost enveloping her, a grounding force amidst the chaos that churned within her mind.

"Good to see you too, Ghost," she murmured, her voice trembling with the weight of unspoken fears and unacknowledged relief.

For a moment, the world narrowed to just the two of them. The burdens of her journey, the horrors she had witnessed, and the uncertainty of what lay ahead all seemed to dissipate in the shared silence. Ghost's steady presence, his unwavering loyalty, seeped into her, fortifying the resolve she needed to face the darkness ahead.

Ghost nudged her gently, his cold nose pressing into her cheek, as if to remind her that she wasn't alone in this fight. Ruiha clung to that small comfort, drawing strength from the snow wolf. She knew that no matter how bleak the path before them seemed, she had Ghost by her side, a constant in an ever-changing world.

She pulled back slightly, meeting Ghost's gaze once more, allowing herself a brief, fragile smile. "We'll get through this," she whispered, more to herself than to him. And with Ghost's silent promise of support, she found the courage to stand again, ready to face whatever awaited them within Hammer's shadowy depths.

They descended further into the underground city, the air becoming cooler and damper with each step. The dampness clung to Ruiha's skin, seeping through her clothes and chilling her to the bone. Hammer should have been a sanctuary, but instead felt like a fortress under siege. The air buzzed with tension, whispers filling the corridors like the rustling of dead leaves, each rumor of Magnus's defeat at Fang adding fuel to the wildfire of fear.

Faces turned toward them as they passed, eyes wide with worry and dread. Ruiha could feel their silent pleas for reassurance, for hope, but she had none to give. The sense of impending doom was palpable, an invisible fog that clouded every corner of the city. Her own fears mirrored in their eyes, and she had to steel herself against the urge to succumb to the growing panic.

They reached the Great Hall, a cavernous space that seemed even more foreboding than usual. There, slumped against a stone bench, was Magnus. The sight of him made Ruiha's breath catch in her throat. His face, usually so strong and resolute, was now a mask of pain and anger. A deep cut across his brow still oozed blood, a stark contrast to his ashen skin. Each labored breath he took seemed to echo in the hall, a testament to the fierce battle he had endured.

Karl and Brenn, the only surviving members of the Snow Wolves, were with him. The weight of their loss was etched into their very beings. Karl's eyes, once so vibrant and full of life, were now hollow and haunted, reflecting a depth of despair that words could never capture. His armor, battered and blood-stained, told a silent story of the horrors they had faced. Brenn, usually the cheeky and jovial one, now wore a haunted look. His usual humor had vanished, replaced by a somber silence as he stared down at his hands trembling on his knees.

Ruiha approached them slowly, her heart pounding in her chest. The scene before her was almost too much to bear. She had fought alongside these Dwarves, had seen them laugh and jest, had shared in their triumphs and defeats. Seeing them like this, broken and defeated, felt like a dagger to her heart.

"Magnus," she said softly, her voice barely more than a whisper.

Magnus looked up, his eyes meeting hers. For a moment, there was a flicker of something—gratitude that she was alive, perhaps, or maybe just relief at seeing a familiar face. But it was quickly overshadowed by the pain and anger that burned in his gaze.

"We were slaughtered," he said, his voice cracking. "Kemp—he was atop the fortress, commanding dark magic. Our forces didn't stand a chance."

Ruiha's stomach churned at his words. Kemp was a friend, perhaps more. The thought of him wielding such destructive power, of him being the cause of so much suffering, was almost too much to comprehend.

Karl stepped forward, his face pale and drawn. "I saw him, Ruiha. It wasn't the Kemp I know; it was someone—something else. The darkness around him—it was alive. It consumed everything in its path. We were obliterated, save for a few of us who managed to crawl away like beaten dogs."

The raw agony in Karl's voice sent a shiver down Ruiha's spine. She could see the battle replaying in his mind, the horrors he had witnessed etched into his memory. She wanted to comfort him, to tell him that it would be alright, but she couldn't find the words. The truth was, she didn't know if it would be.

A heavy silence fell over them, the weight of their shared grief and fear pressing down on them. Ruiha felt a surge of determination rise within her. They couldn't let this defeat break them. They had to fight back, had to find a way to save Kemp from the darkness that had claimed him.

"We'll find a way to save him," she said, her voice steady despite the turmoil inside her. "We have to. For Kemp, and for all those who fell."

Dakarai, standing beside her, nodded in agreement. "We owe it to them to try. Whatever it takes."

Magnus's expression hardened, his voice tight with barely restrained fury. "Save him? He's beyond saving. You've seen what he's become—a danger to us all. A threat. And threats need to be eliminated."

Karl shifted, his eyes darting to the floor as he spoke, his voice wavering. "Magnus is right. Kemp's power—it's too dangerous. We can't afford to risk it, not after everything we've lost already."

The words felt like a hammer blow, and Ruiha's hand instinctively clenched at her side. "So we're just giving up on him, is that it?" Her voice was sharp, cutting through the rising noise. Her eyes burned with a fierce, unyielding defiance. "He's one of us. You don't abandon your own just because it's easier than fighting for them."

Magnus took a step forward, eyes blazing. "This isn't about what's easy, Ruiha. It's about survival." His voice cracked with a bitter edge, years of loss and pain weighing heavy in every syllable. "If we don't end this now, that thing wearing Kemp's face will be the death of us all."

Dakarai moved beside Ruiha, his presence steady, a pillar in the storm. "We don't kill our own because it's convenient, Magnus. If there's a chance—any chance—to bring him back, we take it."

The room erupted into chaos, voices clashing like swords on a battlefield. Magnus's anger met Ruiha's desperation.. The air was thick with frustration and grief, old wounds and fresh pain rising to the surface with every word.

"You want to save him?" Magnus spat, his face twisted with anger. "He's already lost! You're risking all our lives for a man who's not even in control of his own mind!"

Ruiha took a step toward him, her voice dangerously low. "I'll risk everything for him. Because Kemp is worth saving. And if that means standing against you, then so be it."

For a moment, the room froze, the tension snapping tight between them like a drawn bowstring. Dakarai's fists clenched at his sides, ready to act, while Karl shifted uneasily, caught between loyalty and fear.

"Enough," Thraxos's voice boomed, cutting through the rising storm. His gaze swept over them, his tone hard and commanding. "We're not deciding anything right now. We need to regroup, gather our forces, and speak to Gunnar. We're not making any decisions on the edge of a blade."

The silence that followed was suffocating, the weight of unresolved conflict pressing down on them. Magnus's jaw worked as he swallowed back more words, his chest heaving with restrained anger. Ruiha stood her ground, her eyes still locked with his, unbroken.

For now, they had agreed to delay the inevitable, but the decision hung over them like a guillotine.

As the group slowly dispersed, Ruiha's heart pounded in her chest, her mind a whirlwind of emotions. She wouldn't let Kemp fall—not without a fight. And if that meant pushing past every boundary, every threat, she would. Because for her, Kemp wasn't just a friend; he was a reminder of why she fought in the first place.

This wasn't over.

The battle lines had been drawn, and when the time came, there would be no backing down.

31

THE MAN IN THE MIRROR

*"Power's a funny thing—it doesn't ask for your soul,
but it takes it anyway."*

KEMP

Kemp's mind was a battlefield, and the Dragon Crown was winning.

He sat hunched over in the shadows of a dimly lit chamber, the air thick with the scent of sweat, blood, and fear. His shadow hand, wreathed in its dark and purple flames, twitched uncontrollably. The whispers were louder now, more insistent, a cacophony of malevolent voices gnawing at the edges of his sanity.

"Kemp, you're a monster," one voice hissed, dripping with malice. "Kill them all," another urged, seductive in its cruelty.

Kemp clenched his fists, trying to block out the noise. But it was no use. The memories were coming back, relentless and merciless.

Flashes of blood and black flames filled his mind. The Dwarven attack on Hammer, the fear in their eyes, the chaos and destruction that followed. Kemp saw himself moving through the carnage, his shadow hand striking down friend and foe alike.

Magnus's face loomed large, twisted with pain and betrayal.

The realization hit Kemp like a physical blow. The Kwarves were dead because of him. Because of the Dragon Crown. Because he was weak.

He doubled over, a wave of nausea overwhelming him. His stomach churned, and he vomited onto the cold stone floor, the acidic bile burning his throat. He stared at the mess, his revulsion deepening. He felt filthy, tainted, irredeemable.

The thick, acrid scent of smoke clung to Kemp's nostrils, burning the back of his throat. Beneath it, the sharp tang of spilled ale assaulted his senses, its sourness mixing with the stale air. The memories of warmth and laughter twisted painfully against the cold reality of his current torment, the familiar smells now a cruel reminder of what he'd lost.

He was sat at a wooden table with Ruiha, the fire crackling nearby, casting flickering shadows on the walls. They shared a curious meal, laughter and warmth filling the air. Ruiha's eyes sparkled with mischief as he told her of his studies and his time at the academy.

"Kemp, you've got to stop being so serious all the time," she teased, nudging him playfully.

Kemp chuckled, feeling a rare sense of contentment. The weight of his mission to the Scorched Mountains seemed lighter in her presence, and the future, hopeful.

"You have a hero's heart, Kemp. Never forget that," she had said, her voice filled with conviction.

Kemp came back to the present, he wiped his mouth with the back of his hand, trembling. He couldn't go on like this. He couldn't live with the weight of his sins, the constant battle with the darkness inside him. There was only one way to end the torment.

He stumbled to his feet, his legs weak and unsteady. The

chamber seemed to close in around him, the shadows whispering and mocking his every step. He found a dagger on a nearby table, its blade gleaming wickedly in the dim light.

Kemp brought the dagger to his wrist, the cold metal pressing against his skin. He closed his eyes, took a deep breath, and prepared to make the cut.

But the Dragon Crown had other plans.

A searing pain shot through his shadow hand, the flames flaring brighter and more intense. Kemp's grip on the dagger faltered, and he dropped it, clutching his wrist in agony. The dark magic surged through him, taking control, his body no longer his own.

"No," he whispered, his voice barely audible. "No, please..."

But the Dragon Crown was merciless. It tightened its grip on his mind, snuffing out the last remnants of Kemp's resistance. His eyes glazed over, the malevolent power seeping into every corner of his being.

"Death," the Crown commanded. "Destruction."

In the heart of a burning village, Kemp stood tall, his staff a beacon of hope. He had faced down a marauding band of Drogo, his courage saving countless lives. The villagers had cheered his name, their gratitude a balm to his weary soul. He had felt pride, a sense of purpose that now seemed so distant.

"You are our savior," a child had said, looking up at him with wide, trusting eyes.

Kemp's eyes filled with tears. The image of what his life could have been, were it not for the Dragon Crown, was unbearable. He let out an ear-piercing scream, the sound echoing through the dark corridors, a desperate cry against the relentless darkness consuming him.

Then he was gone.

Kemp's face twisted into a cruel smile, his movements no

longer his own. He picked up the dagger, but not to end his life. The whispers of the Dragon Crown filled his mind with dark purpose, guiding his steps as he left the chamber and moved deeper into the fortress.

He was a puppet, a tool of destruction, his old self buried beneath layers of darkness and despair. The faces of those he had annihilated were distant echoes now, drowned out by the Dragon Crown's insidious influence.

Kemp walked through the halls of Fang, the dagger clutched tightly in his hand. The whispers urged him on, promising power, promising vengeance. And deep within him, the last flicker of his true self wept for what he had become.

There was no escape. No redemption. Only darkness. And the Dragon Crown's unrelenting grip.

As Kemp moved through the darkened halls, another memory surfaced, clear and vivid.

Kemp stood in a vast chamber alongside Ruiha, the scent of old parchment around them. She had looked sympathetic as she placed a hand on his shoulder, she met his gaze with determination, her eyes filled with concern. "We're here for you, Kemp. We won't let it consume you."

Kemp's steps faltered as the memory faded, replaced by the all-consuming whispers of the Dragon Crown. He was not the man he once was. Kemp was buried beneath the dark weight of his new master.

He continued on, the dagger a grim symbol of his fate. The fortress awaited, and with it, the next chapter of his grim destiny.

Kemp's journey through the fortress was a march of shadows and echoes, each step a testament to the Dragon Crown's dominion. The whispers promised power. Deep within, the last remnants of his true self screamed against the darkness, but it was a futile struggle.

The man he once was—a man of loyalty, of heart—was now a vessel of destruction. The Dragon Crown had won. And in its victory, it had created a monster, one that Kemp himself had feared to become.

There was no escape. No redemption. Only darkness. And the Dragon Crown's unrelenting grip.

In the Great Hall, his generals waited, their reptilian faces etched with fear and uncertainty. Kemp looked upon them with disdain, their cowardice a stark contrast to the power surging through him. He knew they feared him more than anything else, and that was precisely how he wanted it. But their fear still disgusted him.

"Prepare your soldiers," Kemp commanded, his voice echoing through the hall. "We march on Hammer at dawn."

The generals exchanged uneasy glances, their fear palpable. Finally, General Torak, seemingly the bravest, or stupidest, among them, stepped forward. His voice trembled as he spoke. "My lord, we have lost many Drogo in the Dwarves' attack on our city. We fear that the force we can muster will not be enough to take Hammer."

A tense silence filled the room. Kemp's smile widened, his eyes glinting with a malevolent light. He stepped down from the dais, moving slowly towards Torak. The general held his ground, though his eyes betrayed his terror.

"Do you doubt my power, Torak?" Kemp's voice was soft, almost a whisper, but it carried the weight of a threat. "Do you think I need an army to lay waste to Hammer?"

Torak swallowed hard, shaking his head. "No, my lord. But we must consider—"

Kemp raised his shadow hand, grasping Torak's throat. The

general's eyes widened in terror as the shadowy fingers tightened their grip, lifting him off the ground. Dark flames flickered along the shadow hand, blackening Torak's skin where it touched.

The other generals watched in horror, paralyzed by fear. Torak's struggles grew weaker, his face contorting in agony as the dark flames consumed him. Kemp's eyes gleamed with a cruel satisfaction, relishing the display of his newfound power.

"You see?" Kemp's voice was a cold whisper, silencing any further protest. He looked at his assembled generals, his gaze cold and merciless. "Nergai has given me power beyond your understanding. It is not the Drogo soldiers who will bring Hammer to its knees, but me. My power alone is enough to crush them."

He paused, letting his words sink in. The generals stared at him, their fear now mingled with a twisted sense of awe. Kemp could see the seeds of obedience and submission taking root in their hearts.

"We march at dawn," Kemp repeated, his voice calm once more. "Prepare the soldiers. Anyone who questions my command will face my wrath."

The generals bowed their heads in unison, their resistance broken. Kemp turned away, the whispers of the Dragon Crown praising his dominance. As he walked toward his chambers, he felt a twisted sense of satisfaction. Hammer would fall, and his power would be undeniable.

In the dark recesses of his mind, Kemp's true self screamed in anguish, but the Dragon Crown's grip was too strong. The man who had once been a beacon of hope was now a harbinger of destruction, and there was no turning back.

32

Vengeance First, Mercy Last

"A heart bent on vengeance is a heavy burden, but hope's flame may yet flicker even in the ashes of loss."

Ruiha

Ruiha stood in the dimly lit chamber, her fingers trembling as she adjusted the settings on the SLS, her link to Gunnar and his forces. The sphere flickered to life, and Gunnar's rugged voice came through, lined with worry and fatigue.

"Ruiha," he greeted, his voice crackling through the static. "What's the situation?"

Ruiha filled him in, recounting Kemp's disappearance and his terrifying involvement in defeating Magnus's forces at Fang. Gunnar listened intently, his voice steady but laced with underlying concern.

"Tell me everything," Gunnar pressed, his voice crackling through the static. "What is Kemp's condition now?"

Ruiha took a deep breath, her mind racing. "He is different, Gunnar. It's as if the Dragon Crown has consumed him entirely.

He commands dark magic, powers that obliterated our forces without mercy."

Gunnar's silence on the other end was palpable, a heavy pause that spoke volumes. "And Magnus?" he finally asked, his tone grave.

Ruiha sighed. "He's alive. He's furious, but he's alive," she admitted.

The weight of her words hung in the air, and she could almost hear the tension lift from Gunnar's voice, replaced by a deep, relieved exhale.

"Thank the gods," Gunnar said, his tone softening. "And our remaining forces? How are they holding up?"

Ruiha glanced at Dakarai and Karl, who were preparing their gear with grim determination. "They're shaken, but they're not giving up. Dakarai and I are ready to join you at Claw. We have to find a way to stop Kemp."

Gunnar's tone grew more resolute. "Understood. We'll be ready for you. Stay safe, Ruiha. We need you."

As the connection severed, Ruiha turned to Dakarai and Karl, feeling the weight of their shared mission pressing down on her shoulders. The urgency in the air was palpable, but there was also a glimmer of hope—they had a plan, and they were going to see it through.

Suddenly, the distant, rhythmic pounding of Drogo war drums shattered the tense silence. The sound echoed through the stone corridors, growing louder with each passing moment. Ruiha's heart lurched, and she saw the same panic mirrored in Dakarai and Karl's eyes.

"They're here," Dakarai breathed, his voice a mix of dread and determination.

The fortress erupted into chaos. Soldiers scrambled to their posts, shouting orders and rallying defenses. The once orderly stronghold of Hammer was now a frenzy of desperate activity. Ruiha, Dakarai, and Karl grabbed their weapons and hurried to the battlements, where they could hear the Drogo forces swarming the entrance like a dark tide.

Kemp led them, his presence unmistakable. Though Ruiha couldn't see him clearly, she could feel his ominous aura, and the Dragon Crown's malevolent energy pulsed through the air. His voice, commanding and cold, carried over the din of battle, orchestrating the siege with ruthless precision.

The Drogo warriors surged forward, their war cries mingling with the clash of steel and the roar of siege engines. Arrows rained down from the walls, but the Drogo were relentless, scaling the defenses with an almost supernatural ferocity.

Ruiha found herself in the thick of the battle, her sword clashing against Drogo steel. Each swing was fueled by desperation, her heart aching with the knowledge that Kemp was behind this onslaught. She fought side by side with Dakarai and Karl, their movements a practiced dance of survival.

Amidst the swirling chaos of the battlefield, Magnus swung his axe in wide arcs, cleaving through Drogo ranks with savage force. Blood and sweat slicked his brow, and every blow left a trail of shattered enemies in its wake. But even his immense strength was starting to wane. The tide of battle surged around him, relentless. He bared his teeth in defiance, his roar of fury carrying through the din like the last stand of a dying giant.

Ruiha spun, her blades dripping crimson, just in time to see Kemp—no longer the man she had known—looming above Magnus. Tendrils of dark magic spilled from his hands like living shadows, curling and writhing toward the dwarf with unnatural speed.

"Kemp, stop this madness!" Magnus bellowed, planting his feet, his voice a command as strong as any weapon. But

Kemp's expression was unreadable, consumed by the power now controlling him.

Before Magnus could brace himself, the dark tendrils lashed out, wrapping around his chest, his arms, his throat. He gasped, his muscles bulging with effort as he fought against the magic pulling him from the ground, his boots scraping uselessly against the blood-soaked earth.

"Magnus!" Ruiha's scream tore through the chaos, but it was too late.

Kemp didn't hesitate. His hands clenched into fists, and the dark magic tightened like a vice. Magnus's roar of defiance turned into a strangled cry, his body writhing in mid-air as the shadows constricted around him. The axe fell from his grip, landing with a dull thud at his feet.

Ruiha's heart lurched in her chest as Magnus's body twisted, his breath ripped from his lungs by the crushing force. His defiance never wavered, even as his life was snuffed out. His eyes, wide with pain, locked onto hers in his final moments—just a brief, flickering connection before the dark magic consumed him completely.

With one last agonized cry, Magnus's body crumpled like a rag doll, the sound of his fall lost in the chaos of battle.

"No!" Ruiha's scream was raw, her voice hoarse with grief. Magnus's death hit her like a dagger to the heart, slicing through her composure. Her breath came in ragged bursts, fury burning away the numbness. She had to stop Kemp. Now.

She charged, daggers raised, her rage driving her forward with reckless abandon. But the dark magic met her mid-stride, swirling around her like a storm. The tendrils lashed out, pinning her in place, their grip cold and suffocating. She struggled, but it was like fighting the night itself. Her limbs were frozen, her breath shallow, as Kemp's presence loomed closer.

Kemp, or what was left of him, stared down at her, his aura oppressive, suffocating. The shadows danced around his frame, pulsating with raw power. For the briefest moment, in the depth of his blackened eyes, Ruiha saw something—something familiar. A flicker of the man he used to be, buried deep beneath the darkness.

But it was gone in an instant, swallowed by the void.

Ruiha's heart hammered in her chest, her throat tight with grief. She had lost Magnus, and now she was losing Kemp too. Everything they had fought for was crumbling, and yet she refused to give in.

Through the crushing weight of dark magic, Ruiha locked eyes with Kemp. Her breath caught, her voice barely more than a whisper, trembling with desperation. "Fight it. Please."

For a moment, the battle faded into the background—the chaos, the bloodshed, the screams. There was only Kemp, standing before her, the shadows swirling around him like a living storm.

For a heartbeat, nothing. Then, in the depths of the darkness, his voice, a ghostly echo of the man he had been, slipped through the storm. "Ruiha..." It was broken, hollow, but it was him. "Leave. This place is lost."

Tears welled up, blurring her vision as they streamed down her face. Her voice cracked with pain. "Kemp, please—come back to us. We need you."

But the fragile moment shattered. The shadows coiled tighter around him, and his expression hardened, cold and distant. "There is no going back," he whispered, the man she once knew slipping further into the void. He turned away, lost to her.

Ruiha's legs buckled, her body trembling on the edge of collapse. She reached out, but her hand hung uselessly in the air, the weight of despair pressing down on her chest.

Dakarai's grip on her arm was iron, pulling her back from the abyss. "We have to go, now!" His voice was a lifeline through the fog of grief threatening to drown her.

Karl appeared beside them, his face grim, eyes sharp with determination. They couldn't linger. The city of Hammer was crumbling around them, fire and death swallowing the fortress whole. Together, they fled, their footsteps echoing through the collapsing corridors as the screams of the dying followed them, a haunting reminder of the ruin behind.

As they reached the outskirts of the city, Ruiha stopped, her breath ragged and heart splintering. She turned back one last time.

Hammer was a sea of flames, engulfed in destruction. And there, at the heart of the devastation, stood Kemp. His dark figure was silhouetted against the inferno, motionless, consumed by the power that had twisted him beyond recognition. For a brief, agonizing moment, their eyes met through the smoke and flames. In that instant, she saw it—a glimmer of something. Recognition. Sorrow.

But it was gone as quickly as it came.

Dakarai yanked her forward, his voice a harsh whisper. "Ruiha, don't."

She stumbled after him, her heart aching as they disappeared into the night, leaving the burning city and their lost comrade behind. Each step felt heavier than the last, the weight of what they had lost pressing down on her chest.

The path ahead was uncertain, filled with peril and shadows, but they had no choice but to keep moving. And as they fled into the darkness, Ruiha carried with her the faint, fragile hope that somehow, some way, they could bring Kemp back from the edge.

Because they had to. There was no other way forward.

The night was cold and the air thick with tension as Ruiha, Dakarai, and Karl made their way to Claw, their only foothold in the Scorched Mountains against Kemp's forces. The weight of Magnus's death and the desperate flight from Hammer pressed heavily upon them. Ruiha's mind replayed the brutal scene over and over—Magnus's defiant roar, the sickening sight of dark magic engulfing him, and the final, haunting silence. She clenched her fists, the icy air biting at her skin, each step through the rough terrain a reminder of the loss they had endured.

Dakarai walked beside her, his usually stoic face etched with an unfamiliar sorrow. His eyes were fixed ahead, but his mind seemed distant, lost in thoughts of battle strategies and the friends they had left behind. He had always been a rock for their group, but tonight, the cracks in his armor were showing.

Karl trudged behind them, his heavy footsteps echoing his exhaustion. He carried the weight of their supplies and the burden of unspoken grief. Every now and then, he would glance back toward the direction of Hammer, his heart aching with the knowledge that they had failed to protect their stronghold and their friend.

She felt a pang of guilt, her failure weighing down her spirit like a leaden shroud.

When they finally arrived at Claw, the fortress carved into the jagged mountain stood as a grim reminder of their dwindling hopes. The sight of its high, imposing walls should have brought comfort, but tonight, it felt more like a tomb, a place where the last remnants of their resistance might die.

Gunnar was waiting for them at the entrance, his face a mask of grim determination. His eyes widened as he took in their haggard appearances.

"Ruiha, Dakarai, Karl," he greeted, his voice rough with exhaustion. "What happened?"

Ruiha took a deep breath, steeling herself for the news she had to deliver. "Magnus is dead, Gunnar. Kemp's dark magic overwhelmed him."

For a moment, there was silence. Then Gunnar's face contorted with rage. "Dead?" he roared, his voice echoing through the courtyard. "My brother is dead? By the hands of that traitor Kemp?"

He began to pace furiously, his fists clenched at his sides. "I'll kill him myself. I'll march every Dwarf, every weapon we have back to Hammer and put an end to Kemp's madness."

"No, Gunnar," Ruiha said firmly, stepping in front of him. "We can't. Kemp's power is too great now. Marching on Hammer would be a suicide mission. We need to be smarter than that."

Gunnar stopped, glaring at her. "And what do you propose we do, Ruiha? Sit here and wait for Kemp to come for us?"

"We need guidance," Ruiha insisted. "We should seek out Thalirion and Thraxos. They are the wisest and most powerful allies we have left. They may know a way to counter Kemp's dark magic and reclaim the Dragon Crown."

Gunnar's jaw tightened, his eyes flashing with anger and grief. "You're asking me to do nothing while our enemy grows stronger?"

"I'm asking you to think of the bigger picture," Ruiha replied. "Magnus wouldn't want us to throw our lives away recklessly. He'd want us to find a way to win."

For a long moment, Gunnar stared at her, his chest heaving with the effort to control his rage. Then, slowly, he nodded. "Fine," he said, his voice low and dangerous. "We'll speak with Thalirion and Thraxos. But if they have no answers, Ruiha, we march on Hammer, and we end this."

Ruiha nodded, relief washing over her. "Thank you, Gunnar."

As they prepared to leave, Ruiha took a moment to gather

her thoughts. Thraxos held the amulet, a piece of the puzzle they needed to save Kemp.

Her heart ached as she thought of Magnus, his laughter, his strength, the way he had been there to lift her spirits during their escape from the pit. She vowed silently to honor his memory by finding a way to save Kemp and restore peace to their world.

33

THE PATH OF DRAGONS

"When the path leads into darkness, it's not strength that guides you, but the hope you refuse to let go."

GUNNAR

Before departing for Draegoor, Gunnar gathered the group in the Great Hall of Claw. The hall, a masterpiece of high-vaulted ceilings and intricate stonework, stood as a testament to the skill of its creators. Each carved column and stone archway whispered tales of its storied past. The Dwarves who had once called this place home had long since vanished, their legacy buried beneath the barbaric rule of the Drogo.

For generations, the Drogo's brutal presence had seeped into the very stones, but now, under Gunnar's recent occupation, Claw had become the foothold in the Scorched Mountains they needed to defeat Kemp. The air thrummed with anticipation as Gunnar's voice, steady and commanding, filled the vast space as he addressed Karl. "Karl, I appoint you General in Magnus's stead."

Karl's face, weathered by years spent in the Snow Wolves and, more recently, the fires of the forge, turned a shade darker as he stepped forward, his brow furrowing in resistance. "Gunnar, I'm a Spiritsmith, not a general. My place is in the forge, crafting weapons, not leading armies. Magnus was—"

"Magnus is gone," Gunnar interrupted, his tone as unyielding as the stone walls surrounding them. "We need a strong leader, someone who understands war. You're the best we have, Karl. You must accept this responsibility."

Karl opened his mouth to protest but then closed it, his shoulders slumping under the weight of inevitability. He knew the truth in Gunnar's words, even if he didn't want to admit it. "Fine," he muttered, "but I don't like it."

With the matter settled, Gunnar, Ruiha, and Dakarai set out for Draegoor. The landscape of the Scorched Mountains, with its rugged terrain and harsh beauty, challenged them at every step. The jagged rocks and treacherous inclines mirrored the turmoil within them, underscoring the urgency of their mission and the heavy loss they bore. Gunnar could see the strain etched on Ruiha and Dakarai's faces as they trudged along, each lost in their thoughts, the silence between them heavy with unspoken fears.

During one of their brief rest stops, as they huddled around a small fire for warmth, the conversation turned to Kemp. The firelight danced on their weary faces, casting flickering shadows that seemed to mirror their inner turmoil. Gunnar's voice was low but intense. "We need to end Kemp once and for all. His dark magic is too dangerous. If we don't stop him now, he'll destroy everything we hold dear."

Ruiha looked up from the fire, her eyes reflecting its flames. "There's still a chance to save him, Gunnar. The Kemp we knew is still in there, somewhere. If we can find a way to break the hold of the Dragon Crown—"

"And what if we can't?" Gunnar cut in, his eyes hard as flint. "What if he can't be saved? Are we supposed to risk everything on the hope that he might return to us?"

Dakarai, who had been silent until now, finally spoke, his voice a calm counterpoint to the rising tension. "We don't know enough to make that call yet. Thalirion and Thraxos might have answers we don't. We should gather all the information we can before making such a final decision."

The discussion continued, the air growing colder with each exchanged word. The tension was palpable, a reminder of the fragile balance between their desperation and hope. In the end, they reached no clear resolution, only an uneasy truce as they continued their journey.

Upon arriving in Draegoor, the sight of the fortress brought a mix of relief and apprehension. The towering stone walls, etched with ancient runes and battle scars, loomed over them, both a promise of safety and a reminder of the battles to come. The ancient fortress seemed to breathe, its stone walls whispering secrets of wars long past and victories hard-won.

Gunnar's heart hammered in his chest, a fierce rhythm that matched the pounding of his boots on the cobblestone path. His breath caught as the gates creaked open, revealing the sprawling courtyard within. And there she was—Anwyn.

She stood in the center, a beacon of resilience against the backdrop of worn stone and fading light. Her eyes met his, and Gunnar felt a jolt of something electric shoot through him. Anwyn was nearly fully recovered, her strength and power visibly returning. The once-pallid hue of her skin now glowed with vitality, her posture exuding an unspoken confidence.

Without a word, she lifted her hand, and the air around them seemed to shimmer in response. Gunnar watched, entranced, as she manipulated the very elements with a grace that took his breath away. A gentle breeze swirled around her, lifting her hair like a halo. The rocks at her feet danced to an unseen melody, spiraling upward in a delicate ballet.

Gunnar's throat tightened, a mixture of awe and an emotion he couldn't quite name. Relief, yes—but something deeper, too, something more profound. The sight of Anwyn wielding her regained abilities was more than just a testament to her recovery. It was a symbol of hope, a flicker of light in the encroaching darkness of their uncertain future.

He took a step closer, his eyes never leaving her face. Anwyn lowered her hand, the conjured breeze dissipating into the evening air. She smiled then, a small, knowing smile that spoke volumes. Gunnar felt his own lips curve in response, a silent promise passing between them. Whatever battles lay ahead, they would face them together, united by the strength they found in each other.

As they stood there, surrounded by the ancient stones of Draegoor, Gunnar felt a sense of peace settle over him. The fortress, once a looming reminder of the challenges to come, now felt like a sanctuary. With Anwyn by his side, there was nothing they couldn't overcome.

Dakarai found Elara waiting for him. Gunnar observed from a distance, noting the way Dakarai's tense shoulders relaxed at the sight of her. Their reunion was quieter, more introspective, yet there was an undeniable deepening bond between them. He saw it in the way their eyes locked, in the way their expressions softened as they approached each other.

Gunnar watched as Elara stepped forward, her eyes reflecting a mix of relief and unspoken emotion. Dakarai hesitated for a moment, then closed the distance between them. The embrace they shared was subtle yet powerful—a silent vow to stand by each other, no matter what lay ahead.

In that quiet moment, Gunnar felt a pang of something akin to envy, but also another sign of hope. The bond between Dakarai and Elara was forged in the fires of their individual struggles, tempered by the trials they had faced together. It was a reminder of the strength found in unity, the resilience that came from shared purpose.

Gunnar turned his gaze away, giving them their privacy. He thought of his own companions, the silent promises and unspoken understandings that bound them. In the face of the coming storm, those bonds would be their greatest strength. As he moved away, the sight of Dakarai and Elara's reunion lingered in his mind, a testament to the power of connection and the hope that, even in the darkest times, they would not stand alone.

Finally, they all gathered in the council chamber with Thalirion and Thraxos. The room was lit by a soft, otherworldly glow emanating from Thalirion's staff, casting long shadows on the ancient stone walls. The air was thick with the scent of old parchment and burning incense, a fitting backdrop for the gravity of their meeting.

Thalirion, his wise eyes studying each of his close friends, spoke first. "We seek the truth about the Dragon Crown and the means to save our friend Kemp. The amulet we possess is a key, but the task is not simple."

Thraxos, his voice a rumble like distant thunder, added, "The tome discovered in the Hall of Whispers speaks of a person pure of heart who can break the Crown's hold."

Thalirion's voice cut through the tense silence. "There's more—a saying from thousands of years ago: 'A Dragon's heart is the purest of all.'"

Gunnar's jaw tightened, his fingers tapping the hilt of his axe. "What then? We hunt down these mythical creatures that haven't been seen in centuries? We might as well march on Fang right now and get it over with."

His frustration boiled over, a bitter edge to his voice. The weight of everything—Magnus, Kemp, their entire world—pressed down on his shoulders. How could they chase ghosts while their enemy grew stronger every day?

Thalirion's gaze didn't waver. His expression was calm, resolute, as though he were delivering an unshakable truth. "The Dragons, Gunnar, are real. And I know where they are." His voice softened, but the conviction remained. "Even in the darkest times, there's always a spark of hope. Don't lose sight of that."

Gunnar's brow furrowed, doubt flickering in his eyes. He didn't trust hope. Not anymore. "Dragons are nothing more than stories passed down through generations. Legends. Why would they reveal themselves now? And why the hell would they help us?"

Thalirion exhaled slowly,. "it's said they fled to the inhospitable mountains of Sandarah when the Drogo emerged in the Scorched Mountains. Why they left remains a mystery, one I haven't been able to unravel." He paused, his gaze sharp. "But their hearts, pure and untouched by the corruption that plagues our world, are our only chance. They may hold the key to breaking the Dragon Crown's hold on Kemp."

A heavy silence settled over the room, the weight of Thalirion's words sinking in. Gunnar's mind raced, thoughts colliding, fighting to make sense of this. Could they truly find these creatures? And even if they did, could they convince them to save Kemp?

The crackling of the hearth was the only sound until Ruiha, her voice steady but edged with fire, stepped forward. "If Dragons are what we need, then Dragons we will find. I'll go to the southwestern reaches of Sandarah, to the hidden mountains where Thalirion says they're hiding."

Gunnar glanced at her, pride and fear warring within him. She was relentless, always diving headfirst into the impossible. And this? Dragons? It was insanity. But in her eyes, he saw the same fierce determination that had carried them through countless battles.

The room thrummed with an unspoken resolve as they began to lay out their plan. The air was thick with the weight of what lay ahead. Gunnar's chest tightened. He thought of Magnus, the way his axe had cleaved through their enemies, and the promise Gunnar had made to honor his memory. Whether they saved Kemp or ended his reign of terror, they would make this right.

"This is madness," he muttered under his breath, staring at the flames that flickered in the hearth. The warmth didn't reach him. It hadn't for a long time. But somewhere, buried deep, a spark of hope stirred. It was faint, fragile, but it was there.

They would face whatever lay ahead together, bound by friendship and duty, their resolve as unyielding as the ancient stones of Draegoor. Gunnar straightened, feeling that small spark of hope catch. This wasn't the end; it was the beginning. Their journey would lead them into the heart of a dragon's lair and beyond.

The flames in the hearth danced, casting long shadows on the walls, and Gunnar knew, deep in his bones, that their greatest battles had yet to come. But together, they would prevail.

Because failure wasn't an option. Not anymore.

Thank You for Embarking on The Vellhor Saga!

Your journey through *Dwarven Prince* is just the beginning. To show my appreciation, I'm offering you an **exclusive**, free short story that delves even deeper into the world of Vellhor. Each book in *The Vellhor Saga* comes with its own unique short story, available **only** to my mailing list subscribers.

Sign up today to get your first story and continue your adventure with the characters you've grown to love.

https://dl.bookfunnel.com/duzg5g68q2

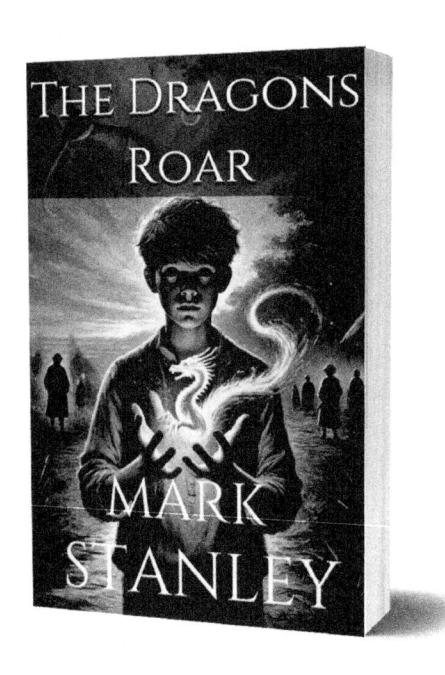

What You'll Get When You Sign Up:

- **Exclusive Short Stories**: Unlock new tales from Vellhor, not available anywhere else.
- **Insider Updates**: Be the first to know about upcoming books, special events, and more.
- **Early Previews**: Get sneak peeks at new releases before anyone else.
- **Special Offers**: Access discounts and offers available only to my mailing list subscribers.

Don't miss out on these exclusive extras

Join now and keep the adventure going!

Stay Connected!

I'd love to stay in touch with you! Follow me on Facebook and Instagram for the latest news, behind-the-scenes content, and to connect with other fans of *The Vellhor Saga*. Plus, be on the lookout for special giveaways and exclusive content just for my social media followers!

Facebook - https://www.facebook.com/profile.php?id=61561728111921

Instagram - https://www.instagram.com/markstanleywrites/

Afterword

A Sneak Peek at Book 4 – Shadow Mage

Kemp stood at the edge of the ravine, a solitary figure gazing into the abyss of the underground city, Hammer. Below, the subterranean landscape was a barren wasteland, illuminated by the pallid light of a waning moon that filtered through the cracks and shafts in the cavern ceiling. The moon's sickly glow cast eerie shadows on the jagged rocks, mirroring the chaos within his soul. He could not see the Dragon Crown, but he felt its sinister presence lodged deep within his spirit, whispering insidious promises and dark secrets.

The memory of the battle at Hammer haunted him, vivid and relentless. The screams of the dying, the stench of blood, the intoxicating surge of power as he unleashed his newfound abilities—all played out in torturous clarity. Once, Kemp had been a man of honor, a champion for justice and protector of his people. Now, he was a harbinger of ruin, a vessel for a malevolent force that sought to consume him utterly.

The wind keened through the ravine, mirroring Kemp's despair. He hadn't sought this fate, but the Dragon Crown chose him, its dark magic coursing through his veins, promising dominion and power.

Afterword

Kemp turned his gaze to the horizon, where dawn's first light began to pierce the darkness. In the distance, the flickering flames of Hammer, now a ruin, could still be seen. The fortress had fallen, and with it, the last vestige of hope for those who had once called it home. His former comrades—Ruiha, Dakarai, Karl—names that once held meaning, now felt distant and irrelevant.

A pang of guilt, a fleeting moment of clarity, surged within him. The man he used to be struggled to resurface but was swiftly drowned by the overwhelming darkness. There was no return. Kemp was ensnared in a grander scheme, one orchestrated by ancient forces beyond his control.

As the sun rose, casting elongated shadows across the ravine, Kemp heard footsteps approaching. Turning, he recognized the figure emerging from the gloom. *Magnus*. Once a fearless warrior, now a shattered husk, twisted by Kemp's dark magic. Yet, defiance lingered in Magnus's eyes.

"Kemp," Magnus rasped, his voice a mere whisper. "This isn't you. Fight it. Fight the darkness."

Kemp's gaze remained cold. "There is no fighting it, Magnus. The Dragon Crown has claimed me. I am its instrument."

Magnus staggered forward, his breaths labored. "You must try. For all our sakes."

For a moment, a flicker of emotion crossed Kemp's face, but it vanished. "It's too late, old friend. Resistance is futile. Only submission remains."

Magnus collapsed at Kemp's feet, his body broken, yet the spark of resistance undimmed. Kemp looked down, feeling a strange detachment. He had not wanted this for Magnus, but the Crown's will was inexorable. It had plans for Magnus—dark, twisted plans.

Turning away, Kemp felt the weight of his actions bearing down on him. A new purpose, a new path, lay before him. The

Dragon Crown's designs would reshape all of Vellhor in its dark image, and Kemp would be its enforcer.

As he descended deeper into the ravine, the first rays of sunlight illuminating his path through the shafts above, a cold resolve took hold. Kemp embraced his destiny, the darkness claiming him completely. There was no turning back.

Firstly I'd like to say a big thank you to all you wonderful readers who have stumbled upon my writing and have stuck around to actually give it a read!

So, born in the amazing 80s (1984 to be precise), I'm Mark Stanley, and my life's been quite a journey, fueled by a mix of optimism and the occasional misadventure.

Following in my old man's footsteps, I did a stint in the British army where I saw some of the best and the worst the world has to offer, but, no matter where I was in the world, there would always be a book in my pack.

Then, I ventured into the world of international intrigue with NATO for a solid three years. Let me tell you, writing international policy is nowhere near as exciting as conjuring up fantasy realms!

Alongside my partner-in-crime (and life), Katie, we run a recruitment agency that's ticking along nicely, all while I'm secretly plotting my next epic fantasy masterpiece.

Family is my anchor in life. Three crazy kids—Luis, Ava, and Owen keep me on my toes, along with our crazy spaniel, Stanley, and the majestic feline queen, Tia.

Fun fact: my love for the fantasy genre? You can blame my mum's creative disciplinary tactic of making me read as a punishment!

When I'm not crafting stories, you'll find me experimenting in the kitchen or sweating it out at the gym, trying (and often failing) to keep pace with Katie.

Now for some insight into my academic credentials: I've got a CIPS Level 3 Certificate in Procurement and Supply and an LLB Hons Law Degree from the University of Hertfordshire. But let's be realistic, formalised education and my ADHD? Let's just say they didn't always see eye to eye.

I am an avid reader and writer inspired by the captivating works of *Michael R. Miller, Philip C. Quaintrell, John Gwynne, Will Wight,* and *Terry Mancour*. Drawing from the rich worlds and compelling characters created by these authors, I craft stories that blend fantasy and adventure, aiming to transport readers to realms filled with wonder and excitement. With a passion for storytelling and a dedication to the craft, I continually try and explore new narratives and share them with my growing audience.

So, that's me in a nutshell—full-time writer, full-time dreamer, family man, and eternal seeker of the next great adventure. Thanks for joining me on this wild ride called life!

Printed in Dunstable, United Kingdom